THE ASSASSIN AND THE SORCERESS

N. R. G. SELOVE

For my wife Jess.
For all the struggles with cancer, fertility, and parenthood that we have tackled together. Life with you is my greatest adventure.

Chapter One

The Assassin

From her vantage point, Jessara scoffed as she scanned the complex.

The courtyard flaunted wealth from ill-gotten gains. A second-floor balcony ran the length of its rectangular frame. Limestone Corinthian columns held up the landing, and the building itself was made of rosewood. Clay urns overflowing with roses and lilies sat at the base of each column. Only the wealthiest echelons within the Compact could afford such elegant architecture. The tacky free-standing fountain fed into a shallow pool in the middle of the courtyard. A true eyesore, but a good place to hide bodies.

Jessara stood atop a three-story building adjacent to the complex. It was windy that night—something to account for when shooting arrows. Jessara's brown hair and black cloak rustled behind her. The moon was invisible behind the clouds, as was she beneath them.

Jessara reached into her satchel and pulled out a drawing of an elven man. She'd already studied this face intensely, but she didn't take chances with her targets. The man had wide eyes, a massive forehead, and long white hair. On the back of the paper was the name "Anuen Ruciel"—a name respected by some and feared by all in the city of Sunderbury.

Ruciel was her favorite type of target—a noble of the Compact, a torturer, a vocal supporter of the purge of humans. The King had declared his life forfeit, and Jessara was more than happy to wield the blade. No sleep would be lost over him.

The breeze against Jessara's face brought the scent of roses and lilies. She closed her eyes and pictured the layout of the compound. The previous day, she'd pickpocketed blueprints from one of the foot soldiers. In her mind, she pictured every corridor, every room, every nook. Her target would be in the back office.

Jessara opened her eyes and turned her attention back to the courtyard. *Three guards: one by the fountain, two on the balcony.*

She preferred thinning the numbers with her bow from a distance, but this would not be an option. The one by the fountain was in plain view, but eliminating him would alert the two grouped on the balcony. A grumble escaped her lips as she planned her approach.

The jump between where Jessara stood and the roof of the other building was around fifteen feet—seven across and ten or eleven down—child's play for an elf of Anwood. Jessara smirked. She took out a tight headband that blended into the color of her hair. The pressure from the band helped her stay focused, while keeping hair out of her eyes. She took a few steps back, balanced herself, and dashed to the edge of the building, bracing her muscles as she'd done hundreds of times. Her cloak rustled behind her as she soared and then landed with a barely audible roll.

Jessara crept until she stood above the two guards on the balcony. Both were elven men wearing the standard leather armor of the Compact—a red stripe through the middle of the cuirass on a backdrop of green. The image of a tower with an eye was stamped in the middle of the chestplate—the Watch Tower—the symbol of the Compact. Jessara still filled with hatred every time she gazed upon that insignia. All that wore it would face the wrath of the assassin.

She stalked the guards from the rooftop as she eavesdropped on their conversation.

"Ruciel finally broke that filthy human," one said.

The other looked at his companion curiously. "Damn leech! Any idea what she revealed?"

"Must have been important...He is in his room dictating a letter to the Watch right now."

"How long did she last?"

"Three hours."

"Fuck! Was there anything left of her by the time she talked?"

The guard's mouth contorted into a nasty grin, making Jessara's stomach churn. "Let's just say her death was a mercy."

Jessara clenched her teeth as she waited for them to turn to the courtyard. They would receive the same mercy soon enough.

"I cannot believe Ruciel wasted seven hundred tecos on that hideous fountain!"

"Of course, he never thinks to kick some of that extra money our way." Both turned their backs on her, looking at the fountain.

Now was her chance. Jessara brandished the daggers on her hips and leapt. With agile precision, she sank a dagger into each of their necks. All they could muster was a quiet groan as Jessara brought them to the ground.

Jessara sheathed her daggers and drew the recurve bow on her back. The guard in the courtyard stood between her and the fountain, and she smiled as she grabbed an arrow, aimed, and let loose. It found the guard's throat, and he fell into the fountain, the water swallowing his scream, turning red with his blood.

Three perfectly executed kills—three fewer soldiers for the Compact.

Jessara made her way through a door to the interior of the complex. Before her lay a hall lined with more Corinthian columns, and generic paintings of pompous elves lined the walls. Decorative weapons also hung there, which Jessara scoffed at. Weapons were tools, not ornaments.

As she judged the decor, footsteps approached. She crept behind the nearest column and listened. *Tap tap tap*—the steps grew louder. Just as their owner was about to pass her spot, she circled around it, positioning herself behind the guard. Jessara grabbed one of her daggers, put her hand on the guard's mouth, and jammed the knife into the elf's back.

As the guard collapsed, Jessara heard footsteps behind her. She spun around to see another guard rounding the corner. She threw her dagger into his throat before he had time to react. Jessara breathed a sigh of relief. *Sloppy!* She could hear her instructors screaming in her ear for allowing herself to be snuck up on. The imagined noise made her wince.

Jessara dashed down the hall to retrieve her dagger and peaked around the next corner. The coast was clear. She swiftly snuck down several corridors until she finally spotted Ruciel's office. Two guards stood at the entrance, an elven woman and an elven man. Both stood in Jessara's way. Both would have to be removed.

Jessara looked back at the hall she'd come down and noticed a window. She snuck over to it and gazed outside. Diagonally from her position was a window to the hall where the guards stood watch. Jessara grinned. She opened the window, grabbed an arrow and shot it, shattering the glass.

"What in Nara?" Jessara heard the woman say.

Jessara darted back and looked around the corner. The guards had their backs turned to investigate the disturbance.

Jessara took a breath and charged. She grabbed an arrow and shot it at the farthest guard, hitting her in the back of the head.

The other turned around just in time to see Jessara sink a dagger into his heart. She covered his mouth as his eyes widened with shock, and she eased his body to the floor, watching life leave him.

Jessara stood in front of the door, her prey on the other side. She edged the door open and saw Ruciel pacing the room. He wore a bright red velvet doublet with long sleeves and gem-encrusted buttons, his clothing alone worth more than the price on his head. An elven woman in a modest white wool dress sat at a desk, scribing on parchment.

Ruciel's voice dripped arrogant elitism with every syllable spoken in his posh, overly articulate Compact accent. "The prisoner revealed that Kingdom forces plan to start making coordinated strikes on our outer villages. What is more, they are planning on making contact with the orcs of the Northern Mountains in an attempt to secure a treaty. While the Kingdom's use of orcish mercenaries is nothing new, this could constitute—"

Before he could continue, Jessara kicked the door open, an arrow drawn and aimed at Ruciel's heart. Ruciel and his secretary froze, and she briefly scanned the room. His desk was huge with custom designs. Behind it hung a massive portrait of Ruciel, which was far more flattering than reality. More weapons, a few tapestries, and the body of a human woman, slumped and chained to the wall.

Jessara was not surprised to see her. She was obviously dead. Her bloodstained clothes were ripped, and cuts and burns covered her body. Jessara was no stranger to death, nor had she expected to find the woman alive, but the sight made her sick with disgust. The poor woman must have endured horrors before the end. *Don't worry, I'll make the bastard pay!*

Ruciel's eyes darted with shock and fear, but he maintained his composure. His scribe was terrified, and as she sat at Ruciel's desk, she looked at Jessara with pleading eyes. Regaining his confidence and noticing Jessara looking at the body, Ruciel smirked. "Admiring my handiwork?"

Jessara's gaze returned to Ruciel. Hatred swelled in her heart, making it almost difficult to keep the bow steady.

"It's sloppy."

"The cleanliness was entirely under her control." Ruciel flashed a nasty grin. "For a leech, she was surprisingly resilient. She lasted three hours."

Jessara hated talking to her targets. She struggled to look Ruciel in the eyes as he spoke. The sight of his grin made her teeth clench so hard, her gums throbbed. "So she broke?"

Ruciel walked over to his desk and casually leaned against it, pretending not to have a care in Dremeria. "Everyone breaks eventually."

Jessara glared but stayed silent.

Ruciel crossed his arms. "You are a Woodlander? Yes, only one of your kind would betray the Compact to fight for the Kingdom." He glanced over at the corpse and chuckled. "Not much of a rescue."

When she spoke, Jessara's voice had a hint of a Woodlander accent. Despite growing up with the humans in Enderdale, she was raised with other elven children, most of whom were also from Anwood. But the biggest giveaway was her olive skin.

"I'm the one who was betrayed." Jessara's eyes narrowed. "And I'm not a rescue." She aimed her bow at the scribe and released. The arrow plunged through her heart, sticking her body to the chair and staining her white dress with blood. Then, Jessara stormed at Ruciel.

"No—wait!" Ruciel held out his hands and tried to step back.

Jessara kicked him to the floor, and he screamed. He hit the ground, and she knelt over him, clutching her daggers. She held them just over his throat, but before she could say anything, footsteps approached the door behind her.

She peered over her shoulder in time to see three guards enter the room with swords drawn. They must have seen the bodies, and Jessara cursed herself for not being more thorough in her approach. When they saw Jessara holding daggers to their boss' throat, they stopped in their tracks.

"Stay back!" Jessara tightened her grip.

"Surrender!" Ruciel breathed heavily as he spoke. "Look at your odds!"

"I like them." Jessara lifted her daggers and brought them down, just below Ruciel's kneecaps, severing the tendon and exposing the joint. She then slammed her fists down on the daggers, and they sank into his leg. His screams made Jessara wince as she drew the hoplite sword on her back and turned to face her opponents.

They attempted to circle Jessara, but she darted at the middle guard, who didn't expect such an aggressive attack. The guard slashed down at Jessara, but his blade hissed over her head as she ducked. As her opponent staggered, Jessara stabbed her sword into his side, puncturing a kidney.

Jessara drew a dagger from her victim's belt before he toppled over. She turned to her next assailant and threw the knife into his throat.

The final guard lunged at her, but Jessara backed up, dodging the blade. Her final opponent was furious and desperate. She attacked again, which Jessara parried with a *clank*. Having overcommitted, the assailant lost her balance. Jessara kicked the guard's leg, bringing her to the ground. With professional precision, Jessara sank her sword into her chest.

The internal voices chastised her sloppiness again, straining Jessara's senses. She hid her reaction as she turned her attention back to Ruciel—who still writhed on the ground, crying in agony.

She knelt beside him. "Here's how this is going to work." As Jessara spoke, every word was devoid of emotion. "I'm going to ask you three questions, and you will answer all three. If you refuse to answer a question, or if I think you're lying, I'll do this." She gripped the daggers lodged in Ruciel's knees and twisted them.

Ruciel screamed as tears collected in his eyes. All trace of his smug elitism vanished. "Please! Please! I'll tell you whatever you want!"

Jessara felt sick for a moment. She looked at the gruesome sight of the human prisoner's body. That was the cause. "How long ago did Laina talk?" She did her best to force eye contact.

"Who?"

Wrong answer. Jessara twisted the daggers in Ruciel's knees. "The woman you murdered! You didn't even bother to learn her fucking name?"

Ruciel shrieked. "Two hours ago! Two hours! Please!"

Jessara loosened her grip. "Have any guards left the complex in the last two hours?"

Ruciel gasped for air. "No. I ordered all guards to patrol the interior tonight, in case someone tried to rescue the prisoner."

"That's not what you should have been worried about. How many guards are assigned to this complex?"

Ruciel hesitated for a second. "Seven."

Jessara gripped the daggers and twisted them.

Ruciel screamed once again. "Please!"

"I killed ten guards tonight." For another brief moment, Jessara felt sick.

"That's all of them! I swear that's all of them!"

Jessara let up on the daggers again. "Prove it."

"My ledger! It has the names of all the guards. It's in the middle drawer."

Jessara walked over to the desk, but didn't take her eyes off Ruciel. She reached into the second drawer and pulled out the ledger. Sure enough, ten names.

She nodded her head, walked back over to Ruciel, and knelt over him.

Tears streamed down the elven noble's face as he made one last pathetic attempt to beg for his life. "Please! Whatever you're being paid—I'll double it. I'll triple it! Just don't kill me!"

"Laina lasted for three hours, and you broke in less than a minute. But it's like you said." Jessara yanked her daggers out of Ruciel's knees, and he screamed one last time. "Everyone breaks." She cross-slashed his neck, and his head rolled across the floor. She walked over to it and picked it up by its white, bloodstained hair. She went to the desk and picked up the parchment the scribe had been writing on. She put it in her satchel and replaced it with the severed head of Anuen Ruciel.

CHAPTER TWO

THE SORCERESS

Asha stared at the bars of her jail cell, where she sat patiently. Her legs were chained to a latch on the ground, and although the rusty restraints chafed her skin, she'd endured worse. The scent of mold filled the air of the drafty cell, and a shadow from the cell's window bars striped the floor next to her. She could hear a large crowd outside, a few blocks from the prison. They'd come for a show.

Asha's chains *clanked* as she adjusted herself, and her back ached from sitting for so long. She had a dry mouth and a nearly empty stomach. They'd given her little water since her arrest, and her "last" meal had consisted of one chicken leg.

A man approached her cell wearing the standard uniform of a Kingdom soldier—a blue gambeson with gold shoulder pads and the insignia of a crown on the right side of his chest, blue trousers, and leather boots. He gave her a smirk full of rotten teeth. "I reckon they're almost ready for you, traitor."

Asha looked up at the guard, smiling. "I've betrayed no one." Every word was calm, defiant, and filled with poison.

"You betrayed your king! You're no better than an elf!"

Asha's smirk widened. "To betray a king, one must feel loyal to him in the first place. I never swore any loyalty to that parasitic son of a whore."

"Watch your tongue!"

"You're right." Asha raised a conciliatory hand. "That was insulting to whores."

"Insulting the King's an offense—"

"Punishable by hanging?" Asha laughed. "You can tell the marshal to add it to my list."

Another guard came up to the cell. A woman in uniform. "They're ready for her."

No, they aren't.

The first guard reached out to open the cell, speaking to the female guard. "It's about damn time. I was gonna kill this bitch myself."

Asha chuckled again. "Fucking try it."

The first guard stepped toward her and drew his sword, but the second stopped him. "She's going to the gallows!"

Asha was unfazed, her heart rate unchanged.

The first guard breathed heavily for a few seconds. Asha could smell onions and garlic on his breath. She preferred the mold.

Finally, he sheathed his sword. "I wouldn't wanna deprive the audience of the spectacle."

"The sorceress drew quite a crowd."

"I'm bloody touched." Asha mockingly put her hand on her chest.

"Stand up!" The second guard clearly had no more patience than the first.

Asha took her time getting to her feet. "Only because you asked nicely."

"Hands behind your back!" said the second guard.

Asha complied, but a smirk never left her face. The second guard took out some rope and started binding Asha's wrists.

She wasn't Asha's type, but that didn't stop Asha from giving the guard a seductive wink. "Normally, a girl has to take me on a few dates before I let her tie me up. Consider yourself lucky." Asha laughed.

The first guard hit her across the face with the back of his hand, and the spot throbbed with pain. She had to shake her head to get her wavy blonde hair out of her eyes, but her expression didn't change. She did not stop laughing. *Just you fucking wait.*

The second guard finished tying Asha's hands. "Let's get this over with."

They unchained her legs, and the guards escorted Asha out of the cell, gripping her upper arms tightly. Asha stretched her back as much as the guards would let her. Despite the circumstances, it was good to be unchained.

Both guards towered over Asha as they walked, which wasn't surprising. She was short for a human. They strode past several other cells of stone and metal. Some had petty criminals that watched grimly as Asha passed by. At the end of the hall was a set of stone stairs, which they descended for several flights, allowing Asha to stretch her stiff legs. At the bottom was a locked door, which the first guard opened with a key.

They were now on the streets of Enderdale, the capital of the Kingdom. The city rested at the edge of a cliff in the southeastern part of Dremeria. It was far enough to the south to be warm and close enough to the sea to be humid. It was a particularly hot day, but high or low temperatures never affected Asha.

Most of the buildings were made of stone with straw roofs—pretty common construction in the commoner part of the city. In Enderdale, wooden houses were a luxury and primarily existed in the noble's district, with a few in the merchant's.

Asha walked past several people on the cobblestoned street—human commoners, based on the women's modest clothing of brown or gray wool dresses and the men's simple white linen tunics. Some looked at Asha with hatred, some with curiosity, but most with fear.

A foul stench filled the air, and it didn't take long for Asha to spot the source. She was escorted past the lifeless bodies of three elves hanging on the side of the street. A sign underneath them read "Magic Users." Based on the decomposition, and the smell, Asha estimated they'd been there for three days.

The smile disappeared from Asha's face as she gazed at the faces of the victims. Two women and one man—all a little older than she. She nodded her head to them in tribute as she passed by, wondering if the King planned to put her up there as well. Usually only elven bodies were displayed, but Asha knew she was a rare case. Not that their plans would matter.

The guards brought Asha to the town square that sat between the commoner and elven districts. The crowd that she'd heard from her cell grew silent when they saw her. Most of the crowd were human commoners, but a few elves and nobles dotted the audience.

The elves were always easier to pick out of crowds in Enderdale. Even without noticing the ears, one could recognize them by their colorful clothing. Despite using much of the same materials as human commoners, the elves had brought their knowledge of clothing dye with them when they had defected to the Kingdom. Nobles were even easier to spot. They wore insultingly expensive velvet doublets or brocade silk dresses of bright colors and florid designs.

Asha wondered how she must have looked to them in her blue satin dress with the embroidered white tree covering its torso—more colorful than a commoner, but not as affluent as a noble.

Among the crowd, barely audible whispers drifted to her ears. Even the birds seemed to quiet themselves out of respect for her, a condemned woman. At the end of the town square loomed the gallows. On the scaffold stood the executioner, all in black with a mask over his forehead, and another Kingdom soldier, the marshal she supposed.

Asha noted details as they brought her closer—the noose, the eleven guards in the crowd, the stone wall on the far end of the town square. Surely, the doorway led up to the Skywall, the system of parapets that circled the city and separated each district. Guards used it to keep track of the populace from above.

When they reached the gallows, Asha's two guard escorts walked her up the stairs and positioned her on the trap door. A small gust of wind kissed her face, and her hair and the noose flowed as if coordinating with each other. Asha looked over the crowd of people, but only grim eyes stared back. Asha heard the footsteps of the executioner behind her, felt him place the noose around her neck and tighten it, cutting her air, chafing her skin.

The marshal stepped forward and took a scroll from his pocket. "Asha Weaver. You have committed the following crimes: treason, magic use, resisting arrest, the assault of several officers of the law and the murder of one, and the destruction of property—"

"And don't forget insulting the King." Asha gave the marshal a proud smile as he looked at her, confused. "I called him a parasitic son of a WHORE!" The crowd started to murmur. Asha tipped her head toward the first guard. "He was there; he can tell you."

The first guard turned blood red as all eyes fell on him. "She did say that."

"What did she call the King?" said the marshal, his eyes narrowed.

"A son of a—" the guard hesitated. "A son of a whore."

"Parasitic." If Asha hadn't been tied up, she might have raised her index finger.

The guard took a nervous breath. "Parasitic son of a whore."

The marshal paused for a moment. "And insulting the King. Therefore, you have been sentenced on this day to hang by the neck until dead. Do you have any final words?"

"Nope."

"Very well. May the Creos have mercy on your soul." The marshal nodded to the executioner. "Proceed!"

The executioner reached for the lever, but before the he could pull it, Asha said, "Actually, wait."

The executioner looked to the marshal, who lifted his hand. "Hold on. What is it?"

"I do have one final statement."

"Fine. Speak!"

Smoke came from behind Asha's back. "If you're going to hang a fire sorceress, maybe don't use rope to tie her up."

At that moment, Asha pulled her hands from behind her back, fiery bits of rope flying in every direction. Balls of fire emerged from her hands as she spun around to launch one at the executioner and one at the marshal. They both jumped off the gallows, ablaze and screaming.

She could hear the crowd panicking behind her. As planned, pandemonium ensued.

The guards drew their weapons as she removed the noose from her neck. Before they could approach, Asha shot more flames, blinding both guards. They howled, dropping their swords, which Asha grabbed and used to shove them off the gallows.

The guards attempted to rush the gallows, but were delayed by the panicking crowd. Seizing the moment, Asha jumped off the scaffold and darted to the doorway of the Skywall. As Asha had hoped, the bowmen above did not attempt to shoot into the chaotic crowd.

One guard managed to slip out and block her way. Asha gripped one of the stolen swords in her palm and produced a blast in her hand that propelled the weapon. It sunk into the guard's chest.

Asha slipped through the doorway and up the stairs. Despite her hunger and thirst, Asha's desperation staved off her fatigue. When she reached the top, she could hear the city alarm bells. She sprinted across the parapet toward the outer wall.

In front of her, another guard charged her, his sword drawn. She stopped, pulled back her arm, and shot the other sword at him. It hit him in the chest, and he fell off the wall into the city below.

She could hear more pursuers closing in behind her, and as she approached the outer wall, she spotted more officers coming in from both sides. By the time she reached the wall, she was completely surrounded. "Bloody Nara."

"You've nowhere to run!" One of the guards pointed the tip of his blade at Asha's heart. "Surrender!"

Asha looked behind her at the 200-foot drop, then to the guards. With a cocky grin, she backed up closer to the edge and stepped onto one of the battlements.

"What in Nara?" said another guard.

"Give the King my regards. Tell him I fucked his mother." With that, Asha jumped.

CHAPTER THREE

THE KING

As Jessara entered the King's office, she noticed the King first, in his lavish garment, and then General Harriot in the corner, with his patented scowl, but she did her best to ignore him. His presence was always an unwelcome distraction. Instead, she looked around the room.

The walls were a mixture of stone and wood, with a window that overlooked Enderdale and drew in a cooling breeze. Parchments layered the King's desk, and an inkwell and hourglass stood on its corner. A map of the continent of Dremeria covered a large table in the center of the room, and decorative armor hung from the walls. It was all too rich, too regimented for Jessara's taste, but to each their own.

"My dear Jessara. You are always a pleasant sight to behold." The King was bald, but with bushy brown eyebrows. A ruby-encrusted crown encircled his head, and he wore a blue silk doublet with brocade golden flowers, which Jessara found overwhelming. He grinned and walked toward her, screeching his nails against a suit of armor.

Jessara could feel the scratching against her skull as she stared at the ground. "The same cannot be said for Ruciel."

"Eyes, Jessara," said the King, and he waited for her to look at him. "I take it the job is done?"

Reluctantly, Jessara met his gaze and nodded. Eye contact with anyone made her uncomfortable. She had never understood why, but since her childhood, the eyes of others made her feel threatened, under attack. The King viewed this as a sign of weakness and frequently tested her.

"You're just going to take her word for it?" General Harriot demanded. He was a large man with brown hair and a full beard, and he wore a golden steel chestplate with the Kingdom's crown insignia. His muscular build made him intimidating to most, but not Jessara.

"Why would I lie?" she snapped at him.

"I don't rightly know why do you do anything," he sneered.

Jessara glared at Harriot; they'd always been at odds. She assumed it was because he didn't trust her, couldn't believe an elf would ever have the Kingdom's best interests in mind. The fact that she'd never failed to complete her contracts wasn't enough for him, and he still, after all these years, questioned her motives every chance he got. But it didn't matter. She didn't need *his* approval.

"Enough!" The King stepped between them. "You can measure your swords later. General, if you would leave us; I will fill you in later."

General Harriot glared at Jessara, then turned to the King. "Of course, your Majesty." He bowed and walked out of the room.

Jessara did her best to hold back a smirk. "What's up his ass?"

The King raised an eyebrow and chuckled. "Glass houses."

Jessara looked at the ground again. "I'm not a people person."

"Eyes, Jessara. Most assassins are not."

Jessara raised her gaze again. Her heart rate increased as she tried to maintain eye contact.

"Did Laina talk?" The King's voice hardened.

"Everyone talks."

"Did she survive?"

Jessara remembered the horrific sight of the poor woman's corpse. "No."

The King sighed. The lives of his agents were never his first priority, but he always made it clear to Jessara that they were *a* priority. "Was Ruciel able to write to the Watch?"

"He tried." Jessara pulled out the paper she took from Ruciel's desk and handed it to him.

He skimmed over it quickly. "Did you contain the information?"

"Of course." Despite a few mistakes, the mission had been a success. Jessara allowed herself to feel a moment of pride.

"Capital!" The King walked over to his desk and pulled out a coin bag. "Your payment. Five hundred drems."

The King approached Jessara and lay a paternal hand on her shoulder. "As always, my dear Jessara, you performed your duties to the letter."

Jessara's chest fluttered. Although she would never admit it to anyone, she craved the approval of the King. She picked up the coin bag, enjoying its *clink* as she put it in her satchel. Money meant booze, food, and weapon maintenance.

"I love that noise." She patted her satchel. "Who's my next target?"

The King grinned. "So soon? Why not take some time off? Maybe go find a nice young man...or woman to keep you company? I do have other assassins."

Jessara raised an eyebrow. This was another game they played. She appreciated that he always offered her breaks from contracts; it made her feel in control. But she hated cities, and Enderdale was the biggest one in Dremeria. The sooner she was back on the road, the better. "None better than me."

The King grinned again. "Indeed."

Another affirmation that Jessara would never admit to enjoying.

The King strode over to the window and looked out into the city. "A situation has arisen that requires a more...delicate touch."

"I'm delicate," said Jessara, impassively.

The King laughed. "I have a question for you. Why is magic forbidden in the Kingdom?"

Jessara looked away. "Can we not?"

The King turned back to her. "Eyes! I asked you a question, Jessara."

Jessara sighed and brought her gaze back to the King's. It was clear she would not escape this lecture. "Because we elves sold our souls to the Creos in exchange for the ability to use magic." Her tone was mocking "Now we're a bunch of husks."

The King snorted at her and shook his head in annoyance. "Do not use that term in my presence. You know I do not believe such a ludicrous thing—nothing more than peasant superstition."

Jessara nodded and gave him the answer she assumed he wanted. "Because humans can't use magic."

"Partially." The King raised an index finger with an emerald ring. "Magic gives too much power and influence to those who control it. But political power must be based on nerve and intelligence, not force."

"Force helps."

"It can. That is the purpose of people like you. But force alone does not rule a kingdom. Do you know what else it takes?"

Jessara shook her head, wondering when he would get to the point.

"Stability and security." The King balanced hands as if imitating a scale. "And uncontrolled magic threatens both. So, sometimes a message must be sent."

Jessara gestured to the window. "Like bodies in the street?"

"I take no pleasure in their deaths." The King frowned and crossed his arms. "But the elves agreed to the terms when I was kind enough to allow them into the city. I appreciate their defection from the Compact after the anti-human extremists took over the government, but precautions must be taken. For nearly thirty years, the Compact has sought to wipe out all humans in Dremeria, and *we* seek only to live in peace."

"Could have fooled me." Jessara knew the King was no saint. In this world, nobody was.

"See, that is why I like you, Jessara." He threw back his head and laughed. "All of my other subjects claim to believe in my vision. I am sure many of them do, but most are too scared of me to voice dissent."

"The bodies hanging in the street might have something to do with that." The treatment of Jessara's kind in Enderdale had never sat well with her. She had no problem with killing the guilty, but she hated the theatrical nature of executions. And she wasn't sure magic users deserved to die.

The King waved a dismissive hand. "As I said, I take no pleasure in their deaths. You make it clear that you do not approve of *all* my methods, and you do not care about my vision. So why are you loyal to me?"

It was finally a question Jessara had a clear answer to. "Because I like killing members of the Compact, and you pay me to do it." Despite her skepticism about some of the King's actions, those two reasons were what it always came down to. She was good at her job—the best of all the King's royal assassins. Such a role gave her more freedom and respect than most people in his service—certainly more than any other elf in Enderdale.

"Exactly! *That* is why I trust you. You are not motivated by a cause; you are motivated by hatred and money. As long as I have money and you have hatred, you will kill for me."

She shrugged casually. "I wouldn't die for you."

The King smiled. "Nor do I want you to. Death is for making martyrs, setting examples, or clearing obstacles. Your death would be of no use to me."

Jessara tilted her head. "I'm flattered. You said you had a job for me?"

The King chucked, then nodded thoughtfully. "I am sending you after a magic user."

Jessara wondered what the point of the lecture had been. "Name?"

"Asha Weaver."

Jessara raised her eyebrows. "That's not an elven name."

"She is not an elf."

"You said she was a magic user."

"Hence its high priority." The King walked over to the parchments on his desk and pulled out a drawing, which he handed to Jessara.

Jessara studied Asha's appearance. Her wavy blonde hair fell below her shoulders; she had soft round cheeks, balanced features, and deep blue eyes complimented by dark eyelashes—an overall delicate face. Jessara might have found her attractive, if she hadn't been fairly certain she'd have to kill her.

Jessara was disappointed by the prospect of the contract. She didn't like being sent after non-Compact targets—mages or otherwise. She still did them, but it wasn't her preference.

"Near about three weeks ago," the King pointed to the paper, "this woman showed up at the front gate. Her clothes were ripped, and she was barely conscious and covered in blood. As soon as the front guards saw her, she collapsed.

"She was taken to a healer, who was able to nurse her back to health. She claimed that she had been attacked by bandits. Once she was released by the healer, she rented a room at the Bunkridge Inn in the merchant's district. The next day, she was seen wandering about the city, but curiously, her clothes seemed to be fully mended, and the blood-stains had disappeared. This aroused suspicion.

"Captain Reston ordered a few men to keep an eye on her. One night, strange lights appeared from the window of her room at the inn. The guards who had been watching her kicked down the door to find her weaving fire from her hands. They attempted to arrest her, but she resisted and began flinging fire at them. Two are still being treated for severe burns; one died right there. On her way out of the inn, an off-duty guard tried to stop her, but she scorched him too, and he is still in critical condition. Luckily for us, she ran into a line of crossbowman and was forced to surrender."

"How could a human have such power?" said Jessara.

"I do not know. But it makes her dangerous and fascinating in more ways than one. This has never happened before. Many assumed that she must be an agent of the Compact. Some thought her an elf in disguise; others believed she had been altered in some way by our enemies. Either way, she represented a threat to the Kingdom, so I signed an order for her execution. She escaped—put on a spectacle for the crowd and killed two more guards in the process. A chase from the streets to the Skywall ended with her jumping from the outer walls of the city. But somehow, she landed without injury and escaped into the wilderness."

"Sounds like my type of woman." Jessara brightened a bit at the suggestion that she might be with the Compact. That would make the contract much more satisfying.

The King frowned. "You jest. But this woman has caused panic and debate within the city. The possibility of humans wielding magic is revolutionary. However, the possibility that the Compact could be using humans or masquerading as them has disturbing implications."

Jessara glanced down at the map of Dremeria and then back up at the King. She recalled the information she'd learned in Sunderbury. "Especially since you're planning to begin coordinated attacks on the outer Compact villages."

The King raised an eyebrow. "You know about that?"

"Yes." Jessara pointed to the parchment she'd handed the King earlier. "And thanks to me, the Compact doesn't."

"I see."

"So, you want me to kill this...Asha?"

"Not necessarily. Her escape has escalated her local profile. Many rumors still suggest that she is part of the Compact. However, as the initial shock has waned, some of the populace, and some of my advisors, have started to think that what she represents is too valuable to be wasted."

Jessara's brows furrowed. "What *does* she represent?"

"The idea of a human doing magic." The King grew excited. "Imagine it, Jessara. The Kingdom could control magic. With an army of mages dedicated to our cause, we could deprive the Compact of their only advantage over us."

It wasn't a bad thought. The mages Jessara had been sent after in the past had been tough contracts, which she'd always had to complete from a distance. Having them on their side would mean more dead Compact soldiers, which was always a worthy goal. "So, tell me what you want."

"I want as much information about her as possible. Find out if she is with the Compact, how she got her magic, and if any others exist. Get the information in any way you wish."

Kneecaps it is. "Then I kill her?"

"Anxious, are we? As I said, she has caused both panic and debate in the city. If you discover that she is with the Compact, bringing back her head to place on a pike would go far in restoring a sense of stability and security. Bringing Asha back alive, and ensuring she is hanged properly, would go even further."

Jessara let out a sigh. She hated taking prisoners. They were unpredictable, tried to escape, and never stopped talking. "And if she isn't with the Compact?"

"Assuming you can verify it, then especially try to bring her back alive. If she could be turned into an asset, she could be useful."

"You'd consider sparing her? Then why'd you try to have her executed in the first place?"

The King had never been a particularly fickle man. "As I told you, death must always serve a purpose. I signed her execution order the first time because the uproar over her actions caused uncertainty over the security of the Kingdom. I had my own personal curiosity, but stability takes priority. As the people have taken time to process the implications of this woman, public opinion has become anything but a consensus. Therefore, if she is more useful alive, then she shall remain alive."

"How much does the job pay?"

"Two thousand drems for her head. Four if you bring her back alive."

Jessara was shocked. "Thousand?" Jessara had been leaning toward killing her target and being done, but that number gave her pause.

"This is not your typical contract, Jessara. I understand that you are normally paid to kill. And you may, if you deem it necessary; I trust your judgment. But bringing her back alive could create a wealth of opportunities for the Kingdom. Regardless of the path you take, you will have your work cut out for you. But I am confident in your abilities. I also know that you prefer to go after confirmed members of the Compact, but remember what I said about the dangers of magic users. That is why this contract is so important."

Jessara looked back down at the picture of Asha. She admitted to herself that her mark was quite beautiful. But that had never given her pause before, and it certainly wouldn't now. "Anything else?"

"One more thing." The King took out a rolled-up paper. "This map was found on her person when she was arrested. It is a map of the Kingdom. Two towns are circled—Turnhol and Farnsville. Recently, there was a fire at a house in Farnsville. A family was lost in the flames. We are still interviewing witnesses, but it seemed to happen just before Asha appeared in Enderdale. This cannot be a coincidence. Turnhol, on the other hand, is close to the border between the Kingdom and the Compact. If she passed through this town, it is quite possible she came from the Compact."

"Sounds good. I'll start at the inn. See if there's anything in her room."

The King gave her a paternal smile. "You are a natural hunter. Can you get this done for me?"

"You know the answer to that." Certainty filled her voice.

"Capital!" The King took a step toward her and put his hand on her shoulder. "Please, be careful. You are valuable to the Kingdom and to me." When he spoke, his voice was genuine and soothing. Jessara wondered if her own father would have talked to her with such warmth, if she'd ever known him.

Jessara considered making a cocky comment, but simply nodded before walking out of the office.

Right outside the door, General Harriot stood with his arms crossed. "Where're you headed?"

Jessara stopped, looked over her shoulder at him, and smirked. He wasn't getting a damn thing from her.

Chapter Four

The Scholar

Jessara entered Room 36 at the Bunkridge Inn where Asha had stayed. By the King's order, it hadn't been rented out and remained the way Asha had left it. Jessara scanned the room. Like most inns in the merchant district, it was made of wood. An unmade bed sat in the right corner and a table with two chairs in the left. The inn wasn't one of the more prestigious establishments, and the accommodations were modest, especially considering the district. Some rotten mutton on the table and a burnt rug on the floor created a foul stench. *Looks like she was about to sit down for dinner.* Jessara turned around to face the doorway and saw more burn marks on the walls. The innkeeper was lucky the entire place hadn't caught on fire—or perhaps Asha had just been careful.

At that moment, an older elven man walked into the room. His gray eyes matched his hair, and he wore a purple woolen robe. His nose was slightly crooked, his chin sharp, and he stood a little taller than Jessara.

"Aleris, thanks for coming." Jessara did not take her eyes off the scorch marks.

"My pleasure." Aleris Rondelio had been a scholar of magic in the Compact for ten years. He defected to the Kingdom thirty years ago, when the purge of humans began. He had no love for the King and frequently expressed dissent to Jessara, but like the other defectors, he couldn't support genocide, so he'd left the Compact.

Aleris looked around the room, and spotting the burn marks on the wall, walked over and ran his hand across them. "No smoke and mirrors; these scorch marks were caused by magical flames."

Jessara squinted her eyes, studying the marks. "How can you tell?"

Aleris framed the burns with his index finger. "The scorch marks are too thick to have been made by natural fire. Also, I've been trained to recognize the odor of magic residue."

"Is she human?"

Aleris grinned. Jessara knew he loved lecturing but was rarely able to do so. The scholar's information had always proven useful, however, so she was usually willing to indulge him. At least he wasn't as self-righteous as the King when he spoke—most of the time anyway.

"She's no elf. Shapeshifting magic *has* been studied and used by the academy, but it requires years to be able to change even the color of your eyes. Only the greatest masters of shapeshifting are able to fully change their appearance to look like another elf. I've only ever known one person that could change into a human. Even so, they were only able to keep the spell up for a few hours. Using magic takes a lot out of someone, which is why few mages exist. Besides, if this Asha were a shapeshifter, she wouldn't be able to use fire magic. Both are specializations, and mages can only have one."

"Specializations?" Jessara had hunted down magic users before, but she usually took them down from a distance. She'd never seen much use in learning about the specifics of magic. Mages were rare and bled just like everyone else. But she was still weighing whether or not she was going for the kill or capture, so it was time to let Aleris do what he did best.

"There are seven known specializations." Aleris' excitement was palpable. "First you have the three elemental specializations: fire, ice, and lightning. Then you have shapeshifting, telepathy, healing." He paused for a moment. "And telekinesis. Asha is clearly a fire sorceress, which means she cannot be a shapeshifter."

"So she's human." Jessara paced as she speculated. "Could she have been altered in some way by the Compact?"

Aleris stroked his sharp chin thoughtfully. "Perhaps. Giving a human the ability to tap into magic was never attempted when I was teaching. But on occasion, mages were able to give untrained elves the ability to tap into their magic for a short time. I don't know why they would let a human do such a thing, but it could probably be done."

Jessara stopped pacing and narrowed her eyes. "So, you think there might be more to this?"

"I do. Perhaps if the King trusted elves more, I could have saved the fool a lot of confusion."

The other elves living in Enderdale usually shunned Jessara because they viewed her as a lackey to the King. Aleris talked to her, but she still felt the need to defend the King's actions, even the ones she disagreed with. In a way, she was defending herself. "I hate when you call him that."

"I hate when he acts like one...so I guess we're both disappointed."

"Can you blame him after what the Compact did to the humans?"

"Blame is irrelevant. His troublesome hostility toward all elves makes defection far less appealing. The Compact wants a war of elves versus humans. The more the King persecutes us, the more ink he provides the Compact to write that narrative. Hence, he's a fool."

Jessara chuckled, knowing she'd brought that on herself. "Why do I even bother trying to argue with you?"

Aleris grinned. "One should relish the opportunity to be proven wrong. It's the only way we can grow."

"Okay! I get it!" Jessara knew he was probably right, but she'd never tell him that.

"My apologies. The persona of the academic is difficult to turn off."

Jessara rolled her eyes. "Especially when you don't want to. Is there anything else you can tell me, Aleris?"

"As I mentioned, magic users only develop one specialization in magic." Aleris started pacing around the room. "There are simple spells that most mages can cast, such as magical barriers, stationary illusions, personal hygiene, or the mending of clothes, as this woman seemed to do."

Jessara tilted her head in curiosity. "Those don't require specializations?"

He shook his head. "Mages usually start with basic spells like those. They rely on tapping into the natural magical forces that exist in the world. Specialization magic comes from within the mage, and it only develops after the user has spent enough time absorbing outside magic and casting spells." He sighed. "Unfortunately, that fact is how the

Compact justifies its atrocities against humans. Elven supremacists in charge are convinced that the presence of humans causes magic to be absorbed by those who can't wield it—meaning that more elves would be able to use magic if there were no humans." He grew enraged as he continued. "The idea is nothing short of foolish! Magic is abundant and constantly being renewed. The imbeciles might as well say that the humans steal sunlight!"

"And that's why they call humans leeches." Jessara shook her head. "You're off on a tangent again. Can we get back to magic users."

Aleris took a moment to settle down and then chuckled at himself. "Forgive me. Where was I?"

"Specializations."

"Ah yes! Becoming a true mage changes both the body and the mind, depending on the type of magic they choose to specialize in."

Jessara pondered for a moment. "This Asha is a flame sorceress. What can I expect from her?"

"Her body is the source of her power, but it can only be released and controlled through her hands. This will allow her to conjure and launch fireballs." Aleris reached into his satchel and pulled out a pair of chainmail gloves. "I've never known of a fire mage who could conjure fire hot enough to burn through metal, at least through normal means. These chainmail gloves should contain her power."

"What do you mean by 'normal means'?"

Aleris shrugged. "Some books have described cases in which a mage can enter a state of nearly limitless power called Altemus, but it can only be achieved through a state of extreme emotion. Cases are so rare that many scholars believe it's just a myth—a tale for fools. I don't know, but regardless, I doubt you'll need to worry about it." He held up the gloves. "Just lock these around her hands and use metal shackles, and her magic will harm no one."

"Thanks." Jessara took the gloves. "Also, what did you mean by altering the mind?"

"A mage's personality tends to be influenced by their specialization. They all, of course, make their own choices, but they may have idio-syncrasies."

"What do fire mages tend to be like?"

"Passionate and impulsive. She may also have a temper. But as I said, these are just emotional tendencies. Different people have different levels of control over their emotions. Mages are no different."

"Passionate and impulsive? That could be problematic." She sighed. "Maybe dead is the safer option. Anything else?"

"You should try to familiarize yourself with more magic for this contract." Aleris reached into his satchel and pulled out a few rolls of parchment. "You mentioned in your message that this was also an information-gathering mission. I prepared some notes for you about magic users. Read all of them, but be thorough in the section about fire mages."

Jessara took the notes and tossed Aleris a bag of coins. "Thanks for the information. Here."

Aleris inspected the sack. "Fifty drems? You must be collecting a glorious bounty for this one."

"I will be." Jessara grinned and started toward the exit of the room.

"Where are you going?" he called after her.

"Farnsville, then Turnhol."

Chapter Five

Turnhol

Farnsville was a small town, a few miles west of Enderdale. Most of the houses were made of wood—a luxury in Enderdale, but common in small towns. Most of the people were farmers or laborers. Their clothes were mostly low-quality wool and cheap linen—the type nobody cared about getting dirty.

The climate was hot and humid, and a few trees dotted the grassy, hilly terrain. Not Jessara's favorite part of the Kingdom, but she appreciated the warm weather.

The people of the town were friendlier toward Jessara than she was used to as an elf, probably because they were far from the border. They hadn't seen the ugliness of the Compact up close. Children played in the streets, and the people strode around town without a care.

In the tavern, the bartender told her that he'd seen a woman in a blue dress the night of the fire. She'd gotten into a fight with some men inside the now burnt-down house. No one in the tavern knew the men or had seen the woman since. It was an interesting visit, but not useful in figuring out where Asha had gone.

Jessara left the town and started her journey to Turnhol. She preferred to travel on foot. Horses were faster, but riding made it easier to be caught off-guard by the occasional brigand or human supremacist.

The trek to Turnhol took about a week's time. Two days passed before she was out of the Capital Region of the Kingdom and into the Midwestern Forest. It wasn't as dense or impressive as Anwood over in the Compact, but Jessara, a woodland elf, enjoyed trees more than hills. While in the forest, a highwayman confronted her, but her knife slit his throat before he could finish his threat. Apart from that, Jessara made it through the forest without incident, and after three more days, she arrived in the Border Region.

The Border Region lay between the Compact of the elves and the Kingdom of the humans—the two major nations on the continent of Dremeria. This region suffered the most devastation from the warring nations. The carnage was a glaring contrast to the vast meadows that spanned most of the area, for the dead, left to rot in the fields, fertilized the local flora. Intermittently, Jessara found seas of corpses from battles—some old, some fresh—and every few miles, the scents would switch from sweet flowers to rotting corpses. The contrast always made Jessara uneasy.

After another two days, she made it to her destination. Turnhol was a small village, with a population of around 150, and was garrisoned by a volunteer militia. This was often the case with smaller towns in the Border Region.

The buildings would make any self-respecting architect cry. The houses were built of poorly measured lumber, with boards sticking out of the sides. Roofs were made from old, rotting straw, and the smell of mud and sewage filled the air. Upkeep was pointless when the Compact could attack and burn everything at a moment's notice.

The people were as shabby as the town itself, making the commoners in Farnsville look like Enderdale nobles. Their clothes were filthy rags, and too many bore obvious bloodstains.

When she entered the town, Jessara could tell everyone was looking at her. Humans in the Border Region were even less tolerant of elves than those in the larger cities, for they were more likely to have been personally affected by the Purge. Violence occurred frequently, and the local militia usually looked the other way or joined in.

A patrolling militia guard, in a clearly failed attempt at a homemade Kingdom uniform, strode up to her, his expression filled with disdain. "You lost?"

"I'm looking for an inn. You got one?" Jessara involuntarily shifted back and forth between looking at the guard and the ground. This was typical behavior for her whenever she met strangers. Eye contact with people she knew was difficult enough.

"You looking to stay the night?"

"What if I am?" Jessara raised a brow. *Think I'd want to stay in a shithole like this?*

The guard scoffed. "Might be too rich for the likes of you."

Jessara almost laughed, but she caught herself. She probably made more in her last contract than some of these people did in a year, but that wasn't their fault. "I'll manage."

The guard eyed her suspiciously. "Down that street and take a left. The Turnhol Inn."

Jessara nodded. As she walked away, she heard the guard mutter, "Fucking husk."

Jessara paused. No matter how many times she heard it, that word dug into her like a snakebite. She could feel the guard's gaze, and considered turning around and saying something. But she kept walking. She was in town to get information—no sense in starting a fight just yet.

Jessara followed the guard's directions and found the inn. It was probably the best constructed building in the entire town, which still left quite a bit to be desired.

As she entered, the smell of whiskey and baked bread greeted her, and as she scanned the room, a loud table in the corner grew quiet. *Drunk bigots. Problematic.* She approached the counter and the innkeeper smiled nervously. A short, middle-aged woman with brown hair speckled with gray, she wore a brown wool dress with a slightly soiled white apron. Still, she looked more prosperous than most of the villagers Jessara had seen.

"Can I help you, good elf?" Innkeepers were usually the least hostile toward elves. They couldn't afford to turn away business, and in Jessara's experience, they were also the best sources of information.

"Beer." Jessara leaned against the counter, scanning the room and straining to keep eye contact. She needed the innkeeper to trust her.

"Two drems."

Jessara reached into her satchel and set five drems on the counter. "The other three are for information." Behind her, she heard the table that had grown quiet begin to buzz angrily, and she felt herself begin to buzz too. Still a little worked up about the guard's comment, she wanted an excuse to punch some racists.

The innkeeper glanced at the table, but said nothing.

"What sorta information?" The innkeeper took the drems, grabbed a mug, and poured the beer.

"I'm looking for a woman. Blonde hair, a blue dress decorated with a white tree—name's Asha Weaver."

Jessara took out the drawing and laid it on the counter.

"You Compact?"

Jessara strained to keep her face from glaring, but she knew better than to antagonize someone she was asking for a favor. "No. But *she* might be."

The woman glanced at the corner table, then began drying the mug in her hands with the corner of her apron. When she spoke, Jessara had to lean in to hear her. "I seen her. Stayed here several weeks ago, she did. Said she was heading to some small town near Enderdale."

"Farnsville?"

"Aye, that's the one."

Excitement stirred in Jessara, but she maintained a blank expression. "She come back through here?"

"Aye, about a day ago. This time, she seemed on edge. Kept looking over her shoulder."

Jessara chuckled under her breath. Evidently, her mark was not good at keeping a low profile. That would make Jessara's job much easier. "Do you know where she went?"

"She asked me about the best path to the Northern Mountains. Lost her map, she must've."

An almost imperceptible smile began to spread across Jessara's face. "What did you tell her?"

The innkeeper grabbed another mug and began wiping it down. "Lake Rune lies north of us, so there's no direct path. I told her she could take the path east of town and then curl round the lake. There's an easy pass into the mountains at the town of Gatewatch. She was scared to go back east, so she asked for a different path. I told her that the only other way lies on the northwestern path. But that'll take you through Compact territory. She didn't seem worried. Bought some food, a sack of throwing knives, and a cloak, and headed northeast. Maybe she *is* Compact."

"We shall see. Thanks for the information." Jessara took out two more drems and gave them to the innkeeper.

"Much obliged. Now you might be thinking about clearing out of here; you seem to be attracting some attention." She flicked a glance at the table in the corner.

Jessara peered over her shoulder to see the three toughs striding toward her. Jessara took another gulp of her beer and put on her headband, telling herself not to kill.

"I think you're done here, husk!" the tallest man said, emphasizing the word "husk".

Again, that word bit, but Jessara didn't show it. She lifted her mug. "I'll leave when I'm finished." She took a long swallow and set it back on the table.

The shortest man picked it up and threw it on the ground, shattering the silence. "You're finished!"

Jessara didn't jump. Instead, she glanced at the innkeeper. "How much was that mug worth?" She wasn't in the mood for this.

The innkeeper was shaking. "No, it's fine. Just leave, please?"

Jessara shook her head. "How much?"

"'Twas a mere drem. No trouble."

Jessara glared at the men. "Pay the woman."

The three men laughed. "I've got me a better idea. You leave now, and you keep your fucking teeth, husk!"

"Last warning." Jessara's sympathy had ended.

The man standing directly behind her grabbed her shoulder. Jessara elbowed his gut, and he retracted in shock.

Another stepped in for a punch. She blocked it with the side of her arm and kicked his knee. A *crack* echoed through the room as he fell, howling.

Jessara's first assailant recovered, and he and the third man attempted another attack. She kicked the first in the chest and grabbed the arm of the third, pulling him to her. She smashed his head on the counter, causing him to fall to the ground, unconscious.

Jessara strode to the first man who was still clutching his chest. She dragged him by his hair and brought him to the counter. She then slammed his head down, while twisting his arm behind his back.

Jessara barely needed to catch her breath; this may have been the easiest fight of her life. "One drem."

"Rot in Nara!" He snarled, although the pride in the man's voice had left.

Jessara twisted his arm, making him cry out again. "One drem or one arm."

"Fine! Fine! Lemme up!"

Jessara released him. He reached into his pocket, produced a drem, and gave it to the innkeeper.

"Apologize." Jessara wanted to make sure he got the message.

The man glared at Jessara and spoke through his teeth. "I'm sorry!"

"Not to me." Jessara motioned to the innkeeper.

The man turned to the middle-aged woman. "I'm sorry."

Jessara turned to the innkeeper. "Thanks for the information." *And the workout.* And then she left the inn with her new heading.

CHAPTER SIX

AMBUSH

In the two days after her visit to Turnhol, Jessara came across three campsites, which she concluded had been left by her quarry. She found the remains of animals which had been cooked, despite there being no evidence of a campfire. The last one she'd found had been warm. She was getting close.

An entry in Aleris' notes mentioned that fire mages were able to raise their body temperatures at will, meaning that they rarely used campfires. Jessara was almost envious.

Jessara was in the Foothill Region of Dremeria, which led to the frost-covered Northern Mountains. The mountains were still far off, but they towered over the land. It wasn't a densely-forested area, but some trees dotted the landscape. The hilly terrain would make it easier for Jessara to ambush the sorceress when she found her. Pity. Hunts through the forest were more satisfying, but at least this was better than the plains.

Temperate weather greeted Jessara for now, but she knew the farther north she traveled, the colder it would get. Hopefully, she'd find her target soon. As she walked, the chirps from several species of birds filled the dry air.

This was Compact territory, so Jessara trod just off the path to hide her prints. During the trek, Jessara continued to ponder what to do with Asha when she found her. Jessara had the means to contain Asha's power, but getting the gloves on her would be a challenge. Aleris' warnings about fire mages rang in her ears. *Impulsive and quick-tempered.* Not exactly the type of person Jessara wanted to haul all the way back to Enderdale.

Jessara had killed magic users before, and she'd interrogated people for information. But she'd used stealth on the previous magic users, and she'd interrogated only normal people before.

After another hour of walking, Jessara spotted someone on the path in the distance, their back toward Jessara. They wore a bright blue cloak with a hood over their head and walked with a woman's stride, but Jessara would need to get closer to see the face. Jessara stalked in the brush as she tried to get in front of the stranger. When she did, she still couldn't make out the face, but it was a woman, and she wore a blue dress beneath the cloak.

Most of the local towns were military strongholds, so very few civilians traveled these roads. The mystery woman certainly wasn't a soldier. But if this was the woman Jessara sought, she was either brave or stupid. Her brass to walk this openly through Compact territory was almost admirable. She wasn't even trying to blend in. Of course, this could just be evidence that Asha was with the Compact.

Suddenly, Jessara noticed movement in the brush on the other side of the path. Six Compact soldiers in their green and red uniforms leapt out and surrounded the woman. They kept their hands on their swords but didn't draw them.

Jessara waited patiently on the edge of the path to watch how this would play out.

"Good morning, ma'am." The soldier wore a red uniform, indicating that he was a commanding officer. "Fine day for a walk, is it not?"

The mystery woman lowered her head, obscuring her face even more. "Indeed."

"Why don't you take that hood off?"

The woman took a moment to respond. "Umm...I have hood hair?"

While Jessara observed from the other side of the path, she adjusted her headband, grabbed her bow, and drew an arrow—although she wasn't sure whom she'd use it on.

An elf behind the woman drew his sword.

The leader shook his head and tsked. "That was not a suggestion."

The woman slowly removed her hood. Sunlight shone on flowing blonde hair. Even from her hiding place, Jessara immediately recognized the deep-set eyes, the dark eyelashes, and the soft, round cheeks on milky white skin. Her mark!

The sound of swords being drawn filled the air as soon as the Compact soldiers saw her ears. "Human!"

"I knew it!" The leader's voice echoed off the surrounding hills as he yelled. "You are coming with us, leech! Your execution will entertain the entire town tonight!"

"See...that doesn't give me much incentive to come with you." To her credit, Asha didn't sound scared in the least.

Jessara couldn't help but chuckle.

The leader took a step toward her and put the tip of his sword against her throat. "Or we could kill you right here. It makes no difference to mc."

Asha took a step back, holding her hands out. "Now wait just a minute. I have authorization to be here."

Jessara pointed her drawn arrow at Asha.

"Just let me show you my papers." Asha slowly reached into her cloak.

Jessara was ready to take the shot. If Asha produced identification, that was all the information Jessara needed. She'd take her head when the soldiers left the area. Two thousand drems would be plenty.

Much to Jessara's shock, Asha didn't produce any papers. Instead, she drew a dagger in each hand and seemed to throw them, but their speed didn't make sense. Both targets had blades in their chests before anybody had time to react.

Jessara watched as the leader came at Asha with his sword. He attempted a side slash, but Asha dodged it.

The elf standing behind Asha moved in to stab her in the back. Jessara made a split-second decision and shot the arrow.

***

Asha heard the sound of metal entering flesh behind her. She turned to see a soldier, with an arrow protruding from his chest, fall to the ground. *What the fuck?* Then a dark figure emerged from the brush and charged into battle. The figure appeared to be a woman. As she ran, she shot an arrow into another soldier with precision unlike anything Asha had ever seen.

Seeing an opportunity, Asha produced another knife and sank it into the neck of the distracted leader.

Seeing this, the final soldier swung his sword at Asha. She dodged the attack, falling to the ground. He was about to stab her when a sword emerged from his chest, staining the green of his uniform with blood. He fell to the ground, revealing the dark-haired stranger behind him.

Asha stared at her savior. It was then that she noticed the ears and realized her rescuer was an elf. Her dark brown hair flowed in the wind, and the sun reflected off her olive skin—a Woodlander. Her green eyes seemed to pierce through Asha's soul. A strong chin held up a defined jaw with small pink lips. Asha thought she'd never seen such a beautiful woman. However, she also acknowledged to herself that she was likely just thankful to be alive.

Asha looked around at the bodies of the soldiers, then her gaze returned to the dark-haired elf—the arsenal of weapons on her back and hips, the black armor made from some unknown hide, the look of curiosity on her face. Her rescuer was clearly a dangerous character. But she hadn't tried to kill Asha yet, so that was probably a good sign. The elf stared at her, and Asha didn't move as she waited for her to speak, but she remained silent. She was clearly thinking deeply about something, but her face gave nothing away.

After silence for what felt like minutes, Asha couldn't wait any longer. "Umm...hi?"

The woman didn't respond.

Asha tried to break the tension with a nervous grin. "See something you like?"

It was then that the woman seemed to realize that she was staring. She quickly turned her head and walked over to pull her sword out of the soldier she'd killed.

Asha watched the awkward woman with both curiosity and amusement. "Thanks for the help."

The elf walked over to the other soldiers she'd shot and retrieved her arrows. Asha noticed that the arrows remained in good shape, which meant they were a special kind of steel, likely made from a unique formula. The mystery woman was some kind of professional with access to top quality gear.

Asha raised a curious eyebrow. "You got a name?"

The woman turned back to Asha and walked over to her. She was tall for an elf and towered over Asha, making her tremble slightly. The woman extended her hand. "Jessara." Her voice was deep and a little unsure.

Asha took the hand of the woman. As Jessara pulled her up, Asha noticed the firmness of her grip.

"Asha. Asha Weaver" She got to her feet and continued to look at Jessara, trying to figure out what to say.

"You should probably grab your knives." Jessara looked impassive, but her voice was strangely nervous.

"Right!" As Asha retrieved her weapons, she wondered what this deadly woman had to be nervous about.

"How'd you propel those daggers like that?" said Jessara.

Asha's eyes widened as she tried to come up with something. "Um...strong flick."

Jessara raised an eyebrow. "Really?"

Asha's face turned red. "Yep."

"Strong flick."

"Uh-huh."Jessara tilted her head and raised her eyebrow more.

Asha decided to return the suspicion. "Wait, what are *you* doing out here?"

"What?"

Asha sized up her appearance. "What's a defector from the Kingdom doing out here?"

Jessara's jaw dropped. "I never said I was."

"Well, you clearly aren't Compact." Asha pointed to the bodies. "You aren't an orc, your armor and weapons are too high quality to be from a village. You clearly aren't a bandit, or you wouldn't have saved me. And your accent is mostly faded. So what else could you be?"

"Traveling merchant," she blurted.

It was Asha's turn to raise a suspicious eyebrow. "Really?" *Well, she's full of shit. Then again, so am I.*

"Yeah."

"Why all the weapons?"

Jessara looked at her arsenal, then back at Asha. "I sell weapons."

Asha had several more probing questions, but before she could say anything, a loud horn sounded behind her. The women turned around to find that one of the soldiers was still alive and blowing an alarm horn. Jessara drew her sword, rushed over to the soldier, and stuck it into the side of his neck. Annoyance filled her eyes when she turned back to Asha. "You didn't make sure he was dead?"

"I shot...umm...flicked a dagger at him—he looked pretty bloody dead."

Jessara pointed an aggressive finger at Asha. "You always make sure they're dead! Always!"

Asha threw her hands up. "I'm sorry; my killing skills are rusty!"

The voices of Compact soldiers began coming from the brush.

"Come on!" Jessara beckoned Asha up the path, and they sprinted to escape.

Asha looked behind her and saw dozens of green and red uniforms emerging. "Shit! How many soldiers do they have?"

"It's the outskirts of Compact territory; they have the entire region secured! Why in Nara did you take this path?"

"I could ask you the same thing!"

At that moment, a dozen soldiers emerged from the brush on both sides of the path in front of them. Several of the soldiers had arrows pointing right at the two women. They stopped and turned around to see that the soldiers behind them had caught up and surrounded them.

Asha slapped her palm on her forehead. "Bloody Nara."

CHAPTER SEVEN

THE DEAL

"Not again," Asha groaned. She was in another cell, this time sitting across from Jessara. It was tiny, of solid iron, and surrounded by walls made of mud and twigs. The dusty air filled her lungs. They sat on the floor with their hands tied to poles behind their backs and their legs tied together, their weapons well out of reach on a rack outside the cell.

"I've escaped from worse." Jessara's face was calm to a point that Asha found irritating.

"How?"

Jessara didn't respond.

She pursed her lips. "Comforting."

At that moment, a red-uniformed Compact officer entered the hut and approached the cell. He unlocked it and smiled nastily at her cellmate. "Welcome to Tarton, Jessara. Your papers indicate you are a defector. No last name though."

"I don't have one."

The officer turned to Asha. A small scar crossed his left eye. "There was no identification on you, however. What is your name, leech?"

Asha shrugged. "My parents warned me not to talk to strangers. You should ask your mother; we're much better acquainted."

Without warning, the officer kicked Asha in the gut. The impact was unexpected and knocked the wind out of her. A little harder, and she might have vomited. She gasped in pain for a few moments before catching her breath. "Fuck!"

She glanced over at Jessara, who glared at the officer. Jessara struggled in her bonds, but it was no use.

The officer turned back to Jessara. "What about you, Woodlander? Do you know her name?"

Jessara remained silent as her face relaxed, her expression blank.

"Come now." The officer unsheathed his sword and pointed it at Jessara's neck. "You can tell me." He held the blade close to her throat. "We are all friends here."

Asha assumed Jessara would flip and tell the officer what she knew. But to her surprise, Jessara pressed her throat against the blade. "Do it."

"Oh, bloody Nara." Asha knew she should stay silent, but her impulsive nature got the better of her. "My name is Asha! Asha Weaver."

The officer sheathed his sword and laughed. "Thank you. We will be sure to update our records. See you both on the gallows." He walked out of the cell, relocking it behind him.

Asha glared after him. *Son of a bitch! After I burn these ropes, I'm scorching your ass!*

Jessara glared at her. "Why in Nara did you do that? They have your name on record now!"

That certainly wasn't the "thank you" she'd expected. "He was going to kill you!"

"No, he wasn't. They want to execute us both publicly."

"They want to execute *me* publicly. I saw the look in his eyes—he was going to kill you." Asha narrowed her gaze and studied Jessara suspiciously. Given how experienced this woman clearly was in life or death situations, she couldn't have mistaken the officer's intent.

Jessara glanced away, as if trying to shrug it off. "Look, we're going to get out of here, and it would have been better if they didn't know your name."

Asha raised an amused eyebrow. "Oh yeah? And how are we going to do that?" She knew her own plan of escape, but she was curious about Jessara's.

"You'll burn through the ropes."

She paused, her heart racing. "What?"

Jessara clearly realized she'd made a mistake. "You know, just burn through the ropes."

Asha tilted her head and tried to remain calm. "How did you know I could do that?" Internally, she was freaking out. *You aren't a telepath, are you?*

Jessara smiled awkwardly. "You...told me...Remember?"

"No, I didn't." She tried to focus her mind, looking for any telltale signs of mindreading. After all the time she'd spent around telepaths, she was well acquainted with how the magic felt. But nothing seemed to have invaded her mind. Jessara wasn't a telepath.

Asha stared at Jessara, right in her beautiful green eyes. *No! Not beautiful eyes! You're suspicious right now.* "The only way you could know that is if..." she finished putting it together. "Is if you were sent here to find me."

"No," Jessara lied.

"You were sent to kill me, weren't you?"

"No!"

Asha gave her a look.

Jessara couldn't meet her eyes. "Not exactly."

"So, you *were* sent to kill me. Brilliant! An assassin."

"*Not exactly.*" Jessara emphasized the words this time.

"So you aren't an assassin?"

Jessara opened her mouth to speak, hesitated for a moment, then looked to the side. "If you want to get technical about it."

"Unbelievable!" If her hands hadn't been tied, she would have thrown them up. "I'm sorry I ever thought you had pretty eyes!"

Jessara's jaw dropped, and her face contorted into utter confusion. "Wait—what?"

Asha realized she'd said that out loud. "Don't turn this around on me! You're the one that's here to kill me!"

"It's a bit more complicated than that."

Asha's eyes widened sardonically. "Oh, is it? Please, enlighten me."

"The King suspects you're with the Compact. I was supposed to find out more information and then..." Jessara hesitated, "...then kill you or take you back to Enderdale."

"So, you *are* here to kill me."

"Or take you back to Enderdale."

"Yeah? And what would happen to me in Enderdale?"

Jessara paused for a second. "Well, if you are Compact, you'll be executed. But if you aren't, then you can potentially be pardoned and become an asset."

Asha didn't know what Jessara meant by asset, but it didn't matter. She'd die before she helped the King with anything. "Good to know."

Smoke rose behind her back as she burned through her ropes. She pulled her hands free, and bits of her bindings flew around the room. "I appreciate you saving me. I just saved you so that makes us even." In seconds, she burned through the ropes that bound her legs. "If it makes you feel better, a small part of me hopes that you find a way to escape." She turned to the door of the cell and realized that it was metal. "Shit." She shot flames at the lock. Nothing happened.

She turned to Jessara with an embarrassed smile.

Jessara grinned. "Problem?"

"Nope. I got it." She continued to try to melt the lock. "Oh, by the Tre—umm—Creos!"

"You're not good at thinking things through, are you?"

She glared at Jessara. "I'm closer to escaping than you are."

Jessara used her head to motion to the cell door. "That's solid iron. You're never going to melt it. And if you keep doing that, the lock will become too hot to pick."

Asha stopped her magic. "Well, I can't pick locks."

"I can."

She turned back to Jessara. "You just said you were here to kill or capture me—no bloody way I'm letting you go."

"Look, I was sent after you because we thought you were with the Compact. You clearly aren't. You're also the only known human that can use magic. Come back to the Kingdom with me, and I'll get you an audience with the King. He's sure to see the value of keeping you alive as an asset."

It wasn't that simple for Asha. "What do you mean by 'asset'?"

"I don't know exactly what he has in mind—probably information. But he told me that if you were useful, then you'd remain alive."

Asha wondered how such a powerful, accomplished warrior could be so naive. With all her skills, not to mention her beauty, why would an elf like her work for a racist tyrant like the King? Asha knew firsthand the type of world he was trying to create. "You have too much faith in the generosity of a tyrant."

"Look at your options. The Compact will arrest you on sight, just for being human, and the Kingdom will keep sending people after you until you die or they catch you. You might as well settle things with them."

"I'll be safe in the Northern Mountains. You people can't touch me there."

"With the orcs? The King's planning on trying to establish a treaty with them soon. Nowhere will you be safe."

"You don't know the orcs like I do. They wouldn't give me up."

"Even if that were the case, hiding among them would be problematic for the treaty and make enemies of the orcs and the Kingdom. You wouldn't want that, would you?"

Asha pondered her options. As much as she hated to admit it, Jessara's words made sense. If her actions brought conflict to the Northern Mountains, it would put people she loved in danger—no way she'd allow that to happen. Then again, the Kingdom had no reason to suspect that she'd be there. She'd been able to stay hidden in the past. Perhaps it hadn't been a good idea for her to have told Jessara about her plans. As always, she'd been too honest.

For a brief moment, she considered letting Jessara out so she could pick the lock and then kill her the first chance she got, but she dismissed the idea fairly quickly. Despite what Jessara had said, she hadn't wronged her yet, and her sense of honor reminded her that so far, Jessara had helped her. Even without the locked cell, Asha didn't want to leave Jessara to her fate. She remembered standing on the gallows as people cheered for her death, and she pictured Jessara with a noose around her neck, with Compact soldiers cheering. To the Compact, Jessara's death would be nothing but entertainment. The thought made her sick.

Light from the sun shone through the bars illuminating Jessara's face, her olive skin, her dark brown hair, her piercing green eyes. *By the Tree, why does she have to be so damn attractive!*

She huffed a capitulatory sigh. "You can get this unlocked?"

"Easily."

"You think the King would pardon me?"

"I'll do everything I can to convince him. You have my word."

Asha didn't believe the King would actually pardon her, but she believed that Jessara believed it. Maybe that would be enough for them to work together, at least for now. When they escaped the city, then she could figure out her next move. She walked over to Jessara and moved behind her. "This'll burn a little."

"Do it."

Asha shot flames out of her hands and burned the rope. *This isn't because I think you're pretty.*

Jessara pulled her hands apart as Asha burned off Jessara's leg bonds. Jessara rubbed her wrists for a moment and stretched out.

"All right." Asha motioned to the cell door as if presenting a prized pony. "Get us out of here."

Jessara lifted the heel of her boot and pulled out a small metal wire. She walked to the door, shaped the wire, and within seconds opened the door.

Asha's eyes widened. "Well, that's impressive."

"We need to move."

Jessara and Asha crept over to the rack that held their weapons. Asha retrieved her knife sack, which held 20 throwing knives, but just in case, she strapped a dagger to each leg.

***

Jessara reclaimed her bow, her quiver of arrows, her sword, and her daggers. Putting on her headband completed her ensemble. It was nice to have her gear back; she felt naked without it. As she re-equipped, she kept a weathered eye on Asha. She wouldn't stab Jessara in the back for now, but Aleris' warning rang in her ears. *Passionate and impulsive.*

When Asha pulled up her dress to put her hidden daggers in their holsters, Jessara noticed her taut calves. When Jessara had first seen the drawing of Asha, she'd known she was pretty, but the likeness didn't do her justice. Her face was proportioned perfectly with round cheeks, soft lips, and lively blue eyes that reflected the sun like the surface of the ocean. Jessara was wondering what her wavy blonde hair felt like when Asha's head came up, and Jessara looked away in a hurry. *Fuck me! Focus! Stop acting like a child!*

Once they were armed, Jessara motioned for Asha to follow her. Jessara glanced through the doorway of the shack and observed the town. The buildings were vastly superior in architecture to those of small towns in the Kingdom. A mix of rock and wood comprised their construction, and none had a stone out of place. The smell of smoke from fire pits in the town was a welcome relief from the dusty cell.

Tarton was a military outpost, so most of the people Jessara saw were in uniform. That would make things easier. She preferred to avoid civilian casualties, if possible.

Several houses dotted both sides of the cobblestoned road which led up to the jail. At the end of the road stood the town gallows, from which two nooses swung. Several guards patrolled the streets. To sneak behind the line of houses across the road would be their best bet, but the women wouldn't get to them without being spotted.

Asha finally broke her concentration. "So, we going to blast our way out, or what?"

"Do you want to alert the entire town?"

"Have I mentioned that I can throw fireballs?"

"We need to be smart about this. Give me a moment." Jessara looked back at her fire sorceress companion. Part of her resented the fact that she had to work with Asha. Everything about her was an unknown, and Jessara hated fights with unknown variables. However, she realized that they did need a diversion, and fire was always a good one. "How far can you throw them?"

Asha gave an excited grin, as if she'd been waiting to be asked that question. "How far do you need them?"

Jessara pointed to the scaffold. "Can you throw one to set the gallows on fire?"

Asha glanced at the scaffold with pride. "Yeah."

Jessara nodded. "All right. On my mark, throw a fireball. Then we run over to that line of houses and sneak through the alley behind them."

"Got it." Asha got into position.

"Ready?"

Asha nodded.

"Now!"

Asha held the palms of her hands together and conjured a fireball. The flames reflected off her eyes created a beautiful contrast of orange and blue, which Jessara found annoyingly difficult to ignore. When the spell reached the size of a human head, Asha launched it at the gallows with a *whoosh*. A loud blast shook the ground, and the guards in the area ran to the burning scaffold to investigate. Jessara and Asha darted across the street to the line of houses.

A guard happened to look back and spotted them. "Hey! The prisoners are—" He was interrupted as Jessara put an arrow in him. He fell to the ground and other guards stopped, trying to find the source of the attack. By this point, Jessara and Asha were behind the line of houses.

They ran through the alley and heard a guard shout, "Check the prisoners!"

"Check the alley!" yelled another.

"Fuck!" Jessara drew another arrow.

The two women picked up the pace. Jessara glanced behind her and saw several guards appear at the end of the alley.

"Three guards, behind us!" Jessara halted and shot an arrow. "Two."

Jessara saw Asha stop and produce two knives, then "flick" them at the other two guards. A *crack* came from her hands.

Jessara was amazed. "How in Nara do you do that?"

"Ask me later."

Three more guards appeared at the end of the alley and charged the fugitives.

Asha held out her arm, halting Jessara. "Stand back." She used the palms of both hands to conjure another fireball. It grew until it was the size of the first, and then she threw the inferno at the three guards. It hit the middle one with a loud *bang*. When the blast cleared up, hardly anything was left of the middle guard, and the two others were smoking piles of red and green armor. Asha lost her balance for a second, almost collapsing.

"Are you all right?" Jessara reached out to steady her.

"Yes." Asha caught her breath. "Keep moving!"

When they reached the end of the alley, the town wall towered before them. Guards closed in from both sides.

Jessara shot an arrow at a guard to the left, then one on her right.

Asha produced two more daggers and shot them at both sides with deadly impact.

"Put your arms around me!" Asha turned her back to Jessara.

Jessara stared at Asha's back, completely baffled. "What?"

"Just trust me."

Trust you? Jessara glanced at the approaching guards again. She didn't have time to question. Jessara put her arms around her companion and smelled lavender on her hair. If they weren't in the middle of an escape, Jessara might have thought it a pleasant embrace.

"Hold on!" With that, Asha produced small fireballs in both her hands and slammed them against to the ground, propelling both women up and over the wall. Jessara almost lost her grip, but she held on. As they fell on the other side, Asha produced two more fireballs and slammed them against the ground as they landed.

"What in Nara was that?" Jessara tried to get her bearings.

"Let's get out of here!"

CHAPTER EIGHT

THE CAMPSITE

Jessara had managed to bag a rabbit in the forest. Four hours had passed since she and Asha had escaped from Tarton, and they had set up camp on a natural ledge overlooking the forest, making it easy to spot incoming patrols. Despite her mistrust of Asha, they had to eat, and hunting was best done alone, so she left Asha to guard the campsite.

On her way back, Jessara considered what to do about her new companion. It was clear Asha wasn't helpless. Reckless maybe, but not helpless. Whether that was a good or bad thing remained to be seen. Was Asha sincere about taking the deal? Would she willingly accompany her to the Kingdom? Unfortunately, Jessara was much better at reading people's intentions during combat than during conversations. It was easier to lie with the mouth than the body.

Before she returned to camp, she considered killing Asha from a distance. It would be easy enough to shoot an arrow from the forest. Jessara paused and took out Aleris' notes to see if they could give her clarity. One passage on fire mages caught her attention. "Honest to a fault and will usually wear their emotions on their shoulders. While anyone is capable of deception, it is not in the nature of a fire mage, and it will rarely be their first impulse. They favor a direct approach to conflict."

Jessara looked toward the camp. Aleris' passage would explain why Asha was so cavalier about everything. Jessara kept in mind Aleris' comments about those behaviors being "tendencies" rather than universal traits, but these notes eased her fears about a possible betrayal.

After all, Asha had saved Jessara twice in Tarton. So far, she'd given her no reason to turn on her. Asha would live for now. If a betrayal occurred, it wouldn't be Jessara's.

When Jessara returned to camp, she found Asha sitting on a log watching the sunset. She gave Jessara a welcoming smile, and Jessara almost felt guilty for considering killing her. Almost. Being cute wouldn't save Asha.

Jessara glanced down at the dead rabbit and back up at Asha. She wanted to avoid building a fire if she could.

"If I skin this, could you cook it?"

"Sure." Asha patted a spot on the log next to her. "But first, come look at this sunset." The sun created an orange reflection over the clouds that spread across the sky.

Jessara rolled her eyes, dropped to the ground, and began to skin the rabbit. "Yes, it's very nice."

Asha giggled. "You didn't even look at it."

Jessara glanced at the sunset again. "*Very* nice." She turned back to the rabbit.

"Put that down; I'm not hungry yet." Asha patted the log again. "We cheated death today. The least you could do is enjoy a sunset."

Jessara sighed. "If it'll make you cook the damn rabbit, fine." She sat next to Asha, maintaining an impassive expression.

Asha shook her head and laughed.

"What?"

"You. You're so dark and brooding."

Jessara studied the ground. "I'm not dark and brooding."

Asha raised an eyebrow as her grin deepened. "Oh? When was the last time you took a day off and had a date or something?"

"I've had plenty of dates."

Asha's eyebrow rose higher. "That didn't end with you killing the other person."

Jessara thought for a second. "I've had...some dates." In truth, they were one-night stands.

Asha laughed again.

"I'm an assassin. What do you want from me?"

Asha grinned. "Nothing—unless you're offering."

Jessara attempted to suppress a smile as she turned red.

"Was that a blush?" Asha's eyes lit up as if she'd discovered hidden treasure.

"No!" *Fuck! Did I really just blush?*

Asha winked. "Don't worry; I won't tell anybody."

A strange feeling brewed in the pit of Jessara's stomach, as if something wanted to get out. This time she had no power over suppressing her smile. "Do you always pry this much?"

Asha shrugged and scooted a little closer. "Depends on if I think there's something to pry."

"There's nothing mysterious about me, if that's what you think."

"Oh, really? You don't even have a bloody last name."

The smile disappeared as sorrow filled Jessara's heart.

"I'm sorry." Asha's tone grew softer.

Jessara shook her head. "It's fine."

"Sore subject?"

"You could say that."

Asha hesitated. "What happened? If you don't mind my asking."

Jessara had never told anybody what had happened to her parents, and the only person who did know was the King. Normally, she coped by channeling her hatred into those who'd wronged her, forging the ruthless assassin that she was. But for a moment, Asha's deep blue eyes put her at ease. Jessara almost never willingly made eye contact, but something about Asha made it easy. Made her vulnerable. And that scared her.

Jessara turned away and looked back at the sunset. It *was* beautiful. There was even a pleasant breeze that carried the sweet scent of a nearby cedar tree.

"Look, if you're trying to be my friend, don't." Jessara sighed. "I'm not a friend person."

"Why not?"

"It's not worth it. People die. Might as well make sure you don't miss them when they do."

"That's a bleak outlook."

"It's a bleak world."

Asha looked back at the sunset. "There is beauty in it too, though."

"The sun only sets once a day."

"There are other things." Asha turned to her companion.

Jessara gazed back, caught by the flirtation in Asha's voice. Asha's blue eyes glimmered, and the sun's last rays glistened on her wavy blonde hair. Asha gently rested her hand on Jessara's arm. Everything she'd learned told her to move back, but she stayed still. The pressure of Asha's hand was pleasant, and she glanced down at Asha's lips.

She's your mark! Jessara came to her senses and stood up. "I should finish the rabbit."

***

Asha frowned in embarrassment. At first, she'd been trying to win Jessara over to reduce the chances of being killed in her sleep. But the more she talked, the more she wanted to get to know her. Asha loved talking to people, and Jessara was especially fascinating. However, the casual flirting may have been too overt. Asha reminded herself that she was flirting with the woman hired to kill her.

"Right. We also need to figure out how we're getting back to Enderdale." Asha still wasn't sure whether she'd comply with Jessara and turn herself in. Before making any decisions, she wanted to know what Jessara's plans were.

Jessara finished skinning the rabbit. "Lake Rune destroys any possibility of a direct path, and it's too dangerous to head south back through Compact territory. A lot of pissed off patrols will be looking for us." Jessara paused and gazed at the sky, as if a map were drawn in the clouds. "The path just north of Lake Rune runs right through another Compact settlement, Robinheart. There's little chance they haven't heard of us."

"So, the Northern Mountains?"

Jessara nodded. "We should be able to find a path to bypass Robinheart and put us back into Kingdom territory."

"Sounds like a plan." It was where Asha had been heading anyway, so she decided she'd stay with Jessara for now. A decent amount of Compact territory remained before they reached the Northern Mountains, and having a deadly assassin on her side might be useful. But their companionship couldn't last, and Asha resented that she'd have to deceive Jessara in the meantime.

"Here." Jessara handed the skinned and gutted rabbit to Asha, who began cooking it with flames from her hands.

Jessara leaned forward as she watched. "How is it that a human can do that?"

Asha shrugged. "You have your secrets; I have mine. And mine don't protect only myself." Even that might be saying too much.

"Can you at least tell me a bit about how your powers work? I know some of the basics, but...I mean, you jumped over a wall."

Asha grinned proudly, deciding no harm could come from sharing that much. "I produce fire from my core and release it through my hands. I build a ball of fire energy to create blast, and the longer I build up the energy, the larger the spell. But magic takes a lot of energy, so the bigger the blast, the more exhausted I get. Sometimes, I can absorb fire around me in order to save energy."

"And you can shoot weapons out of your hands?"

"Yep. I create a concentrated release in my hand, which propels the weapons wherever I'm aiming them. Think of it as a mini-explosion. The spell itself isn't large, so it's a good way to save energy during a fight."

"And the super jump?"

Asha's grin widened as she discussed her favorite trick. "The world is constantly pushing up at you to prevent you from sinking into it. The harder you push the world, the harder it pushes back. I use concentrated blasts in my hands to propel my body upwards and to break my fall when I come down."

Jessara's eyes widened. "That's how you escaped Enderdale. They said you survived falling from the wall."

Asha scoffed. "I didn't fall. I jumped."

Jessara chuckled. "Your powers should prove useful in the mountains."

Asa pulled off a rabbit leg and handed it to Jessara. "At least, we won't have to deal with any people trying to kill us."

"It's the beasts that could be problematic—ice chaulks, snow trolls, frost bats, wolves"—Jessara waved the rabbit leg at Asha—"and mountain bears!"

In truth, Asha knew well the dangers of the Northern Mountains. She knew what they would face when they arrived, but they still had a long way to go before then.

CHAPTER NINE

SPARRING

Asha woke up the next morning to the sounds of birds chirping and frogs croaking. The sweet smell of cedar filled the air as she sat up and saw Jessara skinning their breakfast.

"Rabbit again?" Asha had never been a fan of most small game.

"Not worth trying to carry the meat from larger animals." Jessara handed her the skinned rabbit.

Asha took the animal and began cooking it with her hand. "I'm still alive." She looked at Jessara sideways. "I half expected you to slit my throat in my sleep."

Jessara threw leaves over the place where she'd slept. "Cutting someone's throat is a great way to keep them quiet, but it doesn't kill them immediately—problematic when they can shoot fire out of their hands." She pointed her knife at Asha's chest. "I'd probably go for your heart. You'd lose consciousness before you could do anything."

Asha stared at Jessara, then handed her half of the rabbit. "I feel safer already." Perhaps sticking with an assassin hadn't been the best idea.

"You haven't considered scorching me in my sleep?"

Asha stayed silent. She hadn't been considering it—at least, not anymore.

"The path to the north isn't far from here. We can take it directly to the base of the mountains." Jessara took a bite of meat.

Asha nibbled at her own portion. "Won't there be patrols on the path?"

"There'll be patrols both on and off the path. If it were just me, I'd stay in the woods, but two people are more noticeable. If they catch us, they'll know we're trying to avoid them."

"So, we try to get the drop on them?"

Jessara shook her head. "We try to avoid fighting entirely."

"Why? After yesterday, we've proven we're both more than capable of taking on a few soldiers."

"We were lucky yesterday." Jessara shook her head again. "No, we go with my approach."

"Which is?"

Jessara reached into her satchel and produced a pair of shackles. "Give me your hands."

Asha backed up and raised a finger. "I don't think we're quite at that point in our relationship."

Jessara rolled her eyes. "You're a human in Compact territory. The only way patrols won't immediately try to kill or capture you is if they think you're already captured."

Asha sighed. "So, I pretend to be your prisoner?" More deception.

"Elven bounty hunters turning in humans for execution are not an uncommon sight in Compact territory."

"Look, I know you've probably done this a hundred times, but lying is not something I'm good at."

"Then don't talk."

"Also not something I'm good at."

Jessara threw a bone into some bushes. "I've noticed."

Asha looked at the shackles. "And if it doesn't work?"

"Then we hope the charade gives us the element of surprise, and we improvise."

"While my hands are chained?"

Jessara shrugged. "They'll be in front."

Asha looked between Jessara and the shackles. The idea was terrible, but so far, Jessara had managed to keep both of them alive. She decided to give it a chance. "Fine."

Jessara took Asha's hands and began putting the restraints on. Her grip was firm but not aggressive. She was close enough for Asha to realize that she had a sweet pollen smell to her, the kind a person has when they've spent a lot of time outside. Jessara's piercing green eyes occasionally glanced at Asha as if to make sure she wasn't hurting her, a gentleness Asha had not expected.

When the shackles were securely locked, Asha did not feel vulnerable or unsafe around her companion. In some ways, she felt protected. Asha's breathing rate increased involuntarily as the pressure of the metal on her wrists made her—*Nope! Not the time!*

"We'd best get underway," Jessara said, lifting her satchel.

Asha distracted herself by covering her tracks and visiting the bushes to relieve herself. Then the women headed to the path and began their trek north.

They were silent for the first half hour of walking. Despite their fear of being caught, they enjoyed the beauty of the Dremerian foothills. They passed hilly grassland dotted with a few trees, and dense meadows which greeted them with a sweet flowery scent. Occasional streams soothed them with the sound of rushing water. The Northern Mountains loomed in the distance, the snow-covered range seeming to tower over them as they drew closer.

Asha grew bored as they walked. Long journeys by herself were nothing new, but she was no fan of the isolation. Talking and interacting with people energized her. Sometimes, this got her into trouble as she was prone to oversharing. She never broke her oath, but she had made the mistake of telling people her name in Enderdale. Secrets made her nervous, but she understood their value.

As they walked, Asha kept glancing over at Jessara, hoping she'd notice her boredom and try to spark a conversation. But her impassive companion was oblivious and focused on the path. So Asha did what she did best. Overthinking. Did Jessara hate her? Had Asha said something to upset her? She remembered how upset Jessara had been the previous night when Asha had asked about her last name.

After another few minutes, Asha sighed loudly, trying to give a more overt hint that she wanted to talk. Jessara studied her, but she said nothing, and seemingly satisfied that nothing was wrong, kept moving.

It had to be the last name comment from the previous night. "Hey, Jessara."

Jessara stopped dead in her tracks and looked around for a moment. "Did you hear something?"

"Umm...no."

Jessara scanned the area for a few more moments, putting her ear to the wind. When she seemed convinced that they were alone, she turned to Asha. "What?"

"I'm...I'm sorry if I offended you last night."

Jessara wrinkled her eyebrows, confused. The silence between the two was palpable.

Asha took a deep breath. "I mean when I asked about your background."

Jessara's confusion deepened as she stared. "It's fine." Then she turned her attention back to the path and kept walking.

It's fine? Why was Jessara so cold? After several more minutes, Asha couldn't take the silence any longer. She needed to talk about something, and there was only one thing she knew about Jessara. "So you kill people?"

Jessara didn't look at her and didn't respond. At first, Asha though that she might not have heard the question, and when she spoke, her words were so soft she barely caught them.

"So do you." Jessara still didn't look back.

Asha took a deep breath. "But that's your job."

"It is."

"You like your job?"

"Yes."

"What do you like about it?"

Jessara seemed to think for a few moments. "The killing."

Asha sighed. "Bloody Nara. Work with me here."

Jessara's eyes shot back to Asha. "What are you trying to do?"

"It's a long walk to the mountains."

"So?"

"So, I'm trying to pass the time."

Jessara stopped in her tracks and motioned ahead of them. "Three soldiers." She put on her headband.

Asha looked ahead and spotted the incoming patrol. She slipped a knife into her sleeve and tried to put herself into the headspace of a prisoner. "What do we do if they make us?"

"Let me handle it."

Before Asha could protest, one of the soldiers called out, "Halt! Identify yourself!"

Jessara struck a casual tone and emphasized her Woodlander accent. "I found this leech in our territory. I'm turning her in for the bounty."

The soldier raised an eyebrow and tilted his head. "Is that so?"

Jessara nodded.

"Because it just so happens that we have been informed of two fugitives that escaped justice in Tarton recently." The soldier smirked. "A leech in blue and a Woodlander in black."

Jessara and Asha glanced at each other awkwardly.

"First I've heard about it," said Jessara.

"Truly, who believes rumors these days?" said Asha at the same time.

"Detain them both!"

Without skipping a beat, Asha shot her knife at the soldier on the left.

"Shit!" Jessara jerked at the abrupt start of the fight, but she recovered quickly and drew her sword.

One of the soldiers charged at Jessara, and their blades clashed.

The third went for Asha. She attempted to grab another knife, but her restraints cost her precious seconds. He swung at her, and she lost her footing. "Jessara!"

Jessara was still contending with her own challenger when she glanced back. "Damnit!" She kicked her opponent in the chest, temporarily stunning him, and she darted at Asha's attacker.

He turned his head just in time to see Jessara sink her sword into his chest.

Asha's heart raced as she watched Jessara spin back around to face her final opponent. He charged, but before he reached her, Asha threw a fireball. The soldier screamed as his face became engulfed in flames.

Again, Jessara was thrown off by the spell. After a brief delay, she seized the opportunity and slashed his throat.

As the guard collapsed, Asha pulled herself to her feet. "This was a terrible fucking idea!" She raised her restrained hands.

Jessara turned to face her. "I told you to let me handle it!"

Asha shook her head in disbelief. "What the bloody Nara did you want me to do, just stand here playing with my dick? Not going to happen! Now get these bloody shackles off!"

After a few more seconds of staring, Jessara reached into her satchel and pulled out a key to unlock Asha's cuffs. "Retrieve your knives."

Asha was thrown off by the abrupt change in subject. When her mouth opened, she couldn't find the words to protest. That didn't happen often. In the end, she let out a loud grumble and retrieved her daggers. As she did so, she took a sword off one of the fallen soldiers.

"Do you even know how to use a sword?"

The last thing Asha wanted to hear was another criticism. "Of course I can use a damn sword!"

Jessara gave her a look. "We need to get going."

"And if we run into more patrols?"

"Try to sneak around them or take them out from a distance."

"Are you going to let me help you?"

Jessara sighed. "Do I have a choice?"

"No."

"Fine. Just don't engage until we're on the same page and have a plan of attack."

"Fine." Asha gestured toward the dead soldiers. "Should we do something about the bodies?"

Jessara strapped her gear tighter and turned to leave. "No. We're close enough to the border for others to assume they were ambushed by a Kingdom raiding party. Let's go."

***

They walked for another two hours. The sloppiness of their last fight was eating away at Jessara. She knew traveling with an unknown quantity would be a pain—another person she'd have to try to keep alive. Initially, Jessara wanted to attempt the fake prisoner ruse because she hoped that with Asha restrained, she wouldn't get in her way. Clearly, that was a bust. She wasn't sure if allowing Asha to fight would be much better, but it seemed she had no choice.

Jessara tried to put her frustration aside so she could listen for upcoming patrols. Woodland elves depended heavily on hunting, so most had naturally attuned senses. But even among Woodlanders, Jessara was unique. All of her senses were heightened and far surpassed that of most elves.

In her line of work, heightened senses were useful, but they had their drawbacks. Her senses could easily become overloaded.

Loud noises, large crowds, unwelcome touches, overwhelming smells—even the texture of some foods could make her seize up.

It had been much worse as a child, and she'd learned to control herself better in adulthood. However, she still preferred being on the road or in nature as opposed to cities. Urban centers had too much going on, and they gave her nearly overwhelming anxiety. This was why she took few breaks and loved combat: she could push through sensory overload by staying active. But in other contexts, there wasn't much she could do. For the moment, however, as she scanned for patrols, she was in her element.

Asha huffed another strange breath. Jessara glanced at her, then refocused on the path. That was the third time she'd done that on their trek, and Jessara wondered if she was ill. Trying to read her was fruitless. Jessara still couldn't figure out why Asha had apologized to her earlier. She had no way of knowing Jessara's parentage was a sore subject. When she'd asked, Jessara wasn't angry; she just didn't want to talk about it.

Asha broke the silence again. "So tell me about your most impressive assassination."

Jessara glanced back at Asha, again not sure what to make of her. After their last exchange, Jessara assumed that she would appreciate some silence.

"You're seriously interested?"

"I asked."

She did ask, and Jessara grinned. It wasn't that she hated talking to people; she just hated talking to people about nothing. Most people raised only mundane subjects, such as the weather. Jessara's profession was an artform, but for some strange reason, other people never appreciated her work—so she never found much to talk about.

"I had a contract on a Compact general in Gladerville, a town in the plains," she began. "He'd been behind several raids in the southwestern part of the Kingdom."

"Capture or kill?"

"Kill. Capture contracts are rare."

"So, what happened?"

"Guy was paranoid. Never went anywhere without at least five guards. Normally, I would have just shot him from a rooftop, but he wore heavy armor whenever he was in the street—the kind that's difficult to fight in but arrows bounce off of."

"Damn. Who did he think was out to get him, besides you?"

"Positions fluctuate in the Compact, with people constantly vying for power. Murder and assassination are commonplace, so killing someone notorious is a great way to advance your own position. It's possible that if I hadn't killed him, someone else would've. This particular general was close friends with Supreme Leader Ansod."

"How did you kill him?"

Jessara grinned. "The Kora River flows right through Gladerville. There was a stone bridge in the center of town that crossed it, which he walked over every day. I purchased some mining equipment, and I climbed under the bridge at night, slowly removing stones—not enough for the bridge to collapse immediately or under the weight of just one person."

Asha realized where this was going. "But the weight of six people?"

Jessara winked. "With one wearing heavy armor..."

"And water and heavy armor don't mix." Asha laughed. "How did nobody notice?"

Jessara shrugged proudly. "Like I said, I worked at night. I also left the side stones in place so nobody could see what I was doing."

"Did it work?"

"After three nights of working, the general walked his normal route. When he and all five guards were on the bridge, it collapsed. His *guards* were fine."

"And him?"

Jessara grinned. "They managed to pull his body out of the river a few hours later."

Silence fell over the women for a few moments. Jessara's heart pounded. Had she said too much? Although she was not much of a talker, she was enjoying the opportunity to discuss her work, her special interest. In the past, people had nodded politely and never talked to her again.

"You're brilliant," Asha said.

"Really?"

"Yes!" Asha punched her lightly and grinned.

"Oh."

***

Asha realized that Jessara's reluctance to talk wasn't that she was mad or bitter: she simply didn't like small talk. That understanding made the rest of the day a little easier.

With a little nudging as they walked, she had convinced Jessara to explain her plans. Now, when they encountered small patrols, she let Jessara take the lead, and they were able to avoid another confrontation. It wasn't the approach Asha was used to, but she understood Jessara's intentions better, and she couldn't argue with the results.

As evening approached, they made camp for the night in a secluded spot. Just in case, Jessara used some string and branches to create noise traps around the camp.

Jessara left to hunt while Asha watched the campsite. While she waited, Asha tried to get a feel for her new sword. She gripped the blade tightly and swung it around, trying to mimic Jessara's form.

"What in Nara are you doing?" Jessara said behind her.

"Practicing." Asha tried to keep her focus on the blade, hoping Jessara would be impressed and trust her more in fights.

Jessara let out a barely suppressed laugh. "Your form is terrible."

Asha lowered her sword in disappointment. "How?"

Jessara pointed to her legs. "You're entirely off balance. You said you've handled swords before."

"I can take care of myself."

"Really?" Jessara dropped what looked like a dead squirrel and drew her own sword. "Okay—attack me."

"Seriously?"

Jessara nodded and raised her sword.

Okay fine. I don't need magic to fight. Asha tried to slash at her, but Jessara moved to the side, and with one swift motion of her legs, brought Asha to the ground. Jessara knelt over her, holding her sword over Asha's throat. "Slash. You're dead."

Okay, maybe I do need magic. She opened the palm of her hand. "Whoosh. You're scorched."

A slight smile spread across Jessara's face, and Asha started to laugh.

. "I killed you first." Jessara sheathed her sword and extended her hand to Asha.

"I usually use magic alongside the sword." Asha brushed dirt off her dress. "It's easy to stab somebody blinded by fire."

"And if you couldn't use spells, or you're fighting multiple opponents at close range?"

"I don't know. Wing it?"

Jessara scoffed. "How have you survived this long?"

"Fine." Asha set her fists on her hips. "What am I supposed to do?"

Jessara shrugged. "I can *try* to show you a few things."

Asha raised her sword. She was determined to prove herself to Jessara. Besides, how often would she have the chance to learn sword skills from a trained assassin? At the least, it would give them more to talk about.

Jessara raised her own blade. "First, you need to center your balance. Form an 'L' shape with your feet, and make sure you aren't leaning forward or backward when you move."

Asha shifted her body to Jessara's instructions.

"The number one rule when entering a fight is to know your assets. Assets can be your weapons or tools." Jessara advanced.

Asha took a step back, but tripped on a rock and fell on her butt. "Bloody Nara!"

Jessara pointed her sword at Asha, then lowered it as Asha pulled herself to her feet.

"Assets can also be your surroundings." Jessara motioned around them. "Note the battlefield and figure out what you can use. Now attack me."

Asha advanced toward Jessara and went in for a slash. Jessara dodged, and Asha's blade hit the ground. Jessara's sword returned to Asha's throat. The cold metal made her heart skip a beat.

"If you overcommit to an attack, and it doesn't land, you leave yourself vulnerable." Jessara took her sword off Asha's throat. "You need to leave yourself room to recover. Again."

Asha normally didn't think about strategies; fighting was always instinctive, driven by emotions. She advanced, trying to remain balanced. She glanced down at her feet to make sure she was putting them in a proper "L" shape. Before she could look back up, Jessara had knocked the sword out of her hand, and in another swift motion,

Jessara had used her arm to push Asha backwards and her leg to trip her to the ground. Before Asha could even curse, she was on her back with Jessara holding a dagger at her throat.

"Fuck! Was that necessary?"

Jessara got up and sheathed her dagger. "Never lose focus on your opponent. Want to stop?"

"No!" Asha seethed as she stood up. Jessara would pay for that.

Jessara's grin was smug. "Okay then. Whenever you're rea—"

Before Jessara could finish, Asha attacked. Jessara parried her sword and put out an elbow, which Asha ran straight into. In the next moment, Asha lay on the ground, clutching her forehead. "Damn you!"

"You're angry."

Asha let out a loud grumble. "Bloody right, I'm angry!"

Jessara slashed her sword in a figure eight. "That's why you keep failing. Anger can sometimes make you feel strong, but the sword isn't a weapon of strength. You need strategy and balance. You lose both when you're angry."

Jessara offered her hand, but Asha glared at her. Anger fueled her magic and made it more powerful; she was used to relying on it. However, she acknowledged to herself that although her anger strengthened her magic, it also made it more chaotic. The events of Farnsville played through her mind, and Asha decided it would be worth learning to rely on more than passions in a fight.

Asha's eyes relaxed as she took a deep breath and accepted Jessara's hand. "Is this how you learned?" Asha rubbed her forehead.

"No. They actually hurt me." Jessara let out a laugh.

Asha did *not* laugh. "That explains a lot."

The smile faded from Jessara's face, and her voice softened. "Is your head okay?"

"Fine. Shall we continue?"

"If you want to." Jessara's voice was gentle.

Both women raised their swords. This time, Asha did not rush in for an attack. Instead, she circled Jessara slowly, observing her surroundings without taking her eyes off her opponent. She took a small step forward. Jessara clicked her blade, and Asha immediately stepped back.

"Good job not overcommitting," said Jessara.

Asha nodded with a half-smile before advancing toward Jessara, who took a step back. A tree with a few low-hanging branches stood behind Jessara, giving Asha an idea.

She advanced again, and Jessara took another step back. Another, and Jessara made contact with her sword. Asha slowly circled her opponent until she positioned herself underneath the tree. She then swiped at one of the tree branches, and it fell on Jessara, distracting her. Asha jumped at her, and Jessara dropped her sword. Asha brought her to the ground, straddling her, her sword at her throat. Asha grinned.

The feel of Jessara's body underneath her gave Asha confused feelings. The sweet smell of pollen emanated from Jessara's hair, and for a brief second, she forgot she was holding a sword to her throat.

Jessara raised an eyebrow. "Not bad."

"Got you!" Asha gave a proud smirk. "Always be aware of your surroundings."

"I was just about to say the same thing." Jessara's eyes motioned downward.

Asha glanced at where she'd looked and realized Jessara was holding a dagger against her side. "Oh."

"Yeah."

The women stared into each other's eyes for a while longer. A smile crept across both of their faces as they started to laugh.

"You want to get off me?" said Jessara.

"Yes. Of course." Asha got up. Although "want" was not the word she would have used.

***

Jessara continued instructing for another hour. She tried to ease up a little—less sparring and more slow instruction. She wasn't used to teaching, but she kind of enjoyed it after Asha started listening. As the practice continued, Jessara noticed Asha's balance gradually improving. It still was far from adequate for a professional like Jessara, but it was a start.

Eventually, dusk settled, and it became difficult to see well enough to continue.

Although it was getting colder the farther north they went, they didn't risk lighting a fire. Asha cooked the meat, and as night fell, it became almost pitch black—they'd be well hidden.

As they lay on separate parts of the campsite, Jessara listened to the sounds of the wilderness. When the nerves of being in enemy territory made it difficult for her to sleep, Jessara would listen to the various animal noises and try to imagine the bird, frog, or insect that made each.

Jessara's thoughts were interrupted.

"So why do you do it?"

Jessara sighed under her breath. "What?"

"The whole assassin thing."

There were many reasons, which Jessara had no intention of sharing. "Because I hate the Compact."

"I thought you were supposed to avoid anger?"

"Anger and hate aren't the same thing. I control my emotions when I fight."

"Why do you hate them?"

Another question that would not get a full answer. "Who doesn't?"

"I reckon there are plenty of elves that don't. The ones that do usually have a story."

Jessara did have a story. But despite the fact that she was slowly becoming less annoyed by the presence of her companion, it wasn't a story she would be sharing anytime soon. "It's late, and we have a long day tomorrow."

The air was filled with silence for several moments. Finally, Jessara heard Asha say, "Right. Good night."

For the next three days, Jessara and Asha continued their journey to the Northern Mountains. On their trek, Jessara tried to teach Asha how to stay out of sight, and they were able to avoid further confrontation. During rests, Jessara continued to instruct Asha on form and footwork. She steadily improved, but Jessara could only teach so much in the short time they had.

By evening on the third day, they were almost to the mountains. The range towered above the women, the terrain more rocky and hilly. The air grew colder, chilling Jessara to the bone.

Suddenly, Jessara stopped in her tracks and held out her hand to halt Asha.

"What is it?"

Jessara knelt down and placed her hand on the ground. She closed her eyes for a few seconds and felt vibrations. "Company." She motioned for Asha to follow her, and they ran off the path to their right and climbed a hill overlooking the path. Within moments, a group of five elves came into view. However, they weren't wearing Compact colors. Instead, they wore animal skins and plain leather armor. A human man, his arms chained behind his back, was in tow.

Asha gave Jessara a puzzled look.

"Bounty hunters," said Jessara. "Like I said, you often come across them taking humans for execution. Poor bastard."

Asha looked horrified. "We have to do something."

Jessara shook her head. "Not much we *can* do. And we already have enough people looking for us."

Jessara noticed Asha staring at the man. He was frail and emaciated with a filthy tunic, his body drenched in sweat, his forehead streaked with blood. Asha looked back at Jessara with obvious intention in her eyes.

Jessara gave her a warning glare. "Don't do it."

Without another word, Asha jumped from behind the rock and darted at the bounty hunters.

"Fuck me." Jessara grabbed her bow, put on her headband, and ran after Asha.

Chapter Ten

Rescue

By the time Jessara had made up her mind, the bounty hunters had noticed Asha charging.

Asha produced daggers in both hands and shot them—one into the chest of the leader and the other at a second hunter who she missed by inches. Then she drew her sword as three of the remaining hunters rushed at her, the fourth remaining with the prisoner. With her free hand, she shot a fireball at the closest assailant, and blinded, he ran right into Asha's blade.

Jessara sprinted to the fight and shot an arrow into another hunter.

The next hunter attacked Asha just as she'd recovered from the first assault, and although she parried his sword, she lost her balance. Taking the advantage, he elbowed her face.

Jessara holstered her bow and darted to Asha as she hit the ground. Before Asha could use her magic in defense, her assailant's blade was slashing down at her. Jessara intervened just in time. If anybody was going to kill Asha today, it would be Jessara.

Seizing the opportunity, Asha launched a fireball at the hunter's face, his scream suddenly interrupted when Jessara finished him off. Together, she and Asha turned to face their final foe.

He stood behind the prisoner, holding a knife to the human's throat. "One step closer, and the leech dies!"

The human was terrified. Pleading eyes fixed themselves on the women before him.

As if she'd heard nothing, Jessara reached for her bow, drew an arrow, and shot the bounty hunter between the eyes. He fell to the ground, leaving the prisoner unharmed.

"Creos!" said the prisoner, collapsing to his knees.

Ignoring him, Jessara's blood boiled as she turned and glared at Asha. Once again, she'd started a sloppy fight that had almost gotten her killed. Jessara's fury bubbled. "You ever do that again, and I'll kill you myself!"

Asha stared at Jessara as if it was *she* who was crazy. "I had to do something!"

"No. You *decided* to do something."

"Okay then—why'd you *decide* to help me?"

Jessara wasn't entirely sure why she hadn't just let Asha die. Jessara could have remained in her hiding spot and collected Asha's head once the bounty hunters cleared the area. The rest of the journey would have been a lot easier without Asha constantly blundering into trouble. But as Jessara imagined cutting Asha's head off her dead body, something churned in the pit of her stomach, a sense of loss and sorrow. The loss of what, Jessara didn't know. In the end, she decided it was all for the extra bounty; that was the only rational reason. "Retrieve your daggers!"

Asha silently seethed, but complied.

"Milady, good elf, I don't know who you are, but you have me thanks," the prisoner said, raising his head with an effort. He might have been thirty or fifty—his brown hair streaked with gray, his forehead wrinkled—but his signs of age appeared to be more from hard living than years.

Asha found a key on one of the bodies and unlocked the prisoner's restraints.

"You're welcome. And when you're recaptured, try not to mention you saw us," Jessara said, wiping blood off her sword, then sheathing it. It might have sounded cruel, but Jessara was serious.

Asha glared at her. "Jessara!"

Jessara stalked toward her until she was inches from her face and pointed at the man. "This is why you don't just charge into battle. You think you've saved him, but he can't follow us where we're going, and he's too deep in Compact territory to make it out. Recklessly trying to save everyone just-gets-people-killed!"

A change spread across Asha's face the moment Jessara finished speaking. Despite Jessara's struggles to read faces, the look was unmistakable. Pain. Something about Jessara's comment had devastated Asha, and it pierced through Jessara's stoic demeanor. She felt remorse, a feeling she barely knew. Tears threatened to spill out and she had no idea why. With all the death and pain she'd caused in her life, why was this causing her guilt? She had no time for this, so she tried to bury it with fury. "Fuck!" She turned around and slammed her fist against a tree. Her fist throbbed with pain as she slowly composed herself.

For a few moments, the only sound was the rustling of the forest around them. Jessara glanced at the prisoner, expecting to see anger or fear in his face. Instead, she saw what appeared to be sorrow and concern. She felt for the man, but nothing more could be done. She put her bow on her back and turned toward the path. "Let's go."

"Begging your pardon." The prisoner took a step toward Jessara, his hands open in supplication. "I know I've no right to ask anything more, but...they got me boy!"

Jessara kept walking. The King had always told her that any emotion—besides hatred—was a liability on missions.

"I'm sorry. But your son's lost."

"Please, good elf—he's but eight!"

Jessara stopped in her tracks. She turned to look at him and attempted to strike a more empathetic note. "I truly am sorry. But nothing can be done." Nothing could. That was the truth.

"I know where the camp lies," said the man. "Clearly, you both know how to fight. Please, good elf, he's a child."

Asha put her hand on the man's shoulder. "How far?"

"Asha," Jessara said, her tone calm, but firm. "We can't get involved."

Asha stormed up to Jessara and stared into her eyes. "How can you be so heartless!"

That comment hurt Jessara more than she expected. She wasn't being heartless. The man was in no shape to accompany them in the Northern Mountains, and it certainly would be no place for a child. Even if they could mount a rescue, both the father and son would be recaptured before making it back to the Kingdom. It was the truth, and emotions wouldn't change that. Jessara had spent a lot of time in Compact territory, and she regularly came across groups of bounty hunters with human prisoners. She'd never attempted to rescue them for the same reasons. But as Jessara looked at Asha's judgmental eyes, she couldn't help but feel sickened by her own indifference.

"Fuck me!" Jessara turned to the man. "How many are in the camp?"

"At least six."

Jessara sighed. "How far?"

"Two miles to the west."

Jessara looked at Asha. "Fine. But you do exactly what I say when I say it. I make the plan, you listen to it, and you follow it to the fucking letter! Are we clear?"

"All right." Asha gave a confused half smile.

"I can't thank you enough." The man was almost in tears.

Jessara stalked toward the path. "Don't thank us yet."

Asha and the man scrambled to follow her. This rescue plan was a bad idea, but Jessara felt too confused by her own actions to be angry. She certainly wasn't angry at the man; none of this was his fault. But neither could she be truly angry at Asha. Jessara couldn't help but admire Asha's idealism, but it was a trait she knew she'd never share.

"What's your name?" said Asha, as the man led them west. The farther they traveled, the rockier the terrain became. Brush and trees remained, but they were less frequent. The air seemed to take on a grayish light, and left a dry taste in Jessara's mouth.

"Gorno," said the man.

"And your son?"

"Storn."

"We'll get him back," Asha said. "How did you end up out here anyway?"

Jessara glanced at Asha, saying nothing. She'd been taught never to make promises she couldn't keep.

"Storn and me live on a small farm near the border," said Gorno. "Normally, hunters don't bother you unless you cross it. But as the Kingdom's been stepping up attacks against the Compact, the price on humans has doubled in some towns. Near a week ago, this gang raided me farm and took us both."

"A week?" Asha's tone was grim. "They've kept you for that long?"

"Bounty hunters typically hold onto captured humans longer," said Jessara. "The bounty for humans is different depending on the town, and they often compete with each other for access to 'entertainment'."

Asha looked horrified. "That's terrible!"

"Yes, well, the Compact's evil—welcome to Dremeria."

Asha frowned and turned back to Gorno. "Why were you separated?"

Gorno shook his head. "I don't know."

Jessara wished she didn't know the answer. "They still pay bounties on children, but they don't normally make public spectacles out of killing them. Bad for morale, I guess. Bounties on them are usually paid by the military, who hold private executions."

"Oh Creos." Tears streamed down Gorno's cheeks, and Asha shot Jessara a look.

"You asked." Jessara hadn't intended to be callous. She felt a twinge of guilt, but guilt wouldn't save his son.

"Is it just you and Storn?" Asha asked.

"Aye." Gorno tried to regain his composure. "Sickness took me wife three winters ago—boy's all I got left."

Another tear ran down Gorno's face, and a tightness gripped the pit of Jessara's stomach.

"I'm sorry," said Asha. "We'll do all we can."

Gorno wiped his face with his shirt. "If you don't mind me asking, how is it you produce fire from your hands, milady?"

Asha grinned. "Trade secret."

The trio walked for another half hour. Rock covered more of the terrain the farther they went. Evening was falling, and the scent of a campfire saturated the air as Jessara noticed smoke coming from behind a rocky hill.

"That's them." Gorno whispered, pointing at the smoke.

"Stay down and follow me." Jessara led them to the top of the hill, which she hoped would give them a good vantage point. She was correct. She and her companions lay prone at the crest and below them, six tents surrounded a campfire. Jessara counted four bounty hunters—one patrolled the perimeter of the camp, while three others sat around the fire either eating or staring at the flames. Two poles were stuck in the ground nearby. A child was tied to one—Storn—and the other restrained an elven bounty hunter. A curious sight, but a question to be answered later.

To Jessara's relief, Asha and Gorno stayed silent as she formed a plan and adjusted her headband. The patrolling bounty hunter had a brief window during his route where a tent blocked him from the view of his companions.

Jessara turned to Asha and wondered what to do with her. Despite Jessara's preferences, her previous attempts to convince Asha to sit out fights had failed. Furthermore, although Jessara probably could take down four bounty hunters by herself, it would be sloppy without help. So Jessara thought about how she could use all of her assets, including Asha. The most useful Asha had been so far was when, as in Tarton, she'd been a distraction. That gave Jessara an idea.

"Asha, I'm going to take out the patrol," she whispered, nodding to the man below. "As soon as I do, I need you to create a distraction. Get their heads turned away from me."

Asha nodded, and Jessara left the group. The hills and rocks around the camp provided plenty of cover for Jessara to get in position without being spotted. She wasn't used to working with other people on jobs and putting her trust in Asha wasn't easy. But Asha hadn't gotten either of them killed yet, so that was a good sign.

Jessara took position behind a rock, waiting for the patrolling bounty hunter. She clutched her dagger tightly. He looked primitive, wearing a badly sewn bear skin which swayed back and forth as he walked, his eyes on the surrounding hills. With more ease than it should have been, Jessara crept behind him, covered his mouth, slit his throat, and eased his body to the ground.

***

Asha emerged from her hiding spot and casually strode to the group of bounty hunters, who were noticeably confused when they saw her.

"Hey there, boys!" Asha noticed one of the hunters was a woman. "And girl! I'm a human with a massive bounty on her head, and I'm looking for some bounty hunters so I can turn myself in. Do you know any?"

The bounty hunters stood up, but didn't go for their weapons. They were too dumbstruck to do anything besides stare with dropped jaws.

That's right. Keep your eyes on me.

"What are you playing at?" said one of the bounty hunters.

"Well...if you don't know any, I guess I'll just be off." Asha turned around and began to slowly walk away.

"Wait...stop!" said another bounty hunter.

As planned, all backs were turned to Jessara. Asha turned and tried not to glance at Jessara as she crept behind the closest bounty hunter. Before the hunter took another step, Jessara snapped his neck.

The hunter beside him never even noticed, for with one fluid movement, Jessara had sunk her dagger into her side, eliciting a death scream.

The final bounty hunter whirled around in time to see Jessara's sword diving into his chest.

Asha watched the scene with amazement. The fight, if one could call it that, had lasted only seconds, and Jessara had moved through the bounty hunters like smoke. If that was the type of precision Jessara was used to, no wonder she'd been so annoyed with Asha. Everything about the execution, from her steps to her weapons' play, was perfect, and Asha realized how much she could learn from her companion. Perhaps she could prevent future mistakes like the one she'd made in Farnsville.

Jessara sheathed her weapons as Gorno emerged from his hiding place and sprinted to his captive child. "Storn, me boy!"

"Papa!" The boy wore a dirty white tunic with a brown vest and trousers. He had his father's puffy cheeks and small forehead, but his hair was blonde. Asha suspected he'd gotten that trait from his mother, and she smiled as she watched the reunion.

Gorno struggled to undo the child's ropes, and Jessara handed him one of her daggers.

"Thank you, good elf." Gorno gladly took the knife. "A thousand thanks!"

Jessara turned to the captive elf. "What's going on here?"

Asha had been curious about that herself.

The child pulled his hands free. "Tiriel tried to save me, Papa!"

Asha squinted at the captive. He was young for a bounty hunter, late teens or early twenties. Fear filled his eyes, but behind that fear was a certain fire.

Jessara knelt to eye level with the bounty hunter. "Is that true?"

Tiriel hesitated, then nodded. "He is just a child. This is not what I signed up for." The young elf was slender and short, with hair as red as the dried blood on his face.

"You signed up to hunt humans for the Compact." Jessara's voice was slow and lacked emotion in a way that made Asha tremble.

"Yes," said Tiriel. "But most of the lee—humans we've captured meant us no harm. Certainly, a child does not. I thought being a bounty hunter would be adventurous, but I cannot keep doing this. Innocent people have died because of me. I tried to save the child last night—killed one of my clan in the process, but the rest overpowered me."

"You think that redeems you?"

"Nothing ever will. You might as well kill me. I deserve it."

Can't argue with that. Although Asha decided to keep her thoughts to herself; after all, she'd agreed that Jessara could call the shots on this rescue. But she didn't see any reason why the bounty hunter should be spared, and she assumed Jessara would feel the same way. Even if he felt bad later, he still stole a child. Nobody deserves a second chance after that.

"No!" Storn struggled in his father's arms. "He's me friend!"

Asha looked at the child. *Poor kid.* Then she brought eyes back to Jessara.

Jessara looked at Gorno and Storn. The son had pleading eyes, but the father remained stone-faced. He held his child again, and that was all that seemed to matter to him. Then her gaze met Asha's, who'd already assumed that the bounty hunter's fate was sealed. Finally, Jessara returned her attention to Tiriel. The young man's eyes made it clear he was ready to die.

"Give me back my dagger." Jessara held out her hand to Gorno.

"No!" Storn tried again to pull himself free, but Gorno held tight and handed the dagger to Jessara.

Asha was fully prepared to watch Jessara slit the elf's throat, but to her surprise, Jessara walked behind Tiriel and cut his bonds.

Tiriel rubbed his wrists in confusion. "I do not—"

"Get them out of Compact territory." Jessara nodded toward the father and son. "Keep them restrained and openly use the path. If you run into any soldiers, you're a bounty hunter turning them in. You're already dressed for the part. Nobody's looking for them, so as long as you don't say anything stupid, they should believe you."

Asha hadn't considered any of that. She would have killed Tiriel without a second thought, and she would have been wrong. After that moment, Asha looked at Jessara with a new respect.

***

Jessara did not take her eyes off the confused bounty hunter she'd spared.

"I do not deserve your mercy, Woodlander," said Tiriel.

Jessara shook her head. "No, you don't. Now get moving!"

Gorno got up and walked over to Jessara, looking between Asha and her. "I'm in your debt. How could I repay you?"

For a moment, Jessara considered asking for money. But the glow of admiration in Asha's eyes warmed Jessara in a way she'd never experienced, and she didn't want that feeling to go away. "Survive—so it wasn't for nothing."

Gorno nodded. "Come, boy. We're going home." Tiriel, Gorno, and Storn parted ways with the women.

Jessara watched them leave with a sense of satisfaction. The fight had been clean, the mission a success, and probably not for nothing. And now they could continue with her mission.

She scanned the camp, ignoring the dead bounty hunters on the ground. "We should search the camp for provisions and move. We'll put some distance between us and here, and then we'll settle in for the night."

Asha nodded and began searching the tents. The women found some bread and a bit of cooked meat, which they chewed as they hiked. Asha had remained silent, and Jessara wondered what she was thinking. Then she wondered why she cared.

The silence between the two lasted until they found a spot to sleep for the night. It was cold, so they decided to risk a fire. Again, Jessara created some noise traps around the camp.

The women sat around the fire watching the flames. Jessara wanted to break the silence, but she had no idea how. What would she say?

Fortunately, Asha broke it for her. "I'm sorry I called you heartless. You did a good thing today."

Jessara shrugged. "If they survive."

"You gave them a fighting chance."

"I suppose."

Asha gave a half smile. "Why did you do it? I mean, rescue the kid. What changed your mind?"

Jessara searched Asha's face. The flames from the fire reflected off her blue eyes, creating a beautiful contrast. She wasn't sure how to answer. She wasn't sure what the answer *was*. So, she went with what she thought the answer should be. "You would have gone anyway. Probably would've gotten yourself killed or captured. It was logical."

"No, that's not it." Asha's gaze pierced through Jessara's mind. "You care."

"I care about hurting the Compact." Jessara picked up a stick and poked at the fire. "At least we deprived them of their twisted satisfaction."

"So it's hate?"

Jessara shrugged. "That's what it's always been."

Asha shook her head. "But that can't be everything."

"Why not?" Hate was all Jessara had ever needed.

"Because what would that leave if the Compact were ever defeated?"

Jessara had never thought about that before. In the back of her mind, she'd convinced herself that her assassinations supported her goal to defeat the Compact, but she'd never considered what that would mean for *her*. "We're far off from that."

"Well, I hope that you find something else worth fighting for before that day comes."

Jessara glanced at Asha. She'd never talked this much to one person before. Conversations with the King or Aleris were almost always work related. Occasionally, she found men or women in Enderdale bars for one-night stands, but those encounters rarely involved much talking. For a moment, she forgot that Asha was her mark.

"Besides, with an enemy like you, I'd say their days are numbered." Asha grinned. "The way you moved around those bounty hunters was bloody incredible! I've seen you fight, but that was something else. And

I'm...I'm sorry I keep rushing into fights. You have more experience, and I keep throwing you off."

"Thanks." Not a word Jessara was accustomed to using. "It's just...I'm not used to working with anyone."

"I understand. But you have to admit, we did well today."

Jessara had to give her that. "Your distraction was helpful—and amusing."

Asha grinned proudly. "Nothing's more distracting than a harmless woman saying exactly what you want to hear."

Jessara chuckled. "*Harmless* is not how I would describe you."

Asha raised an eyebrow, and her grin deepened. "That sounded like two compliments in a row."

Jessara playfully shrugged. "I don't know what you're talking about. I'm heartless, remember?"

Asha crossed her arms. "Hey! I feel bad about saying that."

Jessara laughed. "So it's something I can hold over you? Good to know."

They stopped talking, and Jessara found herself staring at Asha's lips. She tried to focus on her eyes, but then she started noticing...other parts of her body.

Hoping Asha hadn't noticed her wandering eyes, Jessara said, "We should probably get to sleep. We'll be in the mountains by midday."

"Sounds good." Asha's tone was flirtatious.

Shit, she definitely noticed.

Jessara lay on the ground, pondering. Friendly banter was not something she was accustomed to, but she found it easy to talk to Asha. Easy and enjoyable. Asha was genuinely interested in what she had to say, and Jessara could be herself, at least a version of herself that she liked. This immediately made Jessara suspicious. The King had always taught Jessara that people were only kind when they wanted something. Once they had it, they left you.

Jessara pulled out Aleris' notes, needing answers. A passage in the section on fire mages caught Jessara's eye. "Fire mages develop strong bonds. They are fiercely loyal to those they care about and will go out of their way to protect friends, family, and loved ones, at the risk of great injury or harm to themselves. However, on the inverse side, they are not known for being forgiving, and once trust is lost, it is nearly impossible to get back."

Jessara put the notes down and glanced at Asha, who was already asleep. They were still far from friends, but perhaps having someone like Asha on her side wasn't a bad thing.

Then she remembered that Asha was her mark. She thought about the agreement they'd made, and for the first time, she found herself hoping that the King would pardon her. Despite her rash behavior, Asha was a good woman. But Jessara knew it wouldn't be up to her. *People die. Might as well make sure that you don't miss them when they do.* Jessara let out a silent sigh and rested her head on the ground. *No use worrying about it now.*

Chapter Eleven

Into the Northern Mountains

The cold was already getting to Jessara when she reached the base of the Northern Mountains, and as they climbed, the temperature continued to drop. Jessara had been trained to survive the cold, but her body wasn't built for it. The forests of Anwood were warm, and despite how little time Jessara had spent in the region, her biology preferred the heat.

Asha demonstrated what Aleris' notes had already told Jessara. Fire sorceresses were able to keep themselves warm in the coldest of climates, her body a walking fireplace. At one point, she'd offered Jessara her cloak. Jessara's own was made for stealth, but it did little to protect her from the environment.

At first, she'd refused, remembering the King's lesson that the day she started relying on others would be the day she sealed her fate. However, the second day in the mountains brought a chilling snowstorm. The snow crystals stung like shards against Jessara's face, and her ears grew so cold, she thought they'd snap off. Her limbs tensed as if her very tendons and ligaments had frozen, and walking grew so difficult, she was slowing them down. Asha became more insistent, so Jessara swallowed her pride and accepted Asha's offer.

When Jessara put the cloak on, the warmth it had absorbed from the fire sorceress instantly rejuvenated her. Her ears thawed in the warm hood, and she was comforted by the lavender scent from Asha's hair. Soon, she was able to pick up the pace.

As they trekked, Asha asked Jessara to tell her more stories of her assassinations, and Jessara was flattered. Asha didn't revel in killing, but she seemed to admire Jessara's abilities.The King only gave light praise after she'd completed her assignments, which, as she hated to admit, she craved almost as much as the gold. But he always treated her successes as nothing more than transactions. Perfection was expected of her, so he wasn't surprised when he got it. Asha was different.

"So basically, if your task had been to kill me, I'd be fucked?"

"Yeah," said Jessara.

"Does that mean you would have killed me the moment we escaped from Tarton?"

"Yes." She didn't want to tell her that she'd strongly considered doing it anyway.

Jessara had never thought she could talk to someone this much, let alone enjoy it. Most of her time was spent on jobs, always by herself. Whenever she'd had down time, she'd usually spent it drinking, brawling, or having casual sex with someone she'd picked up. Often, she simply ran out of things to talk about, since she could only explain so many times all the ways she knew how to kill.

Asha, on the other hand, listened carefully to Jessara's stories, appreciating her insights, and seeming to learn from them. After some of the fights they'd already had, Jessara figured that teaching Asha how to plan would help her.

They trudged through a long pass, curiously flat, which ran to the east within the mountains. After another hour, Jessara spotted a white figure moving up ahead, that blended into the falling snow. "Hold up."

"What is it?"

"I'm not sure." Jessara motioned for Asha to crouch down, and the two women crept closer. The snow made it difficult for Jessara to make out its exact features, but she studied its movement. Its arms were longer than its legs, its back hunched, and it walked as if limping on both legs. Jessara could recognize that walk anywhere.

"Snow troll." Jessara pulled out her bow and put on her headband.

"You've killed trolls before though, right?" Asha's voice shook.

"Yeah." Jessara drew an arrow and aimed at the troll. "They aren't difficult if you can get the drop on them."

Jessara held her breath and prepared to release, but before she could, the ground broke beneath the troll. A giant white snake-like creature shot into the air and pulled the troll into a frozen lake.

Asha nearly lost her footing. "Bloody Nara!"

Jessara lowered her bow. "Ice chaulk!" she said, trying to hide her terror. "This could be problematic."

"But it's okay, because we aren't over that lake, right?"

Jessara knelt down and dug through the snow. After nine inches, she hit a slippery surface, causing her heart to nearly jump out of her chest. "Stand. Completely. Still."

"You've killed ice chaulks before, right?"

"Yeah." Jessara tried to force a confident smile.

Asha gave her a look.

"Okay, it was a regular chaulk." Jessara pursed her lips. "And there were twelve of us."

"We're going to die."

"Shhh!" Jessara put her ear to the ice of the lake. The sound of water moving rustled under them. For a moment, time seemed to stop. The wind died down, and even the falling snow seemed to slow in fear of the monster beneath.

"We need to run." The movement in the water grew louder. "Now!"

Jessara and Asha leapt from their spot. Moments later, the chaulk shot up from the ice where they'd been standing. Asha threw a fireball at the beast, but it curled its head down, causing the spell to hit its protective scaly layer.

"Shit!"

"It's got a tough layer on top." Jessara quickly glanced back at the beast. "Nothing's getting through that!"

Jessara ran faster than she ever had in her life, and to her surprise, Asha kept up. The ice chaulk periodically reemerged, barely missing them each time. Glowing red eyes tracked the fleeing women each time the beast emerged, and it's mouth opened in four directions with razor sharp teeth, its snout exhaling visible breath.

"How did you survive the first time?" said Asha, panting.

"Most of us didn't."

"Well, that's fucking comforting!"

Memories of her previous encounter flowed through Jessara's brain. "It's got a soft underbelly!"

At that moment, the ice chaulk crashed through the ice in front of them.

"Fuck!" Jessara slid a few paces as she tried to slow herself.

The beast curled its head, preparing to strike, and lunged at the two women. Jessara pushed Asha out of the way, and the beast barely missed them as the women lost their footing.

Asha slid across the ice away from Jessara. The ice chaulk had disappeared back into the lake, but the water moved beneath Jessara. She jumped backwards as the ice chaulk shot up again, separating her from Asha.

The force from the beast cracked the ice, and the chunk Jessara stood upon separated from the rest of the lake.

"Fuck! Fuck! Fuck!" Jessara grabbed her sword as the chaulk prepared for another strike. When it came down, Jessara slashed, stopping its advance and cutting beneath its chin.

The beast roared and snapped down at Jessara. She tried to duck, but one of its fangs sank into Jessara's right shoulder, breaking through her armor. Pain shot through her body as she screamed at the top of her lungs.

A large fireball hit the back of the beast's head, causing it to release Jessara. Blood poured out of her shoulder as Jessara saw Asha circling around the hole in the ice, trying to get the ice chaulk's attention.

"Over here you ugly snake!"

The "snake" turned to Asha, presenting Jessara with an opportunity. She grabbed her bow, but the pain from her shoulder made her scream again. The muscles in her shoulder seized as she tried to ignore the agony.

She nocked an arrow, and more blood poured from her shoulder and onto the ice. With her last strength, she aimed and let loose. The arrow hit the chaulk in the bottom of its neck, and its shriek shook the ground as the beast retracted into the water. Jessara collapsed, clutching her shoulder.

"You got it!" Asha threw a fist in the air.

"It's not dead!" Jessara tried to breathe through the pain. "It's just assessing my strength. It'll be back."

"You need to get back here. Can you jump?"

Jessara was still floating on the free ice chunk. Between her blood loss and having only one usable arm, getting to her feet was a struggle. The edge of the hole was about ten feet away.

"I think so."

Jessara backed up, ran to the edge of the ice chunk, and leapt. Asha darted to the edge of the hole as Jessara landed on the ice, but it broke under her, plunging her into the icy water.

***

"Jessara!" Asha leaned over the edge of the ice, seeing Jessara's head bob above the surface and then sink back into the water. She knew Jessara's muscles would soon seize from the cold, and when that happened, it would be too late to save her. Asha got to her knees and reached her hand in, wishing she could swim. She frantically tried to grab Jessara, finally reaching her arm and pulling her out. She was a lot heavier than she looked.

Weak from the cold and her injury, Jessara lay collapsed on the ice.

Asha knelt over her. "Can you walk?"

To Asha's dismay, Jessara could barely move her legs, and she waved her hand dismissively.

"Get the Nara out of here!"

"Not a chance!"

At that moment, the ice chaulk shot up again and towered over the two women. It poised itself to strike. Asha grabbed Jessara and dragged her across the ice. She pulled Jessara behind her, standing between her companion and the ice chaulk. The creature reared its head for another attack, and Asha charged up a fireball.

When the chaulk surged again, she launched it at the beast's head.

The blast knocked Asha off her feet. From where she lay, the underside of the chaulk's head was exposed. Quickly, she grabbed her sword and shot it at the beast, hitting it in the throat. The beast screamed as it fell backward and collapsed on the ice. After a few weakening roars and quakes, it went silent and still.

Asha breathed a sigh of relief. But then she looked over at Jessara, who was barely conscious and rushed to her.

"Oh no! Come on, Jessara, stay with me!"

Asha checked her injury. The cold had slowed down the bleeding, but blood still poured out and Jessara was looking pale. The bleeding had to be stopped.

"This is going to hurt." She conjured fire in her hand, and when she pressed it against the wound, Jessara let out the third loudest scream Asha had ever heard. She hated to hurt her, but it was all she could think to do. The smell of burning flesh seeped into the air, and Jessara panted from the pain.

"Can you walk?"

Jessara tried to say something, but she was drifting in and out of consciousness. She'd lost too much blood to walk.

With all her strength, Asha hoisted Jessara over her shoulders. Even with her wound cauterized, she would freeze to death without shelter. The fireball had weakened Asha, but she pushed on as Jessara settled heavily on her back.

Chapter Twelve

The Cave

For ten agonizing minutes, Asha carried Jessara on her back. She struggled across the base of the mountains, desperately trying to find shelter. Jessara shook violently. All Asha could do was pray that the warmth of her body would sustain Jessara through her clothes. But the harder Jessara shook, the more Asha's hope waned.

Finally, Asha spotted an opening. At first, she feared she'd imagined a cave, but the closer she got, the more unmistakable it became. Normally, Asha hesitated when going into caves because of the rats, but she had little time. When they entered, Asha noticed an abandoned campfire and a stack of wood—doubtless from an orc who'd taken shelter. She carefully set Jessara down next to the fire site. Jessara's body was practically jerking at this point as she curled into a fetal position. Asha grabbed some of the wood and used a spell to make a fire.

She then turned her attention to Jessara.

"How are you doing?"

Jessara looked at her with fear in her eyes and didn't speak.

Ice crystals covered Jessara's clothes, making her condition worse. Asha took a deep breath. "I need to get those clothes off you so they can dry. Can I do that?"

Jessara barely nodded her head, looking uncharacteristically vulnerable.

"I'm sorry about this." With that, Asha removed Jessara's armor. The wound Asha had cauterized didn't look good, but at least it wasn't bleeding. Next came the clothes under Jessara's armor, and then her undergarments and breast band. Out of respect, Asha avoided looking at her body.

Naked and continuing to shake, Jessara huddled near the fire. Asha put her hand on her companion's back. It was cold as ice, and her breathing was slowing. The fire wouldn't be enough. She was dying.

Asha knew there was only one way to save her from freezing to death. "Jessara. You're in the second stage of hypothermia. I can help you. I can raise my body temperature and use my skin to warm you up. Can I do that—please?"

***

Jessara gazed at Asha. She was disoriented but she knew exactly what Asha was asking. Jessara had never been this vulnerable before—naked, weak, and closer to death than she'd ever been. Asking anyone for help went against everything she'd been taught, but her desperation was greater than her pride. Breathing grew difficult, and she felt herself slipping away. She begged the Creos not to let her die. Not like this. But the Creos couldn't help her; only one person could. So Jessara nodded her head.

Asha began to undress, and Jessara looked away. After a few moments, footsteps approached her. "I'm going to turn you around so that your back is against the fire."

Jessara looked at her and nodded. For the first time, she saw Asha's body. Her arms were soft, but her legs were defined. Her breasts were slightly bigger than teacups, and her nipples were wide and pink. Perhaps it was the hypothermia or her desperation to stay alive, but Jessara couldn't help but stare. For a moment, Jessara could have sworn she saw a divine glow reflecting off Asha's fair skin. Everything about her was the most beautiful sight Jessara had ever beheld.

Jessara's muscles relaxed as she let Asha guide her body. Her hands brought a refreshing heat that made Jessara long to feel the rest of Asha's warm skin. She got her wish as Asha pressed her body against hers and put her arms around her to hold her tight. The warmth of the fire sorceress' body was everything Jessara had been desperate for.

The skin-to-skin contact soon soothed her shivers, and even in her weakness, she enjoyed the intimacy. Asha's body was gorgeous, but it wasn't just desire that she felt—it was care. A sigh of relief escaped her mouth as their naked breasts pressed against each other. Their legs intertwined, and she looked into Asha's beautiful blue eyes. The scent of lavender wafted from her companion's hair.

But Jessara had not stopped shaking yet. Although she felt better, her mind was fuzzy. Control of her limbs had left her, and she was terrified that this was what dying was like. Was it already too late for her to survive? The only part of her body she seemed to have control over was her eyes.

Jessara focused on training her gaze on Asha's. As long as she could see Asha, that meant she was still alive. The light from the fire reflected off those blue orbs as Asha's blonde hair flowed over her face and brushed across her lips.

Asha reached her palm out to touch Jessara's cheeks. Jessara wasn't sure if Asha was having similar intimate thoughts or if she was just checking her temperature, but right now, that didn't matter. Those gentle hands were warm, and more of her was touching Jessara. Her face thawed as Jessara let out another breath. She still didn't know if she was dying, but the more she kept her focus on Asha, the more content she became. Whatever might happen, she wasn't alone. Her eyes drifted to Asha's lips—pink and glistening in the light of the fire.

"Kiss me." She had spoken those words aloud, and her heart raced as she realized what she'd just asked.

Apart from a slightly raised eyebrow, Asha seemed unfazed by Jessara's request. Perhaps she'd been thinking the same thing. Asha looked at Jessara's lips and slowly moved closer. Jessara closed her eyes and felt the warmth of Asha's breath tickle her skin, her lips brush her cheek. She desperately wanted her mouth on hers.

Asha finally closed the gap, and as soon as their lips touched, Jessara's body grew warm both inside and out. She hadn't realized how cold her lips had been until she felt Asha's warm lips against them. She stopped shaking, and with her uninjured arm, she pulled Asha closer to her. Asha's tongue brushed against her own as their bodies remained locked together. They were the softest lips Jessara had ever kissed. The fear of death finally left her, but she was still tired. Slowly, the mouths of the women parted as their eyes opened, and they stared at one another.

Jessara was safe in the arms of Asha, content. Blood loss still weakened her, but life was returning. It was as if Asha's kiss had captured her soul before it could leave her body. Jessara felt herself drifting off to sleep. Before she did, she softly whispered, "Thank you."

CHAPTER THIRTEEN

SPELUNKING

Jessara awoke to find her body still pressed against Asha's. As she opened her eyes, Asha's beautiful face came into focus. She was still asleep, looking peaceful, and Jessara smiled. Although Jessara was still weak from blood loss, she was no longer feeling any effects of hypothermia.

Asha's warm body against hers made her feel euphoric. Cold air surrounded them, but her companion's body protected her, and she didn't want their embrace to end. Those soft cheeks, those gentle lips, those long eyelashes—all these belonged to the woman who'd saved Jessara's life.

Aleris' notes played through her head. *Fire mages develop strong bonds. They are fiercely loyal to those they care about and will go out of their way to protect friends, family, and loved ones at the risk of great injury or harm to themselves.*

Even so, Jessara couldn't believe all Asha had done to keep her alive. She'd fought off and killed an ice chaulk; she'd carried Jessara on her back through a snowstorm; and she'd saved her from freezing to death. Since they'd met, Jessara had been questioning why she kept putting herself at risk to save Asha without hesitation. Now she wondered if a small part of her had known that Asha would do the same for her.

Jessara glanced at Asha's lips, part of her wanting to kiss her companion awake. Their kiss last night had been divine. But now that her senses had returned to her, she remembered that she'd have to turn Asha in to the King. Whatever happened after that was anyone's guess.

"They" could never happen. They could never be. She gently cupped Asha's cheeks, trying not to wake her. *Could they?*

No. Asha was human and Jessara elven. Interracial relationships weren't forbidden, but they were rare. In Enderdale, if a human married an elf, they gave up all of their special rights as humans. They were forced to live in the elven district and were legally considered elves. The same status was given to their children, even if the mother was a human and therefore birthed human offspring.

Asha blinked, and her eyes slowly opened. She smiled when she registered Jessara. "Hey. How are you feeling?"

That smile warmed Jessara's heart as much as her skin had warmed her body.

"Not great, but not hypothermic." Jessara didn't try to hold back her smile this time. "You sleep well?"

"All things considered."

They lay together for several moments, just looking at each other, neither saying a word.

Asha curled her hair behind her ear. "Listen, about the kiss."

Jessara's smile disappeared. She wanted so much to kiss Asha again. She tried to read Asha's tone to figure out where she stood, but halted, remembering the long-term reality. This couldn't happen. She was Jessara's mark and an enemy of the King. The kiss shouldn't have happened, and it could never happen again.

"I'm sorry." Jessara frowned. "It was a mistake. I thought I was dying, and the hypothermia went to my head."

Asha was silent for a few moments. "Right. People do all sorts of things when they're out of their heads. No need to apologize."

"Good." It was the right thing to do. Even if Asha *did* feel something—*especially* if she felt something—it was best to stop it right then.

The disappointment in Asha's eyes was clear, but she took a deep breath, put on a strong face, and sat up. "Your clothes should be dry now."

"Right." Jessara tried to get up, but as soon as she put weight on her arm, the surge of pain in her shoulder made her gasp.

"I'll get them." Asha stood and walked over to their clothes, which hung near the fire. She held up Jessara's armor and examined the crack caused by the ice chaulk attack. "What material is this?"

Jessara chuckled. "Remember when I told you I once fought a chaulk?"

Asha nodded.

Jessara motioned to the armor. "After we took it down, we harvested its hide to make armor for all of the royal assassins."

Asha's eyes widened as she held up the armor. "This is chaulk hide?"

"From a regular chaulk. Black ones that prey on fishermen in deep lakes." Jessara snorted. "Ironic, isn't it?"

Asha grinned. "I can repair this for you. Would you like me to?"

Jessara nodded, remembering what Aleris had said about mages mending clothes. She was curious to see it for herself.

Asha hovered her hand over the armor. Strange green beams of light descended from her palms, and the armor seemed to slowly repair itself. Within moments, the hole was completely gone.

Jessara was awed. "Amazing. Can all mages do that?"

Asha shrugged. "The mending of fabric takes a little while to master, but I was taught the skill at a young age."

She handed Jessara her clothes.

"By whom?"

Asha's grin disappeared. Jessara would not be getting an answer, which was fair. She tried to stand but stumbled, still woozy.

Asha caught her before she fell. "You lost a lot of blood. You need to take it easy."

Asha helped Jessara to a boulder in the cave and sat her down. Jessara tried to put her clothes and armor back on, but it was a struggle. Her right arm could barely move.

Asha walked over to her own clothes, and Jessara watched as she dressed herself. A pang of guilt came over Jessara—Asha had risked a lot to save her. "You didn't have to do that—save me, I mean."

Asha smiled. "That's why it meant something."

Jessara couldn't help but smile back. "Still though. Thanks."

Asha finished dressing and walked over to help Jessara. "You're welcome." She handed a canteen of water to Jessara, who took a long drink and then glanced outside.

"The blizzard's stopped. We should get going." Jessara tried to stand, but immediately sat down again.

"You're in no condition to travel. It could take weeks for you to recover from your blood loss."

"We don't have weeks."

"I know." Asha appeared to be pondering something. Conflict reflected in her eyes. "Look, there are some...people I know who live in these mountains. They can help us."

"The orcs? Look I got nothing against orcs, but they usually tear people apart, not put them back together."

"Do you trust me?"

The question threw her. The only people she'd ever come close to trusting were the King, and maybe Aleris. Even as she'd warmed up to Asha, she hadn't shaken the feeling that Asha was biding her time until she could escape—probably soon, here, in the mountains. But here they were, in the mountains, and Asha hadn't abandoned Jessara after the ice chaulk attack. Instead, she'd saved her life. At this point, Jessara couldn't think of any reason not to trust her. "Yes."

"The caves in these mountains were built by orcs during the final years of the Shadow War, to travel through the mountains. There's a large settlement on the other side, Coshgromar. That's where my..." Asha paused. "There are people there who can help us. If we can get through this cave, it shouldn't be too difficult to find."

As they'd traveled together, Jessara had noticed several words or phrases from her companion that she'd only ever heard from orcs. Asha must have spent a good deal of time with them.

"Are you sure?" said Jessara.

"Yes."

Jessara remembered that Asha had been heading to the Northern Mountains originally, possibly to hide with these mystery people. If Asha had planned to ditch her in the mountains, she certainly could now.

"You *should* just leave me here," said Jessara.

"Don't you bloody say that again!" The force in Asha's voice made Jessara jump.

"All right."

"You should eat something before we go."

"*We* should. There's some bread in my satchel."

Asha grabbed Jessara's bag and pulled out some frozen rye bread. After thawing it with her powers, she handed it to Jessara.

Jessara pushed the bread back to her companion. "You take half; that's the last of it."

"You need it more."

"I need you to stay nourished. If you're going to carry me, you need the energy."

Asha conceded reluctantly and pulled the bread apart. "Which half do you want?"

Jessara pointed to the slightly smaller half, but Asha gave her the larger one. Before Jessara could protest, Asha shot her a look that said *Don't even think about it.*

They ate their bread together. It was stale and soggy at the same time. Every bite tasted of lake water, but at least it provided nourishment.

Once they'd finished, Asha wrapped Jessara's arm around her shoulders and lifted her. Jessara tried to hurry, but she was weak and moved slowly. A ball of fire conjured from Asha's palm lit their way as they walked into the depths of the cave.

The tunnel was clearly artificial, with no stalactites or stalagmites—just cold, dusty dirt. The arch of the cave was smaller than Jessara found comfortable, and the only thing preventing a cave-in was frost and prayers to the Creos.

Jessara nearly tripped on a rock, but kept her balance. "Anything you think we need to worry about in here?"

Asha stopped dead in her tracks for a moment as if remembering something. "Keep an eye on the ground."

Jessara's eyes immediately went to the dirt floor. "Why? Venomous snakes?"

Asha shook her head. "Rats." Her voice was uncharacteristically serious for such a carefree woman.

Jessara nearly burst out laughing. "You aren't serious."

"Dead serious. Mountain rats burrow through these caves the deeper you go."

"You're afraid of rats?"

"No." Asha's response was more defensive than she likely meant it to sound. "I have a healthy distaste for them."

Jessara smirked. "Healthy distaste?"

"Rats were responsible for the Mahgarian plague of 1016. A quarter of Dremeria's population was wiped out because of rats."

"Asha, that was over three hundred years ago."

"Exactly! We're due for another plague. Do you want to be patient zero?"

Jessara shook her head and chuckled. "Fine. But are there any threats that *aren't* the size of my boot?"

Asha shook her head. "I'm not sure. Ever since the Northern Mountains Treaty was signed, orcs don't use these tunnels much. We should still be on our guard."

Jessara tried to remember what she'd learned about the Shadow War. Her education in the palace barracks had given her some details, and Aleris had filled in most of the blanks. Humans and elves had fought each other on and off for most of recorded history. In only one instance had they worked together. In 1153, around two hundred years ago, an army of orcs had landed on the southern shores of Dremeria and raided villages, threatening humans and elves alike. The conflict was called the Shadow War because nobody knew where they'd come from or what had provoked them.

After a year of fighting independent wars against the orcs, both the Kingdom of the humans and the Compact of the elves coordinated their strikes with each other. Their alliance was tense but effective. After another two years of fighting, their combined armies cut off the orcs' access to the sea. This deprived them of fishing, a major source of food. The allied armies spent the next three years slowly pushing the orcs north along the borders of their lands.

Eventually, they pushed the orcs all the way to the Northern Mountains, where they established permanent bases to hold off the advance of Compact and Kingdom forces. Two more years passed, and their strikes became more of a nuisance than a major concern. Eventually, the chieftain of the orcs, Grollush, sent an emissary to the leaders of the Compact and the Kingdom requesting a meeting. The King of the humans and the Supreme Leader of the elves reluctantly accepted. Historians speculated about what had caused Chief Grollush to seek peace, but neither Jessara's palace teachers or Aleris had ever provided a solid answer.

At the meeting, the three armies signed the Northern Mountains Treaty. The orcs agreed they would end all hostilities if both armies recognized the mountains as orc territory. The mountains were treacherous, cold, infested with dangerous beasts, and had few resources, so the humans and elves agreed. The eight-year conflict ended and sparked a time of peace between the humans and elves for the longest period in history. Both nations were inherently nationalistic, so occasional disputes over land and resources cropped up, but it never resulted in armed conflict.

This lasted until thirty years ago, when elven supremacists staged a coup and took over the government of the Compact and the Purge began. Anti-human sentiment had always been present among the elven nation, but after the coup, racism became genocide. Humans within Compact territory were massacred by the tens of thousands, along with any elves caught aiding them. The brutality sparked a war between the Kingdom and the Compact. Jessara had always wondered where the supremacist faction managed to get the resources to stage the coup in the first place, but it wasn't her job to know or care.

The orc nation had maintained a neutral stance in the conflict between the humans and elves. Individuals would sometimes offer their services as mercenaries to the humans, but when the Purge began, the orc nation cut off trade with the Compact. Peripherally, they supported the humans, but they were reluctant to get officially involved.

Jessara had met a few orcs. Green, with tusks that protruded from their lower jaws, the average orc was about a foot taller than the average human. A barracks in the elven district in Enderdale housed mercenary orcs that had been hired by the Kingdom. Every now and then, Jessara would be challenged to a fight, which she always eagerly accepted. Orcs had superior strength, but she had agility. She usually won.

Jessara had never met an orc that wasn't a mercenary. She knew they had a nation and she'd even been in the Northern Mountains several times, but she'd never visited an orcish city. It still wasn't clear to her how they could help her, but Asha seemed certain they would. Either orcs had an understanding of medicine that far surpassed the rest of Dremeria or there was something significant Asha wasn't telling her.

***

A half hour of Asha pulling Jessara through the cave passed. To Asha's great relief, they did not encounter any rats. As they walked, she thought over what had transpired between them the previous night. She kept beating herself up for the kiss. It should have been obvious that it was the desire of a delusional, dying woman. But in the moment, it had felt so real—like they had a true connection.

Asha hadn't considered that something might be growing between them until last night. Sure, she'd been attracted to Jessara when they'd first met, but she found lots of women attractive. Sure, Jessara was interesting, impressive, and funny in her own way, but she was an assassin—an assassin that killed for the King. An assassin that planned to deliver her to him. An assassin that, until quite recently, Asha had planned to abandon. But the more they'd talked, the fonder of Jessara she'd grown, and now the thought of abandoning her felt like a betrayal.

Then the ice chaulk had attacked, and everything had changed. All thoughts of leaving Jessara had vanished, and she'd cared only about keeping her safe. Then, the moment their bodies had pressed together, she'd realized how much she longed for her. She'd been desperate for that kiss before Jessara had asked for it, and it had felt like the most natural thing in the world. When it was over, she'd wanted to dance in her excitement.

Now, all she felt was embarrassment mixed with guilt. Had she taken advantage of Jessara? Was Jessara angry at her? No. She'd thanked Asha. And despite what she'd said about the kiss, she'd been kind all morning. Maybe nothing serious could ever be between them, but Asha hoped they could at least try to be friends.

Asha's thoughts were interrupted as Jessara suddenly went dead weight on her.

"Jessara? Jessara? You still with me?"

"Ye-yeah." Jessara had nearly passed out.

"We're going to take a break here." Asha slowly set her down.

Jessara leaned her back against the wall. "How much farther?"

"Hopefully, not long. How are you feeling?"

Jessara forced a grin. "Like death."

"Well, you certainly look like it."

At that moment, Asha heard voices ahead of them. The accents were elven.

"What in Nara?" Jessara looked in the direction of the voices.

Asha's heart raced as she tried to figure out what she needed to do. Jessara was in no condition to fight. Asha scanned the area and saw a few boulders on the side of the cave, big enough to hide one person. She dragged Jessara behind them.

"Stay quiet." Asha put out her light. The voices grew closer, and she spotted torches. Two soldiers marched her way. She made out the familiar red and green colors of the Compact. *Shit! What are they doing here?*

"These orcs are much better at being fodder than building tunnels," said one.

"Just keep moving," said the other. "The commander is going to want a full report when we get back."

"Can we not forge the report? It is not like we are going to use this tunnel."

"I am going to pretend you did not say that. We must look at all possible paths."

The two elves drew closer. Asha feared using magic, as any explosion could cause a cave-in. There was nowhere to hide or run. Fighting was her only option—fighting without her magic against trained soldiers.

Asha snuck over to Jessara and reached for her sword. Jessara tried to stop her, but Asha lay her hand on hers.

"Trust me."

Asha wasn't sure she trusted herself, but she had no other choice. Reluctantly, Jessara allowed her to take the blade.

Asha crouched down and waited for the two elves to get closer as she tried to remember what Jessara had taught her—about planning out motions, thinking through attacks, using all of her assets. These soldiers likely had years of experience, and she nearly panicked as her heart pounded.

The two elves approached the boulder where Jessara was hiding. The biggest asset Asha had was the element of surprise, and she was about to lose that. It was now or never.

Asha jumped out of the darkness and sank her blade into the nearest soldier. A cry echoed as he fell to the ground.

Asha quickly pulled out her sword and tried to swing at the other. He was surprised, but he managed to block her. Asha assumed the fighting stance Jessara had taught her and retreated just in time to dodge a counter attack.

While her opponent recovered from his failed advance, Asha went for his neck with a thrust. He whirled his blade up at the last second to parry. As their swords *clashed*, he kicked her in the gut, and she fell, the wind knocked out of her.

The soldier dropped his torch, and it rolled in front of Jessara. Out of the corner of her eye, Asha could see Jessara reach out to grab it. Then she chucked the torch at the soldier's face, and the flames hit his eyes, temporarily blinding him.

That was all the time Asha needed. She jumped at the soldier and jabbed the blade into his chest.

The biggest sigh of relief she'd ever drawn left Asha's lungs. She could hardly believe she'd survived that fight.

She walked back to Jessara and returned the sword to its sheath, and then she leaned against the wall to catch her breath.

Jessara nodded in approval. "Nice job."

Still breathing heavily, Asha tried to force a playful smile to calm her nerves. "What? You're not going to tell me how sloppy that was? How problematic'?"

Jessara smiled back. "Oh, it *was* sloppy. But I've also learned to avoid insulting someone when you're half-dead and relying on them to carry you."

"That happen a lot?"

Both women laughed.

Jessara glanced at the corpses of the elven soldiers, and her smiled faded. "What the fuck is the Compact doing here?"

"Nara if I know. The orcs need to hear about this." Asha helped Jessara up so they could continue their trek.

"How do you know the orcs so well?"

"I've...been here before. I promise I'll explain everything when we get to Coshgromar."

"Don't you trust me?"

"I do. That's why I'm taking you there." She desperately wanted to explain everything to Jessara, but she wasn't going to break her oath.

***

Jessara decided not to press any further. She had her own secrets and no intention of sharing them. "We should warn the orcs about the Compact patrols. Their days of neutrality might be numbered."

Asha shook her head. "I hope not."

"Why? The Kingdom could use them."

"Yeah. *Use* them."

Jessara raised an eyebrow. She'd never been one to discuss politics, but she assumed that most humans were already on the same page when it came to the war. "So you want the Compact to win?"

"I didn't say that. But the Kingdom is only a beacon of hope to certain people. You, of all people, should understand that."

Jessara frowned. "What's that supposed to mean?"

"Elves are forced to live in the slums of the city. Crimes committed against them go unpunished, but crimes against humans are punished severely. If an elf so much as lights a bloody candle using magic, they're executed."

Jessara gritted her teeth. "You don't need to explain to me what it's like to be an elf in the Kingdom. In Enderdale, humans don't even look at us. Outside of Enderdale, I can't buy a drink without having to fight off a bunch of drunken bigots. I see the bodies hanging in the streets."

"Have you ever almost been one of those bodies?"

Jessara paused for a second. "No."

"The Compact is evil, but the Kingdom doesn't deserve your loyalty—not while it depends on the suffering of others."

"I'm not loyal to the Kingdom—I'm loyal to the King, and only because he pays me."

"The soldiers of the Kingdom get paid as well, but that doesn't mean they aren't tools. The Compact pays too. If it were only about money, why not kill for them?"

There was sense in Asha's words, but this was the only life Jessara had ever known. She'd always told herself that she was different from the rest of the people that fought for the Kingdom. The King had convinced her of this. No contract had ever been forced on her—not that she'd turned down any—but the King had always presented them as her choice.

The King respected her, and he'd looked after her since she'd been a child. He'd saved her from her parents' fate and had given her the means to enact her revenge, even though it meant she fought for a nation that oppressed her kind. The conversation made her sweat.

At that moment, Jessara spotted daylight at the end of the tunnel and jumped at the change of subject. "There's the exit!"

Asha glanced at her, clearly knowing that she was trying to avoid the question. To Jessara's relief, Asha didn't push the matter further. "We'll rest at the mouth and then start looking for a camp."

CHAPTER FOURTEEN

THE ORCS

After resting at the mouth of the cave, Asha decided it was time to set off. A severe wind chilled the mountains, so she gave Jessara her cloak again. As Asha had predicted, they soon noticed a small smoke cloud to the east. Asha let herself feel hope, and she glanced at her companion. She'd have much to explain when they got to Coshgromar, but she'd finally be free of her oath.

As they trekked through the snow, they occasionally discovered the bodies of orcs. Some appeared to have frozen to death, while the wounds on others suggested lost battles with mountain creatures. At one site, three dead orcs lay next to the bodies of two snow trolls. Asha's heart raced as she looked at the mangled corpses. She'd killed a snow troll once, but only with help, and Jessara was in no condition to fight.

It had begun snowing again, and she could just barely make out the spires of the surrounding mountain ranges. Suddenly, Asha heard movement behind them, halting her in her tracks. She and Jessara turned slowly. The snow blinded them, making it impossible to see what followed. Asha set Jessara down and grabbed her sword. The fight in the tunnel had given her more confidence, but she needed to see what she was up against.

Asha moved in the direction of the noise. Something lurked, and she refused to let it sneak up on them. Asha gripped Jessara's hoplite tightly as she peered through the white sheet of snow. She looked back at Jessara, who had drawn her bow and was struggling to notch an arrow.

Jessara's eyes widened as she pointed to something behind her. "Asha!"

But it was too late. Something knocked Asha off her feet and made her drop the sword. She hit the ground, the wind knocked out of her.

A snow troll had been hiding in the white, waiting for prey. Its red eyes penetrated Asha's very soul as it leapt upon her. It dug its claws into her flesh, and pain seared through her. She screamed, but managed to shoot a fireball at the troll's chest. It released its hold and let out a blood curdling cry.

***

During the fight, Jessara tried to draw her bowstring, but every movement was excruciating and made her lightheaded. She could only watch as the troll retreated and grabbed snow to put out the fire on its chest. Asha struggled up and pulled out two knives, but the troll had recovered, and swiped them out of her grasp with its claws.

Then the troll balanced on its hands and swung its legs forward, kicking Asha in the chest. A loud *crack* echoed off the rocks as she fell on her back, gasping for breath. The troll cocked its arm, ready to slash down at her.

Gripping the bowstring with her hand was impossible. Instead, Jessara wrapped her arm around the string and pulled her bow forward. She tried to ignore the pain in her shoulder, but she was in agony. She released the arrow, but it only grazed the troll's back.

The creature roared and scanned the area for the source of the arrow. When it spotted Jessara, the beast beat its chest and charged her. Jessara grabbed a dagger and tried to stand, but the strain made her collapse.

She anchored herself as best she could, and when the creature raised its arm to slash at her, she sank her dagger into its hand. It cried out and swiped its other arm at her, which sent her flying through the air. She hit the ground, pain jolting through her body as she rolled several times. Her shoulder wound reopened, and she stained the surrounding snow with blood. All strength left her. She couldn't have moved even if she'd had the will to do so.

The troll charged her again, and she waited for the inevitable. Suddenly, another figure charged in from the side. The troll was knocked backward, but managed to stay on its feet. Two other figures joined the battle. Orcs! They must have heard the fight from their camp.

The troll attempted to swipe at the first orc, but it overextended itself. One of the others brought her axe down on the troll's arm, slashing it off. The troll roared as a third orc cleaved the creature's skull from behind with a loud *crack*. The beast collapsed, its legs twitching until it finally grew still.

Jessara gave a sigh of relief, but she had to fight to stay conscious as blood oozed from her shoulder. An orc woman, who appeared to be the leader, approached her.

"It's a bloody elf." The orc woman wore animal skins decorated with bones. Her black hair was braided and kept together by large wooden beads.

"Compact?" said another orc.

"Ain't wearing Compact colors."

"Don't mean she ain't fucking Compact," said the third.

Jessara was disoriented, but she knew that Asha needed help. Asha lay on the ground, gripping her chest, and Jessara pointed to her companion. "H-h-help."

The orc glanced over and spotted Asha.

"What she say?" said one of the other warriors.

The leader pointed in the direction of Asha. "There's someone over there!"

The other two orcs ran to check. "It's a bloody sorceress! Chaulk's balls! I think it's Asha!"

The leader looked surprised. "How is she?"

Asha tried to speak, but all she could do was lean to the side and cough up blood.

"A fucking mess! We gotta get her to the temple."

Jessara tried to pull herself up, but the orc leader stayed her with her hand.

"Hold still, elf."

"H-help her."

"We got you both." The leader turned to one of the other orcs. "Prugo! Get to the camp! Tell the rest of the unit to bring stretchers."

Prugo nodded and ran out of sight.

Jessara drifted in and out of consciousness, and lost all sense of time. Vaguely, she saw Prugo come back with a half dozen more orcs with stretchers made from animal skin. Orcs lifted Jessara and placed her atop one, and she saw Asha loaded onto the other. The orcs hoisted the stretchers and marched them through the mountains. For a while, all Jessara could hear was the sound of snow crunching beneath their rescuers' feet.

Once during the march, the orcs brought their stretchers side by side. When she saw her friend, her heart trembled. Asha was barely conscious as she looked back at Jessara. Her breath faltered, and blood dripped out of her mouth. Jessara reached out her hand, and Asha weakly took it. The warmth of Asha's hand comforted Jessara, but she knew that they were in bad shape. That was the last thing she remembered before fully losing consciousness.

Chapter Fifteen

The Sisterhood of the Miracle Tree

Jessara slowly opened her eyes. A stone ceiling with a large tree mural that seemed oddly familiar came into focus. Blankets warmed her body, and a soft bed lay beneath her. A woman sat at a table next to her, mixing what appeared to be a red liquid in an alembic. She was human, close to Jessara's age with black curly hair and a black satin dress similar to Asha's. Jessara tried to rise, but she was too weak.

"Easy. You've been through a lot, yeah?" The woman's voice was as soft and soothing as her soulful brown eyes. "Just lie back."

Jessara tried to calm herself, and reality slowly returned to her as she caught her breath.

The woman leaned in as if inspecting Jessara's face. "It's okay; you are safe."

Jessara stared at the woman, not sure what to make of her. As uncomfortable as it made her, she forced eye contact and studied the woman. She was quite pretty, with a long face, winged eyebrows, and thin cheeks.

"Can you tell me your name?" Every motion and syllable made by the stranger seemed designed to put Jessara at ease.

But she remained silent, still trying to orient herself.

"My name is Anea." The woman smiled.

Even for one as naturally suspicious as Jessara, it was difficult to feel threatened by Anea's demeanor. "Jessara."

"How are you feeling, Jessara?"

To her surprise, Jessara felt pretty good, at least compared to how she'd been. She was warmer, less lightheaded, and her shoulder felt better. Her right arm was still stiff and a little painful, but she could move it. As she put her hand on her shoulder, she realized it was bandaged. The cauterization burn still pained her, but the inside of her shoulder was almost normal. "Fine. How long have I been out?"

"Two days. Drink this, would you please?" Anea poured what she'd been mixing from her alembic into a ceramic mug.

Jessara eyed the cup suspiciously.

Anea winked and took a small sip herself. "It's okay; it's a remedy."

I guess if she wanted to kill me, she would have done it already. Jessara took the cup and sipped. It had a salty, sweet taste. She took a gulp and the clouds in her head parted ways.

Anea took the mug. "Is that better?"

"Thank you." Within seconds, Jessara's mind was clear. She looked around the room, trying to get an idea of where she was. The ceiling was solid stone, and the walls appeared to be made of white translucent glass. The room was small, only furnished with the bed Jessara lay in, the stool Anea sat on, and the table littered with several herbs and the alembic.

Jessara still wasn't sure where she was, but she was clearly safer than she'd been before she lost consciousness. She relaxed, sank her head into her pillow, and tried to remember how she'd gotten here. The ice chaulk, the cave, the troll, Asha. She jerked her head up again. "Asha!"

Anea's smile faded, causing Jessara's heart to sink. Anea's eyes were red and swollen, as if she'd been crying. "Where is she?"

"She..." Anea struggled to get words out. "She took a bad hit to the chest."

"Is she...?" Jessara couldn't finish her sentence.

Anea lowered her head. "She's still with us, but we can't guarantee she'll recover. You understand?"

Jessara didn't know what to say. Her brain was floating six feet above her as she processed the information. After all Asha had done for her and what they'd survived together, she couldn't die. Tears threatened, but she halted them at the last moment. "Where is she?"

"She's being worked on by one of our healers."

"I need to see her!" Jessara forced herself out of the bed.

"I think you need to rest."

Anea put out her hand, but Jessara shook her off.

She took a deep breath and forced herself to look at Anea's eyes. "Please."

Anea hesitated and squinted her eyes at Jessara. After a few seconds, she relaxed and gave a slight smile. To Jessara's surprise, she nodded. "Can I help you up?" Anea took Jessara's arm and got her to her feet.

For the first time since her fight with the ice chaulk, Jessara was able to walk on her own. Somehow, her blood seemed to have been restored. Despite still being drowsy, she was no longer helpless.

"This way." Anea led Jessara out of the room and down a hallway. Like the room she'd come from, the walls were made of white translucent glass with stone columns at each corner holding up the ceiling. While they walked, they passed other women wearing satin dresses of different colors but similar design. Each looked at Jessara with fascination.

Anea stopped in front of a glass wall and turned to Jessara. "It's important that you remain calm, all right?"

Jessara nodded. Anea waved her hand across the translucent glass, and it turned transparent. Through the clear wall, Jessara could see Asha, eyes closed, lying on a bed in the middle of a room. An elderly woman in a red satin dress hovered her hands over Asha's chest and head. A strange green light emitted from the woman's palms. It was similar to the light Asha had used to mend her armor, but much brighter.

Jessara's heart raced as she tried to make sense of what she was watching. "Can I go in?"

"Not right now; I'm sorry. Healing magic requires a great deal of concentration, and Asha is very fragile." Anea raised an eyebrow. "You must have many questions, yeah?"

A thousand questions raced through Jessara's mind. Where was she? Who were these women? How could these humans perform magic? Evidently, Asha wasn't the only one. But she couldn't bring herself to ask about anything other than Asha. "What were her injuries?"

"She had a cracked rib, which punctured a lung." Every word for Anea seemed to be a struggle, as if something else choked her words. Pain?

"When she got here, she was hardly breathing. Her brain had been deprived of air, which put her in this state. We managed to get the internal bleeding to stop, but in her fragile state, we've had to go much slower than usual with healing magic. We're still working on her lung. However, the state of her brain is unclear. You understand?"

In any other situation, Jessara would have attempted to hide her emotions, hide her worry. But right now, she didn't care. "What are her chances?"

Anea frowned. "That's hard to say. It's much easier to repair the body than the mind."

Jessara noticed the concern in her voice and wondered who Anea was to Asha. "You can't let her die."

Anea's expression turned to anger, but then softened. "And we won't. But that's in the hands of the Tre—" She paused. "The Creos."

A single tear dropped as she played Asha's voice in her mind, to make sure it was preserved. And Jessara thought about the kiss, the one she'd pretended to brush off. How could she have been so callous, so dismissive? Asha had been the only person to ever show her genuine affection—genuine care. And Jessara had pushed her away out of fear.

As if reading her mind, Anea said, "Who is she to you?"

Jessara pondered this question. Who was she? Her mark? Her job? Her companion? Her friend? Or something deeper than that? "It's complicated."

Anea nodded, clearly unsatisfied. "Very well."

Jessara understood that nothing more could be learned about Asha's condition. She decided to satisfy her curiosity in other areas. "Where are we?"

"The orcish city of Coshgromar, in the temple of the Sisterhood of the Miracle Tree."

Jessara looked around the halls of the temple. "I take it you're all sorceresses?"

"She didn't tell you about us?"

"No."

"Good, then she kept her oath."

"Oath?"

"When a sister reaches maturity, she's allowed to leave the city. But she must also swear a lifelong oath to never discuss the Sisterhood with an outsider."

Jessara squinted. "Why are you telling me now then? Am I not an outsider?"

"You're inside, aren't you?"

Jessara laughed. "Very literal."

Anea shrugged. "Isn't that the nature of oaths?"

"Are you all human?"

"Yes."

"How is this even possible?"

"Humans using magic?"

"Yes."

Anea took a step closer to Jessara, staring at her eyes intently, then her face softened. "I suppose that Asha wouldn't have led you here if she didn't trust you. It's a long story though. You sure you want to hear it?"

Jessara glanced back at Asha. "I'm not going anywhere. I have time."

Anea gave a slight smile. "Have you ever wondered why Asha has a tree on her dress?"

"I just assumed she liked the design."

Anea shook her head. "Three hundred years ago, around the 1050s, during one of the many conflicts between elves and humans, there was a village in the northwestern part of the Kingdom, Crisdale. It stood at the base of the Northern Mountains and had been under constant attack from the Compact for some time. The King had sent platoon after platoon to try to defend it, and they had been able to hold off the onslaught of the Compact, but the losses were great. Eventually, the King decided that it wasn't worth the cost, yeah? He ordered his soldiers to retreat, leaving the town defenseless."

Jessara grunted. "It seems not much has changed in three hundred years."

Anea chuckled and continued her story. "Compact forces closed in on the settlement. The men fought while the women retreated into the mountains, for at that time, few female warriors existed. About eighty women managed to escape the carnage. For five days, they wandered the mountains with plenty of water from the snow, but limited food or blankets."

"How did they survive?"

"Many didn't. By the end of the fifth day, half of the women had perished. The remaining ones found a cave, the very cave in the middle of this city. As they explored it, they encountered a large tree with a white trunk that bore an unfamiliar fruit with a strange warmth radiating from it. The stories say that when the starving women found the tree, they ate the fruit and each was nourished. But the fruit did more than satisfy hunger. Are you with me so far?"

"Yeah." Jessara tilted her head with curiosity. "What else did the fruit do?"

Anea nodded. "The women developed magical powers. The ability to freeze objects, to conjure fire, to produce lightning—telepathy, telekinesis, healing—more were discovered each day."

Jessara remembered what Aleris had told her. "The mage specializations."

Anea lifted her head and looked at Jessara thoughtfully.

"An acquaintance of mine is a scholar," said Jessara.

"I see." She waved her hand. "They did not develop all seven of the specializations though. No shapeshifters."

"Why is that?"

"We're not sure. We know little of the origins of the magic, only that it exists."

"What became of the women?"

Anea continued the story. "They taught themselves how to use their powers to find food and fend for themselves. There also seemed to be some sort of ancient magic in the soil of the mountains. They discovered several plants with magical properties, which they used to make elixirs."

"Like the potion you gave me?"

Anea nodded. "Some even claimed to see spirits of the dead, but most of us believe that part is exaggerated. Eventually, some took to this new lifestyle of self-reliance. However, others longed to return to the Kingdom. An agreement was reached that those who wanted to could leave, but they had to swear an oath to keep the location a secret from all outsiders. Eighteen stayed and built this temple. The rest went back into the Kingdom to live out their lives."

"So, descendants are hidden in the Kingdom?" Jessara wondered if she'd ever encountered one.

"Absolutely. The women who left kept their oaths, though. They didn't tell their eventual offspring or partners. The ones who stayed, discovered a way to reproduce using the spiritual bond between female lovers, so we were able to replenish ourselves. The Sisterhood of the Miracle Tree was born. However, we had a small population, not enough to sustain ourselves, yeah? So, after the first generation died out, the Sisterhood began to search for the descendants of the women who'd left."

"Any luck?" Considering the size of the Kingdom, Jessara would have been surprised.

Anea smiled. "Yes. It was then that we discovered magic could only be passed to women and the spirit bond could only produce female offspring. It could be *passed* by men, but they could not use magic. Also, many descendants' powers will remain dormant and never be discovered. But as soon as one uses magic, we can detect it. The Sisterhood started sending out sisters to invite these descendants to return. However, the Sisterhood soon discovered that we were not the only ones looking for them, yeah? A secret order of humans called the Red Daggers was hunting them down and taking them."

The idea was barbaric to Jessara. "Why would they be hunting down children?"

"Based on what captured members have told us, they believe magic is too powerful a force to let just anyone wield it. They view it as a matter of keeping order, if you can believe it."

That sounded uncomfortably familiar. Jessara wondered if the King would ever try to recruit them. "So, you can detect any magic use?"

Anea shook her head. "Only the first time the descendent uses it."

"What if a child is born here?"

"We enchanted our temple with a concealment charm. The Compact has never been able to detect the high concentration of magic users. But every time a new descendent is revealed in the Kingdom, it becomes a race to get to the child before the Red Daggers can."

"What about the parents?"

"The Red Daggers only care about magic users. Once the child is taken, the parents are left alone." Anea frowned for a moment. "If the parents aren't killed defending their child, we usually erase their memory of the child with a potion created by a telepath like me. The younger the child is, the easier it is to erase memories." She sighed. "Ethically, a questionable solution, but there's no acceptable alternative, you see? If the child remains in the Kingdom, she will be hunted until she's killed."

"You're a telepath?" Jessara realized why Anea kept squinting her eyes at her.

"Yes."

"Are you going to erase my memory?" Jessara's voice was uneasy.

Anea squinted her eyes again. "Probably not. As I said, it appears that Asha trusts you, which is good enough for the Sisterhood. Also if you meant us harm, I would know."

Jessara tried to think really hard, *I mean you no harm!*

Anea chuckled. "I figured that out already, yeah?"

"So why are you in the middle of an orc city?"

Anea tilted her head and smiled. This was a story she clearly enjoyed telling, and Jessara assumed she didn't get much chance to do so. "You know the history of the Shadow War and the Northern Mountains Treaty?"

"As much as most people. The orcs randomly switched from wanting to kill everything that wasn't an orc to wanting peace."

Anea smiled. "It wasn't random. After the orcs were pushed to the Northern Mountains during the war, their chief, Grollush, discovered our temple. He tried to pillage it, which didn't work out so well, yeah? The Sisterhood displayed their magical prowess in a way that humbled the chief. He was forced to order his soldiers to stop attacking. At first, he believed the Sisterhood to be forms of the Creos, and he ordered the rest of his army to bow before us. Eventually, he came to understand who we really were. They sought our guidance and eventually, we convinced them to establish a treaty with the Kingdom and the Compact. Now do you see?"

Jessara chuckled. "So that was you all."

Anea nodded. "Orcs aren't evil by nature, but they need constant challenges. In the past, this took the form of bloodlust on the battlefield. However, we taught them to turn these mountains into their battlefield. It's a constant struggle to stay alive in these parts, yeah? We developed a symbiotic relationship. They help us retrieve food and guard us while we use our magic to help them in other ways, such as with healing, building, and growing crops."

Jessara looked at Asha. "What's her story?"

Anea turned back to the room. "I think she should be the one to tell you that."

"Will she be able to?"

"As I said, it's too early to say for certain. I'm sorry."

At that moment, the green lights disappeared from the palms of the healer who'd been working on Asha.

Jessara tensed. "Why did she stop?"

"Miland has done all she can for now. We can go in, if you'd like."

"Thank you."

Both Jessara and Anea entered the room while the healer was gathering her things to leave. She was an elderly woman, a little shorter than Jessara. Her long gray hair clearly didn't receive a lot of care, and her face was deeply wrinkled.

When they entered the room, the woman didn't turn to look at them. Anea slowly walked up behind her and put her hand on her shoulder. "Miland, this is Jessara."

The woman turned to Jessara and gave a forced nod. "Pleasure." When she spoke, her voice was gravelly, yet much more energetic than Jessara would have predicted. Her light blue eyes looked like they'd seen much.

"Are you done in here?" said Anea.

"For now. Got to let it run its course."

"May we sit with her?"

"Do whatever you want." Miland got up and walked out of the room in an abrupt manner. Clearly, she was not a patient woman.

Jessara pulled a chair next to Asha's bed and sat. The light of the room reflected off her fair skin, and Jessara fantasized about her waking up at any moment. But that wouldn't happen, and Jessara knew it. She glanced over at Anea. "May I take her hand?"

Anea nodded.

Jessara cupped Asha's hand between her palms. It was still as warm as always. There was much Jessara wanted to say, much she decided she would say if Asha woke up. "What did she mean 'Run its course'?"

Anea frowned. "With grievous wounds, it's important to give the body time to adjust to the healing magic. This is why you were asleep for so long."

"So, you restored blood to my body?"

"In a manner of speaking. Healing magic works by speeding up the body's natural healing process. Your body is designed to replace lost blood—we merely sped that up, yeah? Because of how long that would normally take, your recovery took a while."

"And my shoulder?"

"We were able to heal the muscle, but the burn is another matter. That's the type of tissue damage that we need special oils to repair. It's already been rubbed under that bandage, and it will take a day or two to heal completely. I hope the pain has lessened at least."

"That's *still* quick."

Anea grinned. "What can I say? Magic is a wonder."

Jessara's eyes rested back on Asha. "I can never repay what you've done for me."

"According to the orcs who saved you, Asha would already be dead if it weren't for you. When you help the Sisterhood, we help you, yeah?"

"Well, *I'd* be dead if not for her." Jessara looked at Asha's lips and once again, her thoughts returned to the night they'd kissed. She'd been quick to decide that could never happen again. Not because it didn't mean something, but because it did, and that terrified her. Jessara hoped Anea wasn't reading her mind.

"Would you like me to leave you alone?" said Anea, confirming that she was.

Jessara nodded gratefully.

"Come get me or one of the sisters if you need anything, yeah?" With that, Anea waved her hand, and the transparent glass became translucent again. Then she stepped out of the room.

Jessara was alone with her unconscious companion. She took a deep breath before speaking. "Hey, Asha." She held back tears with an effort. "It's me. I'm fairly certain you can't hear me but..." Jessara paused, losing the battle with her tears. "Please don't die. Because you were right. There is beauty in the world. I didn't believe it existed, but it's right here. And I don't want to go back to a world without it. Please wake up." Jessara gripped Asha's hand and held it to her heart. "Please, Creos don't let this woman die!"

Sobs erupted, sobs that made her chest hurt, her eyes swell, and her nose run, but she didn't care. She didn't care that she'd allowed herself to become emotionally involved, that the King would disapprove, that she was as vulnerable as she'd ever been. All she cared about, in that moment, was Asha.

Five minutes passed before she caught her breath. She pulled herself back to the chair and studied Asha. No change. Crying wouldn't bring her back to life.

There had to be something else that could be done, something the sisters hadn't thought of. Jessara pulled out Aleris' notes. Perhaps he had insights they didn't. They were isolated, and he worked for the academy, so it was certainly possible. She flipped through the pages until she found the section on the physiology of fire mages. Unsure about what she was looking for, she skimmed as much as she could.

"The same chemical compound found in smoke runs through the blood of all fire mages, meaning that they can breathe smoke like regular air." *Not helpful.* "Fire mages can control their core temperature to be—" *Already knew that.* Finally she found a section marked "Self-healing". "Fire mages can heal from superficial injuries quickly, as cuts are able to cauterize themselves to prevent excessive bleeding."

"Fuck!" Jessara threw the notes across the room and lay her face in her palms. She squeezed her temples as she turned her attention back to Asha on the bed. Again, a part of her hoped that if she stared long enough—with enough will—Asha would come back to her. She looked at her eyes hoping that they would open. She sat for an hour, then two hours, then three. No change. She almost didn't notice when Anea and Miland came in.

Anea carried a tray of food. "Are you hungry?"

"I'm fine." Jessara's gaze remained on Asha.

"You just recovered from losing a shit ton of blood. Eat!" said Miland.

Jessara was startled, but she knew she was right. Jessara grabbed the tray. "Thank you." Seasoned bear meat and fresh rye bread, it was the best food Jessara had eaten in a long time, but she kept her attention on Asha.

Anea took a step toward Jessara. "May I sit with you?"

Jessara nodded.

Anea pulled up a chair. "The other sisters are worried about you."

"I'm not the one in a coma."

"They heard you earlier; it sounded like someone dying," said Miland.

Anea flashed her a look. "Miland!"

"I'm sorry," Jessara said.

"No need to apologize. It's okay to feel for Asha. It's okay to grieve." Anea looked down at the unconscious woman. "You aren't alone in that, yeah?"

Jessara shook her head. "Grief is for the dead; she's still breathing."

"Listen." Miland tried to strike up an empathetic tone. "If the magic was going to work, it would have by now."

Jessara's heart sank. "What are you saying?"

"As I said, repairing the mind is much harder than repairing the body." Anea's own eyes watered.

Jessara looked back down at Asha's closed eyelids. "So, she's going to die?"

Anea paused. "I'm sorry."

Jessara didn't know what to say. After all she and Asha had been through, it couldn't end like this. She wouldn't let it. "There has to be something we can do. Some kind of magic."

"I admire your dedication." Anea gave her a slight smile. "But beyond what we've done, magic that could help her is...inaccessible to us."

Jessara's ears perked up. "So there is magic that can help her?"

"That's inaccessible to us," repeated Miland.

"What is this magic?" Jessara looked between the two women.

"I think you're missing the operative term here—'inaccessible,'" said Miland.

Jessara shot her a glare. "Nothing's inaccessible to me." She didn't care if she had to journey to the capital of the Compact itself.

"Look." Anea put her hand out. "You know how I told you that healing magic works by speeding up the body's natural process? There's a special flower called the Kai Plant which does the opposite. If used properly, it can reverse injuries. Basically, it restores the injured organ to a time when it wasn't injured. You understand?"

Hope returned to Jessara as she stood up. "Where is this Kai Plant?"

"Inaccessible!" said Milland.

"They grow in a cave to the east," said Anea. "We used to have access to them, but a group of renegade orcs are holed up there now."

Jessara's brow furrowed. "Renegade orcs?"

"Not all orcs are accepting of our teachings. They believe that fighting is the orcish way, rather than simply overcoming adversity. The renegades create small towns and camps, and attack anyone not from their clan."

"How many?" Not that it would matter to Jessara.

"At least thirty."

"Which brings us back to the whole 'inaccessible' part," said Miland.

Jessara shrugged. "I've had worse odds. Where's my gear?"

Anea nearly chuckled. "I assume there's no way we're talking you out of this?"

Jessara straightened her posture. "Read my mind and tell me."

Anea gave her a thoughtful smile. "Perhaps who Asha is to you is not as complicated as you think, yeah?"

The comment did not make Jessara uncomfortable, even though she thought it should have. "Perhaps."

"Follow me."

Chapter Sixteen

The Kai Plant

Jessara wasted no time setting off for the renegade camp. As soon as she grabbed her gear, and Anea pointed her to the exit, she left the temple. Coshgromar was built into a mountain on an incline, so it wasn't difficult for Jessara to figure out how to get to the front gate—just go down.

On her way out, some of the orcs looked at her admiringly. Some tried to address her, but Jessara was so focused on her goal that she didn't notice. At one point, she thought she saw a strange glowing light out of the corner of her eye, but she ignored it—probably a torch or campfire.

Despite the circumstances, it was good to be back on her feet and active. The Sisterhood's magic had worked wonders on Jessara's injuries. Even her burn was nearly healed.

Jessara had never had this much drive before an infiltration job, although she'd be lying if she said she wasn't nervous about what she was up against. The few brawls she'd gotten into with orcs had demonstrated how tough they were as fighters. And those had been one on one fights, not one on thirty.

Orcs would always have strength on her. Stealth, agility, and skills would be her advantages. Despite what she'd told Anea, she knew this would be a tough mission, but that didn't matter. The only thing she cared about was saving Asha. Creos help anyone who stood in her way.

Luckily for Jessara, the wind had died down, and the snow had stopped. It was still too cold for comfort, but not enough to slow her down. At one point, she noticed a snow troll ahead of her. The sight of the same beast that had injured Asha filled her with rage.

Jessara drew an arrow, got closer, and sent it through the beast's skull.

After a two-hour trek, Jessara saw smoke ahead, indicating she was close to the encampment. As the base came into view, she studied its layout and put on her headband. The encampment reached out from the base of the mountainside like a horseshoe. A wooden-stake wall with three entrances surrounded the camp. Many of the stakes were crooked or leaning—not aesthetic by any means, but they were enough of a barrier to make Jessara's job difficult.

Going through one of the main entrances would be a bad idea—too many eyes watching them. Jessara scanned the wall, trying to find lower spots. Several orc lookouts stood on scaffolds just behind the wall—another complication to consider.

Fortunately, it was getting dark, and Jessara could take advantage of that. Keeping low, she drew closer to the edge of the wall, and studied the head movements of the orc lookouts, planning her advance accordingly.

Between the cover of night and the falling snow, she made it to the wall without being spotted, then snuck along the wall toward the base of the mountain. When she reached it, an orc lookout stood above her—an obstacle that needed to be removed.

Jessara glanced through a crack between the wooden stakes to get a good look at the orc. His breath was visible in the mountain air, and his crude animal-skin cloak fluttered in a gust of freezing wind.

A quick scan of the area assured her that there'd be no witnesses. Jessara grabbed her bow, but hesitated. These orcs had done nothing to her or the Kingdom. Despite what Anea had said about them attacking outsiders on sight, Jessara had no quarrel with them. But the image of Asha lying on the infirmary bed returned. She didn't feel good about what she was about to do, but she didn't have time to hesitate. *I'm sorry.*

Then she drew string, stepped backward, and shot an arrow at the orc. It sailed through the bottom of his chin into his head. *Thud.* Jessara used the corner of the mountain and the side of the wall to climb her way into the camp.

Jessara ran over to the orc body and rolled it over the edge of the wall, before whirling around to scan the encampment. White tents of various heights and shapes sprinkled the area. Jessara was surprised to see no permanent structures. The place looked more like a military camp than a permanent base.

Jessara followed a path beside the mountain that brought her in view of the cave entrance. Two orcs stood guard, so she would need a diversion. She wished for Asha, remembering when she'd lit the gallows on fire in Tarton. Perhaps Jessara could try something similar, but she'd need a flame. Jessara noticed that most of the tents were lit up on the inside. Candles. She could get her fire from there.

Suddenly, she heard snow crunch behind her. As she turned around, she saw an orc coming her way. He hadn't spotted her, but he would at any moment. She grabbed her bow and shot an arrow into his throat. The body fell in the open with no obvious place to hide it, so Jessara dragged it closer to the edge of the wall. Hopefully it would be unnoticed. Orc bodies were heavy, but Jessara's strength had returned to her.

Her search for the right tent brought Jessara to one on the outer row close to the wall. As she stood next to it, she could hear an orc breathing inside. She grabbed her daggers, snuck around the corner of the tent, and peered inside. An orc woman stood with her back to the entrance. She appeared to be hunched over a table looking through some papers. Jessara crept into the tent, got behind the orc, and sunk her daggers into the orc's sides, puncturing her kidneys. She died quickly.

Jessara used one of her knives to cut a piece of cloth off the wall of the tent. She then took an arrow and wrapped the cloth around the head. After using a candle to light the cloth, Jessara stepped outside. Making sure the coast was clear, she shot the arrow at another tent. The blaze didn't take long to rise.

The confused voices of orcs shouting echoed through the air. Jessara slipped out of the tent and dashed to the entrance. Only one orc stood guard this time. Jessara drew an arrow and shot it between the eyes. After dragging the body to the nearest tent, she slipped into the cave.

Past the narrow entrance, Jessara came to a larger cavern. Orcs, with their backs toward her, were digging on jerry-rigged scaffolds;

she seemed to have stumbled upon some type of mining operation. Unfortunately, no plants were in sight.

Jessara spotted another tunnel at the end of the cavern. Carefully, she prowled to the opening. As she approached, two orcs emerged from the passage. She ducked to the side of the tunnel and drew her daggers. As soon as they passed, Jessara got behind them both and stuck a knife into their sides. They collapsed in different directions.

She sheathed the daggers and started through the tunnel. The cave wasn't as cold as the outside, but it certainly wasn't comfortable for the Woodlander. The air was stuffy, and the water dripping from stalactites echoed through the cavern.

At the end of the tunnel, she spotted what appeared to be a throne room. An orc sat atop a crude throne, presumably the chief. Two orc guards stood by his side. To the left of the throne, a garden full of glowing blue flowers lit up the cavern. The Kai Plant!

Jessara hadn't been spotted yet. She drew her daggers and took a deep breath, and then ran into the tunnel and threw the knives into the throats of the standing guards.

The chief drew his axe, and Jessara shot an arrow, but he deflected it with his weapon and charged.

"Shit."

The orc bashed her with the side of his axe, and she was flung backwards.

The chief attacked again. As his weapon hurtled toward the ground, Jessara rolled out of the way. She kicked the chief in the side, causing him to roar, but he managed to keep his footing. Jessara got to her feet and drew her sword to face her opponent.

The chief charged at her with a war cry. She parried his axe to the ground and swung her sword at the wooden handle, slashing it in half. A loud *snap* echoed through the cavern.

The orc glared at her. He swung his arm and hit her in the chest. The shock of the blow made her drop her sword as she was sent flying.

She hit the ground, knocking the wind out of her for a moment. Gasping for breath, she tried to pull herself up, but the orc threw the handle of his broken axe at her. It struck her in the chest, sending shockwaves throughout her body and knocking her on her back.

Seizing his advantage, the chief stormed to where Jessara lay and jabbed his foot on her throat. With all the strength she could still muster, Jessara tried to keep the boot from crushing her windpipe, but all she could do was slow down the inevitable as she lost the ability to breathe.

Jessara stared up at the orc's glowing yellow eyes as he crushed the life out of her. She thought about Asha in the temple, hovering near death. Without Jessara's help, that death would come. But it wasn't too late.

Jessara closed her eyes and quickly ran through the fight, trying to remember what assets were still available. Her knives were still in the throats of the guards, her sword was on the ground out of reach, her arrows were being crushed under her back. Then she remembered the axe handle that the orc had thrown at her. Where was that?

She pulled a hand from beneath the orc's boot which added more pressure to her neck but allowed her to feel around for the axe handle. Finally, her hand grazed the broken weapon. Her fingers eased it toward her until she managed to get a grip. Then, with all the strength she could will, she jabbed it at the chief's groin.

He staggered back, releasing Jessara's throat. His roar was so loud, it shook the cave.

The sweet air in her lungs was rejuvenating as she got to her feet. It was payback time. Gripping the axe handle, she stormed over to the chief and bashed him in the skull. He fell to his knees as Jessara landed another blow. A *crack* echoed in the room as he hit the ground. Jessara continued to smash his head in until she was certain his legs had stopped kicking.

Then she tossed the axe handle to her side and leaned over with her hands on her knees to catch her breath. It was a sloppy fight, at the end of a rushed mission, with no strategic benefit beyond the saving of one life. The King would have never approved of such recklessness, but he wasn't there.

Jessara quickly did a self-inspection and determined she had no major injuries from her fight. She'd be sore tomorrow, but otherwise, she could continue with the mission. After retrieving her weapons, she approached the Kai Plant.

The flowers had a strange glow to them. They were blue at the end with a hint of white toward the base of each petal. Jessara was not attuned to magic, but even she could feel the power pulsing from the petals when she touched the plant. She didn't know how much she'd need, so she picked several and put them in her satchel.

Jessara started back through the tunnel to the mining cavern. The mission accomplished, it was time to save Asha.

Suddenly, she heard an alarm horn ahead of her. When she reached the opening into the mining cavern, she saw three orcs standing over the bodies of the two she'd killed earlier. *Fuck me.*

"Alert the chief!" said one of the orcs.

"Fuck! Fuck! Fuck!" she whispered.

The other two orcs marched through the tunnel in Jessara's direction. She'd have to fight her way out, as if this mission weren't sloppy enough already.

Jessara took out a dagger and threw it at one of the approaching orcs. It struck him in the eye as the other roared with shock. She pulled out her sword and ran at the remaining enemy. Jessara went in as if she were attacking the throat, causing him to pull his axe up in defense. As soon as he did this, Jessara swung her sword down and struck his chest.

The fight alerted the other orc at the opening of the tunnel. She pulled out her bow and shot an arrow into his forehead.

Jessara retrieved her dagger as she ran by the bodies.

The orcs who'd been mining on the scaffolds were descending their ladders. On top of that, five orcs sprinted into the cave from the entrance.

Jessara ran over to one of the scaffolds as the newcomers shadowed her. As soon as the assailants got closer, she took out her sword and broke one of the support beams holding the scaffold.

Jessara jumped out of the way as the scaffold collapsed on four of the renegades.

One of the orcs managed to jump partly out of the way, but he caught his leg in the rubble. Jessara could have finished him off, but he no longer posed a threat. He growled after her as she passed.

After reaching the exit, Jessara was met by another orc. He swung his axe at her neck, but Jessara ducked her head and then slashed at the axe handle, breaking it. Then she dug her sword into the orc's side.

When she got out of the cave, several furious orcs rushed the entrance. She took out her bow and ran along the base of the mountain to the outer wall.

Three more renegades appeared ahead of her. She shot an arrow into the farthest one.

With her bow in the other hand, she drew a dagger and moved on the nearest orc. When she got close, he went in for a sideways slash. Jessara threw her body to the ground and slid on the snow, avoiding the axe and stabbing up through his gut.

Jessara sheathed the dagger as the third orc swung his axe. It narrowly missed her as she rolled out of the way and jumped to her feet. She ran up the steps to one of the outlooks and jumped over the wall. She landed on the other side with a roll and sprinted away from the encampment as she heard roars behind her. The noises died down as she escaped into the mountains.

Chapter Seventeen

Stories in the Moonlight

Jessara wasn't sure how much time Asha had before she'd be beyond help. She made haste back to Coshgromar. Her trek took about an hour and a half as she pushed through exhaustion, and so much adrenaline pumped through her veins that the cold almost didn't register. A lookout must have let her through the front gate, but her march through the city was a blur as she focused on returning to the temple. After she entered, she stormed past several sisters who were surprised to see her, but she barely acknowledged their presence either. She gripped her satchel as she barged into the infirmary.

Anea, who still sat next to Asha's bed, was startled by her entry. "Jessara?"

Breathing heavily, Jessara tossed her satchel to Anea. "I got the flower."

Anea looked astonished as she reached into the satchel and produced the Kai petals. "How?"

"I used violence. Now, do what you need to do."

"I'll get Miland." Anea ran out of the room.

Jessara looked down at Asha—still in her coma, but still breathing. "Hang on."

A moment later, Anea returned with a sleepy Miland.

"How in Nara are you not dead?" said Miland.

"I got the flowers." Jessara pointed to the satchel. "Bring her back."

"It wouldn't kill you to say 'please.'" Miland reached into the satchel and pulled out a flower. "I only needed one."

"Keep the rest."

"All right. This'll require concentration, so shut up." Miland took the flower and ground it up with a mortar and pestle. She then took an alembic and a few other ingredients that Jessara didn't recognize. The bits of the flower were poured into the alembic and mixed with the rest of the ingredients, and after the ingredients dissolved, they were transferred to a bowl which Miland dipped her hands in. With flat palms from which green lights shot out, she held her hands over Asha's forehead.

The droplets from Miland's hand appeared to sink into Asha's skin as if absorbed by a sponge. Miland dipped her hand in the bowl again and repeated the process three more times. On the third, she cupped some of the liquid in her hands, sprinkled it on Asha's head, and conjured an almost blinding light. Jessara stared at Asha's eyes, hoping they would open. Each passing second in which they didn't made her heart pound faster.

A few minutes passed that seemed like centuries. Jessara's breath cracked. *Please wake up. Please, by the Creos, wake up. I...I think I've fallen for you.* At that moment, Asha's eyes opened. She took a deep breath as Miland's magic ceased.

"Creos!" Jessara smiled, tears of joy streaming down her cheeks. She practically leapt at Asha to embrace her. A surprised Asha hugged her back, and those blue eyes warmed Jessara's heart.

Miland threw up her hands. "Careful!"

Jessara loosened her grip on Asha's body and let her lie back down.

"How do you feel?" Anea's voice was both relieved and excited.

Asha rubbed her temple. "Like someone stuck a sword through my head."

Jessara laughed through her tears.

Asha turned to Jessara. "Good to see you on your feet. How long was I out?"

"Nearly three days," said Anea. "It's good to see you, sister."

Asha adjusted herself. "What happened?"

"A troll broke one of your ribs and punctured a lung." As usual, Miland's bedside manner left something to be desired. "You were deprived of air, and you've been brain dead for the last two days. We've kept you alive with magic."

Anea motioned to Jessara. "She retrieved a Kai Plant. It restored you."

Asha's eyes rested back on her companion as her brows rose thoughtfully. "Jessara?"

Her look made Jessara feel warm and a little jittery.

Anea must have noticed or maybe she'd read Jessara's mind. "We'll give you the room, yeah?" She motioned Miland to follow her.

"Don't be long," said Miland. "She should rest."

"I've been resting for three days," Asha chuckled.

"Fine! But if you die again, someone else is going to have to bring you back."

"Miland!" Anea pulled her out of the room, closing the door behind them.

Asha turned her attention back to Jessara. "The Kai Plant has been in a renegade camp for the last three years."

Jessara hesitated for a moment and then nodded. "Yes."

"You didn't have to do that."

Jessara smiled. "That's why it meant something."

"Thank you." Asha sat up in her bed, put her feet on the ground, and attempted to pull herself up.

Jessara reached to ensure her friend remained steady. "Should you be walking right now?"

"It's probably fine. Although, feel free to catch me if I collapse." Asha stood up and took a few steps forward. Her movements were slow and stiff, but she kept her balance. "Come on. I want to show you my room." She took Jessara by the hand, and they both walked out of the infirmary. Their fingers interlocked as Jessara enjoyed the feeling of Asha's soft palm against her own.

Jessara was amazed Asha could even walk. The nature of magic continued to be a mystery and a marvel. Part of her wished she'd paid more attention to Aleris during the many times he'd tried to lecture her.

They passed a few sisters who greeted Asha as she walked by. Jessara tried to give the sisters a polite acknowledgement, but she kept her attention on Asha.

Asha led her down several more halls of the same translucent glass "So, I guess you know about the Sisterhood now."

"Yes," said Jessara.

"I take it you have some more questions for me." Asha took a deep breath. "Go ahead. No more oaths prevent me from telling you the truth."

Jessara motioned to the walls of the temple. "Is this where you grew up?"

"Yes. I spent most of my life in these halls." The women came to a stone staircase where the walls went from glass to mortar. Pictures of various women in satin Sisterhood dresses lined the walls leading up the stairs.

As they ascended, Asha strained a little, but she made it up with a little support from Jessara's hand on her back. At the top lay a stone hallway lined with doors.

"These are the living quarters." Asha led Jessara down the left passage.

"Are your parents here?"

Asha frowned "No...This is mine." She opened the door and showed Jessara in. The room had a fireplace on the right side with a stack of wood beside the hearth and two wooden chairs with velvet upholstery in front. A large bearskin rug lay on the floor with a desk in the corner. A large bed with linen sheets and a down comforter rested against the middle of the back wall. To the left of the bed stood a glass door, which led to a balcony overlooking the city.

On the other side of the bed hung a picture of two women. One had red hair, blue eyes, and wore a blue dress like Asha's. She also shared Asha's soft round cheeks and compact build. The other woman in the picture had wavy blonde hair and a blue Kingdom army uniform. Her eyes were hazel and as deep set as Asha's. She stood tall with a firm posture and an athletic body.

Asha strode over to the fireplace and grabbed some wood.

Jessara stared at the picture of the two women. "Where are they?"

"Dead." Asha put several logs in the fireplace.

That was something they had in common.

Asha lit the hearth which Jessara deeply appreciated. Jessara had been able to ignore the cold while her adrenaline was pumping, but with that gone, a fire was welcome. Asha walked over to the balcony and opened the door. Her eyes rested on the stars as she leaned against the rail.

Jessara followed her. A bright full moon lit up the city, and Jessara finally had a moment to take it in. Coshgromar was a warrior's city, and it looked like one. The houses were clearly designed with function—not aesthetics—in mind. Most were two or three stories high with wood reinforcing the corners and stone making up the walls. The roofs were tiled and of mansard design. Barrels, tanning racks, and anvils lined the cobblestoned roads. In the distance stood the spires of snow-covered mountain ranges.

It was a beautiful city. If it weren't for the cold, Jessara likely would have thought it a pleasant place to live. At one point, she thought she saw a bright floating light disappear down an alley, but she didn't get a good look at it. Instead, she looked back at Asha, who still watched the sky with a bittersweet sadness.

Jessara assumed she was bothered by the mention of her parents. "Tell me about them." She wondered if that was too forward or out of bounds. Then again, Asha had said she'd answer questions.

Asha looked over her shoulder at Jessara. "Members of the Sisterhood have learned how to tap into the spiritual connection between female partners. We're able to use that connection to allow one to bear a child without a father. The child will have traits from both mothers. My birth mother was a sorceress, and my spirit mother was a soldier of the Kingdom."

"How'd they meet?"

"Did Anea tell you about descendants?"

"Yes."

"And the Red Daggers?"

Jessara nodded.

Asha's eyes turned to a distant mountain range. "A girl of three years had been revealed to the Sisterhood. My birth mother, Reana, was tasked with seeking her out. She was in the small town of Olive Tree in the south-western part of the Kingdom, a long way from the Northern Mountains. When she arrived, the Red Daggers were already inside. The girl's parents had tried to fight them off, but both had been killed.

"Mother Reana was a fire sorceress, and no stranger to combat. She attacked the Daggers, but there were five of them. My spirit mother, Caris, had been a guard on patrol at the time and heard fighting in the house. She rushed in to find that Mother Reana had killed off most of the Daggers, but they'd managed to wound her. Together, they finished the rest.

"From the moment they'd first seen each other, they knew there was a connection."

Jessara knew that feeling.

As if reading her mind, Asha blushed. "Mother Reana used to say the Tree itself had brought them together. Mother Caris helped her and the child escape the town. Mother Reana wasn't allowed to explain anything at the time, but she invited Mother Caris to come with them, which she accepted. When they got to the temple, my spirit mother was introduced to the Sisterhood."

Jessara heard the distant sound of a dog barking. "What was the child's name?"

Asha smiled. "Anea. She was raised as my adopted sister. Not long after my spirit mother came to the temple, she and Mother Reana fell in love. After a year, they were wed."

"This was allowed by the Sisterhood? Even though Caris was an outsider?" Jessara wasn't just asking on behalf of Asha's parents.

Asha took a step closer to Jessara, which made her tremble with desire. "It's rare but not forbidden." Asha's voice shook when she spoke. "Once an outsider is allowed within the temple, they're no longer considered an outsider. After another year, I was born."

Jessara looked back at the painting. "That picture in your room?"

"Them."

"They were beautiful."

Asha gazed up at the moon and sighed sadly. "That picture can't do them justice."

Jessara hesitated. "What happened to them?" Again, she worried she'd overstepped. "I'm sorry. You don't need to tell me."

Asha paused, looking at the city below. "You deserve to know. I...I want you to know." She took a deep breath. "I was sixteen years old. Mother Reana was still going on regular missions to retrieve descendants. She'd been training Anea and me for the last several years to take over. One day, a child was revealed to the Sisterhood in the town of Bloomfield, in the southwestern part of the Kingdom. My birth mother decided it was time for us to come with her as observers. Mother Caris insisted on coming along. Bloomfield wasn't far from Olive Tree where she'd grown up, so she knew the area. When we arrived in Bloomfield, the town was under attack by Compact soldiers. My mothers told Anea and me to hide in the trees on the outskirts of town, and they joined the fight. It was the first time I'd ever seen battle."

"Were you scared?"

A slight grin spread across Asha's lips. "Not as much as Anea, but a little. Mostly, I was impressed with how fierce my parents were. They must have taken down at least a dozen soldiers. But the town had only a small militia, and they were overwhelmed by numbers. Mother Reana sent Mother Caris to find the girl in the town. They separated. Mother Caris managed to find the house and save the girl, but..." Asha paused for a second, and her eyes filled with tears.

Jessara gently put her hand on Asha's shoulder. "It's okay."

"Like I said, the numbers were too great." Asha's voice thickened. "Soldiers circled my birth mother and one...stabbed her through the heart from behind. My spirit mother had just returned with the girl, but it was already too late. The moment Mother Caris saw the body, she screamed so loudly that it almost drowned out my own screams. I still hear us in my dreams.

"When Mother Caris got her bearings, she demanded that we run. She insisted that we go to Olive Tree, since they had a proper garrison, to get reinforcements for Bloomfield. When we arrived, she told Anea and me to hide with the little girl, and then she told the captain of the guard about the attack and begged him to send troops. But he recognized her. They'd been soldiers together in Olive Tree before she'd met Mother Reana. He demanded that she tell him where she'd been all those years, but she kept her oath. He accused her of desertion and treason. She pleaded for Bloomfield, but he refused to listen. We watched as they dragged her into the forest and tied a noose to a tree. Then..." Asha choked on her words.

"Hey, come here." Jessara held Asha against her shoulder.

"No trial! No hesitation!" Asha put her arms around Jessara and gripped her back as she spoke between wails. "They didn't even cut her down. They just left her body to rot!"

Much began to make sense to Jessara. "That's why you hate the Kingdom."

Asha wiped her eyes. "It's why I hate the King. Plenty of well-meaning people live in the Kingdom. But they're led by that bloody tyrant. The penalty for almost everything is death, and they rarely hold trials.

He may not have signed the order to execute my spirit mother, but he's the reason she's dead."

"I'm sorry." Jessara tightened her grip around Asha.

"Thank you."

"Your mothers sound like amazing people."

"Yes, they were."

"Dremeria is the lesser for their loss."

"Yes, it is." Asha pulled herself away from Jessara and looked into her eyes.

"Did the girl make it?"

Asha's lips curled into a smile. "Yes. She lives in the temple with us. She's nearly a woman herself."

"What's her name?"

"Relic. You'll probably meet her at some point. She's wonderful. Despite the loss of my parents, saving her made me want to continue retrieving descendants."

"What about Anea?"

Asha frowned. "She couldn't do it again. She hasn't left the mountains since."

The moonlight reflected off the blue eyes that Jessara had learned to be comforted by. Asha had trusted her with a painful secret, and she was honored. Flashes from Jessara's own past played through her head, and she realized that she wasn't alone in her pain. "I never knew my parents. That night at the camp, you asked me why I didn't have a last name."

"You don't have to tell me if you don't want to." Asha put her hand on Jessara's shoulder.

Jessara closed her eyes; it was time to let another in, and she wanted it to be Asha. "I want to." She opened her eyes. "I was born in a small village close to the border in Anwood. I don't even remember the face of my father. The only memory I have of my mother was her leaning over my crib, dead—blood dripping from her mouth onto me. The Purge had been going on for several years, but it hadn't come to Anwood yet. Several villages had given refuge to humans trying to escape. My village was one of them.

"The Supreme Leader at the time decreed that there would be no more exceptions. Any village found to be hiding humans would be sacked, and all of the villagers killed. I was three at the time. All I remember is an arrow piercing my mother's chest as she ran into my room. A Compact soldier reached down to take me. I couldn't see his face, but I could see the symbol of the Watch Tower on his armor."

Jessara's expression hardened. "I'll never forget that symbol. Kingdom soldiers broke into the room and killed the soldier before he could take me. The King personally led a platoon to defend our village. They were trying to get humans out of Compact territory. Nobody knew my family name. They only knew my first name because it was stitched to my blanket. The soldiers brought me to the King, and he took pity and brought me back to Enderdale.

"There was a barracks within the palace where he'd housed other orphaned elven children rescued from the Compact. We were all raised together. As soon as we could pick up a sword, they started training us to be assassins. Any humans seen in Compact territory are killed on sight. It was logical to use elves for assassinating targets in the Compact."

A horrified look spread across Asha's face. "You were children! He turned you into weapons!"

Jessara understood Asha's reaction. She knew how the story sounded, but to Jessara, the training was the best thing the King had ever done for her. "We had everything taken away from us by the Compact. We were children, helpless to defend ourselves or our family. The Kingdom gave us the ability to fight back. We were fed and taken care of. Once we finished our training, we were paid handsomely for jobs. I know it may seem like we were tools to the King, but he was the closest thing I had to a father. He never demanded loyalty from us. He trusted that our compensation would keep us loyal. I've been content with being a weapon against the Compact."

"You're more than that." Asha put her palm on Jessara's hand.

Jessara glanced at her companion. "You're the only person who's ever made me question."

"Question what?"

"If a weapon is what I want to be. If I could ever be something else. If hatred isn't the only thing worth fighting for."

"And?"

"I don't know. For the first time, I set out to preserve life, not end it. I wasn't paid, but I've never been so motivated to succeed. I killed tonight. But for once, it wasn't to hurt those I hate; it was to save someone that I couldn't stand the idea of losing."

Asha tilted her head thoughtfully. "So you are a 'friend person'?"

Jessara took a gentle step toward Asha as her heart raced. She was terrified of what she was about to say, but she refused to let that stop her. "I don't want to be just friends."

Asha's lips curled into a surprised smile. "Really?"

Jessara took a deep breath. "Yes. I...I've felt this way since the kiss."

"I thought you said it was a mistake."

Jessara moved in closer, putting her hand on Asha's cheek. "Maybe it was. But I don't care. I almost lost you tonight. We still have a long journey ahead of us. I don't know what'll happen when it's over. But I don't care about that either. All I know is that right now, I'm here with you. That's all I want." Another deep breath. "I don't know if you feel the same way. It's okay if you don't. We can be friends. But I had to tell you where things stood for me."

The silence lasted between the women for a few moments. Jessara held her breath as she waited for Asha to respond. She seemed to be in deep thought. In that moment, Jessara wished she were telepathic.

Finally, Asha shrugged her shoulders. "Maybe the kiss was a mistake."

Jessara's heart sank. Of course, Asha would never be interested in an assassin like her. How could Jessara have thought this would go any other way?

But then, Asha's lips slowly curled into the most beautiful smile Jessara had ever seen. "You want to make it again?"

Chapter Eighteen

Joined

"Yes!" The answer came out more forcefully than Jessara had meant it to.

The moonlight glistened off Asha's lips as she slowly moved them closer to Jessara's. Asha closed her eyes.

Right before their lips made contact, Jessara hesitated for a second. She could feel the breath of desire coming from Asha. Then she closed her eyes and pressed their mouths together. Asha's lips were as warm as the rest of her body. They were soft and inviting. In the cave, their kiss had been one of desperation. But here, it was a kiss of pure comfort. Jessara felt like she was in a dream. She put her arms around Asha and held their bodies together as their tongues touched.

"Just to be clear." Jessara spoke between kisses. "This means you *do* feel the same way?"

Asha giggled. "Yes! By the Tree, yes!" She pressed her tongue against Jessara's, then trailed kisses across Jessara's cheek and down to her neck. Each sensation made Jessara more needy.

"There's only one bed." Jessara could barely find words as she enjoyed Asha's mouth on her skin.

Asha brought her lips to Jessara's ear. "I know." Her breath sent a tingle down Jessara's spine as Asha returned to Jessara's neck and ran her tongue against it.

Jessara let out an aroused sigh. "Would you like me to take the floor?"

Asha pulled back and pressed their foreheads together. "No. I want you to take me to the bed."

Jessara's heart pounded louder. "Are you sure you're up for this?"

"Yes." Asha winked.

Jessara looked at the bed, knowing she wanted this. The longing between her legs was overwhelming. But she also knew Asha had been through a lot. "Sure?"

"Yes!"

Jessara's legs pulsed. "It's been a while. Show me what you like."

Asha reached for Jessara's chaulk-hide chestguard and gently undid the straps. While she worked the armor loose, she gave her neck another kiss. Jessara worked on removing the rest of her armor as her neck tingled from Asha's touch.

Normally, Jessara hated having her armor off. Even during previous sexual experiences, it gave her an uncomfortable sense of vulnerability. But for the first time in her life, it was freeing. The world was so much lighter.

Asha undid her own dress and pulled it down her body. The more skin Asha showed her, the more desperate Jessara grew. Then, to Jessara's excitement, Asha took hold of her breast band and slowly slid it up over her head, revealing what lay beneath.

Jessara studied Asha's gorgeous figure. This wasn't the first time she'd seen Asha's body, but the night in the cave, she'd been half-conscious and delusional. Now her head was clear, and she could enjoy her partner's beauty in the moonlight.

Asha had pink nipples with wide areolas. Her arms and abdomen were soft and undefined. Jessara tried not to stare, but she couldn't help it. She needed to touch her partner.

As if reading her mind, Asha gently took Jessara's hand and held it against her breasts. Jessara rubbed around her nipples, causing Asha to arch her head back. "Somebody's sensitive."

Jessara pulled away for a moment and removed her under armor and breast band. As the linen brushed against her own nipple, she could feel herself getting goosebumps. She was nervous about exposing herself, but as soon as she did, Asha's eyes lit up at the sight of her body. Asha wanted her!

Comparatively, Jessara had a significantly more athletic build. Her arms were toned and her abdomen was well defined. Her breasts were a little smaller than Asha's with small dark nipples. A breeze from the window made her shiver as it hit her bare chest.

Asha took Jessara's hand and pulled her partner to the bed. Jessara lay across it, and her skin tingled with Asha's every touch. Each kiss held both desire and care. Nothing was rushed, and it was clear that Asha's only goal was to make Jessara as comfortable as possible—a goal that was well achieved.

Jessara sighed with lust. Asha sat back, beckoning Jessara with one finger, and Jessara lightly pushed Asha down so she could get on top.

Then she repaid the tenderness from Asha by running her own tongue against her neck. As she did, she felt Asha's soft hair brush against her cheek as the wonderful smell of lavender filled her senses.

"Right there." Asha pulled Jessara's chest toward her and ran her tongue against her nipples.

The sensation sent pulses through Jessara's entire body. "You're not the only sensitive one."

Each press of Asha's tongue grew more firm and desperate. She wanted more, and Jessara was more than happy to give it to her.

Jessara brought her hand down Asha's chest and down her stomach. She slid it into Asha's undergarments and held a finger just above Asha's clit. Those gorgeous blue eyes reflected pure joy as she lightly teased.

Asha giggled. "Please."

Jessara brought her lips down to Asha and kissed her—a little more aggressively than before. Then she started rubbing and for the first time, she felt how soaking wet her partner was.

Asha's lips clenched with need as she let out a soft moan. "That feels bloody amazing."

Jessara stopped for a moment and gently pulled Asha's undergarments down. She ran her hands across Asha's inner thighs and worked them apart. Asha's hips and legs were significantly more muscular than the rest of her body—doubtless from all the traveling.

Jessara's eyes scanned up Asha's body and rested back on her eyes. "Can I taste you?"

The words made Asha tremble. "Yes! By the Tree, yes!"

Jessara slowly kissed down Asha's body, down her chest, down her stomach, and she stopped just above her core.

She looked back up at Asha, wanting to see the desperation in her eyes, the lust. What she saw was the most beautiful woman she'd ever beheld—eyes begging for the pleasure Jessara was eager to give to her.

Jessara gently brought her mouth down where she knew Asha wanted it. As soon it made contact, Asha moaned loudly. "Yes!"

Jessara pressed her tongue up against Asha and licked steadily, the taste divine. Every stroke from Jessara's tongue drove Asha wild with ecstasy and lust. Asha moved her pelvis up and down to rub herself against Jessara's mouth.

Jessara knew she was pleasuring her partner. The thought of giving Asha what she needed made Jessara wet.

This was the first time Jessara had done this for someone she truly cared for. For the first time, she cared about giving someone pleasure, not because of the promise of reciprocation, but because of the desire to give them what they truly deserved.

Asha deserved the world. She deserved more than Jessara could ever hope to give her. But that fact only drove Jessara to focus on nothing else but her partner's pleasure.

Jessara slowed down her licking and then sucked on Asha, who grabbed Jessara's head and nearly screamed.

Jessara continued as Asha moaned louder, building up more and more. She was close. Careful not to press too hard, Jessara went faster. Asha tightened against her, and she let out another gasp. Then she squeezed Jessara's head between her thighs as she let out a series of moans.

Her climax pulsed against Jessara's tongue, and Jessara knew her partner was satisfied, at least for now.

Asha slowly relaxed into the bed. Jessara crawled her way up Asha's body and kissed her. She lightly ran her finger between Asha's legs and she twitched. Too sensitive. As their tongues played with each other, Jessara started running her finger in circles between Asha's legs, occasionally pressing on the middle.

When it was clear that Asha had recovered, Jessara kissed down her body again until she was back between her legs.

Asha's voice shook in anticipation. "Please, I need your mouth again."

Jessara was more than happy to oblige. But first, she licked around Asha's lips, specifically avoiding where she knew Asha was aching for her to touch. She kissed down her thigh on one side and then the other.

"Don't tease." Asha's legs quaked with anticipation.

"You'll get what you want." Jessara pulled her tongue away.

"Please! I need—"

Without warning Jessara pressed her tongue firmly against Asha.

"Fuck!"

Jessara guided the rough edges of her tongue against those wet, inviting lips.

Asha moaned with desire once again. "Lick me!"

The begging made Jessara pulse between her legs. Although she would be enjoying this regardless of whether or not Asha could pleasure her back, she was looking forward to the idea of Asha's tongue on her.

But Jessara needed to be closer to her partner. "Can I use a finger?"

"Yes!" Asha was barely able to talk between moans.

Jessara slid her finger inside Asha, feeling the wet walls of her partner. She rubbed Asha's spot in rhythm with her licks.

Asha rode Jessara's finger and tongue. "You can use two."

Jessara gave Asha a firm broad stroke with her tongue as she put another finger inside her. Asha tightened and pleasured herself. The intimacy of being inside Asha was a level of closeness that Jessara hadn't known she'd needed until she had it. This was what sex should feel like.

Asha moved against Jessara's tongue and on her fingers. Like they'd done so many times, they were working together to accomplish their goal. Only this time, that goal was giving Asha an amazing second orgasm.

"Just like that!" Asha's breath rate increased. She tightened around Jessara's fingers as she gasp again, louder than her first climax.

Jessara looked at the face of the woman she was pleasuring. Not only did she want to make sure Asha finished, she wanted to see it.

Asha squeezed Jessara's head between her legs. The pressure was soothing—almost like the headband she used to concentrate.

Asha giggled. "By the Tree, you know what you're doing."

Jessara couldn't help but smirk at the flattery.

"Come here—I need you." The desperation in Asha's voice hadn't subsided. Asha pulled Jessara to her and kissed her as she caressed Jessara's breasts. The passion and longing was palpable as Jessara enjoyed those soft warm hands running across her skin.

Asha pushed Jessara on her back and climbed on top of her. The deep pressure of Asha's body relieved tension that Jessara hadn't realized she had.

Asha reached down and slid Jessara's undergarments down her legs. Jessara almost stopped her, but she restrained herself as she hoped her partner liked what she saw.

Asha's gaze scanned Jessara's body. As she looked between Jessara's legs, her eyes grew hungry. The reaction didn't completely cancel Jessara's self-consciousness, but it waned as Asha crawled up her body with renewed vigor.

Their naked bodies pressed together, almost every inch of Jessara's skin touched Asha's warmth. She was so close to Asha that it was as if their bodies could sink into one another and meld to become one.

Asha ran her finger down Jessara's body and stopped between her legs. She licked her partner's breasts, and the bumps of Asha's tongue massaged Jessara's nipples. She wanted Asha to take care of her.

Once again, Asha seemed to read her mind. "I need to taste you."

"Please."

Asha kissed down Jessara's body. Each time she felt those warm lips, Jessara arched her back. Asha hovered her mouth between Jessara's legs and began to breathe exactly where Jessara wanted her mouth. The air against her made her more desperate for that soft warm tongue.

Asha looked up at her partner. "Beg me for it."

Jessara narrowed her eyes and smiled. "Now." Sweet, but firm.

The dominance of Jessara's voice made Asha shiver. "Yes, ma'am."

Ma'am. She liked the sound of that. And as soon as Jessara felt that tongue against her, the rest of the world stopped. The sensation she'd been aching for was finally happening. She'd never been so wet, so aroused, and so comfortable in her entire life.

It wasn't just that Asha was pleasuring her; it was that she knew Asha wanted her to be pleasured.

Jessara reached down and touched Asha's head, stroking her soft hair. Asha ran her tongue firmly and slowly between Jessara's lips. Each time she got to the top, Jessara gasped.

She looked down at Asha, whose attention was focused between Jessara's legs. She placed her hand on Asha's head and stroked her hair again. "You're the most beautiful woman in Dremeria."

Asha looked up at her partner. Those blue eyes sent a spell that caused throbbing between Jessara's legs.

Jessara lay back on the pillow, enjoying the building ecstasy. Asha's skills had put Jessara into a trance-like state that she never wanted to leave.

Asha gave another firm press of her tongue. "No one can match you, my dear."

"You're such a li—" Jessara was cut off as Asha went faster, making her grip Asha's head.

She had trouble calming her mind, but she was enjoying the sensation.

She thought only of Asha. The bond they'd created together. The times they'd saved each other's lives. The fact that for the first time since they'd met, they were safe.

Jessara relaxed and trusted Asha. That beautiful sensation built higher as she moaned. "Don't stop."

Asha gave a bit more pressure with her tongue, exactly where Jessara needed it.

Everything else slipped away. Jessara looked at Asha's face once again.

Those gorgeous blue eyes looking up from between her legs brought Jessara to the top. It washed over her as she gripped Asha's head. Time stopped as she moaned. She didn't take her eyes off Asha as she enjoyed the most intense orgasm of her life. Slowly, as the sensation dissipated, her legs stopped shaking.

She pulled Asha up to her and kissed her lightly as Asha slowly rubbed around her sensitive core without touching it. With her other hand, she groped Jessara's breast. Her head spun from all the sensations.

Asha slid down and sucked on Jessara's breast. Her nipples hardened as Jessara lay back and gave herself to Asha. She was willing to let Asha do whatever she wanted.

As Jessara recovered from her climax, her clit became desperate for contact once again. "I need more."

Asha pulled her mouth away from Jessara's breasts and grinned. She ran her tongue down her chest and back between her legs.

This time, Asha did not tease. As soon as Jessara felt that talented tongue, she knew it would be easier. But something was missing. She looked down at her partner. "Use your fingers. I need to feel you inside of me."

Asha smiled between strokes of her tongue and slowly worked her fingers inside of Jessara. A tight fit at first, Jessara felt full of her partner as those talented fingers slid in and out of her.

For a moment, Jessara was tempted to ride her finger, but she decided she wanted to let Asha take care of her.

Asha's fingers filled her and her tongue worked magic between her thighs.

This time, Jessara's mind did not wander. The events of the day no longer existed, and neither did tomorrow. There was no past or future, only the present, a present that no force in Dremeria could pull her out of. They were the only two people that existed—that had ever existed. "You're amazing at that."

"Bloody right I am." Asha diversified the movements of her mouth. As Asha's tongue ran against her again, Jessara felt herself starting to build quicker than she expected. Her second orgasm was inevitable.

"Asha! Please!" Jessara let out a moan as she felt another climax wash over her. It was even more intense than the first time.

Every part of her body tingled as she watched Asha. She wanted to make sure that face was a part of the world of pleasure she was experiencing.

Jessara jerked her body a few times, squeezing Asha's head between her legs. That soft blonde hair caressed her skin as she relaxed into the bed. "Come here."

Asha softly petted her partner as she brought her mouth back to Jessara's for more kissing. "I can keep going."

Jessara shook her head. "Just let me hold you."

Asha lay down next to her, and they pulled each other close, looking deeply into each other's eyes. But her hand did not move from between Jessara's legs. She lightly rubbed as they continued to make out.

Jessara knew that she wouldn't be able to climax again, but this was a perfect way of basking in the afterglow of the two best orgasms of her life.

Jessara pressed her lips against Asha's ear. "You were incredible."

"You were amazing."

They lightly kissed, and Jessara closed her eyes, feeling Asha's warm skin against her body. She was content. She was happy. And she let herself drift to sleep.

CHAPTER NINETEEN

THE CHIEF

Asha's eyes peeked open. She was still cuddled against Jessara's naked body. Careful not to wake her partner, Asha attempted to sit up to stretch her arms, but they were still strained. Although she was much better than the previous night, it would be a least another day before she was back to full strength. She gazed down at her new partner, still sound asleep, looking peaceful and beautiful.

Based on where the sun was, Asha guessed it was midmorning. She smiled as she reminisced about the previous night. What they'd said to each other. What they'd done to each other. It had been a while since she'd been in a relationship. Asha had forgotten how nice it felt to wake up next to someone she cared for. She leaned in and pressed her lips against Jessara's, who stirred before kissing her back.

Asha smiled at those beautiful green eyes when they opened. "Hey, you."

Jessara returned her smile. "Hey, gorgeous."

They silently gazed upon each other for a few minutes. Asha was embarrassed by how sappy she felt, but Jessara seemed to feel no different.

Finally, Jessara broke the silence. "What do we do today?"

Asha scooted herself into her partner's embrace. "Lie here. Hold each other. Never leave this comfy bed."

Jessara chuckled. "Sounds nice, but we can't stay here forever."

Asha sighed. There was so much uncertainty about their new relationship and their path forward. Several confessions lingered in the back of her mind that she would need to make eventually. But as long as they stayed in bed, she could pretend it was still last night. Reality could wait. "Maybe not. But we can do it for longer than we should."

Jessara's face became nurturing. "How are you feeling?"

Asha's smile widened. "Like I just woke up from a night of the best sex of my life."

That nearly elicited a laugh. "I meant health-wise."

"Much better. Much better than brain dead."

"You still need to take it slow."

"I'll be fine." Asha gave her partner a playful push when she saw Jessara's doubtful look. "No really."

"Let me get you food." Jessara pulled the covers off and retrieved her clothes. As she stepped off the bed, Asha stared at her firm muscular rear. Clothes lay scattered across the floor in a path leading from the balcony to the bed. Jessara dressed as Asha watched, disappointed that Jessara would no longer be naked. Jessara started toward the door, but then paused for a moment and turned back to Asha. "Where do you go for food?"

"We'll go together." Asha shook her head and got out of bed to retrieve her own clothes.

Jessara grinned. "But I was hoping you'd stay naked."

Asha smiled and rolled her eyes. "How do you think I feel?"

When she finished dressing, Asha took Jessara's hand and led her out of the room. They walked down the stone hallway, down the staircase, and back to the section of the temple with the translucent glass walls. After making two left turns, she brought Jessara into a room with a large wooden table. Miland, Anea, and about a dozen other sorceresses sat around the table. They all wore Sisterhood dresses, each a different color, and were helping themselves to breakfast. It was good to see her family again, and Asha couldn't wait to introduce them to Jessara.

When the couple entered, the sorceresses applauded. Asha could feel Jessara's heart rate pick up. She looked over at her partner, who was awkwardly staring at the ground.

"There she is!" said a young woman dressed in black. "You look good for dead!"

Asha threw her fist in the air. "I got better, Relic."

"What about you, Jessara?" said Anea. "How's that burn on your shoulder?"

"It faded yesterday." Jessara continued to avoid eye contact. "I removed the bandage on my way back from the orc camp."

Asha wondered why her partner was staring at the ground. Was she okay?

"How did she burn her shoulder?" said Brina, another sorceress in black.

"Asha cauterized her." Miland pointed a crooked, accusatory finger. "This poor young woman got bitten by an ice chaulk, lost several pints of blood, fell into a frozen lake, and got hypothermia in the middle of a blizzard. So naturally, Asha decided she should burn the shit out of her shoulder. Because why not?"

The room erupted in laughter.

"I stopped the bleeding, didn't I?" Asha feigned innocence and shrugged her shoulders.

"Just put some pressure on it or something." Milland rolled her eyes. "By the Tree, you elementals have no respect for how much bloody work you make for us healers."

"But without us," Asha approached Miland and kissed her cheek, "there'd be no need for you."

"Please, eat." Anea motioned to the table. "You've both earned a hot breakfast after what you've been through, yeah? Take as much as you want."

They both sat down and filled their plates. It was Asha's first full meal in days, and she wasted no time. The orcs frequently brought the Sisterhood meat from hunts in the mountains, and many of the sisters were master cooks. Today, the table was full of bear sausage links, fried goose eggs, and mountain red berry pastry—freshly cooked and still hot from the oven.

Asha enjoyed the thrill of adventure while on the road. But the temple came with many securities, food an important one. The meal nearly brought her to tears after days of stale bread and unseasoned rabbit.

"About a dozen orcs arrived in the city this morning," said Anea. "Said they came from the Kai Plant camp. They wanted to return to the fold."

"Really?" Asha glanced at Jessara, who kept her eyes on the floor.

"Yeah." Anea was trying not to grin. "Apparently, some crazy wood-land elf single-handedly killed their chieftain and over half their clan last night."

All eyes in the room rested on Jessara, who awkwardly took a bite of pastry. "What?"

Even with all the amazing feats Asha had seen from Jessara, she was shocked. "You killed half a camp to get the flower?"

"No!" said Jessara. "Some of them were killed after I'd already gotten the flower."

Anea shook her head and chuckled. "Anyway, they apparently be-lieved that they lost their direction. Orcs believe that might makes right, so after a major defeat, they are prone to change their ways, yeah? In this case, they decided that meant returning to the Coshgro-marians. I also have other news. Progmash, the chieftain of Coshgro-mar, wants to speak with you, Jessara."

Asha got excited. It had been a while since she'd seen Progmash, and she was quite fond of him.

Jessara looked up for a moment before her eyes went back to the floor. "What for?"

"He said he had a favor to ask," said Anea.

Jessara shrugged. "I guess I owe them."

"I'm coming with you." Asha kissed bear sausage grease off her fingers.

Jessara held out her hand in protest. "You should probably stay here and rest."

Asha smiled and shook her head. "Not a chance."

Jessara sighed. "Where's the chief?"

"In his hut," said Anea.

"I'll show you." Asha motioned with her head toward the door.

"I guess I'll go put my armor on." With that, Jessara got up, gave Asha a kiss, and walked out of the room.

"She needs her armor for a simple meeting?" said Drana, a sorceress in green.

"She's...slow to trust," said Asha.

"And what about that kiss?" Anea had a smile that was half mocking and half curious. "I asked her who you were to each other. She said it was complicated."

Asha looked in the direction Jessara had left. "It got simpler last night." *Also I know you already read her mind. You probably knew what she was going to tell me before I did.*

Anea feigned indignation. "I would never read such personal thoughts from another."

Asha raised a brow. "Anea, that last part wasn't aloud."

"It wasn't? Shit."

Asha laughed.

"So, are you together?" said Brina.

"Yes." Asha knew that Brina was only asking because they'd previously been in a relationship.

"Does that mean she'll be staying with us?" said Anea, before anything could become tense.

Asha thought for a second, as all of the things they'd need to work out came back to her. She hadn't intended to accompany Jessara back to Enderdale, and she had yet to confess that. Eventually, she'd have to. Part of her was looking forward to not needing to hide it. She hated deceiving people, but she cared more about her oath and the safety of her family. Still, she feared what the fallout would be when she told Jessara the truth. Her smile faded.

"Probably not."

"And you?"

Asha paused again. She was back in Coshgromar, where she had always intended to be. But things were different now. The previous night, she'd considered the possibility that Jessara and she would be going their separate ways, but she pushed it out of her mind and focused on the best sex of her life. Now she knew she'd need to make a decision. "I haven't figured it out yet."

Miland wagged her finger at Asha. "If you leave, remember your oath."

Asha waved a dismissive hand. "I will."

"We never discussed what happened on your retrieval mission, yeah?" said Anea.

Asha frowned as her heart flooded with guilt. "I was too late. I'd rather not talk about it."

"Too late for what?" Jessara reentered the room wearing her armor.

Asha smiled at her. "Sisterhood talk."

Evidently, Jessara didn't notice the pain in Asha's voice. "All right, let's go see the chief."

"This way." Asha led Jessara out of the room and down several more glass hallways to the temple exit.

When they reached the outside, Asha told Jessara to stop for a moment, so she could take in the beauty of her home. Since she'd been unconscious when she'd arrived, Asha hadn't seen the outside of the temple in several weeks. From the outside, the temple was a large stone building three stories high with a gabled roof and ionic columns. The first generation of sisters had known what they were doing. Asha had always wondered if they'd been master builders before they came to the mountains, or if that had been a skill they'd been forced to develop.

When she was satisfied, Asha took Jessara through the city in the direction of Progmash's hut. The sounds of weapons *clanking*, dogs barking, and orcs shouting filled the air. It was nice to walk through the city again; she'd missed Coshgromar.

Jessara broke the silence. "Anything I should know before I meet this Progmash?"

"Leave your prejudices at the door."

Jessara raised a brow. "Why? Will he bludgeon me if I say something problematic?"

Asha sighed. "No. But you did just make my point."

"Right, sorry. Most orcs I've met I've either gotten into brawls with or killed."

Asha stepped in front of Jessara and put her hands on her shoulders. "The orcs of this stronghold are family to me. Please treat them as such."

Jessara nodded. "All right. I'm known for my people skills."

They soon came to a circular hut, and she motioned for Jessara to step through its door. Coshgromarians didn't believe in giving chiefs perks beyond the power they wielded. So the hut was the crudest building in the city. While most buildings were sturdy and made of solid stone, the chief's hut was primarily clay wrapped in animal skin. Bone chimes and trophies from mountain beasts hung on the walls.

Progmash sat on a crude wooden throne by himself in the hut. When Asha had visited him in the past, he would occasionally have family or advisors with him, but as chief, he was expected to be able to defend himself. Therefore, he wasn't allowed personal guards.

When he saw the women, he smiled pleasantly. "You must be Jessara. I've heard damn high praise of you from both your friends and enemies. You got some bloody fucking talent. I am Progmash."

Progmash was large, even by orcish standards. He wore a troll skull for a helmet and the pelvic bones of two different animals as shoulderguards. Braided black hair swung at the sides of his head, and a bear-skin loincloth covered his groin. His green chest was exposed, revealing massive pectoral muscles, biceps the size of Asha's head, and chiseled abs. If Asha hadn't know him so well, she might have been intimidated by him.

"Pleased to meet you, Chief." Jessara bowed her head awkwardly, and Asha noticed her straining to keep eye contact with him.

"I got to thank you for returning some sheep—not to mention our dear Asha."

"Good to see you too, Prog." Asha approached the chief to give him a hug; orcish hugs were always firm.

Jessara bit her lip. "You're not pissed that I killed half a camp of your people?"

Progmash shook his head. "By choice, they weren't my folk. I respect them who don't want to follow our way. But the culling of their clan made them see they weren't stronger without us, as they'd thought."

Jessara tilted her head. "Are the survivors pissed?"

"A bit. But more out of bloody fucking embarrassment. You proved yourself the better warrior."

"Some might say that my use of stealth made most of those kills dishonorable."

Progmash stroked his chin. "Yeah, orcs prefer open battle. But a warrior's got to use all of their weapons. Regardless, they're bloody fucking dead and you're not, so your way must have been better."

"In that case, you're welcome." Jessara bowed her head again. "However, I assume that's not why you summoned me."

"Yeah." Progmash stood up from his throne. "Tell me, who has your loyalty?"

Asha glanced at Jessara uncomfortably. She too wanted to know how Jessara would answer.

Jessara looked back as if to apologize. "I have no loyalties. I kill for the King because he pays me, and I hate the Compact."

Asha shook her head in disapproval. *Still using that line?*

"An elf hating the Compact?" Progmash tilted his head and raised a curious brow. "Always a story there."

Jessara shook her head. "Not an interesting one."

That was a lie, but it was Jessara's business whom she told, so Asha bit her tongue.

"All right." Progmash paced around the room as he talked. "As you know, the orcs are neutral in your conflict. While we don't approve of the Purge, we got no bloody fucking love for the King either. Also, the Compact ain't attacked us yet. However, there's been some troubling shit lately."

"What kind?" Asha thought about the Compact soldiers from the cave. Did they have a connection?

"Hunting parties have seen scouts in Compact colors of late," said Progmash. "One night, one of my best scouts followed a patrol to see where the fuck they were coming from. Turns out the Compact's holed up in the ruins of Fort Chaska, a shitty old fort from the Shadow War."

Jessara glanced over at Asha. "We ran into a few soldiers in a cave as well."

Asha's heart skipped a beat. The Compact encroaching on orcish territory could be the beginning of something big. "Isn't that a violation of the Northern Mountains Treaty?"

Progmash nodded, his expression grim. "Yeah. We ain't trying to go to war with the Compact. We'd be in our rights to attack them, but I don't want to escalate this shit."

"Sooner or later, you'll have to contend with the Compact." Jessara took a step toward Progmash. "You think they'll stop with humans?"

Asha silently grimaced at the comment.

"We can talk about that later." Progmash returned to his throne and took a seat. "For now, I'd like to hire you."

Jessara raised her head. "Hire me?"

"You're an assassin."

"Well, yes, but I work for the King."

Progmash raised a brow. "I thought you worked for money?"

Jessara didn't respond.

"I'd pay you good," said Progmash.

Jessara seemed to be considering the offer. "What do you want me to do? Wipe out an entire fort of Compact soldiers?"

"I wouldn't shed a bloody fucking tear if you did, but that ain't what I need. I need to know why they're here, and if they're trying to start something."

Jessara furrowed her brows. "Why send me? You've got a whole city of warriors."

Progmash gave a quiet laugh. "Orcs ain't known for subtlety. I send my warriors, it'll be fucking carnage. Like I said, I don't want to start a war unless I bloody fucking need to. You—on the other hand—you're Kingdom, and from what I've heard, you're a right fucking master sneak. Even if you were seen, they've no reason to think you're working for us."

"Plausible deniability," said Asha.

Progmash pointed his index finger at her. "Right."

"I assume that means you don't want me to kill any of them?" said Jessara.

Progmash shook his head. "As long as it can't be traced back to my folk, you're free to fuck them up all you want. I just need the information."

"What's the pay?"

"Five hundred drems. And a scout to take you back to Kingdom territory. That's where you're heading, right?"

Asha glanced at Jessara, wanting to know the answer.

"It is." Jessara bowed her head one last time. "You have a deal."

Asha frowned. The answer wasn't surprising, but it was still disappointing.

"Be careful, Jessara." Progmash leaned forward thoughtfully. "I'm not trying to send you to your death."

"I've faced worse." Jessara turned to leave the hut.

Asha followed, knowing that it was time to tell Jessara the truth. Considering Jessara was planning on going back to the King, Asha was afraid that it would be the end of their brief relationship. But she couldn't hide it any longer.

Once they were outside, Asha took a deep breath and turned to her partner. "An escort back to Kingdom territory...you're still planning on returning to the King, aren't you?"

Jessara frowned. "I didn't think those plans had changed. Have they?"

Asha tried to play it off as a joke. "You mean the plan to present me to the King like a prize and hope he doesn't hang me? I can't imagine why we might want to rethink that."

"I thought we'd already agreed on this. When we explain how you can be an asset to the Kingdom, he's sure to see reason."

"There's no reason in that man."

Jessara stopped, turned to Asha, and put her hands on her shoulders. "Look, the Kingdom will never stop looking for you, and if they find you here, it will mean war with the orcs. Do you want that?"

"Of course not. But I don't trust the King."

"He'll listen to me. I thought we had a deal?"

Asha was silent for a few moments as she stared at the ground, shame burning her cheeks. "Jessara, there's something I need to tell you."

Jessara examined her face for a few moments before nodding in recognition. "You never intended to follow me to Enderdale. Did you?"

Asha's heart sank. This was it. "Jessara, I—"

Jessara held up a gentle hand. "It's all right, Asha. I already suspected. You had no reason to trust me."

"I trust you now."

"Then believe me when I say that I'll make sure you're safe."

Asha sighed. Jessara was being naive, but Asha had also been stressing over how she'd react when Jessara found out the truth. Relief washed over Asha. "We can talk about this when we get back from Fort Chaska."

"We?"

"I'm coming with you." Asha still wasn't sure if a future with Jessara was possible, but if it was, they'd need to continue learning to work together—meaning Asha needed to learn strategic thinking, and Jessara needed to learn cooperation.

"You were brain dead yesterday."

"I'm not now, and I know these mountains. I can lead you right to the fort."

Jessara shook her head. "You're not coming."

Asha raised a finger. "We're partners now. I'm not letting you go alone."

Jessara was quiet for a second.

Asha raised an eyebrow and crossed her arms. Her stare did not leave her partner.

"No!"

Asha stared and said nothing.

"Absolutely not!"

She still said nothing.

Jessara sighed and grumbled. "All right, fine. But we leave tomorrow. I want you to at least spend today resting."

"Fair enough."

CHAPTER TWENTY

SELF-HATE

Jessara tried to push her concerns over the future to the back of her mind when she returned to the temple. They could figure it out when they got back. For now, they were together, and they had a task.

While at the temple, Asha introduced Jessara to the other sisters. She met Lea, Mila, and Rana, all ice sorceresses; Idola, Grata, Opie, and Brina, lightning sorceresses; Alia and Tila, flame sorceresses; Cli and Prenda, telekinetics; Trainis, a telepath like Anea; and Wedly and Drana, healers like Miland. Several younger sorceresses also lived in the temple. Jessara met Relic, the young woman that Asha had told her about, as well as Erel, Una, Halia, and Napin.

Jessara liked the Sisterhood. She'd never been in such a large group of welcoming people. Her time in Enderdale had been spent being scoffed at by the human residents. She didn't have a poor relationship with the other elves of the city, but none had any desire to be around an agent of the King. The other children she was raised with had always been pitted against her. The closest person she had to a friend was Aleris, but they only ever talked business, and the closest thing to family was the King. However, the temple was a family through and through, and since Jessara was with Asha, they treated her as one of their own.

After introductions were made, Asha decided to retire to her bedroom, and Jessara accompanied her. Even though she liked the sisters, she wasn't comfortable being alone with them.

In her room, Asha lay on her bed while Jessara sat on the velvet-upholstered chair next to the fireplace. Jessara looked over at her partner with contentment.

Asha noticed Jessara's gaze and smiled. "See something you like?"

Jessara grinned and returned her gaze to the fireplace.

Quiet fell for a brief moment before Asha spoke again. "Can I ask a personal question?"

"Sure."

"I've noticed that eye contact with other people makes you nervous. You barely looked at any of the sisters, and you appeared to be straining yourself to look at Prog."

Had it been that obvious? Jessara glanced back at Asha with a guilty frown. "I'm sorry. I'll try harder to focus with the sisters."

Asha chuckled and shook her head. "No, I'm not asking you to change anything. I'm just wondering why?"

Jessara paused for a moment. "Honestly? I don't know. I've always struggled with it. Everyone else seems to do it naturally, but I have to focus. I'm better than I was as a kid, but if a lot's going on, it's a struggle."

"If it's such a struggle, then why do it?"

"The King always taught me that making eye contact is the only way people will trust you."

Asha grunted. "I should have known he had something to do with this. You never seem to struggle when it's just us. But if it makes you uncomfortable, then you don't need to with me."

Jessara looked up at Asha, her lips curling into a smile. "You're different. Your gaze makes me feel comfortable."

Asha blushed. "That's sweet. Even so, that goes for the Sisterhood as well. We're all a bunch of misfits."

Jessara was silent for a few seconds. "Your sisters are kind."

Asha's brow furrowed. "You sound surprised."

"They realize I'm an elf, right?"

Asha gave her an amused smile. "No offense, but the ears kind of give it away."

"I know, I mean...how do they know they can trust me?"

Asha looked confused. "Because I trust you."

"But they're humans."

"And?"

"How do they know I'm not Compact?"

Asha finally seemed to realize what Jessara was implying. "You can't understand why they don't show prejudice toward you?"

Jessara nodded, as if it was the most obvious thing in Dremeria. "Yes. It's only natural."

Asha frowned and shook her head. "No, it's not. Hatred's taught. While the Sisterhood has no love for the Compact or the Kingdom, we never teach our pupils to hate entire races."

"Hatred is only a mask for fear; fear is a defense."

Asha tilted her head. "You sound defensive of bigoted humans. Don't you frequently get in bar fights with them?"

Jessara sighed. She wasn't used to arguing with people about this. This is the way things had always been. People treated her differently because she was an elf. "I'm not defending it. But that prejudice comes from somewhere."

"It comes from ignorance and superstition."

"It comes from watching their families get slaughtered." The answer came more quickly and aggressively than Jessara meant it to.

Asha was quiet for a second. Then she glanced up at the picture of her parents. "You mean like I did?"

"I'm sorry. I didn't mean..." Jessara stopped herself for a second, not wanting to say anything to hurt her partner. "It's just that you of all people should understand."

Asha was silent for a moment, seeming to fight back a glare. "My birth mother was killed by elves, and my spirit mother was killed by humans. Which should I hate?"

Realizing she'd overstepped, Jessara didn't answer.

"The Compact killed your family, Jessara," said Asha. "You hate them for it and rightly so. But you also hate yourself."

That dug at Jessara. "I don't hate myself!"

"Then what do you hate?"

"I hate the fact that I'm an elf!" It was a truth Jessara had never admitted to herself. "The Compact took everything from me! Parents I never knew and a life I never had! For what? Some bullshit belief that humans are stealing magic? Because my village refused to partic- ipate in genocide?" A tear streamed down Jessara's cheek as her voice softened. "I defend myself from drunken idiots that just want to pick a fight with a soulless husk like me. But sometimes, I feel like I have more in common with them than I do my own kind. And maybe deep down I..." Jessara paused.

"You think they're right to hate you." Asha's voice was calm and gentle, just as Jessara needed it to be.

She looked at Asha, knowing she was right. Although Jessara knew that the belief that elves had no souls was nonsense, the brutality of the Compact did nothing to fight that idea. These were feelings that she'd never told anyone—that she hadn't even admitted to herself. Normally, she hated being vulnerable, but with Asha, it was refreshing to let someone in.

Asha got out of bed, approached Jessara, and knelt down next to her. Trying to hold back more tears, Jessara looked away. Asha gently put her hand against her cheek and pulled Jessara's face down to look at her. Her blue eyes glistened as they reflected the flames from the fireplace. She pulled Jessara in closer and pressed their foreheads together.

"The Compact kills humans because they think themselves superior. They can justify it all they want with their bullshit about humans absorbing magic, but that's what it comes down to." Asha gave her forehead a gentle kiss. "People who think they're special because of their race are just trying to give themselves power without earning it. The Kingdom oppresses elves for the same reason. Perhaps the King doesn't believe elves have no souls, but he bloody well benefits from others believing it."

She stroked Jessara's chin while giving her an empathetic smile as she continued. "At the end of the day, what matters is who we become as individuals. I've seen you do amazing things. You've fought squads of Compact soldiers, dangerous wild beasts, and even an entire stronghold of renegade orcs. You did all this, not because of who you were or weren't born as, but because you've disciplined yourself. You've trained more than anyone I know, and it's inspiring. You've made me want to be like you."

Jessara smiled, but shook her head. "You don't want to be like me. I'm dark and brooding—remember?"

Asha laughed. "But in battle, you're smarter than I could ever hope to be. You're a badass woman, and you made yourself one."

Jessara turned to the fire. "The King made me one."

Asha sighed as she shook her head. "That's what he wants you to think. He needs you to believe that as an elf, you'll always be below him. Dependent."

"But the fact that I'm an elf does matter. It affects where I live, who I know, and what I can do."

"True. But none of that is your fault. It's the way the Kingdom's organized. You don't deserve to be treated that way, and you need to stop blaming yourself for it."

The silent bliss between the two women lasted for a while. Jessara pulled Asha closer. *I'll never deserve her. What the fuck does she see in me?* She put her hand on Asha's cheek, feeling the warm skin of the woman she now called partner. "Thank you."

"For what?" Asha tilted her head curiously.

"Everything." Jessara planted another kiss on her lips. "When it comes to understanding people, *you're* smarter than I could ever hope to be."

Asha nodded playfully. "That's probably true. I guess we'll need to stick together for a little longer."

Jessara wondered how long that would be, but then she put that out of her head. She and Asha would at least have the fort mission together. They could figure out if they had a future afterwards. For now, they had time.

"You should probably get some more sleep. We have a long day tomorrow."

"I'm not ready to sleep yet." Asha stood and grabbed Jessara's hand. With a devious, seductive grin, she began pulling Jessara to the bed.

Jessara smiled. "What are you trying to do?"

"Take off your armor."

Chapter Twenty-One

Fort Chaska

The prospect of another trek through the snow-covered mountains was not one Jessara looked forward to. That being said, she was still a little excited about her infiltration job—to be back in her element.

After a hearty breakfast of elk and vegetable stew, Jessara and Asha gathered supplies and set off. It was a long hike, and they watched for snow trolls and mountain bears. With both women aware and on their feet this time, it was easy to either avoid the beasts or take them down from a distance. Snow fell, but the wind was bearable as long as Jessara kept moving. While they walked, they discussed strategy.

"I've been to the area around Fort Chaska." Asha pointed in the direction they were heading. "I've never been inside, but I've seen it from a distance. There's a cliff that overlooks the place. We can use that as a vantage point."

Jessara considered strategies she'd employed in the past. Infiltrating a military fort was no easy task, but she'd done it before. "We might want to wait until cover of darkness before starting our approach. Do you know how many entrances there are?"

Asha shook her head. "No. Like I said, I've only seen it from a distance."

Jessara gazed at the white desolate landscape. "Does the Sisterhood spend a lot of time exploring these mountains?"

"It's part of our training for retrieval missions. If we can survive the mountains and its dangers, Red Daggers should be no problem."

"Do all sisters train for retrieval missions?"

"No. And the ones that do are usually elemental sorceresses. Currently, the only sisters who are actively assigned retrieval missions are Rana, Brina, and Idola."

Jessara glanced at her. "And you."

"Yes."

"That's why you were in the Kingdom." Jessara internally beat herself up for not figuring that out sooner.

"It was."

Jessara paused. "What happened?"

"Can we focus on the fort? I don't want to talk about that right now."

"Okay." Even Jessara could see the sorrow in her partner's eyes, so she decided not to press the issue.

The couple walked for several hours before they reached Fort Chaska in the late afternoon. As they approached, they could see banners that bore the insignia of the Watchtower, and as Asha had mentioned, a cliff that towered over the northern side of the fort.

As part of her assassin training, Jessara had studied ancient battles and historical war tactics. With that came a library of knowledge about the architectural reasons behind the layout of forts and other structures. For example, she knew that many forts in the Northern Mountains had been built near cliffs to limit the number of angles an army could attack from. But the Compact had never expected an army of two.

After a little searching, the couple managed to find a path that led up the cliff. As they climbed, they searched for a ledge with a decent vantage point. Eventually, they found a small space where they could set up camp and observe the fort about a quarter mile from the structure. Because of the elevation, Jessara had a good view of the layout.

Jessara put on her headband and scanned the fort to get an idea of how to infiltrate it. Fortunately, it wasn't snowing enough to impair her vision. The fort was made of granite and hexagon shaped. Each point had a turret, and a parapet lined with battlements ran on top of the wall. The wall itself was nearly a hundred feet tall and behind it stood five buildings. They were difficult to make out, but three appeared to be barracks and another a small rectangular structure which Jessara could only speculate over. A kitchen? Hospital? Armory? The final structure stood in the middle of the courtyard—a two-story building with a cylindrical tower at the back.

Jessara pointed to the gate. "Only one entrance. Problematic."

"I can make another." Asha conjured a small fireball in her hand.

Jessara looked over at her nervously. Subtlety in this job was paramount, and one mistake could bring the whole fort down on them. But subtlety was not Asha's strong suit, which was partially why she hadn't originally wanted her to come along. However, Asha had expressed a desire to learn, so she would teach her. "Too loud. The fort's old and made of stone. I should be able to climb up the wall. Do you think you can fire jump it?"

"You think I can't climb the wall?"

Jessara raised an eyebrow. "Can you?"

Asha glanced between the wall and Jessara a few times. "That's hardly the point. Yes, I think I can fire jump."

"I'll make sure the area's clear of patrols, and then I'll signal you to come up." Jessara pointed to the building in the middle of the fort. "Our target is that tower."

"How can you tell?"

"Standard Compact fort hierarchy. They always put the commander at the highest place as a reminder of their superiority. The commander's room will have any correspondence between them and the Watch. Also, if we can get the commander alone, we can interrogate them. Either way, the tower's where we need to go." Jessara paused for a moment as she tried to figure out a way to word her next statement. "Look, while we're in there...well...this is my area of expertise."

Asha nodded. "Yeah, yeah, I know. You call the shots."

"Unless it goes south. In which case, feel free to start blowing shit up." Jessara decided not to mention that "blowing shit up" would probably be their last stand, but she wanted to impress upon her the stakes. "Keep in mind, a fort this size probably has about fifty people. Not a huge force, but there are only two of us, and you don't have a sword."

"Hey, the ones the orcs make are too big for me. I'm sure I'll pick one up inside."

Jessara shrugged. "We'll wait for cover of night."

Jessara was no stranger to improvising, and thus far, she and Asha had worked well together. On top of that, she'd learned over the years that if you doubt yourself, you're dead. She needed to have faith in Asha, because they wouldn't be successful without it.

Jessara and Asha waited on the ledge, the cold biting deeply, numbing her face. It was too dangerous to build a fire so close to the fort. She rubbed her hands together to try to generate heat, but her core was freezing and she trembled.

Asha opened her cloak. "Come here."

"I'm f-f-f-fine."

Asha chuckled. "I can see that. Bloody get over here and hold me."

Jessara conceded and joined Asha. Her partner wrapped the cloak around her and held her close. The warmth of the fire sorceress was like being near a fireplace. Heat radiated from Asha's body, which meant that she'd raised her body temperature for Jessara, and her lavender scent made Jessarra smile. She looked into Asha's beautiful blue eyes and kissed her. Limbs thawed, and Jessara's core finally returned to normal.

Asha gave her a peck on the forehead. "How did you manage before me, my dear?"

Jessara shrugged. "Targets were always in Compact territory. I've only been in the mountains once, and I've never been this high."

Asha looked at her curiously. "What type of contract brought you to the mountains?"

"A fugitive orc—killed some pompous military commander along with several guards that tried to arrest him."

"I like him already. What happened?"

Jessara had finally warmed up enough to stop shaking. "The King gave me a contract to kill the orc or capture him for a bonus. I asked around at several villages and eventually learned that he was fleeing to the mountains."

"That seems lucky."

Jessara smirked. "I'm really good at tracking, and orcs stick out in human villages. As soon as I found a village he'd been to, it wasn't difficult to figure out where he was going. I found campsites that were clearly made by an orc."

"How could you tell?"

"Everything was bigger. Once I got to the mountains, it was easy enough to follow the dead mountain beasts until I came across my mark. I prefer to take down targets with stealth, but it was snowy. I needed to be closer to get a good look at his face. As soon as he saw me, he attacked on sight—tough son of a bitch."

"Yeah, but you're tougher." Asha grinned.

Jessara pulled herself tighter against Asha's body, loving every minute of that warm embrace. "We'll never know. Because it turns out we were fighting on top of a frozen lake."

"You're kidding."

"No. Ice chaulk broke through the ice and devoured the orc almost immediately."

"Bloody Nara! What did you do?"

"I ran my ass off. The orc was dead—contract fulfilled."

"No bonus though."

"Yeah, but I assumed that would be the case. When the mark is a fugitive, the King usually puts in a bonus opportunity if they're captured alive."

"So they can be brought back to be made an example of." Asha had an uncomfortable edge to her voice.

Jessara had never thought much about the reasons behind capture or kill contracts. "Yeah, I suppose. I always preferred to just kill my targets. I've captured prisoners before, but it's always a hassle. They try to escape; they try to kill me..."

"You sleep with them." Asha's lips curled into an awkward smile.

Jessara gazed at her. Sometimes she forgot that Asha was her mark—that she was a fugitive from the Kingdom. Or maybe she just wanted to forget. What would happen when she brought Asha before the King? Was Asha still planning on going with her? Jessara was confident that she could convince the King to spare Asha, but a part of her wondered if her partner was right about the King's plans for her.

"None of them could kiss like you." Jessara put on a fake smile.

Asha laughed nervously.

The smile slowly disappeared from Jessara's face as she sighed. Her train of thought reminded her of a secret she needed to share. Asha had admitted to deceiving her about returning to Enderdale, but now it was time for her own confession. "Asha, there's something I need to tell you."

"Yeah?"

"The day we met. The arrow that I shot into the soldier behind you...that was a last-minute decision. When I drew the arrow, it wasn't intended for him."

Asha nodded slowly. "I see. I thought that might be the case."

"I'm sorry. I...I also considered killing you after we escaped from Tarton."

"Why didn't you?"

Jessara reached into her satchel and took out Aleris' notes, moving her hand out of the warmth of Asha's cloak so she could show her. "This was a big part of it."

Asha took the paper. "What's this?"

"Before I left Enderdale, a scholar acquaintance of mine, Aleris, wrote these notes for me."

Asha flipped through the pages. "It's information about magic users."

Jessara nodded. "I've been studying the section about fire mages as we've traveled together. According to Aleris, you all aren't known for betrayal. I knew you weren't telling me the whole truth, but I didn't think you'd stab me in the back either. So I decided that if anyone broke our deal, it wouldn't be me."

"If I ever meet this Aleris, remind me to thank him." Asha read the notes for a few moments. "These are in depth; he knows his magic. Does he practice?"

"Probably, but it's not something we've ever talked about."

Asha handed the notes back to Jessara. "What about the other part?"

"What?"

"You said Aleris' notes were 'part' of the reason. What was the other reason you didn't kill me?"

Jessara was silent for a moment. "I told myself it was because of the extra bounty, but the truth is, I didn't want to."

Asha chuckled. "That's kind of sweet."

"Maybe on a very generous bell curve."

Both women laughed.

Jessara rested her hand on Asha's cheek. "You won me over...even before I'd realized it."

Asha smiled and leaned in. Jessara closed her eyes as her partner kissed her. What a relief to have told Asha the truth. For a moment, she forgot about the infiltration job and settled into the arms of her partner. When they finally parted, Jessara let herself cuddle with her woman as they waited for night to fall.

A few hours passed, and it grew darker and colder.

Jessara left Asha's embrace. She didn't want to, but she knew it was time. "Should be dark enough by the time we get down there. Let's go."

They descended the cliff and headed to the fort. It was cold, and snow fell all around them, while the wind blew faster than earlier. The wind would mask their sounds inside, but it wouldn't make it easier to climb the wall.

As they approached the fort, Jessara put her hand on Asha's shoulder and pushed her into a leaning posture. "Stay low."

When they reached the wall undetected, Jessara scanned it to look for a section with stones out of place.

Eventually, she found a good spot. "When the coast is clear, I'll give you a signal to come up. Before you do, conjure a flame so I know where you are."

"What's the signal?"

"I don't know. I'll wave my arms or something."

Asha looked up the wall. "I can barely see the top."

"I'll figure something out." Jessara approached the wall and started climbing.

"Wait."

"What?"

Asha walked up to Jessara, pulled her in, and kissed her. "Don't die."

"I've climbed worse." Jessara grabbed the wall, but when she put her foot on one of the stones, it slid and she almost lost her grip. "Fuck."

"Jessara?"

"I'm fine." Jessara continued to climb, but in truth, she *was* concerned. Her hands were cold, the stones slippery. Gusts of wind hammered her face and numbed her ears. But after making it halfway up the wall, Jessara' s confidence grew. Despite the snow, she had the grip of a Woodlander.

The top was in sight when a stone Jessara was using to pull herself up gave way. She struggled to keep herself on the wall as she hung on with one hand. Her heart pounded as she fought the urge to panic. Jessara scanned the wall for a new stone to grab. A prominent one stuck out, and she reached for it, but it was too high.

Jessara scraped her feet against the wall to give herself extra momentum. With one motion, she pushed herself up and gripped the stone, stabilizing herself. She breathed a sigh of relief and continued her climb.

As Jessara turned her attention to the parapet above, she noticed a soldier patrolling. She climbed out of sight until she was right under him. A quick scan of the area ensured no witnesses would interfere, so Jessara waited for the soldier to turn around. As soon as he did, she pulled herself up the rest of the way and crawled between two battlements. Then she grabbed one of her daggers and stabbed him silently in the neck.

The coast was clear; time to give the signal. She peered over the edge of the wall, but as Asha had predicted, visibility was low. Jessara needed to improvise. She looked around, and her eyes fixed on the body of the soldier.

***

Below, Asha was getting nervous. Watching her partner almost fall to her death was horrifying, plus she had no idea what type of signal she was supposed to look for. But as she was thinking this, she got her answer. *Crash!* She jumped as a figure hit the ground next to her—the body of a Compact soldier.

"Okay." Asha conjured a flame to signal her position to Jessara. Then she closed her eyes and concentrated. She conjured fire in her hands and slammed her palms on the ground, propelling her upward. On the parapet, Jessara was waiting with her hand outstretched. As soon as Asha was high enough, Jessara grabbed her hand and pulled her in.

Jessara gave her a once over. "You okay?"

Asha grunted. "I'd be better without a dead body thrown at me."

"It worked, didn't it?"

"Really? A dead body? There's something wrong with you."

Jessara shrugged. "That's already been firmly established. Now keep your voice down, stay low, and follow me." The couple snuck along the parapet, heading to the nearest turret.

Asha tried to stay calm and trust Jessara to make the right calls. Stealth had never been a skill of Asha's. Her fights were fairly head on, and she wasn't used to this level of coordination. But she remembered Jessara's stories about her infiltration jobs, and she knew Jessara's skills were their best chance for success.

As they approached the next turret, they spotted another soldier. She was leaning over the battlements with her back to them.

Jessara motioned for Asha to stop as she assessed the situation, then for Asha to stay put. Jessara snuck over to the soldier and unsheathed her daggers. When she was close enough, she stuck her daggers into the soldier's sides. The soldier gasped as Jessara sheathed her daggers and gave the soldier a push. She fell over the side of the wall as Jessara beckoned to Asha.

"By the Tree, you *do* hate the Compact."

"I assume all the turrets have lookouts." Jessara inspected the walls of the fort. "Our time in the compound will be easier if there's nobody up here."

"All right—what's the plan?"

"I go left, you go right. Take out any patrols or lookouts you see. We'll meet on the far turret."

Asha was nervous about separating, but she refused to be a liability, so she agreed. Besides, this was her chance to prove her worth. "All right."

"Keep it quiet."

"I kind of figured that."

"Also, dump the bodies off the edge of the fort."

Asha curled her nose. "I have to lift dead bodies?"

"If they find the bodies, they'll know we're here."

Asha sighed. "Fine."

"Be careful."

"You too."

With that, the women split up and swept the parapet. Asha knew it would be child's play for Jessara, but Asha wasn't used to sneaking around. Fortunately, she had snow that made her harder to see and wind that made her harder to hear. When she shot daggers, it made a small *crack* sound, but the wind covered it up. She didn't encounter anyone patrolling the parapet, and it was easy enough to shoot daggers from a distance at the turret lookouts.

One immediately fell off the wall. *Damn. Not getting that knife back.* The other lookout's body fell against battlements. Asha retrieved her knife and pushed the body over the edge. It was heavy and made her extremely uncomfortable. By the time she reached the far turret, Jessara had already taken out the final lookout and was working on picking the lock to the trapdoor.

"What took you so long?" Jessara didn't look up from her work.

Asha looked around again to triple check that they were alone. "Unlike some, I wasn't trained from childhood to become a ruthless assassin."

The trapdoor opened. A ladder led to a landing at the top of a spiral staircase. As Jessara lowered herself down, she flirtatiously said, "At least you're pretty."

"Fuck off," said Asha playfully as she followed Jessara down.

"Quiet." Jessara tensed as she listened.

Asha heard footsteps coming up the stairs. Jessara motioned for Asha to get down as she grabbed her bow and waited.

The footsteps drew closer. Any minute they would come around the bend. Asha saw the red and green, and within a fraction of a second, Jessara shot an arrow. It hit the guard in the chest, and she fell down a few stairs. Jessara darted down and stopped the body from falling any farther. She was quiet as she listened for other patrols. When she was satisfied, Jessara pulled her arrow out of the body and put it back in her quiver, motioning for Asha to follow her.

Both women descended the staircase. A few torches hung on the wall lighting their way, showing brickwork as old and worn as the exterior. Asha was surprised the fort was still standing.

When the couple reached the bottom, they found a circular room with two guards sitting at a table, talking. Asha waited for Jessara to signal a plan as she listened to the conversation.

"So, whose ire did you invoke to get sent to this wasteland?" said the farther one.

"I chose the post."

"Seriously?"

"I do not mind the cold."

"And you could not resist the trolls and orcs constantly trying to kill you?"

"Leeches are predictable. Killing them can get painfully dull."

"Never gets old for me."

Fucking assholes!

Jessara grabbed her bow and looked at Asha. She pointed to herself and pointed to the guard on the left, then she pointed to Asha and pointed to the one on the right. Asha nodded in understanding.

Jessara drew string and took aim while Asha drew one of her knives. "Now."

Thud.

Thud.

Asha's target let out a death yelp before lying still. The women retrieved their weapons and approached the door. Jessara cracked it open, and they both surveyed the courtyard.

Now that Asha could get a closer look at the buildings, she could tell they'd been aging since the Shadow War. All color from their cedar construction had been eroded. The barracks and the strange rectangular building had snow-covered hip roofs and very few windows. The central structure had a curved roof and a conical one on the tower protruding from it.

Asha didn't see any patrols. "That's fortunate."

"Makes sense; most are probably asleep. They won't expect to deal with threats inside the wall. And in this weather, these elves won't be outside unless they need to be."

Jessara pointed to the central building. "And that means there shouldn't be a lot of people in there."

Two soldiers emerged from one of the barracks on the far side of the fort. They marched to the small rectangular structure in the middle of the courtyard and entered.

"What's that building?"

Jessara stared at the building intensely. "I'm not sure. But I'll bet it goes underground."

"How can you tell?"

"A small building like that would be out of place unless there was more to it." With that, Jessara opened the door and beckoned to Asha. "Follow me."

The women stayed low and crept to the main building. They checked the side entrance. Locked. Jessara picked it and cracked open the door to peer inside. Several hardwood tables stood in rows in the room. A mess hall.

Two soldiers sat at one of the tables together. In the back of the mess hall stood the door to the tower. Two more soldiers stood guard on each side of the entrance. The room was dim with a few bear fat candles on the ceiling lighting up the space. The cedar tables were as old and worn down as the rest of the fort, and cracked stone columns held up the sagging ceiling.

Jessara inspected the obstacles. "This could be problematic."

"Time to start blowing shit up?" Asha said brightly.

Jessara gave her a scared look.

"Kidding." Asha put on a serious face. "What's the plan?"

Jessara nodded, looking relieved, and turned her attention back to the mess hall. "We need to time this correctly. You get behind that column." Jessara pointed to the column closest to the soldiers at the table. "Get two daggers ready to shoot and wait for my signal. I'll take care of the other two."

"What's the signal this time?"

Jessara grinned. "Same as last time."

"So dead bodies falling. You have issues."

"Again—firmly established."

Both women snuck into the building. Asha's column was right next to the door. She crouched down and got her daggers ready, and then she watched as Jessara crept from column to column. *She's good!* Jessara appeared to be observing the soldier's head motions to time her movements accordingly. Hardly any time had passed before she was behind the column closest to the stationed guards. When she was in position, Jessara took out her bow and drew an arrow.

Asha gripped her daggers tightly. As soon as she heard the first guard hit the floor, she shot her knives at the sitting guards. Both let out death gasps as they fell to the ground. Asha glanced back in Jessara's direction in time to see her pull her sword out of the second guard. After retrieving her knives, Asha rejoined her partner.

Jessara put her hand on Asha's shoulder. "Well done."

A warm feeling of pride washed through Asha, knowing they'd flawlessly pulled that off. They were a good team, and Jessara seemed to be recognizing that. Asha grew more confident in her own abilities.

They both came to the entrance of the tower, where a spiral staircase led both up and down from where they stood.

Asha pointed to the lower level. "What do you think's down there?"

"Probably the armory or storage. We need to go up."

With that, both women ascended the staircase. One level up stood a doorway to the second story of the main building. Through the door, they could see more tables lining a room—another level of the mess hall. When they approached the top of the tower, Jessara motioned for them to slow down. At the top was an entrance to a room with a window on the far side. There was a large bed with rich linens, an ornate walnut dresser, and a small mahogany dining table. All of the furniture was out of place in an old fort like this.

An elf who appeared to be the commander of the fort sat at a desk at the far side of the room. Long green hair poured down her back. Fortunately for Jessara and Asha, the commander's back was to the door.

Jessara motioned for Asha to stay put as she snuck behind the commander and slowly drew a knife. When she was close enough, she put her hand on the commander's mouth and held the knife to her throat. Startled, the commander tried to struggle.

"Stay still!" Jessara pressed her knife firmly against the commander's neck. The commander panted but complied. "I've got a few questions to ask. You yell when I remove my hand, and it'll be the last sound you ever make." Her voice was eerily impassive.

Slowly, Jessara removed her hand from the commander's mouth.

"How in Nara did you get in here?" The commander's attempt to hide her fear fooled no one.

Jessara looked back at Asha. "Didn't I say that I'd be the only one asking questions?"

Asha tilted her head and looked up as if genuinely trying to recall. "No, but you strongly implied it."

Jessara turned her attention back to the prisoner. "Then let's try that again. Tell me what the Compact is doing here."

"We are fucking your mother!"

Asha put her hands on her hips and feigned indignation. "That's my line!"

With that, Jessara grabbed one of the commander's hands and shoved it on the table. Then she raised her knife.

Asha realized she was about to stab the commander's hand. "Wait, Jessara!"

Jessara stopped and looked back at Asha.

Seizing the opportunity, the commander slammed the back of her head against Jessara's face.

Caught off guard, Jessara was thrown backward. The commander drew her sword, clutching it with both hands. But before she could do anything, Asha shot a fireball at her hands, causing her to drop the sword. She knelt, gripping her injuries and gasping in pain. Angrily, Jessara walked up to the commander and punched her in the face, knocking her to the ground.

"Jessara, let me." Asha had been following Jessara's lead, but she knew people better than her partner did.

Torture would get them nowhere.

Jessara was still pissed, but she took a step back.

Asha appreciated the trust. She approached the commander, now having a clear view of her adornment. She wore the regular colors and armor of a Compact soldier, but instead of a leather chest plate, hers was made of a red copper that shone as if polished once a day.

Fat lot of good that bloody armor will do for her now. Asha smirked as she conjured a small fireball in the palm of her hand. "You probably know that fire sorcery is released through the hands. But did you also know that a fire sorceress can control the temperature of her hands without even creating fire?" Asha extinguished the flame and then knelt next to the commander. "What about your hands? Do they hurt?"

The commander clutched the burns. "Yes! Damnit!"

"Well, lucky for you then, that you can still feel." Asha flashed a sinister smirk. "Did you further know that a person can be burned so badly that it scorches their nerve endings? They barely feel the pain, but it leaves some bloody ugly scars and renders the victim's skin permanently damaged."

The commander breathed heavily, her eyes wide with fear. Asha slowly moved her hand to press against the coarse skin of the commander's face. "Isn't that fascinating? I could scorch off half your face, and the only way you'd know it would be from the smell of burning flesh." Asha had no idea if that were true, but it sounded like it could be.

"No! Please!" The rebellious attitude had deserted the commander's voice.

Asha put her nose to the air. "Have you ever smelled burning flesh before?" She hated the smell of burning flesh.

"I will have you drawn and quartered!"

"It's been too long since I've smelled it."

"Stop!"

"I've almost forgotten—"

"I'll talk!"

Asha looked back at Jessara, who was visibly impressed.

Then she removed her hand from the commander's cheek. The commander frantically felt her face to make sure it was still intact.

The unstable smile left Asha's face, replaced with a stern glare. "Talk."

The commander continued to pant. "We were sent here to map the region. Scout caves, identify strongholds, find paths."

Jessara took a step toward the commander. "Why?"

"The Compact is considering a move against Coshgromar."

That concerned Asha. "Why would you do that? The orcs have been neutral in the war."

"They never acknowledged our cause or our superiority." She spat on the floor. "Their presence steals just as much magic as the leeches. And they sell themselves as mercenaries for the Kingdom. We have also learned that the King intends to send emissaries to establish a treaty with the brutes."

That caught Jessara's attention. "How could you possibly know that?"

"Some human they interrogated in Sunderbury."

Jessara's eyes widened but she stayed silent.

"But the orcs would never accept such an alliance," said Asha.

The commander shook her head. "Our sources say otherwise."

"What sources?" Asha knew Progmash would never go for a treaty.

"We have orcish prisoners captive here—hunting parties that our forces were able to ambush. Orcs die in these mountains all the time. Nobody notices if a few go missing."

Asha was disgusted, and rage filled her. "You fucking monster! How many prisoners do you have here?"

"About a dozen."

"Where are they?"

The commander pointed outside. "The small building out there goes to an underground prison."

Asha looked back at Jessara. "We have to rescue them."

Jessara approached the commander and crouched on her knees until she was at eye level. "Does the Watch know that the orcs will accept?"

"No. We just recently learned that part. When the storm dies down, we will send a messenger. The Watch will march an army to these mountains, and they will wipe out these pathetic beasts. You will never leave this fort alive!"

"Maybe, but neither will you." With that, Asha drew a dagger and shoved it in the commander's throat. The commander kicked her legs a few times, but she died quickly. Asha took no pleasure in the deed but neither did she regret it.

"I don't understand." Jessara stood and paced around the room. "I know about the human prisoner she referred to in Sunderbury. I contained the information."

"Are you sure?"

"Her interrogator told me that no information she'd revealed had been sent."

Asha raised a brow. "And how did you get that information out of him?"

Jessara was silent.

Asha understood and nodded her head. "Torture rarely gets you accurate information. Prisoners will tell you what you want to hear to get the pain to stop." *Another thing the King was too fucking stupid to teach you.* But she didn't say that part out loud. "That information can't make it to the Watch. The Compact will kill everyone—they'll discover the Sisterhood." Asha remembered how she'd had to convince Jessara to rescue Storn back in Compact territory. A rescue was not in the original deal she'd made with Progmash, so for a moment, she worried Jessara would simply leave.

"I know." Jessara stopped pacing for a moment and glanced at Asha. "So we contain the information."

Asha breathed a sigh of relief. "How?"

"By killing every Compact soldier in this fort."

CHAPTER TWENTY-TWO

ATTACK FROM WITHIN

J essara strode over to the window on the far side of the commander's quarters. She looked at the rectangular building, which she now knew was a prison, and then back at Asha with a thoughtful smile.

Asha's eyes widened. "The orc prisoners!"

"Yes." Jessara was going beyond what she was being paid to do, but that didn't matter. The security of Coshgromar was important to Asha, and that was enough—not to mention that she felt responsible for failing to contain the information in Sunderbury.

Asha stood. "She said there were about a dozen."

"Yes."

"Will that be enough?"

Jessara shrugged. "It'll have to be."

"Not great odds."

"Orcs are tough fighters. Also, we've thinned the fort. We won't need to worry about sentries."

Asha chuckled. "You aren't going to say 'I've had worse?'"

"Honestly, I'm not sure I have." Jessara turned her eyes back to the courtyard and scanned the area. To the right of the central building was one barracks and the prison, and to the left were the two other barracks. All would have multiple Compact soldiers inside. "This won't be easy."

Asha didn't hesitate. "All right. What's the plan?"

Jessara glanced at the doors of the barracks and saw that each had only two exits, something to keep in mind. She looked back at Asha and considered their success so far. Prior to the mission, she'd been worried about taking someone else along on an infiltration job, but so far, Asha had proven herself useful. Maybe having a partner on these types of jobs wasn't such a bad thing. Perhaps that would make Asha valuable enough to the King to keep her alive.

But Jessara couldn't think of that right now. "I'll need some time. For now, let's free the orcs and get them to the armory downstairs—figure out our assets."

Asha nodded. She walked over to the body of the commander and picked up her sword. Its sheath fit perfectly around her waist.

Jessara admired the blade. It was a hoplite sword—similar to Jessara's except much better decorated. The hilt was made of polished steel, embedded with amethyst stones. "It matches your eyes."

Asha smirked at her, and the couple descended the staircase. The mess hall was still empty, apart from the bodies they'd decorated it with earlier. They crept over to one of the side doors and made sure the coast was clear. The night patrols must have been eliminated. Jessara motioned for Asha to follow her, and they prowled over to the prison building. The door was locked.

"Keep watch." Jessara drew her lockpick, and the door was open within seconds. The inside of the building was dark and empty, with a set of stairs leading downward.

Jessara didn't have time to get a good look at her surroundings as she caught sight of two Compact soldiers marching up the staircase. They immediately spotted the women, but before they could react, Jessara drew a knife and threw it into one.

The couple drew their swords as the other soldier overcame her shock. She drew her own sword and rushed the intruders. Jessara parried an attack while Asha buried her sword into the assailant. The soldier collapsed and fell down the stairs.

"What the fuck was that?" said a voice.

Asha sheathed her sword and drew a throwing knife. "Bloody Nara!"

"Come on!"

The women sprinted down the stairs. As Jessara passed the bodies, she grabbed her knife. At the bottom of the stairs stood a hallway lined with cells, full of orc prisoners.

In the hallway, four Compact soldiers charged them with weapons drawn. Jessara darted into combat with her sword and dagger.

Asha shot a knife into the throat of one of the soldiers.

Jessara's blade met with another. She blocked his attack with her sword and stabbed him with her dagger.

Another soldier swung her blade at Jessara's head. Jessara threw herself to the ground, avoiding the attack. After a split second, she heard her opponent cry out in pain. She looked up to see one of Asha's knives sticking out of the soldier's chest.

Jessara got to her feet as the final soldier lunged at her. She parried the attack and knocked the sword out of the soldier's hand. Her blade *hissed* as she swung it at the assailant's neck, slashing his throat. The smell of blood and sweat filled the room as Jessara sheathed her sword, breathing a sigh of relief.

Asha ran up to Jessara. "You all right?"

"Yeah." Jessara was still catching her breath.

Asha smirked. "You're welcome."

"I could have killed her."

"Chaulk shit! Asha! That bloody you?" said one of the orc prisoners.

Asha ran over to him with a smile on her face. "Jorgg!"

"You're a bloody good sight in this shithole. The fuck you doing here?" Jorgg was massive—not as bulky as Progmash, but not far off. His body was wrapped in white troll skin held together by leather straps.

"Prog sent us to investigate the fort," said Asha. "We had no idea you'd be here. Are you okay?"

Based on the bruises all over Jorgg's face and the dried blood on his chin, the orc had been through a lot during his imprisonment. "I've been better. Ain't eaten in days. None of us have."

Asha looked at the dead soldiers and glared. "Bastards!"

Jorgg glanced at Jessara. "And who's the elf?"

Asha motioned to her partner. "This is Jessara. She fights the Compact."

Jorgg's eyes scanned the bodies. "I can bloody see that."

Asha turned to Jessara. "Jorgg is an old friend."

"I ain't got a clue why an elf is fighting the Compact." Jorgg took a moment to size her up. "But if you're with Asha, you must be doing something right."

"Can you fight?" Jessara didn't want to spoil the reunion, but more pressing matters demanded attention.

"I fight better hungry." Jorgg slammed his fist against the bars of his cell. "Time to kill these troll fuckers! Key's in the desk at the end of the hallway."

Jessara grabbed the rusty key and started unlocking the cells of the captive orcs. Many cheered as she set them free. In the end, they released fourteen. A few of them, including Jorgg, grabbed weapons off the dead guards and then gathered around their rescuers.

"Asha, my friend." Jorgg's face grew stern. "They bloody know the Kingdom's negotiating a treaty with the chief, and they think Prog-mash'll accept."

"Does he plan to?" Jessara was genuinely curious. A treaty with the orcs would be a gamechanger in the war.

"No bloody clue," Jorgg said and hung his head. "But I said he did. They...they fucking tortured me. I thought it'd make it stop. I failed my chief."

Asha shot a look at Jessara.

Jessara's mind went back to others she'd tortured in the past. Was the information she'd gotten inaccurate? A tactic to consider changing when she got back to the Kingdom. "Regardless, right now we need to make sure that no Compact soldier leaves this fort. There should be an armory in the main building. Asha and I cleared it on our way here. We'll grab weapons, and then figure out our stand."

"All right." Jorgg threw a fist in the air. "Brethren! Follow the elf!"

Jessara and Asha led the group out of the prison. When they reached the door to the courtyard, they scanned it to ensure no soldiers had awoken in the middle of the night. *Clear.* Jessara motioned for the group to follow her.

Snow crunched under the heavy tread of the orcs, making Jessara's heart pound faster with every sound. She'd never led a fighting force before, and the stress of lives depending on her weighed heavily. She'd gotten used to working with Asha, but this was a different level. Again, she told herself that she had to believe they would pull this off—or they surely wouldn't.

They crept back into the main building and into the mess hall where they descended the staircase. As Jessara had suspected, the bottom floor was an armory. Elven swords, bows, quivers, daggers, and axes lined the walls. Barrels and crates had been scattered around the room, and in one corner lay a pile of orcish weapons. The orcs rushed to the corner, excited to reclaim their arms.

"Check the crates and barrels." Jessara had an idea of what they might contain, and she hoped she was right.

"Hey, this got old oil pots." One of the orcs beckoned Jessara over to an open crate.

Jessara grinned. Now, she had a plan. "From the Shadow War. Useful during sieges." She turned to Asha. "Even more useful when you have a fire sorceress."

Asha grinned back. "Time to blow shit up?" She was so sexy.

"Time to blow shit up. At this point, the remaining soldiers in the fort are asleep in the barracks. We pour oil around the exits of the barracks, get their attention, and when they come out to investigate, we light them up. Should thin their numbers enough to give us a fighting chance."

"Might bloody work," said one of the orcs.

"How we gonna get their attention?" said another.

Asha snapped a finger. "The alarm bells?"

"Perfect!" Jessara's confidence in the plan was growing. "We wake up the whole fort and we set up an archery line in front of each barracks. After we flame them, we attack with a barrage of arrows."

Asha stepped forward. "Right! Let's go up fuck up these bastards!"

The orcs cheered quietly as Jessara smiled at her partner. What they were doing was good, not just in terms of their chances of success but in terms of their goals. These orcs were good people, who didn't deserve the fate the Compact had in store for them. The orcs of Coshgromar had saved Jessara and were far kinder than anyone she'd encountered in the Kingdom. They deserved to be safe from a Compact attack, and Jessara could use her skills to spare them that.

The orcs armed themselves with an assortment of the available weapons. Jessara found a quiver of arrows—the right size for her bow—and replenished her supply. After they were armed, several of the orcs picked up oil pots. Jessara led the group back up the stairs to the door of the mess hall. The group gathered in the courtyard as Jessara instructed the orcs to pour oil at the exits of the three barracks.

When the oil was in place, Jessara set up lines of archers. The alarm bell stood at the entrance to the fort. When everyone was in position, Jessara instructed one of the orcs to get ready to sound the bell.

Jessara looked at Asha, who nodded. Jessara took a deep breath. Open combat wasn't her preference, but she had plenty of experience with it. "Ready arrows."

The orcs drew string.

Jessara surveyed the orcs, knowing they were eager for revenge, and she was excited to see them in action. A palpable rush of anticipation saturated the air as she turned her attention to the orc at the alarm bell. The freezing mountain wind blew against Jessara's face, but she had too much adrenaline pumping through her veins to feel cold. Snow continued to fall in the courtyard, snow that was about to be stained with the blood of battle.

"Now!"

The orc rang the bell several times, and a commotion erupted inside the barracks with soldiers arming themselves. Soon, several Compact soldiers exited the buildings.

One soldier pointed his sword at the small army before him. "The orcs are escaping!"

Several of the soldiers emerging from the barracks were now on top of the oil.

Jessara motioned to Asha. "Light 'em up!"

Asha launched fireballs at the emerging soldiers. When the flames made contact with the oil, circles of fire engulfed all within.

Screams and the scent of burning flesh filled the air. As the flames dissipated, more soldiers emerged from the barracks.

It was time for Jessara to give the next signal. "Loose!"

A barrage of arrows shot into the emerging soldiers from all sides. In seconds, a half dozen were eliminated.

Those that remained charged the line of orcs. The former prisoners threw down their bows and pulled out axes and swords to meet their opponents.

Jessara shot arrows at will. Two more soldiers were brought down before the groups clashed.

The number of elves now matched the number of orcs. Metal clanked as the warriors viciously fought each other.

Jessara noticed a soldier charging at Asha. Before she could assist her partner, Asha blocked the attack with her sword and shot a fireball into the assailant's face.

She could take care of herself. Jessara drew her own sword and stormed into battle.

The bodies of elves fell on the ground as limbs and heads were hacked off by the superior orcish fighters.

Two soldiers attacked Jorgg as Jessara entered combat. She cut down one of the distracted opponents, which caused the other to lose focus. With one slash, Jorgg lopped the elf's head off.

Jessara turned into the rest of the onslaught, just in time to see an orc fall to the ground after being slashed by an elf. Jessara took out one of her knives and threw it at the killer, striking him in the eye.

Few foes remained. Three attempted to flee the fort, sprinting for the entrance.

"Asha!"

Asha turned to Jessara who pointed at the fleeing soldiers. The women darted after the cowards in pursuit.

Asha shot a knife into the back of one of them.

Jessara shot an arrow at another.

The final elf made it to the entrance of the fort and attempted to escape into the mountains. Breathing heavily, Jessara approached the entrance and spotted the enemy. She drew an arrow and held her breath. The soldier was in her sights. The arrow loosed, and the elf collapsed. A sigh of relief washed over her as Jessara turned to her partner.

"Nice shot." Asha was still catching her breath.

"You too."

The clashing had ceased. The women returned to the courtyard to find only victorious orcs. Three orcs had been lost in the battle, but all the Compact soldiers had been eliminated.

"Brethren!" Jorgg threw up a fist. "Victory!" The orcs cheered with joy. Their cries echoed around the fort.

Jorgg ran up to Jessara and grabbed her hand. "My elven friend! It was a right bloody honor to fight at your side! This was the best fucking fight I've had in a long bloody time. You helped me fix my fuckup, and you restored my honor. Know that Jorgg calls you friend!"

Jessara was surprised and had no idea how to respond to such praise. "Umm." Jessara glanced at Asha, who was smiling but offering nothing. "Thanks, you're a friend too." Not sure what else she was supposed to do, Jessara awkwardly bowed.

The orcs roared with laughter.

"Chaulk shit! I bloody like this elf!" Jorgg slapped Jessara on the shoulder.

"Never thought I'd hear you say that!" said one of the orcs.

Jessara was embarrassed as Asha joined her and held her hand.

"Well, anyway." Jessara addressed the orcs. "We should sweep the fort in case any survivors are hiding."

"And you should all find something to eat before we head back," said Asha.

"Right." Jorgg beckoned to the rest of the orcs. "Brethren! You heard the ladies!"

The orcs spread out and searched the fort, leaving Jessara and Asha alone in the courtyard. Asha turned to Jessara and put her arms around her.

"Hey." Asha kissed her. "You saved a lot of people today."

Jessara took pride in her work, but she was still bothered by the big picture. She frowned "This isn't the last base the Compact will set up here."

"No. But it'll be awhile until they send out another expedition. Enjoy the victory."

"All right." Jessara held Asha close. As her combat adrenaline wore off, she could feel the cold air against her face once again. But as always, her fire sorceress brought warmth. She pressed her lips against Asha's and enjoyed the taste of victory.

Chapter Twenty-Three

Triumphant Return

Asha was relieved when she, Jessara, and the freed orcs reached the gates of Coshgromar. Cheers erupted as they paraded through the streets to the chief's hut. Family and friends of the freed orcs rushed to greet them, and Asha saw her own sister approach.

"Welcome back, Asha." Anea embraced her firmly.

"We have a Nara of a story to tell." Asha pulled away from her sister. "Got to report to Prog first."

"Of course. I'll let the sisters know you're back, yeah?" With that, Anea ran in the direction of the temple.

When the women entered Progmash's hut with their orcish companions, the chief stood in surprise. Asha couldn't wait to share the news of their success.

"Jorgg, Truga, Klod!" Progmash scanned the group excitedly. "Bloody fuck! I thought the wilds had taken you." The chieftain ran into Jorgg's embrace.

"Not the wilds," said Jorgg grimly. "The bloody Compact."

"What?"

Jessara awkwardly took a step forward, not wanting to interrupt the hug. "They were collecting prisoners at the fort."

"Why?" Progmash pulled away from Jorgg.

"Interrogation. They suspected you were planning to sign a treaty with the Kingdom." Asha said, and desperately hoped he wasn't. The wonderful thing about living in Coshgromar was not needing to worry about the yoke of the King.

"Did they hurt you?" Progmash gently stroked his hand against Jorgg's cheek and kissed his forehead.

"Not as much as we hurt them." Jorgg grinned as he walked over to Jessara and placed a hand on her shoulder. "Asha and her elven friend saved us. Together we wiped out the pointy-eared troll fuckers!" Jorgg glanced at Jessara apologetically. "Umm, no offense."

"The Watch will not be receiving any information." Jessara turned to Jorgg. "Also none taken."

"You did more than I asked. Bloody fucking more than I expected. You have my thanks, my friendship, and of course, my gold." Progmash approached a cabinet in the hut and retrieved a coin pouch.

Jessara gratefully accepted the payment. "Thank you, chieftain."

"Friends don't use bloody fucking titles. It's Progmash to you."

"Or Prog." Asha smiled pleasantly, satisfied that her partner and her friend were getting along.

Progmash laughed. "Now that, only you're allowed to call me." He turned back to Jessara. "Jessara, I promised I'd lend you an escort. One of my best scouts can take you back to the Kingdom, whenever you're ready."

"Thank you, Progmash." Jessara bowed her head. "There's one other thing, however, if I may speak freely."

Asha tensed, knowing what her partner was about to say.

Progmash held his arms out. "You can always speak freely with friends."

"The Compact clearly views you as a threat." Eye contact was a struggle for Jessara once again. "Fort Chaska was just the beginning. I don't know where you stand on a treaty with the Kingdom at this time, but you may not be able to fight the Compact off if they return in force."

As he listened to the argument, Progmash stroked his chin. "You think I ought to join my folk with the Kingdom?"

Asha glared at Jessara. It wasn't surprising she took the opportunity to speak out for the King, but Asha still hated it. *Seriously? After all that son of a bitch has done to you?*

"Yes," said Jessara, not noticing her partner's disapproval. "The Compact will not stop until every non-elf is dead or enslaved."

"Maybe." Progmash brought up an index finger. "But they ain't gonna find us easy prey. The mountains themselves will wreck their numbers."

Jessara shook her head. "It won't be enough."

"I respect your counsel, Jessara. And I'll think about it. But the Kingdom you know may not be the one I do. In the early days of the Purge, I was a mercenary for the Kingdom. My unit raided villages in Compact territory—so-called 'retaliatory strikes'—but we didn't discriminate in who we killed." Shame spread across Progmash's face. "Too many innocents were slain by me in those days."

Asha grunted, knowing that was just the tip of the iceberg.

Jessara's expression turned to confusion, then defensiveness. "That couldn't have been on the King's orders."

"I don't know." Progmash shrugged his shoulders. "The commander gave us the orders; we followed them. I didn't ask where they came from. Regardless, I ain't allowing anybody under my command to be involved in such bloody, fucking butchery."

Jessara looked at the ground. "I understand. The Kingdom is not perfect. Atrocities are committed in war by both sides. But I hope you'll reconsider."

Again, Asha glared at Jessara, appalled by her callous defense.

"As I said, I'll think about it." Evidently, Progmash had also missed the tension from Asha. "But now ain't the time for bloody fucking politics. Our city will have a warrior's celebration tonight for those who've returned. I hope you'll be there."

Jessara politely held up her hand. "I'm not one for parties."

Progmash grinned and shook his head. "You ain't been to an orc party."

"She'd love to come." Asha walked up behind her partner and put an arm around her. "Wouldn't you, darling?"

Jessara glanced back at Asha, puzzled.

Asha shot her a final glare.

The message appeared to be well received. "I'll be there."

"Right!" Progmash clapped his hands together. "See you at dusk."

Jessara and Asha exited the hut and headed back to the temple. Asha didn't say a word as she silently seethed at her partner. When they entered the temple, they went straight to Asha's room. Asha put some wood in the fireplace and ignited it. Despite her anger, she wasn't going to let Jessara freeze.

"Thanks for making a fire," said Jessara, awkwardly.

"Yep." Asha's reply was as cold as the mountain air. The silence between the two lasted for a few moments.

Jessara slowly approached Asha. "What is it?"

Asha turned and glared at her. "You couldn't resist, could you?"

"What?"

"You're still defending the King! You're still being his bloody representative."

"This isn't about the King. It's about survival."

Asha's forehead creased. "You seriously think the King gives a shit about the orcs? All he would do is use them for his own ambitions."

"He's ambitious, but that doesn't change the facts." Jessara tripped over her words as she spoke. "The Compact is a threat to everyone."

"The King is a threat to everyone."

Jessara threw her hands in the air. "Damnit, Asha! You're so blinded by your hatred that you're missing what's right in front of you."

"Look who's calling who blind." Asha almost laughed at that. "*You're* blinded by your misplaced devotion."

"It's not devotion it's...it's..."

"What?"

"I don't know!"

Both women were silent for a long time.

Asha knew that despite their relationship, Jessara's plans hadn't changed. "You still want to take me to him, don't you."

Jessara raised a gentle brow. "I still think it's our best course of action." The tension in her voice had tempered.

Asha sighed. "He's going to kill me. You realize that, don't you?"

Jessara walked over to Asha and took her in her arms. "I won't let that happen."

"It won't be your call."

Jessara took a deep breath. "Look, I've been thinking about this a lot. I know how to convince him you can be an asset."

Asha sighed. "You said he wanted information on how a human can do magic. That's what he wants me alive for. You know I'll never tell him anything."

"Yes, I know."

Asha's heart pounded, knowing what she needed to ask. "Are you going to tell him about the Sisterhood?"

"No." The lack of hesitation in Jessara's voice put Asha at ease. "I swear to you that I will keep the secret of the Sisterhood. And I don't expect you to betray your oath."

"Then what makes you think he'll spare me?"

"Asha, he wanted to kill you when he thought you were with the Compact—you aren't. He said if it was more useful for you to stay alive, then you'd stay alive." Jessara gave her a crooked smile. "Well, I've seen firsthand how useful you are against the Compact."

Asha tilted her head. "What are you saying?"

"Look, I know you have no love for the Kingdom and the King. But you agree that the Compact needs to be defeated, right?"

Asha's mind when back to the moment her birth mother had died at the hand of a Compact soldier. "Perhaps."

"Then I convince the King to let you work with me."

"Work with you?"

"Why not? We worked well together at the fort." Jessara took Asha's hands again. "We could be together."

"I thought you worked alone?" Asha still wasn't sure about the proposal. But Jessara's offer implied that she'd been impressed with her skill at Fort Chaska. Despite her emotional state, she felt somewhat flattered.

"I don't have to. The King has always given me full freedom when it comes to my jobs. I can use whatever resources I need. There's no rule against me using a partner."

Asha frowned. "There's that word 'using' again."

Jessara sighed. "You know what I mean."

"Do you honestly think he would go for that?"

Jessara nodded with more optimism than Asha was used to seeing from her. "He trusts me. If I tell him you aren't a threat, he'll believe me."

"A monster like that doesn't trust." Asha stepped out of Jessara's arms.

Jessara stood in silence for a few moments. "This is the only way we can close the contract on your head. And...and this is the only way we can be together."

Asha glanced back at Jessara. "Or you could stay here. We could hide in the temple together. You don't have to return to the King."

"Asha." Jessara shook her head dismissively. "I can't just abandon the fight against the Compact. This is the only life I've ever known."

"And this is the only life I know," she said, wounded. "So where does that leave us?"

Jessara hesitated for a few moments, then nodded sadly. "I'll rest up here for the next two days, and then I'm going back to the Kingdom. I...I won't make you come with me."

Asha's heart sank. "What happens if you return without me?"

Jessara paused, then shrugged her shoulders. "I don't know. I've never returned without completing a contract before, especially one this large."

"This large? Wait. How much am I worth?" Asha realized she'd never asked.

Jessara looked at the ground. "Four thousand alive. Two dead."

Utter shock filled Asha's eyes. "By the Tree! What's a standard contract?"

"Most are in the 400-to-500 range. The price varies based on the urgency, the imminent threat of the individual, how much intelligence we started out with, and the high-profile nature of the target."

Asha went silent for a few moments. If she could sweat, she might have started to. "The King really thinks I'm that big of a threat?"

"I don't know. But he really wants you."

That gave Asha pause. There was much to consider, and she realized several things. If Jessara returned without her, the contract wouldn't be lifted. If anything, it would raise the price on her head. More people would be sent to look for her, and they'd never stop. If she were traced to Coshgromar, it could mean war between the orcs and the Kingdom, and would risk the exposure of the Sisterhood. With the King sending emissaries to the orcs, her chances of being discovered would increase. She couldn't put the Sisterhood or the orcs at risk. She couldn't hide here, she couldn't hide in the Kingdom, and she certainly couldn't hide in the Compact.

Asha looked up at her partner, who was also worth considering. What would a monster like the King do to her if she came back without finishing the job? Asha couldn't put her at risk either. Her mind turned to Jessara's offer. There was no way the King would go for that. If Asha went with Jessara, it would only end with her on the gallows.

At that moment. Jessara pulled Asha in and pressed their foreheads together. "Whatever you choose, I'll respect it. But if you do come with me, I promise I *will* protect you."

The words of her partner didn't take away Asha's concern, but she believed Jessara sincere. That gave her a small sense of calm. The idea of her assisting Jessara with assassination jobs was not her ideal line of work, but it would be better than any of the alternatives. Maybe it would be okay. Maybe Jessara could convince the King. And if she couldn't, Asha was still willing to die to protect those she cared about.

Either way, Asha had made her decision. "I'm coming with you. Whether Progmash negotiates an alliance or not, if the Kingdom ever discovered me here, it could mean war. I can't put my family in danger."

Jessara walked over to Asha and held her. "You're making the right choice."

Asha wrapped her arms around Jessara and kissed her. "I hope so." She forced herself to smile, deciding she could worry about the future when it came. For now, she knew where she and Jessara stood.

Jessara's expression softened and became casual. "So why are you dragging me to this celebration tonight?"

"For one thing, I was pissed at you." Asha grinned. "And for another, you haven't lived until you've partied with orcs!"

"I used to get in drunken brawls with them back in Enderdale."

Despite Asha's propensity for blindly rushing into fights, she couldn't imagine herself ever brawling with an orc. But Jessara was a different story. Her history wasn't surprising. "Well, you'd better be prepared for that. Try not to break yourself too much."

***

Jessara was relieved that Asha had agreed to come with her. Their relationship had a path forward now, and she fantasized about working together. It would take some getting used to, but at least they would be together.

The partners spent the remainder of the day resting. Asha talked about some of her friends in the stronghold. She told Jessara about how she'd grown up with Jorgg, and how she had gone on hunting expeditions with him as a teenager. Apparently, Asha had also been in a brief relationship with one of the other sorceresses, Brina, when she'd been in her early twenties. That subject made Jessara uncomfortable.

Later in the day, they sparred with wooden swords they'd gotten from the orcs. Jessara remained a vastly superior fighter, but she instructed Asha as she had before.

Finally, dusk came, and the couple went into the streets of Coshgromar. Music thumped in the cold mountain air. They came to the center of the city where the great hall stood. The roof of the building was a jerkinhead shape, with sturdy granite walls.

The couple entered the building to find rows of tables with feasting orcs. They were drinking mead and gorging themselves on bear meat, charred mountain goose, elk, baked bread, and fresh red mountain berry pastry. In the middle of the hall, two brawling orcs fought in a ring, cheered on by onlookers. A fireplace was built into each wall, and in the back left corner of the hall, several orcs played animal-skin drums and gut-stringed lutes. The room smelled like cooked meat and alcohol. On the far side of the hall, Progmash sat at the center of a large oak table. The other sorceresses from the temple were also in attendance.

As soon as Jessara and Asha entered, Progmash stood and teetered, visibly drunk. "Ah! The women of the hour!" Everyone in the great hall cheered. Jessara was uncomfortable with the attention, but she saw that Asha loved it. She grabbed Jessara's hand and raised it up as the orcs applauded. Jessara couldn't help but smile. Most crowds ignored her, and the ones that didn't were usually elf-haters. Back in Enderdale, people avoided her. As awkward as she was, it was good to be appreciated by the orcs. Asha and Jessara made their way to the main table.

"Get these women some bloody fucking mead!" Progmash motioned toward the couple with his mug, spilling some mead on the table.

Jessara and Asha were both brought full wooden mugs. The loud noises were beginning to overwhelm Jessara, but alcohol often helped her through sensory overload.

Progmash raised his drink. "To our heroines. May the blood of our enemies flow right quick!"

"And may the mead flow quicker!" Asha raised her own mug.

They *clinked* their cups, and each took gulps of their mead. It had a sweet honey taste, but it was stronger than other meads Jessara had tried before. It burned her throat but in a soothing way. At that moment, Jorgg emerged from the crowd holding his own mug and stumbling all over the place.

"Jessara!" Jorgg's speech was heavily slurred. "My friend!"

"Jorgg."

Jorgg raised his mug. "A toast to our slain enemies! May the stink of their corpses reach the rest of those troll fuckers!"

"I'll drink to that." Jessara *clinked* mugs and took a small sip.

Progmash laughed dramatically and shook his head. "This mead ain't to be sipped! The girl fights more aggressively than she drinks."

Jessara took that as a challenge. "Girl?" She quickly chugged the rest of her mug and then slammed it down on the table. The surrounding orcs cheered.

An orc that Jessara hadn't seen before aggressively marched up to her. "So, you're the elf that slayed half my tribe. Don't look like much to me."

"Ah!" Progmash smiled pleasantly and motioned to the newcomer. "Jessara, meet Torp. He was at the camp you fucked up."

"I figured that." Jessara sat silently for a few moments. "This is awkward."

"Oh, no." Torp held out a reassuring hand. "Don't mistake me. What you did was bloody impressive. But I do wonder how you are in a true fight."

"Was that a challenge?" Jessara raised a brow.

"You and me." Torp pointed to the middle of the room. "The battle ring."

The surrounding orcs hooted and whistled their excitement.

Asha took a sip from her mead. "She's going to kick your ass." She wrapped her arm around Jessara and kissed her cheek.

Jessara nodded, excited by the challenge. "I accept. What are the rules of the ring?"

"Try not to kill, and try not to die," said Progmash. "Match is done when someone steps out of the ring or gets knocked out."

Jessara looked between Torp and the ring before bowing. "After you."

The challengers made their way to the circle. Jessara could feel the mead that she'd chugged, but it wasn't enough to impair her. The excitement of the crowd filled the great hall.

Jessara and Torp stood in the middle. She put on her headband and cracked her knuckles, preparing herself for battle.

"Fight!" said Progmash.

Immediately, Torp charged Jessara. She stepped to the side and kicked him in the chest.

He staggered, but he shook it off as he swung at her. She threw herself to the ground to dodge the blow and tripped him with her legs.

The orc collapsed. Jessara rolled herself upright and punched Torp in the jaw. He lay on the floor, not moving.

As usual, orcs had brute strength, but that only helps when they can land a blow.

"He's out!" Progmash raised his mug, and the whole hall erupted with applause.

An orc walked up to Torp and poured mead on his face. Torp shook himself as he got to his feet. "What in Nara?"

"Told you." Asha reached out to embrace Jessara. "I think you've earned this." She gave Jessara a slow kiss.

When she did so, the crowd cheered.

Jessara felt a little awkward kissing like that in front of people, but she wasn't going to complain.

"A damn beautiful display, Jessara!" Progmash drunkenly slammed his fist on the table, making it shake. "Join me at my table! Have another drink." Jessara and Asha took their seats.

"An entertaining fight, if a bit short," said an orc woman sitting next to the chief. When she spoke she was much more eloquent that other orcs Jessara had met.

"Jessara, this is Corgsa." Progmash put his arm around Corgsa.

"Pleasure." Jessara still wasn't used to being around this many people; the noise made it difficult to focus. She took a drink of her mead and struggled to make conversation. "Are you married?"

Corgsa looked puzzled while Progmash laughed.

"I'm sorry," said Jessara, afraid she'd offended.

"Don't apologize." Progmash waved a reassuring hand. "Marriage ain't a big part of orc culture. We have many mates that we love dearly and raise children with. But, life on the mountains is damn harsh."

"A simple hunting expedition can end in death," said Corgsa. "If a mate dies, we miss them, but we can turn to our other mates for comfort."

"In battle, we stay close to our mates," said Progmash. "It gives us motivation to protect each other."

Jessara finished her mug as another orc rushed to refill it. She scanned the other orcs sitting at the main table, wondering how many others were in Progmash's mating group. Progmash had given Jorgg a kiss on the forehead earlier that day. Were they also together?

At this point, the mead was beginning to cloud Jessara's mind, otherwise she wouldn't have asked her next question. "So if everyone is having sex with everyone, how do you know which kids are yours?"

Her comment made Asha laugh, but seemed to confuse Corgsa. "They're all children of the stronghold. They're family to all of us. Their strength is based on their own dedication, not their parents."

"Then how do you decide who the next chieftain is?" Jessara took another drink. The room spun as the effects of the mead took root.

"Being chieftain ain't hereditary," said Progmash. "A chieftain's got to have strength and the consent of the tribe."

"Consent of the tribe?"

Progmash smiled at the question. Clearly, he didn't often get to educate people about orcish culture, and he was enjoying the conversation. "When a new chieftain's got to be named, candidates come forward and argue for themselves, and to be considered, they got to have the consent of the tribe. We have an election."

Jessara finished another mug and slurred as she talked. "An election?"

"Yes. All Coshgromarians get to vote. They raise their weapons," he jerked his axe in the air abruptly, "for who they want. The candidate with the most wins."

Jessara was given another mug. "And they become chieftain?"

"Not yet." Progmash swung his head back and forth and took a gulp. "The winner's gotta complete a challenge of strength. They got to find and slain a bloody fucking snow troll! Noooo weapons allowed!"

Asha laughed. "Hence why I never became chieftain."

"Hold on." Jessara took another massive gulp from a fresh mug of mead, and when she spoke, heavily slurred her words. "You killed a shnow...a show troll with your bare hands?"

"Damn right!" Progmash downed his own mug. "Hardest fight of my bloody fuuucking life!"

Even with Progmash as big as he was, Jessara had trouble believing him. "How the fuck did you kill a snow troll?"

"Oh, please don't tell the story again." Corgsa put her palm against her face.

"What kind of bloody fucking host would be deny...would I to deny...such an epic tale?" Progmash smirked. As he told the story he stumbled from his intoxication. "I tracked the beast for free...for three days! I had an empty stomach, and I lived off of drinking...errr...eating snow. The troll's camp! Oh bloody fuck!" He paused, losing his place. "Wait...yes! I found the troll's camp! The snow was dead with the dead...er...red with blood of victims...dead victims. I charged in with leapt...I...I leapt at the beast! The beck...the neck That was my target! But it grabbed me and whooosh! Me on the ground. Shit! We were like it for nearly an hour. Those bloody fuuucking claws! But no! No, that pain kept me focused. Finally broke the fucker's legs. Then!" He slammed his fist down on the table. "I crushed its filthy neck. Had to drag the damn corpse all the way back to the city. This is him." He pointed to the troll skull on his head as several of the surrounding orcs let out a war cry.

"If you were aaaanyone else, I'd say you were full of shit!" Jessara finished another mug of mead.

Progmash laughed. "And if you were anyone else, I'd take that as a bloody fucking challenge."

"A challenge!" Jessara raised an index finger. "It's a challenge! That's it!"

"Umm Jessara," said Asha, poking her in the ribs. "What are you doing?"

"A challenge!" Jessara frantically nodded her head. As she did, the whole world shook with her. "I want a challenge!"

"Do you challenge me?" Progmash stood up and stumbled.

"Yes!" Jerssara tried to stand from her chair but ended up falling to the ground. "Shit." She slowly pulled herself to her feet and rocked, attempting to stand in place.

"Jessara, maybe you should have some water." Asha went over to try to pull Jessara away.

Jessara looked at her and drunkenly smiled. "Asha! You're so beautiful!"

"Yes, you're beautiful too." Asha placated her, obviously alarmed. "Let's not kill ourselves tonight."

Jessara planted a kiss on her lips. "I love you!"

Asha froze. "Oh. Jessara—"

"Besides! It's fine!" Jessara was oblivious to what she'd just said. "You aren't supposed to kill in the ring, remember?"

"Exactly!" Progmash almost tripped over a chair. "Let us battle!"

"Bloody Nara." Asha rubbed her forehead as Progmash and Jessara stumbled over to the ring. They stood in the middle, facing each other.

"Wait!" said Jessara. "Who says fight if you're the one fighting?"

Progmash stared at her blankly for a couple of seconds, processing her words. "I don't know. I think still me. That's what I usually do."

"All right! Fight! Or you fight me. I mean you say fight me, so we fight!"

"Fight!"

Chapter Twenty-Four

Hangover

When Jessara awoke, she felt like her head had been split in two. She found herself in Asha's room at the temple with no memory of how she got there. A fire burned, and she was fully naked on the bed. An attempt to move resulted in pain from almost every part of her body. Her chest felt like it had caved in on itself, and her eye and jaw felt swollen. *Shit, that's probably a black eye.* She licked her lips, tasting blood and feeling more swollen tissue. Bruises covered the rest of her body. After taking inventory of her injuries, she lay back and groaned.

About a half hour passed, and Asha entered the room and put her fists on her hips. "You're an idiot. How do you feel?"

It even hurt for Jessara to turn her head to look at Asha. "Like death. What in Nara happened?"

Asha crossed her arms. "You challenged the chieftain of the orc nation to a brawl. You know—the one twice your bloody size."

"Oh, yeah." Memories of the previous night flashed through Jessara's head. "How'd I do?"

"You went at it for like twenty minutes. In the end, you were both so drunk and weak from repeatedly clobbering each other that you both just collapsed on the ground and passed out. It was funny to watch, but you're still an idiot."

"Hey. You're the one that dragged me there in the first place." Despite her current condition, Jessara had enjoyed herself.

Asha shook her head and rolled her eyes. "Well, I'm glad that you had fun at least." She walked over to her partner and gave her a kiss on the forehead. "You should try to get some rest. Miland will be in to heal you in a bit."

Jessara groaned. "Aren't I in enough pain?"

Asha laughed and started toward the door.

Suddenly, Jessara remembered something from the previous night. "Wait. Asha."

Asha stopped and turned around.

"I...I said something last night. I used a word I've never used before."

Asha sighed and looked at the ground. "Did you mean it?"

Jessara felt herself deflate. "I don't know. Maybe? But, I don't think I'm ready to start using that word yet."

Asha looked disappointed but she nodded. "Okay. Fair enough."

Before Jessara had time to feel guilty, Miland barged in. "You fucking moron!"

"Yes." Jessara groaned. "That has been firmly established."

"She'll live." Miland shot a glance at Asha. "Do I really have to heal her?"

Asha grunted. "Yes. We need to leave within the next day or two. We have a long way to go."

"Fine!" Miland threw up her hands in indignation. "But I'm leaving the hangover!"

Asha glanced at Jessara and then back at Miland. "Okay." She turned to leave the room.

"She's kidding right?" said Jessara. Asha ignored her and left the room. "She's kidding, right!?"

***

After Asha exited, she stood outside for just a few seconds pondering what Jessara had said—both last night and just now. She turned around and placed her palm against the door. "I think I love you too."

CHAPTER TWENTY-FIVE

DEPARTURE

Jessara enjoyed the rest of her time in Coshgromar. She and Asha stayed in the city for another two days before preparing to depart. During that time, Jessara studied the maps of the Northern Mountains provided by the orcs.

While in the stronghold, Jessara found she enjoyed the company of the orcs. In Enderdale, elves and humans alike seldom looked at her. Here, people celebrated her in the streets and exchanged tales of hunts and battles. Nobody made her feel like she didn't belong, despite the fact that they had every right to. Furthermore, the orcs were refreshingly blunt. Jessara never had to guess what they were thinking because they never failed to speak their minds, often with as much vulgarity as they could muster.

On the day of their departure, Jessara and Asha visited Progmash in his hut one last time. When they entered, Progmash immediately stood from his throne to greet them. Some cuts and bruises lined his face from the fight, and Jessara cringed when she saw the souvenirs she'd left.

"Ah, my friends." Progmash opened his arms. "I hope you're better after our brawl, Jessara."

Seeing the marks on Progmash made Jessara a little self-conscious about using healing magic. "I took the easy way out."

"Well, it's probably for the best. Maybe someday, we'll do a rematch. In the meantime, I understand you're heading out."

Jessara shrugged sadly. "Indeed. You've been kind and hospitable while I've been in your city."

"By taking out that fort, you may have saved our whole bloody fucking nation." Progmash's tone went from banter to sincerity. "It's the least we can do. Your scout should be waiting at the main gate."

"Thanks for everything." Jessara bowed her head.

"You'll always be welcome in Coshgromar. I'll also think about what you said about that treaty with the King. However, I still say you should be careful about trusting the bastard."

This made Jessara uncomfortable. She'd been questioning her relationship with the King recently, but he was still the man who had raised her.

"It was wonderful to see you again, Prog." Asha approached the throne to give him a farewell embrace. "Try not to die while I'm gone."

"And try to keep this one from doing anything too bloody fucking stupid." Progmash pointed to Jessara.

Asha laughed. "Like challenging an orc chief to a brawl?"

Progmash smiled. "Exactly."

The women exchanged their final goodbyes and started toward the main gate. As Jessara walked, she looked around the city with a frown on her face.

"Hey." Asha took Jessara's hand. "You all right?"

"I'm fine. It's just..." Jessara tried to think of the words.

Asha gave a half smile. "You're going to miss it here."

Jessara's eyes met her partner's. She couldn't deny it. "Yes."

"Why do you think that is?"

"I don't know. I guess it was nice to not feel like an outsider, even though that's what I am to these orcs."

"Well, the orcs themselves have always been outsiders. They live in these mountains away from a world that doesn't want them."

"I suppose I can relate." Jessara took in the city one last time—the *clanking* of weapons, the voices of orcs conversing with each other, the echoes of dogs barking. Cold wind tickled her face as she thought about the offer Progmash had made. She'd always have a place in the city. Her immediate reaction was to dismiss it, but the more she thought about it, the more she wished she could accept the offer. But that would require her to walk away from the fight against the Compact. To walk away from the King. To leave the only life she'd ever known—something she'd already told Asha she'd never do. Maybe she could visit again someday. Hopefully by then, she and Asha would be working together.

When the women arrived at the front gate, Anea and the orcish scout greeted them.

"You must be my date! I'm Lashgra. Good to meet you, Ears," said the scout.

Jessara raised an eyebrow. "Ears?"

Asha shook her head and laughed. "She calls me 'Blue'."

"That's because names never make any bloody sense." Lashgra shrugged. "So I give people ones I'll remember."

Jessara was taken aback, not sure what to think. "So I'm Ears? I feel like I should be offended."

"Are you?"

Jessara thought for a moment. "I don't think so?"

"Right then!" Lashgra clapped her hands together. "Ears it is!"

Short for an orc, Lashgra carried a personal arsenal of a bow and a short sword. Most of her kind preferred larger weapons, but scouts were trained to move and kill quickly. Long brown locks wrapped in a ponytail swung behind her, and her skin shone a darker green than other orcs.

After Jessara's back and forth, Asha turned her attention to Anea. "Hey, sister." They embraced. "Come to see us off?"

"Yeah." Anea nodded and motioned to Jessara. "But there's also a matter I must discuss with Jessara."

"I'm all...ears," said Jessara, then instantly felt ashamed.

Asha and Lashgra chuckled.

Anea held back a laugh of her own. "Can you give us a minute, Asha?"

Asha glanced at Jessara, uncertainty in her eyes.

"It's all right." Jessara motioned to the front gate. "I'll catch up."

Asha nodded and beckoned to Lashgra.

Anea watched her sister for a moment, then turned her attention back to Jessara. "As you know, the survival of the Sisterhood is heavily dependent on secrecy."

"Your secret's safe with me. I've already promised Asha."

"I know." Anea pointed to her head. "I'm telepathic. I know when you're lying, yeah? However, it's required for all sisters and friends of sisters to swear a traditional oath of secrecy before leaving, if you would?"

"All right, What do I say?"

"I, Jessara."

"I, Jessara."

"Swear upon everything I hold dear."

"Swear upon everything I hold dear." Jessara glanced at Asha who had reached the gate.

"That I will keep the location and existence of the Sisterhood of the Miracle Tree secret from outsiders until my dying day."

"That I will keep the location and existence of the Sisterhood of the Miracle Tree secret from outsiders until my dying day."

"Thank you."

Jessara nodded and turned to the gate.

"There is one more thing," said Anea. "A personal question from a concerned sister, if you'll indulge me."

Jessara stopped and glanced back at her.

"Will you protect her no matter what?" Anea's question felt less like a question, and more like a command.

"Yes." Jessara did not hesitate.

Anea paused. "Do you love her?"

CHAPTER TWENTY-SIX

THE SCOUT

Asha stood next to Lashgra outside the walls of Coshgromar. The scout was in her own headspace, doubtless making plans for the journey. So Asha stood in silence as she took in the city for what she feared would be the last time. It was more likely than not that she was walking to her own execution. Even if Jessara could manage to convince the King to spare her, and even if she began working with Jessara, she doubted there'd be a chance to return. Once again, she told herself it was all to protect those she loved.

Asha's eyes fell on Jessara talking to Anea. She assumed her sister was making her swear the oath, but they'd been talking longer than expected. Then Jessara turned around and ran to catch up.

The wind wasn't blowing, but it was still cold and snowy. Although the cold didn't affect Asha, she knew it would be tough for her partner.

When Jessara caught up, Asha said, "She make you swear the oath?"

Jessara paused for a moment as if processing her words. "Yes."

Asha had learned that the impassive look on her partner's face meant she was trying to hide something—usually an emotion that made her uncomfortable. "She say anything else?"

"Nothing you don't already know." Jessara smiled awkwardly.

Asha noticed the nervousness in Jessara's voice. There was more to her conversation with Anea. But before she could say anything, Lashgra said, "I remember swearing the oath when I was a teenager."

"Orcs have to swear the oath too?" Jessara jumped at the chance to change the subject. This made Asha even more curious, but they had a long journey ahead of them and could talk later.

"Yeah." Lashgra's voice was gravelly, with a hint of youthful excitement. "At least, if we ever want to leave the chaulking mountains."

"You didn't go outside the mountains until you were a teenager?" said Jessara.

Asha herself hadn't left until she was a teenager. "Most orcs never leave."

"That's right," said Lashgra. "It's usually only scouts. I was raised as one from one of my tribe fathers."

Jessara gave their orcish scout a curious look. "Tribe father?"

"Humans and elves give way to many shits about bloodlines," said Lashgra. "We don't give a chaulk's ass. Kids born in mate groups consider all adults within to be tribe parents."

"If you don't know who your real parents are—"

"*Real* parents?" Lashgra let out a confused scoff. "They're all bloody real."

"She means biological." Asha tried not to laugh at her partner.

"How in the chaulking damn does that make them real?" Lashgra's confusion grew. "Are people not flesh and blood where you come from, Ears?"

"No, they are." Jessara turned red with embarrassment. "I'm sorry. I mean, how do you prevent...you know?"

Lashgra turned to Asha. "Seems she's is better at fighting than bloody talking."

"Incest?" said Asha.

This made Jessara turn Compact red.

Lashgra laughed. "We don't chaulking mate with our own ages inside our mate circles. Kids in the circles are brothers and sisters."

"She's not used to talking to people," said Asha.

Jessara held up a defensive hand. "That's not true."

"That she isn't trying to kill." Asha considered adding "or fuck," but she decided Jessara was already embarrassed enough.

Jessara didn't have a comeback.

Lashgra laughed again. "An elf after my own heart! No matter, Ears. You can't bloody kill mountain beasts by talking them to death."

"I've never been this far in the mountains." Again, Jessara was desperate to change the subject. "Any concerns?"

"Damn right! We need to haul ass to the next ridge before night," said Lashgra.

"Because of the chill?"

"Because of the frost bats. Chaulking things are half the size of an orc and can fuck you up with their teeth. They also have a Creos awful shriek."

Asha had faced frost bats before. They were terrifying beasts with glowing yellow eyes, claws the size of daggers, and sharp teeth that could bite through flesh like butter. Fortunately, their mouths weren't large, so as long as a potential victim kept moving, the bats usually couldn't get a grip. Usually. Asha's fire magic proved to be an effective defense. Beyond their teeth and claws, the worst part of them was their shriek. Asha was not looking forward to hearing that again.

Asha glanced over at her partner, noticing her eyes widening with what appeared to be fear. In the time they'd spent together, she'd rarely seen fear from her. The only other time was when she'd been dying in the cave. Was she afraid of frost bats?

"Will we make it before it gets dark?" Desperation infused Jessara's voice.

"Let's hope," said Lashgra. "You never bloody know what you might run into out here."

The trio hiked southeast for several hours through the white desolate landscape. It was midafternoon. They passed the time with conversation and stories, and Jessara and Asha had plenty to share regarding their journey so far. Asha also took the opportunity to tell her partner some stories about Lashgra and her. When they'd been teenagers, Lashgra had trained to become a scout, while Asha had trained for retrieval missions. That training involved braving the dangers of the mountains, which meant they had spent a lot of time exploring together. In those days, they'd saved each other on several occasions. Lashgra could be trusted to keep them all safe in the mountains.

After several hours of climbing the rocky terrain, they came to the next ridge. They marched west along the base until they approached the entrance of a cave, or what used to be one.

"Chaulk's shit!" Lashgra inspected the opening. "Cave-in."

"Where's the next cave?" Asha tried to picture where they were based on maps she'd seen, but she didn't have a great sense of direction.

"A few miles west," said Lashgra.

Jessara looked up at the position of the sun. "Will we get there before dark?"

"Not bloody likely."

"Fuck me." Jessara put on her headband.

Again, Asha noticed fear behind Jessara's words.

Lashgra pointed to Jessara's weapons. "Be ready to grab that bow, Ears. We'll need it."

The three travelers continued to trek along the bottom of the cliff. As hours passed, Asha grew more anxious. The darker it got, the more she started hearing shrieks in the distance, and the trio was out in the open.

"At least we'll know when they're coming." It was unclear if the shakiness in Jessara's voice was from the cold or nerves.

"They only shriek when they attack," said Lashgra, grimly. "That sound is probably the last thing some poor bastard is hearing."

They picked up the pace. Asha's heart pounded against her chest as if trying to escape. Even at a distance, the shrieks stabbed into her skull. She glanced at Jessara whose face was tightening.

"We're almost there. I can see it." Lashgra pointed to an opening in the mountain. Suddenly, the distant shrieks ceased.

"Hold up." Lashgra raised an arm, stopping Jessara and Asha in their tracks. Lashgra motioned for them to hug the cliff wall. Asha put her ear to the wind, listening for wings flapping—not daring to make a sound.

"I don't think they know we're here." Lashgra beckoned to the others. "Move slowly and be quiet."

Asha's heart pounded so fast she feared the frost bats would hear it. The crunching of snow at her feet seemed louder than usual.

They got closer to the cave, and suddenly, Lashgra stopped dead in her tracks. Asha listened to the air and heard flapping. It grew louder with each passing moment. She looked to the night sky and spotted movement.

"Run!" said Lashgra. But the bats were already upon them.

A half dozen swarmed the trio and let out a horrific shriek.

Asha sprinted for the cave. The gust of flapping wings followed close behind as one of the beasts barely missed her. As she approached the cave, she heard a scream from behind, but it wasn't from the bats. It sounded humanoid. It was then that Asha realized Jessara wasn't with them. She whirled around and watched in horror as bats descended upon her partner. Jessara was seized up on the ground yelling—her hands gripping her ears as she rocked back and forth.

"Jessara!" Asha immediately darted back for her partner.

"Wait, Blue!" But Lashgra's warning was ignored.

***

The moment Jessara heard the shrieking, her whole body seized up. It was as if somebody were drilling into her ears and crushing her skull.

All she could do was grab her ears to try to drown out the screams, but nothing could. She knelt on the ground, rocking back and forth as her ability to move completely left her. A bat flew into her, knocking her off her feet. It tried to attack with its teeth, but her armor protected her.

In all the chaos, she heard a blast, but she couldn't focus on anything else as she desperately tried to drown out the shrieks. Jessara squeezed her eyes shut as she pressed harder against her ears. She thought she'd crush her skull with her own hands. Part of her wanted to—at least that would stop the noise.

A few more blasts rang out, and a moment later, she felt familiar arms around her body. "Jessara, get up!" The arms jerked as she heard another blast. "Please, come on! It's me!"

Jessara felt hands on her chin pulling her upwards. Finally, she opened her lids and saw the blue eyes of Asha staring back at her. Asha wrapped her cloak around Jessara's head and covered her ears, drowning out the shrieks enough for Jessara to get to her feet.

Asha pulled Jessara to the cave entrance. Jessara tried to push through the noise and muster the ability to run. Footsteps crunched in snow behind them, which she assumed belonged to Lashgra. The ground beneath her feet went from snow to rock, and she registered that she'd made it to the cave. After a few minutes of running through the tunnel, the shrieks died down. The bats didn't follow, and soon, they were no longer heard.

The group stopped, and finally had a chance to catch their breath. Jessara's head was still wrapped in Asha's cloak, and she made no attempt to move. So much sensory overload shot through her head that it was as if her very consciousness were trying to escape her body. But the pressure against her head kept her grounded.

Jessara saw Lashgra take out a torch which Asha lit. Then Lashgra took a seat on the cave floor on the opposite side of the couple. Jessara was finally able to take her head out of Asha's cloak. Still quaking, she lay on the ground. Her hands flapped as she tried to calm herself and keep from hyperventilating, but every time she thought about the shrieks, her breath rate picked up again.

Asha sat down next to her. "Can I hold you?"

Jessara nodded frantically, and Asha put her arms around Jessara, holding her tightly. The pressure of her partner's embrace was exactly what she needed. She wanted to ask Asha to squeeze tighter, but words still eluded her. Asha's hair against her face and the familiar scent of lavender gave her something to focus on as she slowly got better.

A half hour went by. As the shaking passed, the guilt set in. The guilt of putting Asha and Lashgra in danger. The guilt of needing to be saved. The guilt of being a liability. She looked at Asha while trying to hold back tears. "I'm sorry. I'm so sorry."

Asha put her hands on Jessara's cheek and spoke softly. "Hey. Don't worry about it. I'm just glad you're all right."

Jessara squeezed Asha tighter. "I almost got us killed. You should have—"

"Don't you finish that sentence!"

Jessara looked at Asha. She thought about her answer to Anea's question earlier that day. Her heart pounded again but not from the bats. "Are any of you hurt?"

Asha shook her head and looked at Lashgra.

Lashgra inspected her own arms. "A few cuts. What happened?"

"High-pitched noises do something to me." Jessara took a deep breath as she tried not to relive unpleasant memories. "Ever since I was a child. I thought I'd learned to control myself but..."

"Everyone has their limits." Asha ran her fingers gently through Jessara's hair. "Lea and Cli at the temple are the same way."

Lashgra grunted. "Are those the two crazy fucks that are always asking for the bodies of trolls to dissect?"

Asha chuckled. "That's them."

"I'm sorry." Jessara buried her face in Asha's shoulder again.

"We're fine, and that should be the last we see of them," said Lashgra. "They chaulking hate caves, and they stick to the inner mountain ranges."

"Bats that hate caves?" said Jessara

"It's because of their size." Lashgra cupped her hands behind her head and lay back against the cave wall. "At least, that's what I think."

Asha pulled Jessara to her and kissed her forehead. "We should rest here for the night."

The others agreed and laid out their cloaks to sleep on. The cave was cold, so Asha held Jessara in her arms to keep the recovering elf warm, while Lashgra put out the torch to conserve it for the next day. Jessara still tried to get the bats out of her head. She hated how helpless they made her. An hour passed, and Jessara lay in the pitch black, unable to sleep. Then she felt the warm lips of Asha against her forehead.

"You're awake?" Jessara tried to speak quietly so as not to wake Lashgra.

"Yes."

"I'm sorry."

"You ever going to stop apologizing?"

"I'm just angry at myself."

Asha tightened her grip. "Everyone has their weakness."

Jessara sighed. "I thought I'd overcome this one."

"What do you mean?"

"I told you about how I was raised with other elven children rescued from Compact villages?"

"Yes."

"Everything was a competition with us." Jessara adjusted herself against her partner, as she prepared to go back to one of the darkest times of her life. "Our trainers were trying to teach us to only rely on ourselves, so we were pitted against each other. During sparring days, the child that lost the most was forced to sleep outside."

"That's horrible."

"Sparring didn't happen every day. And it taught us independence."

"It taught you hate." Asha's voice was stern.

"We already had hate." Jessara had no desire to rehash old arguments. "Anyway, I was the best of all my peers, and they knew it. Every time someone was pitted against me, they knew they were fucked.

One day, I was up against one of the other children, Kelya. She'd been insulting me all day. I was angry, so I broke both of her legs in a sparring match. She screamed louder than I'd ever heard anyone scream. That was the first time I seized up."

"How old were you?"

"Nine. After that, the other kids realized they had an easy way to beat me. Every time they put me in a sparring match, they'd scream in my ears and beat me while I was seized up."

"The trainers allowed this?"

"Yeah. They said that there were no rules in real combat. So, they tried to force me to get over it. I had to be perfect. They would have the other kids hold me down and scream in my ears for minutes at a time. Whenever I reacted, they were instructed to scream louder. I used to think that what they did worked. Now I'm wondering if I just taught myself how to cope as I got older."

The part Jessara decided not to mention was that the King had interfered whenever he'd noticed this happening. He was the only one who advocated for her to receive any type of respite, and he seemed to realize that Jessara wasn't like the other children. He became something of a private tutor for Jessara, teaching her how to mask her internal struggles, and she had come to view him as a father figure. Jessara wanted to share all of this with Asha, but she knew that her partner didn't want to hear her sing the King's praises. And if she were honest, she herself was starting to question if the King really deserved praise.

"Jessara." Asha paused for a second. "They bloody tortured you."

"They were right though; there are no rules in real combat. You have to be perfect. Me especially."

"That doesn't justify it."

Jessara was silent as she considered it. She'd always thought that everything the King and her trainers had put her through was for the best, that she was broken inside and needed to be fixed. But Asha never seemed to think that way. Sure, she teased Jessara, but she never made her feel ashamed for being different. She wished she could see Asha's face right now. "No, it doesn't."

Asha let out a sigh of relief. "It's so nice to hear you say that."

"I still put you in danger."

"You've also saved my life more times than I can count."

"It's still not enough. I'm not perfect."

"Jessara, you don't have to be perfect to be extraordinary."

Jessara was glad that it was pitch black, because she didn't want Asha to see the dam that had burst from her eyes. Asha had said exactly what Jessara needed to hear. She seemed to make a habit of doing that. Despite being reckless and impulsive with her own physical safety, Asha was impeccable with her words. Jessara loved that about her. "What you did for me tonight...it's the first time anyone's ever done that before."

"What do you mean?" said Asha.

"You comforted me out of a bad episode. Normally, they'd punish me for reacting."

"Even if they change the behavior, they can't change the trauma."

"That was never important to them."

"It is to me."

Jessara held her tighter. Asha cared for her, not just for what she could do, but for who she was. Aleris' notes ran through her head. *Fiercely loyal to those they care about.* Asha cared about Jessara, about her feelings and her happiness.

"Asha?"

"Yes?"

"I..." Jessara took a deep breath. "I love you." Her heart pounded. "And I understand if you aren't ready to say it ba—"

"I love you too." No hesitation.

Jessara smiled the biggest of her life. She wasn't sure if she wished Asha could see her right now or if she was glad she couldn't. All she knew was that she loved this woman. The woman who'd saved her life so many times. The woman who gave her something new to fight for. She loved Asha. She caressed Asha's cheeks, and she could feel her smiling back. Jessara pulled her in and kissed her.

A breath of desire escaped her lungs as she ran her tongue against Asha's. Jessara pulled away and held their foreheads together, feeling Asha's breath warm the air between them. "Goodnight, Asha."

"Goodnight, my love."

Jessara kissed Asha one last time before drifting to sleep in the arms of the woman she loved.

CHAPTER TWENTY-SEVEN

THE GENERAL

Jessara awoke from the abrupt jolt of Asha's body scrambling from their pallet, followed by her scream of terror.

Instinctively, Jessara shot to her feet and drew her sword.

Asha screamed again. "By the Tree! Where is it! Where is it!"

The sounds of Lashgra frantically moving echoed in the dark. "What? What happened?"

"It was on me!" cried Asha.

Adrenaline pumped through Jessara's veins. In the pitch black, she could see nothing. Was a frost bat in the cave? A bear? A wolf? A troll?

Jessara heard a match strike a rock. She looked in the direction of the sound and saw Lashgra's face illuminated by the lighting of the torch.

Another scream rang out behind Jessara, and she turned to see Asha with her back against the cave wall as if she were trying to push herself through it.

"There it is! Get it away!" Asha pointed to the ground.

Jessara followed Asha's finger, and when she finally realized what had caused the commotion, she burst out laughing. On the floor of the cave, standing on its hind legs, was a rat, barely the size of her hand. "Umm, Asha?"

Asha shot Jessara a look of pure contempt. "Get it the fuck away from me!" Her voice dropped so low, it was as if she'd been possessed by something otherworldly.

Jessara became more scared of Asha's wrath than Asha was of the rat.

Jessara grabbed the torch from Lashgra's hand, ran over to the rodent, and waved the fire at it. "Go on! Shoo!"

The rat let out a disappointed *squeak,* then scurried off.

Asha released her grip on the wall, put her hand on her chest, and breathed. Jessara and Lashgra waited, staring.

Asha finally noticed them watching. "What?"

Jessara raised a brow. "'Healthy distaste', huh?"

Asha glared at her. "Oh blow me. And after last night, you can't bloody talk."

It was a good point. Jessara fought her urge to laugh. "You're right; I'm sorry." Jessara approached Asha, put her hand on her cheek, and pressed their foreheads together. "Are you all right, my love?"

Asha's expression softened, and she gave Jessara a kiss. "Yes. Thanks for scaring it off."

Laughter echoed behind Jessara, and she turned to see Lashgra with an ear-to-ear grin. "You know, I think I heard that rat saying your name when it ran away, Blue. I think you made a friend."

Jessara was still holding back her own laughter. "Come on, Lashgra."

"What? I'm not fucking her." Lashgra grinned and started packing up the supplies.

Asha was bright red with embarrassment. As amusing as it was, Jessara felt for her, and she wanted to at least try to provide comfort. So she pressed her lips to Asha's ear and admitted something almost nobody knew about her. "Alligators."

Asha looked confused. "Alligators?"

Jessara nodded. "My 'healthy distaste'—alligators. And frost bats."

Asha's confusion slowly turned into understanding, then appreciation. "I love you."

Jessara smiled at her and stroked her cheek. "I love you too."

For the first time in her life, Jessara was in love. She wished that Lashgra wasn't there so they could be alone, but then she reminded herself that they were in a freezing cave, with rats. Not the best setting for romance.

Jessara tried to estimate how long they'd been sleeping. "Any idea what time of day it is?"

"Hard to say." Lashgra closed her rucksack. "Midmorning maybe."

Jessara looked down the tunnel. "Any concerns about the cave?"

Lashgra shook her head. "I doubt we'll run into any problems."

"Speak for yourself," said Asha under her breath.

Again, Jessara resisted the urge to laugh. "What about renegade camps near our path?"

"Maybe." Lashgra stroked her chin as if trying to picture the layout of the mountains. "If we run into any of their hunting parties, best let me do the talking."

Jessara considered what Anea had said about renegades attacking most people on sight. "Think you can prevent them from trying to kill us?"

Lashgra shrugged. "Not bloody likely, but I have a better chance than an elf. No offense."

"None taken."

With their supplies packed, the group started through the tunnel. Jessara felt the walls closing in; she hated tight spaces. But other than Lashgra tripping over a rock, the rest of their time in the tunnel was uneventful. They walked for what felt like three hours through the dark cold passage before they spotted daylight.

It was nice to see the sun again. The light was bright, and Jessara had to shadow her eyes as she adjusted. Slowly, the view came into focus. A low ridge lay in the distance, and just over it, Jessara could see the land below. "How much farther now?"

"A pathway leads right to Gatewatch at the bottom of the mountains." Lashgra glanced up at the sun. "It's early afternoon, so we should be there by nightfall."

Asha looked lovely in the sunlight. Her blonde hair flowed in the cool mountain breeze, and the snow reflected off her bright blue eyes. Jessara was looking forward to getting to the inn at Gatewatch. As she looked at Asha's soft lips, round bottom, and gorgeous breasts, she thought about all the things she wanted to do to her.

Asha looked up and noticed Jessara checking her out. She raised a seductive eyebrow and glanced over at Lashgra to make sure she wasn't looking. Then she glanced straight down at Jessara's crotch and licked her lips.

Oh, you'll pay for that tonight. Jessara tried to ignore the pulsing between her legs and refocused on getting out of the mountains.

Jessara and Asha followed Lashgra through the snow-covered, rocky terrain. As they hiked, Jessara found Lashgra easy to talk to. Like most orcs, she was blunt, and Jessara respected that. Most people didn't communicate directly, and Jessara frequently misunderstood them. On a few occasions, the subject of the Kingdom came up, but during those conversations, Asha stayed silent.

After about an hour of walking, Lashgra abruptly stopped and held up her hand. She pointed to the air as if to say, *Listen.* Jessara heard the crunching of snow coming from a small crevasse nearby. The scout motioned for the women to follow her. They crept up to the crevasse and peered in. A snow troll paced around a nest of blood-covered bones—some animal, some humanoid.

Jessara took her bow, drew an arrow, and shot it into the troll's head. It let out a confused scream as it dropped to the ground.

Lashgra was visibly impressed. "Fair shot, Ears."

Jessara nodded, and the trio kept moving. They marched for another two hours, coming across one more troll and a few bears. Each time, Lashgra was able to detect the beasts early, so Jessara could slay them from a distance.

This new cooperation came surprisingly easily for Jessara. Prior to meeting Asha, she had never imagined herself working with others. But after the battle at Fort Chaska, she realized how needlessly difficult everything was on her own.

Another hour passed, and the scout held up her hand again. As the group listened, they heard the clanking of metal from behind a nearby rock formation. They crept to the formation and climbed to get a view.

The sight of blue and gold clashing with green and red was unmistakable. About a half-dozen Kingdom soldiers were engaged with a Compact force twice its size. Several had fallen on both sides.

Jessara recognized one of the Kingdom soldiers, who wore a gold-colored chest plate and had brown hair and a full beard.

"Shit. Harriot." She put on her headband.

"Who?" said Lashgra.

"Asshole." Jessara pulled out her bow and drew string.

Asha grabbed Jessara's shoulder. "Wait! Is this our fight?"

Jessara was proud that Asha was thinking through a battle before rushing in, but in this case, she was wrong. "If a Kingdom general dies in the Northern Mountains, who do you think will get blamed?"

"Bloody Nara! Fine!" Asha pulled out her knives, and Lashgra drew her sword.

Jessara shot an arrow into one of the Compact soldiers, and the three of them charged toward the battle.

The elves were distracted by the new foes, and the Kingdom soldiers mounted an aggressive and devastating counterattack. In an instant, three elves were cut down by the humans, while another four were taken out by the new attackers. The numbers were now even.

Jessara saw Lashgra slash apart a Compact soldier, who was unprepared for the strength of an orc attacker. Asha stood at a distance, shooting off knives and fire balls.

Jessara put her bow away and drew her sword and dagger. She weaved her way through the enemies like smoke.

One attempted to slash Jessara with a large claymore, but she dodged to the side and managed to cut the attacker's throat.

Another two charged. After blocking with her sword, she kicked one of them in the knee and with a loud *crack,* he fell to the ground. Jessara sank her dagger into his chest as she used her sword to stab the other attacker.

At the end of the fight, the human forces had lost only one additional soldier. Jessara was proud of her companions. If they could pull off a flawlessly executed battle like this with almost no preparation, imagine what she and Asha could do together with time to plan. She was optimistic about her ability to convince the King to spare Asha.

After the battle, the Kingdom soldiers turned their attention to their saviors. Harriot stormed over to the group.

"Jessara?" he said with disgust, "As if the cold wasn't bad enough."

"You're welcome, general." Jessara was never happy to see Harriot, but she'd saved him, and he knew it.

Harriot surveyed her companions, and when he saw Asha, he drew his sword.

Jessara stepped between them, while Asha held out her hands. "Whoa, easy."

Harriot glared at the fugitive sorceress, but spoke to Jessara. "You better have a good reason for traveling with this traitor, elf."

"I do." Jessara scowled at him defiantly. "And it's none of your concern. I'm on the King's business."

Harriot glared down the blade of his sword. "You're bringing a fugitive into Kingdom territory. She doesn't appear to be dead or a prisoner. I reckon it's *my* fucking business."

"Fine. But we'll talk without an audience." Jessara pointed to the other human soldiers. She dreaded talking to Harriot for any length of time, but he would be too stubborn to let this go.

Harriot glanced at his men. "Very well. But the sorceress stays where my men can see her."

"Deal." Jessara looked back at Asha. She didn't look happy, but she didn't say anything.

"Come, elf." Harriot beckoned Jessara out of earshot of the group. "Explain yourself."

"She's my mark," said Jessara. "I'm taking her back to the King."

Harriot raised a brow. "And she's going of her own accord?"

Jessara glanced back at Asha. "She isn't with the Compact. She could help the Kingdom."

"She violated the law against magic and murdered soldiers in her escape."

"Asha was defending herself. She's also helped me several times on our journey. She's not a threat. We can use her in the fight against the Compact." Jessara internally grimaced as she noted her own use of the word "use."

The general's brow furrowed. "What's going on here?"

Jessara tried to maintain an impassive look. "What are you talking about?"

"You don't take prisoners."

"She's different."

"How?"

"It's complicated."

Harriot crossed his arms. "Simplify it."

"The King is paying me well." She shrugged.

"And?"

"He wants to determine if she could be an asset against the Compact."

"That's it?"

"I don't question the King's commands. I simply obey them. If you need more answers, ask him."

Harriot considered her words. "So, *do* you think she can be an asset for the King?"

Jessara nodded. "And the King said that if she can be, she might be spared."

Harriot's eyes grew suspicious. "Since when have you cared about such a thing?"

"What do you mean?"

"You've never cared anything about the cause."

"I care about defeating the Compact."

"No, you care about killing people within the Compact. That's not the same thing."

Jessara was silent for a few moments. "Maybe you don't know me as well as you think you do." *Or maybe I've changed.*

Harriot took a moment to respond. "Perhaps." He sighed as his expression softened. "Listen, Jessara. Without your help, my men and I would likely be dead. You still don't have my trust, but you do have my thanks."

Jessara nodded. He would never have her trust either, but perhaps a slightly less combative relationship with him wouldn't hurt. "What was this about?" She pointed to the dead from the battle.

"A scouting party." Harriot gazed at the bloodstained, snowy battlefield. "The Compact has been carrying out coordinated attacks on Kingdom villages. The Northern Mountains provide a backdoor."

"And what were you doing in the mountains?"

Harriot looked away.

"Trying to secure an alliance with the orcs?" said Jessara.

Harriot looked back at her.

Jessara gave him a crooked smile. "Mind your manners when you talk to them."

"Will they try and rip me apart if I say the wrong thing?"

Jessara laughed uncomfortably. "No. But if you assume they will, then negotiations will be difficult."

"Fair enough." He sheathed his sword and looked at his men. "I reckon it's time for us to go our separate ways."

"Wait." Jessara looked over at Asha and then back at Harriot, realizing she may have an opportunity to help Asha's case. "Come on." Jessara motioned for Harriot to follow her back to the group.

The King respected Jessara's counsel, but he also respected Harriot's. Normally, that was a liability, but perhaps, with Harriot owing her a favor, it could become an advantage. Harriot now had a reason to vouch for Asha, but Jessara needed to make sure he got out of these mountains alive.

When they returned to the group, Jessara went straight to Lashgra. "How much longer until we're out of the mountains?"

"A few miles east, there's a road that leads to Gatewatch." Lashgra pointed away from the setting sun. "We should reach it by nightfall."

Jessara motioned to Harriot. "Listen. It's important that the general make it to Coshgromar safely. Asha and I can take it from here. You take them to Progmash."

"I chaulking hate that idea," said Lashgra.

"Me too," said Asha, angrily.

Jessara could see the rage in Asha's eyes, but this was the best course of action. "Like I said. If they don't make it, it could cause conflicts between the Kingdom and the orcs. You know the dangers of the mountains, and their numbers have been reduced from this attack. Please."

Lashgra thought for a while. "I still don't bloody like it."

Jessara shrugged. "I wouldn't either, but it's necessary."

"For what it's worth," Harriot put an arm across his chest and gave Lashgra a bow, "I appreciate it, noble orc."

Lashgra looked at him coldly. "It ain't worth much, human, but have it your way."

Asha glared at Jessara during the interaction. Jessara's plans at the inn tonight might need to be postponed, but Asha would get over it. When she had time to cool off, she'd understand.

"I suppose we should get underway," said Jessara.

"Much obliged, Jessara," said Harriot. "I won't forget this."

Jessara approached Harriot and whispered in his ear, "Don't forget Asha's part."

Harriot stared at her for a moment and then nodded.

As the groups went their separate ways, Asha remained silent.

"Something on your mind?" said Jessara.

"Nothing at all." Asha's voice had a coldness Jessara wasn't accustomed to, at least not from Asha.

Jessara tried to strike a casual tone. "Never thought I'd hear Harriot thank me."

"Since we don't have a bloody scout with us, maybe we shouldn't talk." Asha refused to look at her. "Make it harder for a beast to sneak up on us."

"All right." Jessara sighed. "That's probably a good idea."

Silence continued between them for the rest of the trek, and Jessara hated every minute of it. Asha was angry and Jessara knew why, but she'd thought Asha would understand. Now, they acted like strangers again.

Chapter Twenty-Eight

Lover's Quarrel

By the time the couple reached the town of Gatewatch, darkness had fallen, and silence still stretched between them.

As Jessara and Asha strode into the town, the citizens stared at the elf. Some recoiled with fear; others glared as she walked by—typical treatment that Jessara had come to expect, but it made her miss Coshgromar.

Gatewatch was one of the nicer towns in the Kingdom. It was well garrisoned, and the residents weren't stingy about upkeep. The buildings were constructed of cedar, oak, and maple from the nearby forest, and oil street lamps lit up a well-maintained cobblestone road. The people of the town primarily wore wool or linen, but it was not uncommon to spot a more aristocratic citizen arrayed in high quality velvet or fine silk.

Horse-drawn carriages carried the more affluent residents through the streets, and the sounds of children heading in from their play for supper echoed through the town. Jessara had been to Gatewatch before, but only to pass through. She'd never stayed the night.

Jessara flagged down a passerby. "Where's your inn?"

"Fuck off, husk!" He spat on the ground next to her.

Asha shot him a death glare. "Jackass!"

She was defending Jessara from bigots. Hopefully, that was a good sign.

The man returned the glare, but he kept walking. Eventually, the women found the inn. The smell of cooked meats and ale greeted them as they entered. Several tables lined the room with patrons enjoying meals and drinks. A stairway on the opposite wall presumably led to the rooms on the second floor. A large fireplace burned on the far side of the inn with a fourteen-point elk trophy mounted above the hearth. Shields marked with the Kingdom insignia hung on the walls.

As they walked in, a few patrons glanced at them, but continued drinking.

Jessara approached the innkeeper behind the bar. "We need a room for the night."

"Make it two." Asha's voice was still as cold as the mountains they'd descended from.

Jessara frowned at her.

"Deepest apologies, milady," the innkeeper said politely. "Only one is available."

Asha pursed her lips. "Fine."

"Fifteen drems, if you please."

Jessara reached into her pouch to pay the man.

"Room three is yours." The innkeeper handed her a key. "Up the stairs, second door on your right."

The women walked toward the stairway, but a woman in a dark wool cloak with a sword on her hip leaned against the wall next to the stairs. She stared at Jessara and Asha as they approached.

Something about her made Jessara uneasy. "Can we help you?"

"That's a mighty fine dress, good lady." The woman pointed to Asha. "Where'd you get such a garment?" Her voice was devoid of emotion in a way that felt threatening. She had menacing gray eyes, long white hair, and a crooked nose. The woman was at least a foot taller than Jessara.

Asha looked at her dress and then at the woman. "Bought it at an auction."

"I see. I'll have to attend more auctions." The woman bowed her head. "Have a lovely night."

Suspiciously, Jessara and Asha ascended to their room. It was a small space with a double bed and one dresser. In the far corner stood a small table with a few chairs. Nothing fancy, but functional. Some candles stood on the dresser with a match box next to them. Asha lit the room with her back to her lover.

Jessara was tired of the silence between them. "What's this about two rooms?"

Asha didn't turn around. "I didn't think you'd be comfortable on the floor."

Jessara sighed. "We need to talk."

"What's there to talk about?"

"Several things. They needed Lashgra more than we did; the King listens to Harriot, who now owes you and will vouch for you; and if Harriot gets killed in the mountains, any chance for peace is off."

Asha glared at Jessara. "Peace? You don't want peace. You want the orcs to join your war against the Compact."

"They can't stay neutral forever."

Asha threw her hands in the air. "Every time I think I'm getting through to you, you make it clear that you're still his loyal servant."

"I don't serve him—"

"Yeah, yeah, you serve his money. You've said that before." Asha raised her voice. "And we both know that's bullshit!"

"Do you not want the Compact defeated?"

"You still don't get it!" Asha stomped toward her. "You don't have to fight for the Kingdom in order to fight the Compact."

"Do you expect the orcs and the Sisterhood to fight the Compact by themselves? You'll be slaughtered."

Asha let out a humorless laugh. "And what do you think will happen if the Kingdom wins? If they rule Dremeria? Magic users will be hanged, which means everyone in the Sisterhood is dead. Elves will continue to be treated like bloody vermin, if they're allowed to live at all. How does that world sound to you?"

Jessara had been thinking of the King in a more critical light, but this was too far. Flawed as he was, he was Dremeria's best hope against the Compact. "You don't know that the King will kill the sisters. We're taking you to him to demonstrate that human magic users aren't a threat."

Asha turned her head to the wall as her voice dropped. "We've been fooling ourselves."

Jessara's heart sank. She didn't like where Asha was going. "What do you mean?"

Asha frantically shook her head. "This only ends one way—with me on the gallows."

Jessara put her hands on her shoulders. "I won't let that happen! I love you."

Asha's eyes filled with tears. "I love you too, but you can't know that." She pulled herself out of Jessara's grip. "It's about time we were honest. We have no future with each other. I agreed to come with you and turn myself in because I wanted to believe that it would end your way. But I don't, and I never have. You're taking me to my execution. I'm coming with you because I'm willing to die to protect the orcs and the Sisterhood."

"It won't come to that!"

"It will." Asha was crying now. "And when it does, you still won't see the King for who he is. We can't do this anymore."

"What are you saying?" Jessara was terrified.

"We can't be together. One way or another, we're going our separate ways when this is over. You know it, and I know it."

"Please don't do this." Jessara's own eyes filled. "I love you. I've never loved anyone else."

"I hope that doesn't remain true. But you're never going to change—not the way you need to. And it's too painful for both of us to continue this charade."

"What if I'm right?" This couldn't be happening. Jessara tried to wake up from the nightmare unfolding. She couldn't bear to lose Asha.

"What do you think will happen? You know I'll never give him information about the Sisterhood."

"You won't need to. You can work with me. That's how you can prove you're an asset."

Asha shook her head again. "I refuse to be his asset or anything else. I won't take his orders, and I could never be loyal to him. Even if he decides to let me go, we still go our separate ways."

She looked sadly at Jessara and shook her head. "You're never going to leave the Kingdom. And I won't ask you to choose between me and the only life you've ever known. That's why I'm making the choice for you."

"We can't know any of that." Jessara put her hands on Asha's shoulders again and looked into her watery blue eyes. "We don't know what's going to happen. All we have is right now. We can be together right now."

Asha pulled herself from Jessara's grip. "It's too painful."

"*This* is too painful."

"I'm sorry. But for once, I'm the one looking at the big picture."

"No! You're being impulsive!"

"Damnit, Jessara! What do you want me to say? What will make you accept this?"

Jessara crossed her arms. "Tell me you don't love me."

Asha paused for a moment. "I can't."

"Then stay with me."

"I won't."

Jessara was still in tears, but now she was angry. Something broke inside her. "Fuck you, Asha! You're a selfish bitch."

That set Asha off. "I'm doing this for both of us!"

"Bullshit!" Jessara pointed an accusatory finger. "You're doing this to punish me!"

"Believe what you want."

"Don't you gaslight me!"

"It's not gaslighting if you really are crazy!"

"Fuck you! I opened up to you! You told me you loved what you saw!"

"I did. I still do. Maybe your next lover will too—if you don't kill them first!"

"The day we met, when I had you in my sights—I should've taken the fucking shot!"

The silence between the women lasted for what felt like an eternity. Jessara instantly regretted what she'd said. The hurt in Asha's eyes pierced Jessara's soul with more guilt than she'd ever felt.

Asha got up and walked to the door. Before she exited, she glanced back at Jessara. "I wish you had."

With that, she walked out of the room.

Jessara was left by herself, her heart torn out and stomped on. She grabbed her chest as she struggled to breathe and cried as she'd never cried before. She was ashamed of what she'd said, but she was destroyed by Asha's words. Rage filled her—both at herself and Asha. She paced around the room playing her relationship with Asha back in her head.

"Fuck!" she screamed as she fell to her knees. The pain of losing her was too much to bear.

Jessara punched the floor over and over again. She punched it until the skin on her knuckles broke, and blood ran down her hands. But the pain in her fist still didn't outweigh the pain in her heart. It couldn't end here. She had to fight for Asha. She had to make her understand. Most of all, she had to apologize. When she got her bearings, Jessara got up and darted out the door.

"Asha!" Jessara descended the stairs. "Asha!" She scanned the downstairs of the inn, but didn't see her forlorn lover.

She approached the innkeeper, who was drying mugs behind the bar. "The woman I was with. Have you seen her?"

"She slipped out a few minutes ago." The innkeeper pointed to the back exit. "Seemed quite upset."

Jessara sprinted to the back door and ran outside. "Asha!"

She found herself in an alleyway full of crates. As she looked to her right, she saw a group of toughs loading something into a horse-drawn cart. As she focused on the shape they were dragging, she recognized a blue dress. *Asha!*

"No!" Jessara drew her sword as the assailants turned around in surprise.

"Get the sorceress out of here!" said one.

Three of the assailants rushed at Jessara with swords drawn to block her.

Jessara kicked the first one in the chest, flinging her against the wall of the alley.

The second attempted to swing at her, but she ducked and slit his throat with one swift stroke.

The third was a large man that rammed himself into Jessara, knocking her off her feet. She hit the ground, stunned. Behind her opponent, Asha was getting loaded onto the carriage. The kidnappers whipped the reins of the horse as the cart sped away.

"Fuck!"

Jessara's assailant tried to bring his sword down on her, but she rolled out of the way. As his blade hit the ground, Jessara grabbed her knife and sliced his ankle. He screamed in pain as he fell to his knees. With all her anger and might, Jessara swung her weapon against his neck, decapitating him.

She got to her feet to pursue the cart, but it was already gone. In the confusion, Jessara hadn't seen which way it had turned. Asha, the woman she loved, the woman who'd broken her heart, had been taken.

CHAPTER TWENTY-NINE

THE RED DAGGERS

Jessara screamed in rage. She slammed her fists into the ground, which only made her bruised knuckles worse. Attempting to sweep her emotions aside, she inspected the bodies of the assailants. They wore leather chest armor and iron helmets, with crimson red capes that bore the insignia of a red dagger. Jessara remembered the group that Anea and Asha had told her about. Could these be the mage hunters?

Jessara noticed that the assailant she'd kicked was still alive. Removing the attacker's helmet revealed the face of the woman who'd accosted them at the inn earlier that night. Jessara pulled the unconscious woman over her shoulders and carried her back into the inn.

As she walked through the back door, the innkeeper noticed her immediately. "What in Nara's going on?" The innkeeper pointed to the unconscious woman.

"Too much to drink." Jessara didn't even look at him as she stormed up the stairs. No time for distractions.

When Jessara got the assailant into her room, she tied her to a chair with rope from her satchel. She thought of all the ways she'd learned to torture people for information, and the rage inside made her yearn to cause this woman pain. But she also remembered what Asha had said about torture not yielding accurate information. It was more important to learn the truth than to satisfy a bloodlust.

Jessara hadn't cared about such things in the past. She'd been trained and ordered to torture—she'd had no reason to question the information she'd received. The information would be passed along, and that was that. But the orcs at the fort had suffered because she'd failed to contain information in Sunderbury. She couldn't afford inaccurate information now.

The problem was, torture was all she'd been trained to do. Her people skills were naturally terrible, and the fact that her training had never focused on honing them didn't help. Asha could have easily figured out how to make this woman talk. But Asha wasn't here.

Jessara tried to imagine what Asha would do. She glanced at the burning candles in the room and got an idea.

After tearing off a bit of sheet, she wrapped it around the woman's eyes as a blindfold. Next, she grabbed her canteen and splashed water on the woman's face.

The woman woke up, shaking frantically. "What in Nara? Where am I? Who's there!"

"We've met." Jessara's voice was entirely devoid of emotion.

The woman panted as she swung her head around in a vain attempt to get her blindfold off. Her soaked white hair whipped all over the place. "You're the elf who was with that sorceress bitch."

Despite their quarrel, Jessara was in no mood to hear someone insult Asha. She wanted to hit her captive, break her fingers, and shove knives into her knees. But none of that would help get Asha back, and that was all Jessara cared about. So she gentled her voice. "Mind your manners."

"Fuck you!"

Jessara walked in front of the woman, sizing her up before speaking. "What do you know about that woman you took?"

"Fuck. You."

"You should be thinking about your long-term survival right now." Jessara walked behind the woman and picked up one of the candles.

The woman smirked. "Funny, I was about to say the same thing about you."

Jessara was silent as she took a few steps toward the woman.

"What are you doing?" The woman struggled in her bonds.

"How much do you know about fire sorceresses?"

"More than you!"

"Is that so?" Jessara held the flame of the candle next to the woman's face.

As soon as the woman felt the heat, she gasped. "What the fuck are you doing?"

"Then you probably know that *we* can control the temperature of our hands." Jessara gently put the candle down and pressed her fingers against the face of the woman.

"You're a sorceress! My people will hunt you down, elf!"

"Did you also know that a person can be burned to the point where their nerves are scorched, and they can't even feel it?" Jessara wondered if that was true as she placed her hand on the face of the woman again.

"Get your fucking hand off me!" The ropes tying the woman creaked as she struggled.

"I could be scorching your face off, and the only way you'd know would be by the smell of burning flesh."

The woman's head swung back and forth, trying get away from Jessara's hand. "Please! No!" Her voice broke.

Jessara grinned as she tried to channel her best impression of Asha. "Do you know what burning flesh smells like?"

"Stop!"

"Want to find out?"

"My people will kill you!"

"Who are your people?"

The woman was silent, but still breathing heavily. Jessara removed her hand from the woman's face and picked up the candle, moving the flame closer to the woman's face.

"No, please!"

"Who are your people?! And don't bother lying because I'll find out, and I'll scorch your fucking face off."

The woman broke. "The Red Daggers! We hunt magic users."

As Jessara had suspected. "Tell me what you know about the woman you kidnapped."

"She's part of some kind of secret cult of human sorceresses."

"Where'd you take her?"

The woman was silent.

Jessara pressed her hand on the woman's face. "Where did you take her!"

The woman struggled and yelled, but it was fruitless. "We have a camp! It's southeast of town, just off the road."

"How far away?"

"A few miles."

"How many others are at the camp?"

"Forty."

"I hope you understand that if I find out you're lying about anything, I'll come back."

"You won't come back! To set foot in the camp will mean your death."

Jessara said nothing. She walked up behind the woman and punched the back of her head, knocking her out. Normally, Jessara would use curare, a paralytic poison, when she was trying to incapacitate someone without killing them. It was less likely to have any lasting damage. But Jessara decided that the woman had at least earned a concussion for all she'd done. Jessara tore more of the sheet to gag the woman. She considered killing her, but she was her only lead to Asha. If the woman was lying, Jessara would need her alive.

Jessara had a task before her. She looked at the pillows on the bed and grinned. She put the pillowcases and the candles in her satchel. A camp meant tents, and tents didn't like fire. After grabbing her gear, she headed downstairs.

As soon as the innkeeper spotted Jessara, his eyes filled with fear. "Is everything all right?"

Jessara suspected he'd heard the screams. "Could I get a bottle of whiskey?"

"A full bottle?" The innkeeper shook with every word he spoke. "Yes."

"Twenty drems." The innkeeper grabbed a bottle from behind him, his hands quaking as he handed it to Jessara.

He'd definitely heard the screams. Jessara took out sixty drems and laid them on the counter. "Keep the change and buy new pillowcases and sheets. Also, keep that room vacant for the next two days. I might be back." With that, she put the bottle in her satchel and headed out the back door.

Due to the cobblestone road, no tracks could be followed yet. The woman had said the camp was southeast of town. So the first step was to find a road leading that direction on the outskirts. Jessara suspected she'd gotten some dirty looks as she moved through town, but she was too focused on her mission to notice or care.

When she reached the edge of town, the cobblestone turned into dirt. Many tracks made by horse-drawn carriages decorated the ground, but only one set had been made recently, and sure enough, it led to the southeast. Jessara had a heading.

If the attackers weren't too far out of town, the tracks shouldn't fade. The woods in this part of the Kingdom were thick, and it would be difficult to pull a carriage through unless they had a path. Jessara needed to look for either a path or an abandoned wagon on the side of the road.

It was past midnight, and the air was cold against Jessara's face. The surrounding trees were a mix of maple, oak, and cedar, the cedar making it difficult to see far. As she continued to follow the trail, she tried to process the events of the last few hours. Her stomach churned when she thought about what she'd said to Asha. She didn't know what she would say when she found her, but it was best not to think of that now.

Hours passed, and Jessara came across an abandoned wagon. She recognized it as the one the Red Daggers had used to take Asha. Jessara checked the ground; horse tracks led deeper into the woods. She followed them for a half hour as dawn broke.

This region was the Northeast Woodland of the Kingdom, Jessara's favorite area because it reminded her of her home, Anwood. Some settlements dotted the region, but the Kingdom didn't invest much in the area. Therefore, it wasn't heavily patrolled, resulting in a major population of brigand camps. Jessara wasn't surprised that the Red Daggers had set up shop around here. If there was a place to lay low, this was it.

After another half hour of walking, Jessara noticed something above the canopy ahead. As she got closer, she saw the camp. A crude wooden wall with defensive spikes surrounded the encampment. Jessara found an oak tree to climb to get a better vantage point.

She put on her headband and was at the top of the tree in seconds, with a perfect view of the layout. The tents were made of heavy canvas—so cotton—which especially didn't like flames. Several dozen tents big enough to shelter multiple people were set up, with a few even larger ones in the middle of the camp. Small wooden watchtowers manned by archers dotted the edges of the wall. The woman had said there were about forty people in the camp. Too many for a frontal assault. Jessara looked around, trying to figure out which tent might hold Asha. One of the larger tents in the center had six guards out front. Chances were good they were guarding something or someone important.

The center of a camp was not the ideal place for a rescue. It was now daylight too, with the archers on watch. Waiting until nightfall wasn't an option either, as they were unlikely to keep Asha alive for that long.

Even if Jessara managed to make it inside the camp, she'd have patrols to deal with. If she made it to Asha's tent, a fight with the six guards would almost certainly alert the rest of the camp.

She studied the camp for another half hour. She noticed a few horses hitched near the entrance closest to her. They could be useful. The lack of a pattern to the patrols would make anticipating their movements impossible. As she'd suspected back at the inn, the only way she'd be able to pull off a rescue would be with a distraction. She could set a tent on fire like she had at the renegade camp, but she had to make sure that whatever she did, Asha wasn't hurt. Fire would probably be safe for Asha, but Jessara needed to be sure. It was time to consult Aleris' notes again.

She pulled out the papers and found the section about the physiological resistance of fire mages. She read: "Fire mages cannot be hurt by fire or heat. One could walk barefoot on hot coals and not be harmed." Jessara also reread the section that explained that breathing smoke didn't harm fire mages. Part of her was jealous of Asha for her immunities, but they would make the rescue easier.

Jessara took out the pillowcases she'd taken from the inn and began tearing off strips. She took out five arrows and wrapped the fabric around each. Next came the whiskey, which she poured onto the linen fabric. Jessara then pulled the match box from her satchel. Since she'd been traveling with Asha, she hadn't needed to use any matches. Their last conversation played in her head once again. Jessara tried to put it out of her mind because guilt wouldn't save the woman she loved—only action.

Jessara notched an arrow and used a match to light it. She aimed for a tent at the far end and took the shot. It sailed through the air and struck the tent, setting it ablaze. Before the camp was on alert, she lit and released three more arrows at other tents on the far side. It didn't take long for the flames to rise. A bell rang in the camp, and the sounds of yelling soldiers echoed through the trees.

The distraction would buy Jessara limited time. She put the last prepared arrow back in her quiver and descended from the tree.

She darted to the closest entrance to the camp. An archer, stationed as a sentry, manned the nearest watchtower, while another patrolled the entrance. The archer had his back turned, looking at the blaze.

She shot an arrow into the guard at the entrance just as he noticed her.

The archer heard the body fall and turned around just in time to take an arrow in the chest.

Jessara slipped into the camp. As expected, few patrols stood in her way, doubtless tending to the fire.

As she made it through the camp, she met only three of the Red Daggers. Two, she was able to shoot with arrows before being spotted, and the last one, she dispatched from behind with her knife.

When she made it to the center of the camp, the tent she had seen from the trees only had four guards. She pondered her next move. The four guards could be taken head on, but it would cost time, time she couldn't afford. She could use her remaining fire arrow to set Asha's tent on fire. That would get the guards away, and it wouldn't harm Asha. However, it would make it more difficult for Jessara inside the tent. Asha might be able to breathe smoke, but Jessara couldn't. Before she could make a choice, a Red Dagger came running from the blaze to join the group.

One of the guards turned to the newcomer. "What's going on?"

"Four of the outlying tents were set on fire." The newcomer struggled to catch his breath. "By arrows. We're under attack!"

"Orders?" said another Dagger.

"Kill the prisoner." The newcomer pointed to the tent. "We can't risk a rescue."

Hearing this, Jessara drew an arrow and shot one of the Daggers.

"Fuck!" said a guard as Jessara charged the group.

Another guard turned to the messenger. "Get backup!"

While Jessara drew her sword and dagger, the newcomer sprinted away and was out of sight before she could stop him.

The remaining three rushed at Jessara with swords drawn. She threw her dagger and hit one in the throat.

Another swung his sword at her chest, and Jessara blocked it to the side and kicked his knee out. A loud *crack* rang out as he fell to the ground, screaming. However, his screams were cut off by a jab to the chest.

The final guard attacked. Jessara moved her body around the path of the man's sword, and her counter slash opened his gut.

Jessara retrieved her dagger and sheathed her weapons as she ran to the entrance of the tent.

"Over there!" she heard a voice call out. Jessara turned to find that the messenger was returning with dozens of Red Daggers, far too many for Jessara to handle by herself. She grabbed her last fire arrow and lit it before backing into the entrance of the tent. Hoping the flames would keep them away, she used the arrow to light the tent on fire.

She turned to see a familiar blue dress. Asha was kneeling with her hands chained to a pole above her and her legs chained behind her. She wore chainmail gloves like the ones Aleris had given Jessara.

Asha had several bruises on her face, blood dripped from her nose, and a cut ran across her forehead.

Asha looked up and saw Jessara. "What in Nara?" Her voice was frail.

"Well, this is becoming a habit." Jessara reached into her boot to produce her lockpick.

"I think this is a first for us." Asha tried to muster more energy in her voice, but it was clearly a struggle.

Jessara darted to Asha as the tent filled with smoke. She had to be quick. She pulled the gloves off Asha's hands and tried to pick the lock of her arm shackles.

They heard voices outside. "Hold!"

"Surround the tent!" said another. "As soon as they try to leave, kill 'em!"

The locks proved tougher than Jessara anticipated. It was getting harder to breathe or see. The smoke burned her eyes and her lungs as she coughed.

"Jessara?" said Asha, worry in her voice.

"I'm fine." After a minute of coughing, Asha's arms were free, but her legs remained restrained. Jessara grew lightheaded.

"Jessara!"

"Almost there." Jessara worked on the locks on Asha's legs, but staying conscious was a struggle. Her entire chest felt like it was on fire. Each frantic cough ripped apart her throat.

"You need to get out of here! You can't breathe. I *can*."

Jessara said nothing and focused on unlocking Asha's chains. Finally, she heard the familiar satisfying *click* as the lock came undone. She looked up at Asha and mustered a smile through fits of coughing. The tent was completely engulfed as Jessara fell to the ground. She'd done all she could; at least she'd given Asha a fighting chance.

***

After being chained for several hours, Asha was exhausted, hungry, and in pain from being tortured. But she was motivated.

Her eyes closed as she felt the flames within her and around her. She held out her hands and began to absorb the fire. An army stood ready outside the tent, and there was only one chance if she wanted to make it out alive with Jessara.

Power coursed through her as the flames flew from the walls of the tent into her hands. She stepped over Jessara. The safest place would be the eye of the firestorm Asha was about to create.

Finally, Asha released. She spun around as fire exploded from her hands. The blast shook the ground as the tent around them disintegrated. The screams of Red Daggers being set ablaze filled the air. Asha collapsed to the ground, exhausted. The blast took a significant amount of her already depleted energy, and she could barely move.

She lay next to Jessara, who was still coughing and struggling to breathe. The tent was gone, but smoke saturated the air. All the surrounding tents were on fire.

Asha scanned the grounds, but saw no Red Daggers left standing. She got to her feet and reached down to help Jessara up. Every movement strained her body.

"Jessara?"

She didn't respond as she gasped for air. They weren't escaping the smoke fast enough. Jessara fell to her knees.

Asha attempted to pull her up. "We've got to move!"

Jessara looked at Asha and with one final gasp, she managed to push out the words, "I'm sorry." Then she collapsed.

"Stay with me!" Asha lightly smacked Jessara's face. No response. "Please stay with me! Please, Jessara, get up!"

Jessara's skin was cherry red. At least it wasn't blue, but even so, she didn't move.

"Damn it! You stubborn bitch, you're not allowed to bloody die!" Despite having very little strength left, Asha bent over and pulled Jessara over her shoulders. As she carried her through the camp, she did her best to avoid the flames. Every single muscle in her body begged to rest. She screamed in pain as she moved, and tears ran down her face. Nevertheless, she pushed on.

Asha thought about her previous interaction with Jessara. Guilt and sorrow flooded over how they'd treated each other. What if that was her last interaction with the woman she loved?

After several minutes that felt like an eternity, she reached the exit to the camp. She struggled over to a white mare and threw Jessara over the animal's back.

After loading Jessara, Asha fell to the ground, but rest would have to wait. With her last bit of strength, she struggled back to her feet, unhitched the horse, and climbed on top.

Asha spurred the horse into the woods. This part of the Kingdom was unfamiliar, and she had no idea where they were going, but she hoped that they would come across a cottage in the woods, preferably as far away from the camp as possible.

They rode for what felt like hours. Asha was ready to lose hope when she spotted a structure through the trees. As she got closer, it appeared to be some kind of monastery. A large stained-glass window sat above a set of massive front doors. The window had a red circle design with other circles inside it that progressively got smaller.

Asha let herself slide off the horse. The moment her feet touched the ground, her legs gave way and she collapsed. Slowly, she crawled her way to the doors, no part of her free from the pain, her body telling her to give up. But she made it to the door. As hard as she could, she knocked. Echoes came from the other side. The great doors opened, and several robed figures emerged. Asha's vision blurred, and she couldn't make out the faces. The last thing she was able to do with the strength she had left was point to Jessara on the horse and say, "Please." With that, she lost consciousness.

CHAPTER THIRTY

THE CHURCH OF THE EVERLASTING SOUL

As Asha opened her eyes, a stained-glass window drifted into focus. She lay in a comfortable bed, wrapped in what she believed to be an excessive number of wool blankets. Shapes in the window slowly took form, and she recognized the symbol she'd seen at the front of the monastery.

Asha slowly sat up, but her whole body ached. Fortunately, the rest had refreshed her mind, and she remembered recent events as if a dam had broken—the capture by the Red Daggers, the torture, the rescue, the fire, and Jessara.

"Jessara!" Asha forced herself out of bed and ran to the door. "Jessara!"

She found herself in a long, stone-walled hallway lined with rooms.

"Jessara!" Asha heard footsteps behind her.

She turned around to see a young woman wearing black wool robes approaching her. "Oh, goodness me! You're awake! Praise the soul, you're awake!"

"The elven woman." Asha's voice shook as she spoke. "Where is she?"

"Oh, she's safe, miss. We're doing what we can for her."

Asha breathed a sigh of relief. "How is she?"

The young woman pondered for a second. "I don't think I'm the one to ask. Our head monk is tending to her. He can probably explain it better than I. May I take you to him, miss?"

"Thank you, yes."

"Follow me, please—oh drat—I almost forgot! My name is Tya." A petite woman with auburn hair, Tya sported brown eyes, light eyebrows, and thin cheeks.

"Asha. Pleasure to meet you." Asha bowed her head politely.

"A blessing to meet you! Good to see you're up, Miss Asha."

As they walked through the hallway, Asha tried to get her bearings. No wall hangings or decorations adorned the halls, just stone walls and wooden doors, which Asha assumed led to additional living quarters. "How long was I out?"

"Almost a day, poor thing. You must've been through a lot."

Asha gave a humorless chuckle. "You could say that."

"I'm surprised to see you up. You had a right terrible fever when you arrived, and it didn't seem to have gone down the last time I checked. You feeling all right?"

Sometimes, Asha forgot that not everyone had the physiology of fire sorceresses. "I usually recover from diseases quickly." In fact, as a fire sorceress, she was immune to diseases.

"Goodness me! Tough one, aren't you? You sure you don't need more shuteye?"

"I'm sure."

Tya led her to another room at the back of the monastery. It was lit with candles and was as humble and as devoid of decorations as the rest of the building. A desk sat in the middle and cabinets lined the walls. At the far side of the room stood a bed with a large, middle-aged man in black robes sitting next to it. Another stained-glass window, also with the circle symbol, decorated the back wall. Asha wondered what it meant.

On the bed, Jessara lay with her eyes shut, her skin cherry red.

As Tya and Asha approached, the man looked up and smiled at the two. "Glad to see you on your feet, lass. With the fever you had, it's a darn miracle."

Asha laughed nervously. "Well, no fever anymore."

Tya motioned to the man. "This is Brother Braun."

"Pleasure to meet you there, Asha." Braun extended his hand. A bulky man with balding gray hair, blue eyes, and gray stubble on his chin, Braun looked friendly, yet purposeful.

Asha shook his hand and raised a brow. "How did you know my name?"

Braun pointed to Jessara. "She's been in and out of consciousness since she got here. She's half delirious when awake, but she's been calling out for you. You must be important."

Yeah, I'm also the woman that broke her heart and got her into this in the first place. Asha stared down at Jessara. "How is she?"

"Her condition appears to be stable for now. Was the lass in a fire?"

"Yes." Asha took it as a good sign that Braun knew enough to deduce that.

Braun nodded. "I thought as much. Her symptoms are consistent with some darn severe smoke inhalation. What's her name?"

"Jessara. Is she going to be okay?"

"Normally, severe forms of smoke inhalation require months of rest." Braun sighed. "However, the toxins from the smoke have affected her blood, and I fear that she won't last that long."

Asha glanced at Jessara in denial. "No. She's red. If the smoke were affecting her breathing, she'd be blue."

Braun shook his head. "Normally, if a person were not getting enough air, that'd be the case. But when the blood is made toxic from smoke," he pointed to Jessara's face, "these are the symptoms."

Asha's heart sank. "How long does she have?"

"Without treatment, I fear a few days. A week at most."

Asha's eyes filled. Not only had she broken Jessara's heart, she'd gotten her killed. A healing sorceress could save Jessara, but there wasn't enough time to find one. "So, she'll die?"

"I said 'without treatment.'" Braun smiled. "Fortunately, we've used a treatment for similar blood conditions before. I won't lie: there are risks, but it's usually successful."

Asha perked up. "What treatment?"

"Jessara's blood is toxic, so we give the lass new blood."

Asha lowered her brows. "I've never heard of such a thing." Of course, most of her knowledge of medicine was magic-based.

"Here, we've had time to learn the ways of science." Braun gave her a professional smile. "It's a process we've used before."

"I've seen it myself." Tya put a comforting hand on Asha's shoulder. "It's miraculous."

Asha looked between the monks. "Who are you people?"

Braun smiled again, proudly. "You are standing in one of four monasteries for the Church of the Everlasting Soul."

"I'm sorry. I'm unfamiliar with that." Asha found religion to be an interesting topic of conversation, but she knew little about smaller sects.

"Most people are," said Braun. "Religious orders, such as ours, that break from the doctrine of the Church of the God Creators, often must seclude themselves."

Asha's forehead creased. "Then why help us?"

Tya shrugged. "Why? Because you need it."

"We believe that we must help all that we can, lass," said Braun.

Asha grunted. "You sure you're a church?"

"I don't follow."

"Sorry. I just haven't had the best experiences with churches." The Church of the God Creators in Enderdale was a major driver of the persecution of magic users, so Asha had never trusted them.

Braun smiled and nodded. "Indeed, I've heard that before."

Asha looked around. "How many of you are in the monastery?"

"A little over a dozen," said Braun. "Most of them are in their quarters meditating."

At that moment, Jessara's eyes squinted open, and she looked around, obviously bewildered. She moved as if in slow motion. "Aaaaashaaa?"

"I'm here." Asha took Jessara's reddened hand and squeezed gently.

Jessara's mouth moved, trying to speak, but no more words came out, only unrecognizable sounds. Her eyes closed and she drifted off again.

"Jessara?" Asha kneeled over her, and began to cry. "Jessara!"

The monks waited silently. Tya stepped away, then tapped her shoulder and offered a cloth.

"Thank you." Asha wiped her faced as she tried to catch her breath.

"Are you all right, lass?" Braun inspected her face.

Asha ignored the question. "Can you use my blood?"

Braun shook his head. "Unfortunately, it's not that simple. We'll need another elf, or her body'll reject the blood."

"Got any lying around?" Asha was only half joking as she looked around the room.

"Not at present," said Braun. "There is an elf in our order, but she's away on an errand."

"Kreatia is due back tonight!" The excitement in Tya's voice made Asha wonder who this Kreatia was to the young woman.

"Until then, there isn't much we can do for Jessara." Braun stood up. "But you are most welcome to use the guest quarters that you woke up in."

Asha didn't move. "I'd rather stay with her, if that's okay."

Braun gave a knowing smile. "I understand, lass. And you are certainly welcome to stay with her. Sister Tya, will you please watch over our guests? The meditation of our brothers and sisters will end soon, so I'll join them to tend the garden."

Tya nodded. "Yes, Brother Braun."

"I don't want to impose on either of you any more than we already have," said Asha.

"It's no imposition, Miss Asha." Tya grinned. "You just got me out of gardening."

Braun laughed. "Be sure to keep her busy. It was a pleasure to meet you, Asha. I'll let you know as soon as Sister Kreatia returns."

"Thank you for your kindness." Asha bowed her head. "We're in your debt."

Braun held up a gentle hand. "We don't believe in debts. You owe us nothing, lass." With that, he exited.

"No debts?" Asha turned to Tya. "Now I know you aren't a real church."

"We believe that we all share the same soul. It'd be quite silly to demand debt from yourself, right?"

"You've lost me."

Tya smiled. "You know about the reincarnation as it's preached by the Church of the God Creators, don't you?"

"Sure. It's the idea that the dead go to Nara, where their souls are recycled into another body by the Creos." Asha was generally familiar with the creation story, but she had never studied doctrine.

"Too right. We also believe in the Creator Gods—in Tello, Drema, and Narde—or the Creos as most call them. We also believe in reincarnation in Nara; however, it is not some linear journey through time. Time is an illusion, and we all share the same soul, but at different parts of development. That symbol of circles that you keep seeing in the windows represents the circle of life's journey and the soul's progress to enlightenment. Neat idea, right?"

"So, you think that you and I are the same person?" Asha tried to puzzle it out. She thought about all the people she'd met in her life—and killed for that matter.

Tya nodded. "In some sense, yeah."

Asha straightened the bed clothes and ran her hand lightly down Jessara's leg. Jessara slept on. "But doesn't experience and memory make up who a person is? We don't have the same memories, so wouldn't that make us different people?" It had been a while since Asha had discussed philosophy or religion, but they were topics she enjoyed.

"Is a person with amnesia a different person? Surely not. They still have the same soul they've always had. Their personality is usually similar as well. Even little ones have personalities before they experience the world. A personality is surely shaped by experiences, so there must have been experiences before life begins." Tya clearly shared Asha's interest in philosophy.

"But why does that mean we all share the same soul?"

"Wisdom and logic come with experience, Miss Asha. Wisdom and logic are how we separate good and evil. Do you believe good exists?"

"I suppose."

"And evil?"

"Certainly."

"If reincarnation is a straight line, then each of us would be on the same part of our soul's journey. Evil lacks wisdom and logic, which means that if evil exists, our souls surely couldn't be at the same level of development."

"Maybe *some* people just have rotten souls." Asha wasn't expecting such wit in a girl as young as Tya. Now that she'd observed her more closely, Tya couldn't have seen more than twenty winters.

"That's a very cynical belief."

Asha looked down with a frown. "I just escaped from people who tortured me; I'm feeling a little cynical right now." She wondered if this was how Jessara felt all the time.

"Oh drat, that must've sounded terribly judgmental of me." Tya bowed her head. "My apologies, Miss Asha. You're at a different part of the soul's journey than I. I can't fault you for a different perspective."

"No apologies needed." Asha laughed. "Also, you can call me Asha."

Tya smiled and nodded. "Very well, Asha."

Asha returned to the discussion. "So, one day I'll agree with you because I'll be you. Is that it?"

Tya shrugged. "Or you've already been me and one day, I'll agree with you. We don't presume to know exactly how far each of us are on the journey."

"Your beliefs are...interesting, I'll give you that. But I think I'll stay cynical for now, if it's all the same to you."

Tya put a hand on Asha's forearm. "I'm sorry you were tortured, Mi—Asha. No one deserves that."

"I can think of a few." Asha knew torture didn't serve a functional purpose in interrogation. But after what the Red Daggers had done to her, she fantasized about returning the favor. That firestorm was too good for them.

Tya glanced down at Jessara. "If you don't mind my asking, what happened to you two?"

"I was kidnapped by a gang of...really bad people."

"Goodness me! Why?"

Asha felt like she could trust Tya. But that information could put people in danger, and oversharing had gotten Asha in trouble in the past. It seemed some of Jessara's caution was finally starting to rub off on her. "I'd rather keep that part to myself, if that's okay."

"Of course."

"Anyway. Jessara rescued me. The camp caught fire, and she inhaled a lot of smoke."

"How many people were in this gang?"

"Several dozen."

Tya's eyes widened. "By the soul. She must be skilled."

"I've never met a greater fighter," said Asha, looking down at Jessara.

"I'm sorry for her condition. I can tell she means a lot to you."

"She does."

Tya hesitated for a moment. "Are you together?"

Guilt fluttered in Asha's heart. "We were."

"But not anymore?"

Asha shook her head sadly. "We said some ugly things to each other before I was kidnapped. It was the last time we spoke. We didn't part on the best of terms."

"I'm sorry to hear that. Are you going to try to mend things?"

Asha was silent for a bit. She didn't want to think of that right now. Breaking things off with Jessara was the hardest thing she'd ever done. She kept trying to tell herself that she'd made the right decision, but after everything Jessara had done to rescue her, she wasn't sure. Jessara was dedicated to her in a way nobody had ever been. Even after Asha had broken her heart, even after they'd said such terrible things to each other, Jessara had mounted a rescue against impossible odds.

Asha thought about the moment before Jessara had lost consciousness at the camp. Those green eyes looking up at her. Her lips saying "I'm sorry".

Finally, Asha looked up at Tya and decided to deflect. "She has to survive first."

"Don't you worry. There isn't much you can do in a monastery besides research and experiment. We've made advancements that go far beyond anywhere else in the Kingdom."

"Why haven't you shared it?" Asha was ready for a subject change.

Tya grunted. "Don't you think we've tried? So far, our attempts have been blocked by the Church of the God Creators."

"Why?"

"There's more money in selling temporary solutions than cures. It seems that the only thing they love more than the Creos is drems."

"You all don't make any drems?" Asha was taken aback.

"Well, we have drems. But money only has value because people decide it does. We use it for trading for essentials but not much else."

Asha chuckled. "You don't value money? Now, I'm not even sure you're human."

Tya laughed. The two women sat and talked for several hours. It was nice for Asha to get her mind off her love life, and she found the beliefs of the church fascinating. She was skeptical, but she admired their approach to the world.

Jessara slipped in and out of consciousness a few more times, but she wasn't able to say anything coherent. Braun came in periodically to check on her. At one point, he brought in chicken meat and fresh cucumbers for Tya and Asha as a dinner. It grew late, and Asha was still sore and drowsy from her own experiences.

Eventually, Braun came back to the room one last time. "Asha, I just wanted to check in before I retire to my quarters. Do you need anything?"

"No, thank you. Has Kreatia returned yet?"

"Not yet." Braun's voice was hiding worry. "No matter. I'm sure she'll be back by tomorrow morning. In the meantime, you should go to bed."

Asha's eyes lowered to the bed where Jessara lay. "I'd like to sleep here for the night, if that's okay."

"Try and get some sleep." Tya stood up. "You've been through a lot."

"Yes, I'll try," said Asha.

With that, Tya and Braun exchanged goodnights and left Asha alone with Jessara.

She rested her hand on Jessara's cheek, frowning. "I don't know where you and I stand right now. But thank you for saving me...again. I will make sure you survive this. We have a lot to talk about. I don't even know what I want to say to you. I'm sure I'll figure it out, but for now, I love you. I never stopped loving you. Keep resting. And I will stay right here next to you."

Asha lay down in the bed next to Jessara, putting her arms around the woman she loved. Their bodies fit together as Asha kissed Jessara's forehead and drifted off to sleep.

Chapter Thirty-One

Out For Blood

"Asha, wake up."

Asha opened her eyes to see Tya standing over her. She quickly checked on Jessara, who was still asleep. After blinking a few times to adjust to the light, she sat up in the bed. "Has Kreatia returned?"

"She hasn't." Tya looked drawn. "Asha, I'm getting worried. She knows these woods too well to have gotten lost. I'm going to speak with Brother Braun."

Asha stood up, stretching off the night's sleep. "I'll come with you."

Tya led Asha down the plain stone hallway, periodically passing other robed monks whom Tya greeted. Under normal circumstances, Asha would have been happy to introduce herself, but she had only one thought in mind.

They came to Braun's quarters. As they entered the room, Asha noticed a stained-glass window, a bed in one corner, and a desk in another. These people had humble accommodations, their head monk no exception.

Braun sat at the desk, looking at a map. "Good morning, lasses."

Asha wasted no time with greetings. "Kreatia?"

Braun did not look up from the map. "She should have been back by now. I fear something's happened to her." His voice was tense.

"Hatred of elves is common around here." Tya approached Braun, desperate. "She could have run into trouble."

"Let's not make assumptions yet." Braun was clearly trying to remain calm.

Asha walked up to the desk and looked at the map. "Where'd she go?"

Braun pointed to a spot on the map. "A family of elves live in the woods a few miles to the north."

Tya crossed her arms. "They keep to themselves on account of bigotry from locals."

"They don't trade much with the nearby villages." Braun shrugged. "So Sister Kreatia took it upon herself to periodically bring food from the monastery."

"Did you send anybody to find her?" said Asha.

Braun stood. "I was preparing to."

"Well goodness! Send me." Tya stepped forward. "I know these woods better than anyone."

"All right." Braun nodded reluctantly. "But I don't want you going alone."

"I'll go with her." Asha wasn't offering.

Braun held up his hand. "You're still recovering, lass."

"Kreatia might be our only chance to save Jessara. With respect, I'm going with Tya." Asha didn't want to be rude, but she would be on this trip—with or without his approval.

"Very well," he sighed. "I won't try to stop you."

"Where did you stash Jessara's weapons?" The Red Daggers had taken her own.

"In the woodshed out back. We don't allow weapons within the monastery."

Asha chuckled. "I probably could have guessed that. We should be off."

"At least eat something before you go."

"I'll pack bread," said Tya. "We'll eat on the way."

"One more thing." Braun scratched his chin stubble as he looked between the women. "In Jessara's condition, the amount of blood we could extract from one elf will be enough to keep her with us, but it won't be enough for a full recovery anytime soon. After Sister Kreatia returned, I was planning on sending someone back to the elven family to ask for another volunteer. While you're out there, if someone from the elven family would volunteer, it will greatly improve Jessara's chances."

"I know the family." A youthful smile spread across Tya's lips. "They're kind elves, and they'll surely help."

With that, Tya and Asha grabbed rye bread from the kitchen and headed to the woodshed. Jessara hated when people touched her weapons, but under the circumstances, she'd understand. Asha grabbed Jessara's hoplite sword and both of her daggers, but left the bow. She could use these weapons, but she'd never held a bow in her life.

She offered Tya one of the daggers; however, she pushed the weapon away. "Oh dear. I'm sorry. I can't."

"Just to protect yourself." Asha pushed it toward her again.

Tya's brown eyes were conflicted, but ultimately, she shook her head. "I'm not allowed to fight, even in defense. I won't judge if you feel it's needed, but I can't help you."

"If you're sure." Asha put the dagger in one of her sheaths, and the two set off. Sure enough, Tya was deeply familiar with the landscape.

Asha hadn't appreciated this region of the Kingdom yet. Neither her kidnapping nor her ride with Jessara had allowed her to take in the beauty of the forest. The sun shone through tree leaves, giving the air a lovely green tint. Oaks, cedars, and maples all towered to the sky. Birds chirped, and squirrels jumped from tree to tree.

Jessara had often told Asha of her preference for forests. Asha frowned, wishing they were together now. Jessara would have enjoyed this walk.

Tya interrupted Asha's thoughts. "This is the path Kreatia always takes."

Asha glanced at Tya and realized she had another reason to worry. Jessara had always called the shots when it came to fights. This region was a haven for ruffians, and there was a decent chance they'd run into trouble. Asha knew she was more than capable of handling herself, but she had Tya to protect as well. After what had happened in Farnsville, Asha had lost confidence in her ability to save another.

But she couldn't think that way. Jessara had taught her well in their time together, and she could use those skills to keep them safe. In the meantime, it was fruitless to stress over hypotheticals.

Asha welcomed the distraction of conversation. "You've made this trek with her before?"

Tya smiled. "Oh yes. Most of the brothers and sisters at the monastery prefer to stay on the grounds. But Kreatia and I have explored these lands since we were kids."

Asha scanned the trees. "These woods can be dangerous. Did the monastery allow it?"

Tya grinned. "Brother Braun tried to stop us, but he quickly learned it was hopeless."

The picture that Tya was painting of her childhood reminded Asha of her own. She frequently snuck out of Coshgromar to explore the Northern Mountains when she was too young to safely do so. "How did you end up at the monastery?"

"My ma and pa were killed in a Compact raid when I was a young one. The monastery took me in and raised me."

Asha frowned—yet another thing she had in common with Tya. "I'm sorry. I know what it's like to lose parents."

Tya shrugged. "No worries. I don't remember much about them. Like I said, I was very young. Many brothers and sisters have similar stories. Most were orphaned, and nobody else would take them in. Kreatia lost her parents when she was a baby, and she's only known life in the monastery."

"You mentioned that you grew up with her. I also notice you don't call her 'sister'. Is she somebody to you?"

"Picked up on that, did you?" Tya smiled. "Yes. But not in the way you mean."

Asha lowered her brows curiously. "How so?"

"She's my best friend, and we *are* life partners. But we don't seem to experience attraction the way others do."

"So, there's no..." Asha tried to find a non-crude way of saying it.

Tya chuckled. "Sex? No. We love each other dearly, but we just don't have those types of feelings. Goodness me, I know that must sound strange to you."

Asha didn't understand it, but she wasn't one to judge. "Tya, I've seen things far stranger than that. I really do hope we find her." Her sister was similar. Anea was sometimes attracted to people, but only after having developed romantic feelings. Otherwise, she avoided sex.

"Me too. For her sake and Jessara's."

Asha let out a sad sigh at the mention of the name. "Thank you. I need Jessara to be okay."

Tya hesitated for a moment. "Forgive me if this too forward, but you said earlier that the two of you had ended your relationship?"

Asha looked at the young woman for a second, not entirely sure how to answer. "Something like that."

"Yet, you clearly love her?"

"Yes."

"And she clearly still loves you."

"Yes."

"So..." Tya gave her a nudge. "You going to make up?"

Asha paused. "We have to save her first. But then, I don't know."

"By the soul, what's not to know? You're in love."

Asha looked at Tya. She should avoid this conversation, but in the short time she'd known Tya, she'd been a good listener. Asha was tearing herself apart over Jessara, and perhaps it would be good to talk to someone. "I don't think we have a future together."

"How can you know that?"

"We're different people from very different places. Our paths are heading in different directions after our journey's over. I don't even know if we'll both be alive at the end." If anything, Asha believed she was sparing Jessara the hardship of watching her lover walk to the gallows. If that was how this would all end, staying with Jessara would be selfish.

Tya had a different take. "Apologies for being blunt, but goodness me, that sounds like a terrible reason to be apart."

Asha tilted her head. "How do you figure?"

Tya took a moment to order her thoughts. "You may not agree with our beliefs, but one thing the church has always taught me is to live in the moment. Time is an illusion, and our journey will take our soul to both the past and the future. That makes both equally unknown. So, the only thing that matters is the now."

"Maybe. But the future will eventually be the present."

"But it's not right now."

"It's a doomed relationship."

"Aren't all relationships?"

Asha let out a chuckle. "Now who's cynical?"

Tya grinned politely. "Still you. It's not cynical; it's the truth. All relationships will surely end. Even those that last end in death. Everyone knows this, but we still fall in love. Now why would we do that if it's doomed to end?"

Asha hadn't thought of this before. She pondered Tya's question for a long time. "I guess it's because they want to enjoy as much time together as they can."

Tya smiled, although it was more of a smirk.

Asha was taken off guard. Tya's wisdom was far beyond her age, and Asha was impressed. "I'll think about what you've said, although, you're a little young to be giving me advice."

Tya laughed. "Perhaps. Or maybe I'm a lot older than you think I am." She winked.

They walked for several miles through the forest, Tya giving her much to ponder. There was logic in the young woman's arguments, but Asha was far from making a decision. She hadn't wanted to break up with Jessara, and it was true that they could be together at present. But how could their relationship work after they got back to Enderdale? For now, she decided to put it out of her mind and focus on finding Kreatia.

After two hours, they noticed something dangling from an oak tree in the distance. Asha strained her eyes trying to figure out what it was. At first, she thought it might have been a broken branch. But as they got closer, the shape of legs came into view. The figure was a person.

"No." Shock and horror infused Tya's voice as she ran to the tree. As she followed, Asha saw that the person was a young elven woman with blonde hair and still eyes. She was hanging by her neck with her hands tied behind her back. Bruises colored her face and she wore a black robe. It looked like she'd been dead for half a day. Tya dropped to her knees and howled.

"Tya?" Asha put her hand on her shoulder.

"It's Kreatia," Tya sobbed uncontrollably.

"Hey." She knelt down beside her. "Come here."

Asha held Tya as she wept into her shoulder, tears seeping through Asha's dress.

Asha felt terrible for the young woman. She looked up at Kreatia's body as she held Tya. The sight sickened her as her heart filled with rage.

"Why?" Tya squeezed Asha tighter. "Who could have done this?"

Asha put things together and came to a terrifying realization. She gently put her hands on the sides of Tya's face. The wet tears soaked her palms. "Tya look at me. Focus on me."

"She's dead! By the soul! They killed her!"

"I know. We'll mourn her and give her a proper burial. But I need you to focus. This looks like the work of human supremacists. You said she was bringing food to an elven family?"

"Yes." Tya tried to regain her composure.

Asha took a deep breath. "How close are we to their house?"

Tya's eyes widened. "My goodness. We have to get to them!"

Asha took out Jessara's sword and cut Kreatia's body down. Nothing could be done for the poor girl's remains right now, but she wasn't going to leave her up there. "Which way?"

"Come on." They both darted through the woods. Asha was furious. She was thinking about Jessara back at the monastery. Had Asha lost her one chance to save her? Part of her felt guilty for thinking more about that than the hate crime she'd witnessed. Regardless, she had to make sure this family was safe.

After ten minutes of running, Asha smelled smoke and saw it rising above the trees ahead. "Tya! Hold up!"

"What?"

Asha pointed to the smoke and placed her finger over her mouth. The two crept closer to the source. Through the trees, they spotted a large flame. As they drew closer, they noticed the flames engulfed a small hut in the middle of the forest. Tya tried to rush to the burning building, but Asha grabbed her arm and motioned for Tya to get behind her.

They approached the house to get a better look. Asha noticed five humans standing in front of the burning home, holding swords. Two corpses lay on the ground next to each other. Three other figures knelt with their hands behind their backs. They were elves, all with dirty blonde hair. One appeared to be in his late teens, one was a preteen girl, and the third was a young boy.

Tya tapped Asha's shoulder and pointed to three nooses hanging from a tree near the house.

Asha's heart sank. "Creos. Fucking monsters!"

"They're going to kill the children." Tya's voice shook. "By the soul! We have to do something."

Asha scanned the field in front of her. Before meeting Jessara, she probably would have rushed in and thrown fireballs at will—strategy be damned. But if she'd learned one thing from her, it was that sometimes, the direct approach was not the best approach. When the lives of others are depending on you, you must take your time and carefully ensure the safest possible approach.

Asha tried to ask herself what Jessara would do. The lessons flashed through her head. *Number one, know your assets*. Asha glanced at the flames from the house. Those would come in handy. Next she needed to figure out a plan. Asha thought back to the rescue of Storn they'd pulled off in Compact territory. Asha had distracted the bounty hunters while Jessara took them out. She looked at Tya, recognizing she had another asset. Not one that could fight, but Asha didn't need her to. She grabbed one of Jessara's daggers and handed it to Tya.

Again, Tya pushed the knife away. "I can't."

"It's not for killing. I need you to free the children. I'll distract and take out the supremacists."

"All five? By yourself?"

"I've had worse odds." Asha laughed under her breath as she realized that she even sounded like Jessara now. "I need you to promise me that whatever you see me do to them or them to me, you will get those kids back to the monastery. Save them, then save Jessara. If anything happens to me...tell Jessara I'm sorry. Tell her...tell her I never stopped loving her."

Tya reluctantly nodded as she took the dagger.

Asha pointed to the area behind the hostages. "Get behind those trees, and get ready to free the children."

With that, Tya left and approached her position.

"One versus five. Where's Jessara when I need her?" The truth was, Asha *had* faced worse odds before. But the more time she'd spent with Jessara, the more she'd realized that her successes were more due to dumb luck than skill. Facing five opponents by herself was nothing to scoff at, and she knew her survival wasn't guaranteed.

Again she tried to remember Jessara's words. *Strategy and balance. You lose both when you're angry.* Asha was still filled with rage. The sight of Kreatia, the parents, and the children boiled her blood in an almost literal fashion. But she knew Jessara was correct. She closed her eyes and took a deep breath to calm herself. The first thing she thought of was Jessara. Just being with her—talking to her. Holding their bodies together. Despite the status of their relationship, Asha felt soothed.

"Strategy and balance." Asha grabbed Jessara's other dagger and put it up her sleeve. She took one more breath and walked into the open.

"Hello, boys!" Asha waved at the supremacists with an over-exaggerated smile.

All five rushed toward her with their swords drawn.

"Who the fuck are you?" Clearly, these men lived rough. Their tunics, too dirty to determine the original color, were little more than rags, and their weapons would have made a blacksmith weep. Scars decorated their faces, and most were missing several teeth.

"I'm just admiring your handiwork." Asha ran her finger through her hair, trying to look as sweet and innocent as possible.

The act was working. All the supremacists had their eyes on Asha. She could see Tya behind them sneaking up to the captive children. "It's awful noble of you to protect frail human women like me from dangerous elven children." Asha took a few steps toward the supremacists, trying to get closer to the flames.

"Not another fucking step!" One of the supremacists pointed his sword directly at her.

"That sounded to me like sarcasm!" said another.

"You one of them husk lovers?" One of the supremacists spat out what looked like yellow goo. She tried not to be sick.

At that moment, Tya reached the first elven child and began freeing his hands.

It was time to strike. "You have no idea." Asha's voice dropped as she shot her dagger into the throat of one of the supremacists.

"What the fu—" another started to say, but before he could finish, Asha shot a fireball into his face.

She drew her sword and rushed over to jam it into the chest of her inflamed opponent.

The remaining three rushed to attack her. One swung her sword, which Asha managed to block, but the force knocked her off her feet. Her attacker jabbed at Asha, but at the last moment, Asha shot another fireball, hitting her opponent in the chest. Asha didn't see where she went next, but she heard her screams.

Asha looked to her right and saw the flaming hut. She rolled toward it and jumped to her feet.

The final two supremacists rushed Asha, but before they could reach her, Asha took control of some fire from the hut and brought it down on one of the attackers, nearly disintegrating his body. The ground shook as the explosion echoed through the trees, knocking both Asha and the final supremacist off their feet. Both dropped their weapons.

The spell took energy and cost Asha precious seconds. Her opponent got to his feet faster than she did. She tried to throw a spell at him, but he managed to duck just in time. He drew a knife from his boot and stormed her. An attempt to get to her feet was interrupted by a kick to the torso.

The flames reflected off the man's knife as he stabbed it down at her heart. She managed to grab his wrist before the blade could penetrate. With all her strength, she tried to halt the man's advance. But she couldn't compete with his brute force as the point of the knife descended on her chest.

Fortunately, she still had one advantage. Her hands were gripping his wrists, so she raised the temperature of her hands as high as she could. The man's skin boiled as he screamed before dropping his knife. Without skipping a beat, Asha grabbed his dagger and shot it into his chest. *Thud.*

Asha lay her head on the ground for a moment, thankful to be alive. She gripped her side. "That's going to leave a bruise."

When she could get her bearings, Asha noticed that the supremacist she'd set ablaze earlier was rolling on the ground, trying to put out the fire engulfing her. Asha looked at where the three elven children had been, but they were gone. Asha smiled as she retrieved Jessara's dagger and sword. The third supremacist now lay still on the ground. The fire was out, but she was too injured to move.

"Help." The supremacist reached her hand out to Asha. Asha walked to her and inspected her wounds. Her burns had blackened most of her skin; she wasn't long for this world.

"I'm going to show you something that you refused to show the innocent people you murdered today. Mercy." Asha knelt next to the supremacist and shoved the dagger into her throat. The supremacist coughed up blood as her eyes went from shocked to still.

"By the soul!" Asha turned to see Tya emerging from the trees and running toward her, the three elven children close behind. "You're a sorceress!"

"Please." Asha felt her heart pound as the adrenaline of the fight wore off. "Tell no one."

Tya nodded. "You have my word."

"Ours too, milady." The eldest of the elven children took a step forward. He wore a basic white linen tunic with brown trousers, and she guessed that he was seventeen or eighteen. His dirty blonde hair was short and feathered, and his green eyes were deep and earnest. His tan skin and muscular body made it clear he was no stranger to hard outdoor work.

"Thank you," Asha said, and put her hands on her knees to catch her breath.

"But how?" Tya looked at the corpses, then back at Asha. "You're human."

"Long story." Asha glanced at the two elven bodies with a frown. "Your parents?"

"Aye." The middle child appeared to be about twelve or thirteen. Her hair, skin, and eyes were the same color as her older brother's. The girl's petite frame was adorned by a brown wool dress with white-stitched flower designs. Tears pooled in her green eyes. "Da stood up to them. They killed him. Ma tried to stop it, but they killed her, too."

"What'll happen to us now?" The youngest couldn't have been older than five. His hair was the same color as his siblings, but unlike them, his eyes were sky blue. His clothing was basic and humble like his brother's. Tears streamed down cheeks that hadn't yet lost their infant puffiness.

Asha walked over to the youngest and knelt down to eye level with the boy. "What's your name, child?"

"Ivir."

"Your brother and sister?"

"Heptor and Vitra."

Asha put her hand on the child's shoulder. "Well, Ivir, I'm Asha. I know a place where you, Vitra, and Heptor can all be safe."

"The monastery." Tya opened her arms as if offering an embrace. "We'd be happy to take you in."

"You and Kreatia been trying to get us to come there for years, Tya." Heptor maintained his composure, but Asha knew he was only doing so for the sake of his siblings. She understood what he was going through better than anyone else probably could. Heptor looked at his brother and sister. "Don't know how safe we'd be on our own, so we accept. Speaking of which, the supremacists mentioned they killed another elf nearby. Kreatia?"

"Yes." Tya looked at the ground.

"I'm so sorry." Heptor bowed his head.

"We know what she meant to you." Vitra gave Tya a hug. "She was family to us too."

Tya glanced at the bodies of the elven parents. "We've all had losses today."

"I don't know how we can ever repay you," said Heptor.

Tya held out her hand. "You know we don't believe in debts."

Asha felt for the children, and she wanted to make sure they were safe. But there was another whose safety she needed to guarantee. "There is one thing you can do to help us."

"Anything, milady." Heptor forced a painful smile.

"There's a woman at the monastery." Asha prayed to the Tree it wasn't too late. "An elf. She's unwell and will die without treatment. I know this may sound strange, but we need a little bit of blood from an elf to save her."

Heptor looked between Asha and Tya. "Kreatia told us about this treatment. This woman means something to you, yes?"

"She does." *The understatement of the century.*

"Then I'll gladly let her have some of me blood." Heptor bowed his head again. "I hope we can save her."

Asha sighed with relief. "Thank you. I suppose we should get underway."

"Ma and Da." Ivir looked at the corpses of the two elves.

"And Kreatia," said Tya.

Vitra pointed to the burning shack. "We've a wagon behind our house we use to transport crops."

"We'll take the...the bodies to the monastery," said Heptor.

Tya gave a slow, sad nod. "It'll be a long trek, but they need a proper burial."

With that, the group pulled the wagon to the bodies of the elven parents so Tya and Asha could gently place them onto it. The man had dirty blonde hair like the children and the woman had brown hair. Their faces were too bloody to discern any major features. Asha normally tried not to take pleasure in killing, but she was glad she'd killed the human supremacists.

The group journeyed down the road and retrieved Kreatia's body as well. A somber silence filled the air as the group marched through the woods in the direction of the monastery.

It grew dark, and Ivir started to have trouble walking, so Asha offered to carry him because he was afraid of the bodies on the wagon. She had empathy for the three children. Asha was only a little older than Vitra and a little younger than Heptor when she had lost her own parents. The bodies of their parents looked to be the age of her mothers when they'd been killed. She had flashbacks to her birth mother being stabbed and her spirit mother being hanged.

Asha desperately wanted to talk to someone about how she felt, but she didn't want to burden the others. The children had just lost their parents, and Tya had lost her partner. She thought about Jessara and how much she wanted to be held by her right now. Worries returned once again. She thought about Tya's grief, and tried to imagine how she'd feel if she lost Jessara. Despite their quarrel, the thought of being without Jessara made her feel empty. And were they already too late? What if they arrived at the monastery, and Jessara had already passed? What if the treatment didn't work? Icy fingers clawed at her heart.

Ivir noticed. "Are you okay?"

"Of course." Asha relaxed the muscles in her face and tried to smile.

Ivir gave her a curious look. "You worried about your friend?"

Asha gently smiled at the child. "Aren't you clever?"

"I hope we help her."

"Me too."

Asha loved children. She spent a lot of time with the children at the temple, and she'd always wanted to have her own. Asha wondered what Jessara's feelings were on the subject. This caused her thoughts to return to Farnsville, and the mission she'd been on before she'd met Jessara—the mission Jessara still didn't know about.

It was the dead of night when the group reached the monastery. Braun sat on the front steps, waiting, and as soon as he saw them, he hurried toward them.

"Thank the soul you're back!" Braun's smile died when he noticed the wagon. "What happened?"

"Human supremacists." Tya walked up to embrace him.

"Sister Kreatia." Braun looked at the bodies of the two other elves, and then spoke to Heptor. "Your parents?"

Heptor nodded. "Aye. We've nowhere else to go. They burned our home."

"I'm sorry, lad." Braun motioned to the doors. "You're welcome here as long as you like."

"Thank you for your kindness, master monk." Heptor gave an appreciative bow. "I also heard you need the blood of an elf?"

"How's Jessara?" Asha's voice shook, fearing the answer.

"Her condition has worsened." Braun's face grew grim. "She's still with us, but I fear that the amount of blood we can safely extract from one elf won't be enough."

Vitra stepped forward. "How about two?"

"You're a but child," said Braun. "It'll be dangerous for you."

Vitra scowled at that. "I'm no child."

Braun shook his head. "I've never taken blood from one so young."

"You said this woman will die without it. Please, I can do this."

Braun looked at the young elf for several moments, pondering her words. "Very well, lass. But I'll take less from you." He turned to Asha. "This means that if Jessara survives the procedure, she'll need time to recover."

Asha didn't like the use of the word "if", but she knew Braun was just trying to be honest. "When can we start?"

"I know you've all had a trying day," said Braun, "but we need to perform the treatment as soon as possible, if there's any hope it'll work."

"No trouble, master monk." Heptor turned to Tya. "Take Ivir to bed. We'll be along shortly."

Tya gently took Ivir's hand. "Let's get you to bed, child." She led the boy into the monastery.

"Come with me." Braun, Asha, Heptor, and Vitra passed through the same door, but turned to the left instead of the right. "I have all the equipment set up. Asha, you should try to get some sleep."

Asha gave him a look, and he rolled his eyes.

"I did say 'should.' But I know you won't, so come with us." With that, Braun led them to Jessara's room.

The walk through the hallway was a blur. Asha felt so anxious that the rest of the world slipped away. The door to Jessara's room stood before her, and she couldn't even remember entering the monastery.

"Listen, lass." Braun led the rest of the group into Jessara's room. "Before we start this, you need to know that although this treatment is effective, I can't make guarantees. She could be too far gone already. Also, sometimes even if we match the correct race, the body rejects the blood and the patient dies. We must also drain some of her own blood in order to replace it. This will limit her body's ability to function even more, and it could kill her. I will do all I can, but you must prepare yourself for the worst."

Asha was not prepared for the worst, but she knew this was the only chance to prevent it. "I understand. Do the treatment."

Braun produced two large cylindrical devices with narrow glass tubes and a sharp end. He also produced a jar of some sort of mushy liquid.

"What's that?" Asha pointed to the cylindrical device.

"An extractor. We use it to remove and transfer the blood." Braun took the jar of the mushy liquid, and poured it into a small opening on one of the cylindrical devices.

Asha had a puzzled look on her face as he worked.

Braun looked up at her. "The mashed up salivary glands of leeches. It prevents the blood from coagulating." He handed her a piece of cloth. "Can you please tie this around the top of her arm?"

Asha complied.

Braun took the extractor that he hadn't poured the glands into and stuck the sharp end into Jessara's arm. He pulled back on a small handle at the top of the device, and it filled with blood. The device had room for at least four pints.

Braun filled the extractor for several minutes. When it reached around three pints, he stopped, set down the extractor, and felt Jessara's pulse. "Lass is still with us. But she's slipping. He picked up the extractor with the glands inside.

He pointed to Heptor and handed Asha another piece of cloth. "Same with him."

Again, Asha complied.

Braun took Heptor's arm. "Please have a seat, lad. This will pinch."

Braun took the extractor and stuck Heptor. The cylinder began to fill up. "You might feel a little lightheaded. That's normal."

Asha watched with curiosity. The operation was unfamiliar to her, and if it weren't a matter of life and death, she'd be asking more questions.

Braun worked for several more minutes. When the device reached about two pints, Braun took the glass out of Heptor, and handed him another cloth. "Put some pressure on that. Now you, young lass." Braun turned to Vitra and repeated the same process, filling the extractor with another pint of blood.

As Braun worked, Tya entered the room and told them she'd put Ivir to bed.

After Braun pulled the extractor out of Vitra, he checked Jessara's pulse again. He nodded and turned to Asha. "I'm going to put the blood in her now. As she's replenished, she'll likely regain consciousness. Her surroundings may cause her stress, but it's important for her to remain calm. Sister Tya, please escort our young elves to their room."

"Yes, Brother Braun."

Braun turned to the children. "You'll need to rest, and eat and drink well for the next several days as your blood replenishes."

"Aye, master monk," said Heptor.

"Thank you." Asha considered hugging the children, but she didn't want to leave Jessara's side.

The young elves nodded and followed Tya out of the room.

Braun turned to Asha. "I'll need your help keeping her calm."

Asha nodded.

Braun took another cloth and tied it around Jessara's arm. Slowly, he stuck the extractor into her. Her body twitched, but she remained unconscious. Very carefully, he pushed down the handle of the extractor, and it started to empty. After several moments, Jessara blinked. As she slowly regained consciousness, she breathed heavily and look around the room.

"Jessara," said Braun. "It's okay, you're safe. Hold still."

"What the fuck are you doing to me?! Where's Asha!" Jessara frantically looked around the room.

Asha grabbed her hand. "Jessara!" She used her other hand to move Jessara's head to look at her. "It's me. I'm here."

Jessara stared at her with wide eyes. "Asha?" She finally recognized her.

"Yes. I'm here."

Tears streamed down Jessara's cheeks. "I'm sorry. I'm so sorry."

"Hey." Asha teared up as well. "Don't worry about that right now."

"I'm so sorry. I love you." Jessara coughed as she cried. Her body started shaking.

"I love you too." Asha put her hand on Jessara's chest, trying to calm her down. "It's okay!"

"Jessara." Braun struggled to keep the extractor straight. "You need to remain calm."

"Jessara, listen to him." Asha wiped away tears. "You must stay calm."

"Asha, I'm so sorry!" Jessara continued to shake.

"She's going to break the extractor!" Braun used his head to motion to the door. "You need to get out, lass! You're distressing her!"

Asha looked at Braun. She didn't want to leave, but she nodded and ran out of the room as Jessara cried out deliriously. Outside the door, Asha sat against the wall and waited. Tears soaked her face as she wept. She kept looking at the door, hoping to see Braun. Once again, guilt riddled her. Their conflict had destroyed Asha's ability to be with Jessara in her time of need. Another half hour passed, and Braun finally exited the room.

Asha immediately stood up. "How is she?" She held her breath.

"The procedure seems to have been a success." Braun smiled. "The smoke still infects some of her blood, but she'll survive."

Asha smiled and hugged Braun. "Thank you. Thank you so much." After fearing for Jessara's life for so long, she could hardly believe it was true. She could finally talk to Jessara and apologize for everything.

"For the next several days, she will need to rest as her blood continues to heal."

"I'd like to stay with her."

Braun gave her a sad smile. "I know, lass, but it's not what Jessara needs right now. She needs undisturbed rest. It's clear that you both have unresolved emotions. I'm sorry, but I must ask that you avoid this room for the time being. She's not ready to face whatever problem you're having. She needs to focus on her health."

Asha frowned. That was not what she wanted to hear. She looked at the door and wanted nothing more than to go inside. To see the woman she loved. But she had to do what was best for Jessara. "That's what she needs?"

Braun nodded. "For now. I'll tell you as soon as you can see her."

The news was bittersweet, but at least Jessara was alive. Asha could take comfort in that. "All right. I suppose I'll retire."

"I trust you know the way to your quarters?"

"I remember." Then Asha went back to her room, alone.

CHAPTER THIRTY-TWO

THE MEMORIAL

Every muscle in Asha's body was sore when she awoke the next day. She hadn't completely recovered from her run-in with the Red Daggers, and yesterday's adventure hadn't helped. As she predicted, a massive bruise decorated the side of her body where she'd been kicked.

It wasn't clear what would be on her agenda today, but she wouldn't figure that out in her room, so she got dressed and exited her quarters.

The smell of cooking meat made her realize how hungry she was. All she'd had to eat the previous day was a little bread.

The smell led her to a large room on the lower level of the monastery. About a dozen monks, of different ages and similar garb, sat at tables on oak wood benches. In front of them were plates of cooked venison and fresh tomatoes. When she entered, they fell silent. She smiled awkwardly. So far, the only two monks she'd talked to were Braun and Tya, and neither of them were present. She hadn't ignored the rest on purpose; she was just too focused on saving Jessara.

Asha decided to break the silence. "Do I have something in my teeth?"

The monks laughed.

"Asha, right?" One monk close to her age beckoned her with a smile. He moved over and patted an empty place on his bench. "Please, join us."

"Thank you." Asha sat down.

"Hungry?" The monk's voice was gentle and welcoming. His light brown hair was short and well brushed, and his hazel eyes reflected sincerity.

Asha nodded faster than normal. "Very."

"Hey, Rody!" He waved over to the monk in an apron. "Get a plate for the lady."

"Coming right up." Rody was plump, elderly, and sporting a full gray beard with long gray locks.

The monk turned back to Asha. "I'm Chez." He motioned to the three other monks sitting at the table. "This is Brand, Lila, and Braida."

"Pleasure to meet you all." Asha loved meeting new people, especially when they greeted her with friendly faces.

Braida leaned in and struck an empathetic tone that reminded Asha of Anea. "I'm sorry about all you've been through, dear."

Rody brought Asha a plate of venison which she wasted no time digging into.

"You must be famished." Braida was an elderly woman with hair as white as snow. Her rough-looking skin was heavily wrinkled, and her brown eyes were cloudy. Wisdom radiated from her demeanor with every word she spoke.

Asha barely slowed down eating to respond. "It's been a rough week." Under normal circumstances, she exercised more table decorum, but she figured the monks would understand.

"I bet," said Chez.

Asha looked around the mess hall. "Where are Tya and Braun?"

Brand laughed. "Our company not good enough for you?" He was a teenager with curly red hair, freckles, bright blue eyes, and a gangly frame, which neither his voice or bones seemed to have grown into yet. The smirk on his face told Asha that nobody enjoyed his sense of humor more than himself.

Asha smiled. "Your company is lovely."

Lila waved her hand dismissively. "He's just messing with you. He's a bit of an ass." Lila had shining black hair, blue eyes, and a delicate face. She was close to Asha's age and a little on the plump side. A pleasant rose smell wafted from the woman, and Asha had to admit that she found her quite attractive.

Brand smirked at Lila, then turned his attention back to Asha. "Brother Braun is with that elf friend of yours."

Asha hesitated. "Any news?"

"He told me this morning that she seemed to be doing better," said Lila. "She's speaking coherent sentences, but she still needs her rest."

Asha was relieved. "And Tya?"

Chez frowned and glanced at the exit of the mess hall. "Sister Tya hasn't left her room since she got back. She's in mourning."

"Poor dear." Braida held her head down. "She was very close to Sister Kreatia."

"Poor Kreatia." Lila frowned. "Kind-hearted, that one."

Asha lowered her eyes as she remembered finding the young woman's body. "I wish I'd gotten to meet her."

"We'll be holding a memorial service for her and those two elves today," said Chez.

That caught Asha's attention. She didn't blame herself for what happened, but she did feel a sense of responsibility. If the monks were holding a service, she wanted to attend. "When?"

"After breakfast, a few of us are gonna head out to dig the graves." Brand took a bite from his food and continued speaking with a full mouth. "It'll be after that."

"I'd like to help the digging." After all they'd done for her and Jessara, Asha wanted to return the favor in some way—however small.

Braida shook her head. "You're a guest, dear. We can't ask that of you."

Asha smiled politely. "You don't have to."

Chez gave her a welcoming nod. "You're more than welcome to join us, friend."

Asha continued to eat and talk with her new acquaintances. As someone that drew energy from interacting with others, the conversation was refreshing and rejuvenating. The monks reminded her of the Sisterhood in some ways. They interacted like a family and seemed to genuinely care for each other.

After she and the monks finished eating, they led her outside. A graveyard stood next to the monastery with several burial mounds marked by narrow slabs of cedar. Names were carved in white on each slab, some of which were eroded by time.

Asha followed the other monks to an undisturbed part of the graveyard. Sticks on the ground laid out the perimeters of three graves. The monks distributed shovels and started to dig. As soon as Asha got hers, she assisted. As sore as she was, the manual labor helped take her mind off the tragedies and hardships of the last few days. Her burdens weighed on her psyche like rubble.

After a few minutes of digging, Vitra exited the monastery and approached the site. She walked slowly and held out her arms to balance herself.

As soon as she was in earshot, Asha greeted her. "Vitra, hey. How are you feeling?"

"Lightheaded, but I've got to be outside." Vitra sat on the ground next to her.

Asha paused in digging. "I wanted to offer my condolences again."

"Thanks." Vitra's answer was as cold as winter.

It was a tone Asha recognized. She'd had the same tone after her mothers had been killed. "How are your brothers?"

"Heptor's resting. Ivir's trying to keep himself busy by caring for him."

Asha imagined the little child tending to his older brother. The image almost put a smile on her face, but she knew such an expression was inappropriate at a time like this. She turned to Vitra. "I know what it means to lose parents. I lost both of mine when I was only a little older than you."

Vitra sighed. "I appreciate what you're trying to do, but I don't know how that's supposed to make me feel better."

Asha shrugged. "Maybe it won't. But sometimes it helps to not feel alone."

Vitra glanced at the graves being dug. "Wish I was alone in this. Nobody should lose their folks."

"No. Unfortunately, what people deserve rarely matters."

Vitra's eyes filled with rage. "Why'd they do it? What'd we do to them?"

Asha gazed into the woods. She'd spent countless hours comforting recently orphaned children at the temple. Sisters who carried out retrieval missions did what they could to limit bloodshed, but they weren't always successful. It was not unusual for parents to be killed. Between the war, bandits, Red Daggers, and harsh laws, orphans were far too common in this world.

Asha continued to face the forest. "Some people define themselves by their hatred. It makes them see enemies in good people."

Vitra's brow furrowed. "I hate the people that did this. Am I defined by hatred?"

Asha shook her head. "They were humans. I'm a human. Do you hate me?"

"No."

"Then no."

"So, hatred's okay?"

"People say hatred is the root of all evil. It's not. Some people deserve to be hated. What matters is the why. Do you hate people for the race they were born as? Where they're from? What they look like? Or do you hate them because of the vile choices they've made? There's nothing wrong with the latter." Asha couldn't take credit for that piece of wisdom. It was something her spirit mother used to tell her.

"I'll try to remember that."

Silence filled the space between Vitra and Asha for several more moments. Asha decided that if Vitra wanted to talk more, she would. In the meantime, Asha continued digging.

With all the monks working together, it didn't take long before the graves were deep enough. The group struggled a bit once it reached the clay layer, but they didn't dig much farther than that. When they were close to finishing, Vitra went inside to get her brothers.

The wagon containing the bodies was pulled to the gravesites. When it got closer, Asha noticed that the monks had wrapped the bodies in linen cloth. One by one, the bodies were carried by the monks and placed in the graves. At that moment, Braun and Tya exited the monastery. A few minutes later, Vitra, Ivir, and Heptor joined them as well.

It was a bright, sunny day. The monks had gathered several arrangements of lilies, and their sweet smell filled Asha's senses. The beauty of the forest created a stark contrast to the sorrow in the air from the assembled mourners.

Braun stepped behind the graves to address the group. "Long ago, the creator gods made this realm of existence for the soul we all share. Tello, the father, created the sky, that we all have something to reach for. Drema, the mother, created the land and water, that we all have ground beneath our feet. Narde, the spirit, created life, that we all may know the beauty of existence. With life came the everlasting soul we all share. For some, this life is long. For some, it is short. Today, we gather to celebrate the life of Sister Kreatia, as well as the lives of two friends of our monastery, Heptia and Ino. They were victims of prejudice and racism. These ideals reject all notions of logic and wisdom in favor of hatred and spite. The people that committed this crime committed it against themselves as well.

"I understand that not all of those present agree with the beliefs of our church. However, I do hope we can agree that this hatred is damaging both to the soul of the individual and to all those they hurt. We can take comfort in knowing that our departed are entering the next stage of their soul's journey. Although we may not see them again in their current forms, we can always visit them in our memories. Would anyone else like to say a few words?"

Asha's jaw hurt from her teeth clenching. Although she didn't know the two elves, she'd spent time around their children—big-hearted children who had jumped at the chance to save Jessara. Whoever Heptia and Ino had been, they must have been good parents.

Heptor stepped forward. "I speak for meself as well as for me sister and brother. Our ma and da were good people. They taught us the value of a hard day's work. They taught us how to farm and care for the animals. I can't believe that yesterday I ate breakfast with them, with no idea that it'd be the last. I don't know about this everlasting soul business, but you folks have always been good to our family. Me folks spoke highly of you. Thank you for taking us in."

"Thank you, lad." Braun embraced the young man. "Would anyone else like to say a few words?"

Tya shyly stepped forward.

Braun beckoned her to the front of the crowd. "Please, lass."

Tya stood before them, her eyes as red as her hair. "I love all of the folks at this monastery. I try to love all those I come across because that is what we're supposed to do. I'm even trying to love the monsters that took my girl away from me. But I've never loved anyone the way I loved Kreatia." Tya paused for a second, trying to catch her breath. "We'd known each other since we were little girls, and we had never spent more than a few days apart since the day we met." Tya paused again. "She was kind. She was loving. She was the best partner a girl could ever ask for. And she didn't deserve this!" Tya grew enraged and started to break down. "I'm sorry. I can't do this!" She ran back to the monastery, and Asha followed her. Tya stormed into her room and slammed the door. Asha approached and heard Tya weeping on the other side. She gently knocked.

"Who is it?"

Asha cracked it open. "It's only me. Do you want to be alone?"

Tya sat on the floor of her room with her back against the wall. "I don't." Like the other rooms Asha had seen in the monastery, Tya's had a bed, a desk, and a stained-glass window. After entering, Asha sat on the floor with her back against the wall opposite Tya.

"I wouldn't want to be alone right now." Asha tried to be as gentle as possible as she spoke to the poor girl.

Tya picked up a rag and wiped her face. "Thank you." Her eyes were swollen and somewhat crusted.

Asha paused for a moment. "Would you like to talk?"

Tya remained silent, and Asha waited for the young woman to speak. She knew the value of being present, even if it meant sitting in silence.

Eventually, Tya turned back to Asha. "When I first saw her, I thought that was the worst thing I could ever feel. Now I'm back here, it seems like I'm supposed to slowly feel better, but every moment just gets harder."

Asha nodded slowly as she thought about her own grieving process. "It was shocking to you. The more time you've had to think about it, the more it hurts."

"I've never lost anyone close to me. My parents died when I was too young to remember them." Tya looked up at Asha. "How long did it take for your parents' deaths to stop hurting?"

Asha choked up. "It never stopped. Not a day goes by that I don't think of them. Sometimes, I start to feel like I'm moving on, that I've cried my last tear. Then something will happen, and I'll feel almost as bad as the day they died. Like yesterday. Seeing the kids lose their parents reminded me of what it was like."

Tya gave a defeated look. "Goodness me. Does it never gets better?"

Asha leaned forward. "The pain never goes away. You'll grieve less frequently as time goes on, but you'll never stop missing Kreatia. All you can do is learn to live with it, and eventually, you find joy in other things and other people."

Tya wiped her eyes with a cloth. "You know what the most painful part is? I'm only nineteen years old. I've known her all my life. But I'm young. I have a life ahead of me. And now, I have to spend it without Kreatia."

Tya began to cry again. Asha moved over to her and held her against her shoulder. Several minutes passed; Asha let the young woman weep as she held her. Asha gently rubbed Tya's back as she let everything out. The pain in Tya's heart was palpable, and Asha wished she could do or say something to make it go away. But she knew from experience that she couldn't. Tya's grief would have to run its course. But the young woman was brave and strong. Someday she'd be okay.

After a few minutes, Tya stopped crying and caught her breath as her head remained buried in Asha's shoulder. After another few minutes, Tya pulled away and nodded her head. "Thank you so much for coming in. You've been a good friend in the time I've known you."

"As have you." Asha could feel a wet spot on her shoulder.

"I think I want to be alone right now though, if that's okay."

"Of course." Asha got up. "If you need to talk, you know where to find me." Asha opened the door and went to exit, but she stopped herself. "Before I go, is it okay if I ask you a personal question?"

Tya nodded.

"If you knew that this would happen." Asha took a deep breath. "Would you have still wanted a relationship with Kreatia?"

"Of course." Tya had no hesitation.

"Why?"

Tya looked up at her with drying eyes. "Because I wouldn't want to waste a second of the time I *did* have with her."

Asha nodded. "Thank you." And she walked out of the room.

Chapter Thirty-Three

Love Rekindled

Another two days passed at the monastery. Asha was regularly updated by Braun as to Jessara's condition. She was gradually improving, but Asha was still instructed to leave her to rest and replenish.

"She's past the worst of it," said Braun, after the first day. Asha was thrilled to hear this, but she desperately wanted to see Jessara. Much had happened since their quarrel. After her conversation with Tya, Asha had made up her mind about what she wanted.

Asha tried to keep herself busy at the monastery. These monks had a foreign lifestyle to her, but she respected it. After eating breakfast, they attended a short service delivered by Braun. Usually, he talked about the need to be good to people because each person is either the past or the future. Asha found the services interesting and began to understand their beliefs. She didn't agree, but she understood.

For the monks, most of the day was spent doing separate tasks based on their interests. The monastery had a library, a laboratory, and even an archery range. Considering how peaceful the monks were, the archery range surprised Asha. However, some of the them had to be hunters in order to feed the monastery. They considered the bows and arrows tools, not weapons.

In the late afternoon, they spent an hour of meditation in their rooms before working in the garden in the evening. Botany wasn't one of Asha's skills, but she tried to assist the monks any way she could.

Tya was finally coming out of her room for meals, but she didn't talk to anyone. Asha visited her when she could, and Tya seemed to appreciate the company. A sisterly affection developed between Asha and Tya. The young woman's beliefs were shaken by her experience, but she hadn't lost her gentle demeanor. A few times, she attempted to ask Asha questions about being a sorceress—all of which were deflected.

Heptor, Vitra, and Ivir settled into their new lives at the monastery. Heptor started helping in the laboratory. He had impressive knowledge regarding herbs and mixtures considering his age. When Vitra recovered, she joined the hunting group. Asha watched her practice on the range several times, and in some ways, the young elf reminded her of Jessara. Ivir helped out in the library. He couldn't read yet, but he enjoyed stacking books. To Asha's surprise, none of the monks forced their beliefs on the children. They weren't required to attend services or to involve themselves in any of the rituals.

With each passing day, Asha grew more restless from her separation with Jessara, although she dreaded their next conversation. Asha had figured out what she wanted, but after their quarrel, she had no idea what *Jessara* wanted.

Toward the middle of the second day, Braun finally approached Asha while she was in her room reading a romance novel about an elf and a human she'd gotten from the monastery library. She'd been a bit surprised to find such content at a monastery, but it turned out the Church of the Everlasting Soul had a much more open approach to the issue of sexuality than other doctrines. While the Church of the Creator Gods condemned things like promiscuity and interracial relationships, these monks had no such qualms.

After a light knock, Braun cracked open the door to Asha's room. "Jessara is doing very well. I have no doubt now that she'll make a full recovery. She'll need to take things slow, and I'd recommend she stay with us for a few more days. But I think that she's well enough for you to see her."

Asha immediately leapt up and hugged Braun. "I'll never be able to thank you enough."

"Not necessary, lass. Come."

Asha's heart pounded against her chest as they approached Jessara's room. Braun opened the door, and Asha saw Jessara sitting up in her bed. She looked much better—at least better than she had when she'd been close to death.

As soon as the door opened, Jessara turned toward Asha and their eyes met. Jessara's eyebrows raised, and she smiled. However, it was a smile with pain behind it. "Asha!" She still sounded frail.

Asha moved into the room. "I'm here."

"I'll leave you two." Braun gave a bow and left the women alone.

Asha pulled a chair next to Jessara's bed. She reached out her hand to Jessara's, scared that she wouldn't take it. But Jessara slowly moved her hand and held Asha's, and both smiled at their clasped hands. Jessara looked as beautiful as ever. It took no small amount of restraint to keep from grabbing and holding Jessara as tightly as she could, but too much needed to be said first.

Jessara finally broke the long silence. "Well, this is becoming a habit."

They both laughed.

Asha immediately felt her nerves calm down. She was still anxious, but if Jessara was making jokes, that was a good sign.

Asha squeezed her hand. "I'm so sorry. I never should've left you."

Jessara's face softened. "I never should have said such terrible things."

"We both did."

Jessara squeezed Asha's hand. "Every day since the moment we met, I thank the Creos I didn't take that shot."

"And I thank the Tree for every moment we've had since."

They spent another moment just looking at each other. Asha studied every aspect of Jessara's face, from her green eyes to the dimples in her cheeks to the creases of her forehead—the face she'd been terrified she'd never see again. She looked at Jessara's pink lips and desperately wanted to kiss them.

Jessara held her head down for a moment. "I spent so much time thinking about what I wanted to say to you."

"Same." Asha let herself smile. "What did you come up with?"

"I don't know how to say it."

"Let me try." Asha was the one that broke their relationship, and she believed it was her responsibility to try to fix it. "I'm terrified of what the future holds. I'm terrified of what happens when we reach Enderdale. I'm terrified of getting my heart broken. But most of all, I'm terrified of losing you. I made a friend here that recently lost her own partner. I was there when she discovered the body. The pain in her eyes was too horrible to describe. She'd just lost the woman she cared for most in this world. It forced me to think about what would happen if we hadn't been able to save you. The fact that you and I had broken apart didn't make that feeling better; it made it worse. It meant that I'd wasted the precious time I had with you.

"I'm still bloody terrified of the future. I'm terrified that my life will end on the gallows. But right now, we're in the present. This present. And right now, we can be together. I want that more than anything. I want to be with you for as long as we can be. Whether it's only a few days, a few weeks, or the rest of our lives, I want us to be together—if you'll have me back."

Jessara smiled, her eyes filling. "That's all I want. That's all I've wanted since that night on your balcony. I know you're afraid of the future. I am too. But I swear to you on the Creos that I will make sure my future involves you. I swear that no matter what, I'll always come for you. I don't know how I'll keep those promises, but as long as I draw breath, I will. Will you believe me?"

"I believe you." Asha smiled as she looked deeply into those piercing green eyes. "And if the only way to protect my family and stay with you is to work with you on contracts, then I'm willing to do it."

"And I'll never make you do a contract you don't want to do."

***

During their conversation, Jessara never stopped holding Asha's hand. Asha pulled Jessara's hand to her lips and kissed it. Her lips were soft on Jessara's skin, and she'd dearly missed them. Jessara pulled her in and put her hand on those warm, soft cheeks. Their mouths moved closer as they closed their eyes and their lips touched. Asha wrapped her arms around Jessara and pressed their bodies together. Her familiar lips and tongue welcomed her home. Jessara pulled her lips away and opened her eyes so she could see her beautiful lover again.

Asha looked longingly at her. "I love you."

"I love you too."

They continued kissing. Jessara had been lonely ever since she'd arrived at the monastery. Most of her interactions had been with strangers, and she had missed Asha even more intensely. Braun had told her that she couldn't see Asha until she'd improved significantly, and that motivated her to push on.

Now, Jessara was at home in the embrace of Asha. She was content. Which is why she was so annoyed when she heard the door swing open.

Asha pulled away and sat back in her chair.

They both turned to see Braun entering. "Oh darn. I hope I'm not interrupting anything, lasses."

Jessara laughed under her breath. "Nothing at all." *Thank you for saving me, but please fuck off.*

"I'd like to try to get you on your feet, Jessara. You think you can try to walk?"

As much as Jessara wanted to be back in Asha's embrace kissing her, she knew it was a good idea to move around. Jessara's head was clear from the treatment, but her body was still drowsy from having been in bed half a week. She tried to sit up, but it was a struggle.

Braun motioned to Jessara. "Asha, help her."

Asha grabbed Jessara's arm and pulled it over her shoulder. She helped her stand as Jessara put her feet on the ground. Even that was a struggle. Her dizziness reminded her of being drunk.

"Take it slow, lass." Braun beckoned them out into the hallway. "You need to adjust."

With Asha's help, Jessara was able to take a few steps toward the door. She stumbled, and Braun had to reach out to catch her. "Slow, I said."

Jessara stabilized herself, and with Asha's help, she was able to walk out of the room and down the hallway. Each step was easier than the previous. After they reached the end of the hallway, Braun nodded his head approvingly. "That's enough for today. Let's take her back to her room."

Asha looked over at Jessara and back at Braun. "Is it okay if she stays with me in my room?"

That was exactly what Jessara had hoped she'd say. There was much she wanted to catch up on, and she hoped they could have some private time to do so.

Braun smiled. "She still needs plenty of rest. But at this point, I see no reason why she can't stay with you."

The women smiled. Asha helped her into her room as Braun followed.

"Will you be joining us for dinner, Asha?" said Braun.

Asha helped Jessara lie in her bed. "I'd like to stay with Jessara for now. But thank you."

Again, exactly what Jessara had hoped she'd say.

"I'll have Chez bring you both some food. Have a lovely evening." Braun began to close the door.

Before it shut, Asha stopped him. "Hey, Braun. If anybody comes to the door, can you ask them to knock first?"

Because we might be fucking.

Braun smiled and laughed. "Of course."

Asha turned toward Jessara and grinned.

Finally, Jessara felt like she could relax as she lay her head against the pillow. "This feels strange."

Asha moved closer to her. "What?"

Jessara shrugged. "This is the longest I've ever been without wearing my armor."

Asha laughed. "You have trust issues, my love."

"Where's my gear?"

"Out back in the woodshed. They don't allow weapons in the monastery." Asha explained to Jessara the beliefs of the church. While she spoke, a monk whom Asha called Chez knocked on the door with plates of food for the two women. He then took his leave.

"Seems a little ridiculous to me." Jessara ate her food, which consisted of chicken, green beans, and baked potatoes. Each was perfectly cooked and well spiced, like all the meals she'd received so far in the monastery.

"Maybe." Asha nodded as she took a bite from her own plate. "But don't tell them that."

Jessara pondered for a moment. "It would really suck if we were all the same soul. I've killed a lot of people."

"It also means that I might be the King someday." Asha laughed.

Digs at the King still made Jessara uncomfortable, but she knew she'd have to get used to them. "It also sounds lonely. If we're all the same soul, then that means we'll always be alone."

Asha looked at Jessara thoughtfully. "I don't know if they view it that way."

"How else?"

"I don't know. I still don't completely understand it myself."

"So, they won't even kill in self-defense?"

Asha nodded. "That's what they said."

"At least they won't mess with my gear."

"Oh, yeah." Asha's eyes widened as her lips curled into a guilty smile. "Speaking of which, I may have borrowed your weapons. I hope that's okay."

If it were anybody else in Dremeria, Jessara might have been enraged. In fact, even if it had been Asha under different circumstances, she might still have been enraged. "Did you have to use them?"

"On some human supremacists."

Jessara gave a satisfied nod. "That's my girl."

Asha told Jessara the story of how she and Tya had saved the elven children. She talked about finding Kreatia's body, the burning hut, and the fight with the supremacists. While talking, they both finished their plates and set them to the side.

Asha had come a long way since they'd met, and Jessara was impressed. "Five all by yourself?"

"What? Is that surprising?" Asha almost sounded offended.

"Well, you're good." Jessara grinned and shook her head. "But you're not me."

Asha laughed. "You can't shoot fire out of your hands."

"You can't hold a bow to save your ass."

"For your information, I didn't hold a bow, and I still saved lots of asses, including yours."

Jessara chuckled, and then her expression softened. "In all seriousness, it is impressive. How's Tya holding up?"

Asha's face melded into a frown. "Seems better each day, but she'll be grieving for the rest of her life."

"And the children?"

"They're strong. They're settling in well with the monastery."

Jessara paused for a second. She'd never been good at understanding what others were feeling. It wasn't that she didn't care; she was just oblivious. But she'd spent enough time with Asha to be able to tell what she was sensitive about. "It must have been difficult for you, considering..."

"Yes." Asha nodded sadly. "The thought crossed my mind."

Jessara ran her hand gently down Asha's arm. "Want to talk about it?"

Asha thought for a moment. "I keep getting flashes of the bodies of my mothers. You know what the worst part has always been?"

"What?"

"There was absolutely nothing I could have done back then. Even if I'd tried."

Jessara adjusted herself in bed. "Some take comfort in that."

"Do you?"

Jessara glanced to the side. "No. Because if we were the people we are now, we could have saved them."

"Exactly. Except we still can't save everyone." Asha let out a sad sigh. "I never told you about the mission I was on before we met."

Jessara brought her eyes back to Asha's. It was something that Jessara had been curious about. The last secret between the two women, but she didn't want to push. "I figured you would when you were ready."

"I'm ready." Asha took a deep breath. "We detected another descendant in Kingdom territory—a young girl about six years old. She was in the town of Farnsville. I traveled there from Gatewatch, and I stopped in Turnhol on my way."

Jessara pictured a map of Dremeria in her head. "That's only a few miles from Enderdale."

Asha nodded. "It's rare that we venture so close to the capital city. I had a bad feeling from the start. When I got to the girl's house, the Red Daggers were already inside."

"Do you fight them often?"

"Sometimes on retrievals, but most of the time, I get there first and never even see the Daggers. Sometimes, I'll be too late, and they're long gone. I've fought them on the road before but rarely in town. Anyway, when I arrived, the Daggers had already killed the girl's father. She and her mother had barricaded themselves in a room on the top floor." Asha's eyes shone in the light.

"You don't need to continue if it's too much." Jessara caressed her lover's cheek.

Asha hesitated for a moment, but then shook her head. "No. No more secrets between us. I rushed in like I normally do and tried to fight off the Daggers. I tried not to use flames at first because we were inside the house. But without magic, you know I'm not much of a fighter. They almost killed me, so I began throwing spells at them. In the fight, the house caught fire. After the Daggers were dead, I tried to rush up to save the child and her mother." Asha paused. "They'd barricaded themselves too well. Before I could get the door open, the house collapsed. I was barely able to crawl out with my life. Afterwards, I managed to escape the town and get to Enderdale. You know the rest."

Silence emerged between the lovers for several seconds. Asha was clearly trying not to break down any more than she already had. But Jessara knew her well enough to know how hard this was for her. "Creos, I'm so sorry."

"When we first met, you would always tell me how bloody impulsive I was. That running head first into fights got people killed. The truth is, I already knew you were right. I'm the reason that girl is dead."

Jessara took both of Asha's hands and squeezed them firmly but gently. "It wasn't your fault."

"They were my flames, Jessara. I've failed before, and I usually move on with an immature sense of humor. I tried to do that, but this time it was my fault."

Some of what Asha had said or did in the days following their initial meeting suddenly made sense to Jessara. "That was why you were willing to learn from me."

Asha nodded. "I hoped you could help me not make the same mistake again."

Jessara's grip tightened around Asha's hands. "Asha, sometimes all the planning in Dremeria isn't enough. From what you told me, there wasn't much more you could have done given the circumstances. You did what you had to to survive."

Asha brought her eyes to meet Jessara's. "And I killed a bloody child in the process."

"If the Daggers had killed you, what would they have done to the child?"

Asha paused for a second. "We don't know what happens when they're taken. We assume they're killed."

"Your death would have accomplished nothing." Jessara leaned in closer to her. "More Daggers would be alive and murdering children. You wouldn't be alive to save them in the future. Also, you wouldn't have been alive to save those three elven children. Which by the way, you did with smart thinking and strategy."

Asha shrugged. "Only because of what you taught me."

"Which worked because you were willing to learn."

Asha was silent for a moment. "I suppose. Thank you for listening."

Jessara brought Asha's hands to her lips and kissed them. "Thank you for sharing."

"It's difficult losing a child. I've always loved children."

"I've never really spent time around them." Jessara chuckled. "Children hated me even when I was a child."

Asha hesitated. "Have you ever thought about having kids?"

Jessara laughed as she motioned to herself. "Have you met me?"

Asha did not laugh back. "I think you'd make a great mother."

Jessara paused for a second as she tried to figure out if Asha was serious. She didn't seem to have a sarcastic tone so she must have been. "I guess I never really thought about it. It was never in the cards for me anyway."

"What do you mean?"

Jessara realized that one more secret remained between them. "When I finished my assassin training, the King had me sterilized."

"Sterilized?"

"They gave me an infection. I don't know the science behind it, but I think they called the process treponemosis." Jessara trembled as she remembered the procedure. "The infection process was...degrading but it was quick. Afterwards, I was sick for a week. When I recovered, they told me I could no longer bear children."

"That's terrible!"

Jessara shrugged. Although the procedure itself was a painful memory, she never thought too much about the result. "The King said it was for my own good. That a child would be problematic to the job. I had no interest in children, and all I'd ever known had been training. I know how it sounds, but at the time, it really didn't matter to me."

Asha paused for a second, clearly wanting to say something.

"What is it?" said Jessara.

Asha gave her a sad smile. "You still could. Have children that is. With me."

Jessara lowered her eyebrows for a bit, confused. Then she remembered what she'd been told at the temple.

"The spirit bond?"

"Yes."

"You would want to do that with me?"

"Maybe someday. Could you see yourself doing that with me?"

"I don't know." Jessara genuinely didn't. "Like I said, it's not something I've ever thought about. It's not something I ever planned."

This time it was Asha who brought Jessara's hands to her lips. "Did you ever plan on falling in love with a mark?"

Jessara chuckled. "I guess plans change." At first the idea seemed silly to her. But if there ever were someone that she'd consider such a thing with, it would be Asha.

Asha leaned in close and kissed Jessara. They both giggled as their lips pressed against each other. Asha wrapped her arms around her lover and brought their bodies together. Jessara saw desire in Asha's eyes, which made her realize she was getting wet.

Asha ran her hand across Jessara's chest. "I want to make love to you."

"I can't do much."

"I'll do everything. I want to take care of you."

"I'm all yours."

Asha stood up, removed her dress, and got back on top of Jessara. The sweet smell of lavender wafted into Jessara's senses. Asha pressed their bodies together as she pulled Jessara's mouth toward hers. Jessara ran her hands across Asha's chest and felt her warm, soft skin. They hadn't made love since they'd left Coshgromar. After everything they'd been through, it was long overdue.

Asha removed Jessara's shirt and trousers, and pulled off her undergarments and breast band. She ran her tongue against her lover's breasts as Jessara let out a breath of desire. The rough ridges from Asha's tongue made her nipples hard. She arched her back, desperate for intimacy.

After all the time they'd spent apart, it was ecstasy to feel the warmth of Asha against her skin once again. Asha slowly removed her own undergarments and breast band. Jessara wrapped her arm around Asha's body and pulled her beautiful perfect breasts to her mouth.

"I missed you so much," said Jessara, as she licked Asha's nipples.

"I missed you. I definitely missed this." Asha brought her mouth down and kissed Jessara's lips. They ran their tongues together. Jessara pulled her body in closer, wishing they could meld together. She'd finally gotten the woman she loved back, and she never wanted to let her go.

Asha pulled away and looked into Jessara's eyes. "May I taste you?"

"Like I said." Jessara lay back on her pillow and opened her legs. "I'm all yours."

Asha smiled and slowly kissed down Jessara's body. Each time Jessara felt Asha's lips against her skin, it sent shivers down her spine. A pulsing throbbed between her legs as Asha got closer and closer to exactly where Jessara wanted her.

Asha kissed down Jessara's abdomen, and finally, pressed her tongue against Jessara's clit. As soon as she felt that beautiful sensation, she forgot about everything else. "I love you."

"I love you." Asha slid fingers inside of Jessara and began moving in and out of her. The gradual start was what Jessara needed. She needed tenderness from her lover, and that was exactly what she got. Every ridge of Asha's tongue pleasured her with each firm broad stroke.

Asha gradually went faster. Jessara placed her hands on Asha's head and ran her fingers through that wavy hair. She moaned louder as she relaxed into the bed.

Days without the touch of one another had taken its toll. Jessara had not expected to be in the right state of mind to be able to climax. But as she stared down at the beautiful blue eyes of the woman she loved, the rest of the world disappeared. As she ran her hands through Asha's soft blonde hair, the monastery disappeared. As she felt Asha's warm tongue and talented fingers, her responsibilities disappeared. All that remained was her, the woman she loved, and the world of pleasure she was receiving between her legs.

"Right there! Please! Please! So close!" Finally, it washed over Jessara. She squeezed Asha's head between her legs as she climaxed. It was as if Asha's spiritual essence were being transferred from her tongue to Jessara's core. It was a physical and mental closeness that Jessara desperately needed. Her legs shook as her orgasm lasted longer than normal. She giggled as she relaxed into her bed. Every limb sank into the comfort of the sheets.

Asha kissed up Jessara's body until she arrived back at her lips. She lay in bed next to her lover. As they continued to make out, Asha held

Jessara close, giving her the familiar warmth of her lover's skin against her body. And once again, they slowly fell asleep in each other's arms.

CHAPTER THIRTY-FOUR

RECOVERY

Jessara spent the next four days building back her strength. The day after she and Asha reunited, she was able to walk around the monastery. Asha still needed to assist her, but her Woodlander biology was giving her a quick recovery. She was even able to join the rest of the monks for dinner that evening. It was awkward to be among strangers, but she appreciated their kindness. After all, they'd saved her life, so she had no reason to be mistrustful.

The three elven children were also in the mess hall. Jessara had wanted to thank them, so she and Asha joined them.

"Heptor, Vitra, and Ivir, meet my friend, Jessara," Asha said. The children looked up from their bowls.

"Glad to see you up and about. How you feeling?" Heptor asked politely.

Jessara tried to smile through her social anxiety. "Much better, thanks. I heard it was you that saved me." She strained to look him in the eyes. "I thank you."

"It was the least we could do for Asha." Heptor motioned toward her. "We owe her a great deal."

Vitra frowned. "Couldn't save our parents though."

"Vitra!" Heptor poked her with his elbow.

Vitra looked at the ground. "Sorry."

"I understand how you feel, Vitra," Asha said. "I only wish that we could have arrived sooner."

Jessara put her hand on Asha's back and gently rubbed her. The deaths of the children's parents was another thing Asha would blame herself for, despite the fact that but for her, the children would be dead too. But what could Jessara say? Her own attitude toward failure wasn't healthy either.

Heptor interrupted Jessara's thoughts. "So Jessara. Asha tells us that you live in Enderdale. Is it true what they say?"

"Depends on what they say." Jessara wasn't sure where this was going.

"Elves and humans living together. Buildings taller than trees?" Heptor spoke as if describing a vacation spot.

Jessara knew better though. "Elves and humans interact more, but make no mistake. We still live in our own district, and we're still treated like second-class citizens. And there are too many bodies hanging in the streets, executed for minor offenses."

"Jessara," Asha said gently, flicking her gaze toward Ivir.

"Right. Sorry."

"What'd they do?" Ivir asked excitedly. Given the subject, Jessara wasn't sure that was normal for a child.

She glanced at Asha. Her lover reluctantly nodded for her to continue. "Usually magic."

"Is that why people hate elves? Because we do magic?" Ivir asked.

"It's one of the reasons."

Ivir frowned. "But my parents didn't do magic."

"They didn't have to." Jessara's voice was more blunt than she'd meant it to be, and Asha shot her another look.

"They didn't have to," Jessara said more softly. She almost never talked to children.

Ivir met Jessara's gaze. "Have the bad people ever attacked you?"

Jessara forced herself to maintain eye contact, which she hoped didn't look strange. "Supremacists? Yeah, they have."

"What happened to them?"

Jessara gave him a proud grin. "Dead or bludgeoned."

Asha put her hand on Jessara's shoulder. "What she means is that she's good at defending herself." She practically spoke through her teeth.

Ivir stood up, put his hands on his hips, holding his body in a heroic stance. "One day, I'll be as tough as you. Then nobody'll hurt me family."

Jessara smiled. The child's comment was as endearing as it was heartbreaking. "It's worth learning a few things, but I *can* still get hurt. That's why your brother and sister here had to save me."

"We should probably get back to our quarters." Heptor took his brothers hand, trying to be as polite as possible. But it was clear he wasn't comfortable with this conversation.

Ivir tried to pull away. "I want to stay and talk to Jessara."

That Ivir found Jessara interesting was surprisingly flattering.

"Ivir." Heptor put his hands on his hips like a parent, which was his new role with his siblings.

"Fine." Ivir bowed to them both. "Goodbye."

The children got up from the table, leaving Jessara and Asha to themselves.

Jessara sighed. "I told you I wasn't good with kids."

Asha smiled. "No, you did fine."

"Really?"

She bumped her with her hip. "Well, you have potential anyway."

The next day, Jessara could walk with no assistance. She asked Asha to walk with her in the woods. Asha expressed her concerns, but Braun told them that walking would aid her recovery. As soon as Jessara stepped out of the monastery and felt the sun on her face again, she felt rejuvenated.

The women held hands as they walked through the surrounding forest. When she'd been rushing through the woods a week ago, Jessara had been desperately trying to rescue Asha, but now she had time to appreciate the wonders of the forest. Oak, maple, and cedar trees dominated the woods, the cedar trees emitting the sweet smell of their sap. The scent filled her senses and made her smile.

"That's something you don't see every day." Asha pointed to her face.

Jessara didn't take her eyes off the woods. "Trees always make me feel safe. Reminds me of Anwood, I guess."

Asha raised a curious eyebrow. "Didn't you leave when you were a child?"

"Yes." Jessara glanced over at her, then turned her eyes back to the forest. "But I had a lot of jobs in Anwood."

"You mean assassinations?"

"Yeah. It was easier to blend in there than in other parts of Compact territory."

"Isn't that the point of having assassin elves? So they can blend in anywhere?"

Jessara paused to listen to the song of a bird. "Elves from Anwood tend to have darker skin. We're not out of place in other parts of the Compact, but we do stick out more."

Jessara put her ear to the wind and heard the gentle sound of rushing water. Through the trees, she and Asha could see a stream. The sound of frogs croaking filled the air as they got closer. Jessara noticed someone wearing black monk robes sitting on a rock, gazing at the creek. When they approached, Asha stepped on a twig and the monk turned around. It was a young woman with auburn hair whom Jessara hadn't met formally, but had vague memories of.

The young woman half smiled when she saw them. "Hey, Asha. Miss Jessara."

"You must be Tya." Jessara awkwardly tried to focus on her eyes.

Tya nodded.

"You were in my room a few times—I think?"

"That was me."

The gentleness in Tya's voice put Jessara at ease. She decided that she could avoid eye contact. Based on what Asha had told her, Tya was not one to judge a misfit like herself. Jessara focused on the water as she talked. "I heard what you did for me. I've been meaning to thank you."

"I'm sorry." Tya frowned and looked back at the stream. "I've been in mourning."

"I'm sorry about your partner."

"We can leave if you want to be alone." Asha motioned back to the monastery.

Tya shrugged. "Nobody owns the forest. Feel free to sit with me."

Several other boulders dotted the bank of the stream. Jessara and Asha sat down on the uncomfortable rocks.

Tya motioned to the creek. "This was our spot. We'd sit here and talk for hours."

Jessara moved her head in the direction of Tya but continued to avoid eye contact. "What was she like?"

"Adventurous. Witty." Tya pointed to some large boulders on the other side of the stream "When we were young ones, she'd try to get me to climb on those rocks with her. Goodness me, I was terrified of falling, so I never did. I'm regretting that now."

The three women sat in silence, enjoying the oasis. The sound of rushing water and birds humming would soothe anyone. Jessara thought about the path ahead of Asha and her. She wasn't sure when they'd have a moment like this again. Jessara wanted to kiss her lover, but even she knew it would be inappropriate in front of a grieving Tya.

Finally, Tya broke the silence. "How are you feeling, Miss Jessara?"

"Better. My strength is returning."

"How long do you all think you'll be with us?"

"Probably only a few more days. We need to leave as soon as I can fight again."

Asha gave Jessara a look which reminded her that the monks were pacifists.

"I mean hunt." Jessara looked at Asha, again who shook her head, suppressing a laugh. "Animals. Hunt animals."

Tya chuckled. "It's okay, I know what you do. I don't judge. Honestly, if Asha hadn't 'hunted' those supremacists, we couldn't have saved the young ones. So maybe it's good to have someone around that can...hunt."

"Does it shake your belief?" Jessara was genuinely curious.

"Jessara," said Asha.

"Inappropriate?" Jessara had never put much stock in religion. She'd been in the room during meetings between religious leaders and the King in Enderdale. The only thing clergy from the Church of the God Creators seemed to care about was politics. Spirituality was secondary, and it gave Jessara a cynical view of organized religion. The Church of the Everlasting Soul was the only religious group she'd ever met that seemed to genuinely care about the principles they preached. But she couldn't shake her cynicism fully.

Tya held up her hand. "It's okay. I thought it might, but it doesn't. Asha did the right thing to save the children. But maybe the right thing for one person isn't the right thing for everyone."

"That doesn't—" Before Jessara could finish, she felt a hand on her shoulder, and Asha pulled her in the direction of the monastery.

"We should probably leave you to it."

Tya turned to the women. "Pardon me but before you go, I wanted to ask. Do you have to leave? The monastery, I mean."

Jessara tilted her head. "What do you mean?"

"You could stay here." Tya motioned around herself. "We have room, it's safe, and it's a respite from the rest of the world."

Jessara looked at Asha, knowing such an offer would be tempting.

"That's kind, but there's something we need to do." Asha looked back at Jessara. "We need to see this through to the end."

"I get it." Tya didn't look surprised. "The offer will stand if you want to come back. It might be safer for people like you."

"Thank you." Asha bowed her head.

With that, the couple started back to the monastery.

When they were out of Tya's earshot, Jessara turned to her lover. "What did she mean by 'people like you'?"

"You—an elf, and me—a sorceress."

Jessara's brow furrowed with concern. "She knows?"

Asha smirked. "My love, we've been over this. The ears give it away."

Jessara rolled her eyes and gave Asha a playful push. "I mean that you're a sorceress."

Asha laughed and nodded her head. "She saw me fight the supremacists, as did the children."

"That's a lot of people to trust with your secret."

"True, but I think they'll keep it."

Asha was far more trusting of strangers than Jessara could ever hope to be. Part of her pitied her lover, but another part envied her. "I hope you're right."

"Honestly, the rest of the monastery probably suspects something." Asha gave an amused smile. "When we first got here, they thought I had some massive bloody fever."

Jessara had to think about that for a moment, but then she understood. "Because you run so hot."

"I woke up with about five blankets covering me," Asha laughed. "I can't even get sick."

"Wait, seriously?" Jessara hadn't heard that before.

Asha nodded proudly. "Yeah. Fire sorceresses can't get sick. I never understood why."

"Hmm." Jessara pondered for moment. Then she reached into her satchel. "I wonder if Aleris knows."

"Your scholar friend?"

Jessara flipped through the pages until she found the section on fire mages. She scanned through until she saw the words *Disease immunity*. "I found it! 'Fire mages are naturally immune to disease. Researchers at the academy determined that diseases come from life forms too small to see, which they refer to as pathogens. The best theory to explain this immunity is that the hotter body temperature kills pathogens before they can harm the host. This would also explain why said immunity goes away during pregnancy. Because the pregnant mage must maintain an average body temperature to ensure the survival of the offspring, they are vulnerable to disease.'"

Jessara looked up from the notes with a grin. "Still want to have kids?"

"Yes." She pursed her lips. "Although that does sound terrible."

Jessara thought about it. "My biggest concern would be the type of world they'd be brought into."

"I understand that." Asha took Jessara's hand and squeezed it. "But there are peaceful places too—like here, for example."

"Tya made a kind offer."

"Was it tempting?"

Jessara chuckled. "Can you imagine me in a monastery?"

Asha looked around the forest. "These are good people. It's also in a forest. There are worse places to settle down."

"I know."

"So, what would your ideal place be?"

"Never thought about it. I've lived in Enderdale for most of my life."

"You like it there?"

"Fuck, no. The city has too many people. That's why I'm always quick to take another job."

"I know how you feel about people." She rubbed her chin. "So, you prefer something more secluded? Something without anybody around?"

"Potentially, yes."

Asha walked in front of Jessara, then turned around to face her, locking eyes. She took Jessara's hand and wrapped it around her waist. "Without *anybody* around?"

Jessara put her hand on Asha's cheek and gave her a kiss. "I suppose I can make an exception for good company." She pulled their lips together again.

Asha ran her hand down Jessara's back and wrapped her palm around her butt. "Maybe it could be out in the woods. A garden out front."

Jessara enjoyed the fantasy as much as the groping. "A forest teaming with game for hunting."

"Maybe a porch that we could sit on and grow old together." Asha kissed her after every sentence. "Away from the world. Away from war. Away from bigotry."

"And the Sisterhood?"

Asha brought her mouth to Jessara's ear and gave it a nibble. "They could come out of hiding and be accepted in the world."

"And the Compact?"

"Defeated."

Jessara smiled as she looked deeply into Asha's blue eyes and imagined this beautiful world she'd created. All Jessara had known was hatred toward the Compact. The idea of it being defeated was a foreign concept. What would she do if the Compact *were* defeated? Prior to meeting Asha, she wouldn't have had an answer. Now, as she gazed at Asha, she wanted a world without conflict. She wanted a world where she and Asha could just be together. "I'd love that world."

Asha grinned. "Well then. When we get back, I'll show you a *taste* of it." And sure enough, much "tasting" was done that night.

***

The next day, Asha was relieved to find Jessara was getting her strength back. At this stage of recovery, Braun insisted that activity would help Jessara renew her blood. Under Asha's watch, she climbed trees in the woods and ran around the monastery. The tree climbing nearly gave Asha a heart attack, considering how weak her lover had been the last few days.

Jessara also wanted to try the archery range. When she and Asha arrived, they found Vitra practicing by herself.

As they approached, Vitra shot an arrow just below the bullseye of one of the targets.

"Not bad." Jessara sounded mildly impressed.

Considering how tough Jessara had been on her during sparring, Asha was relieved by her tenderness.

Vitra turned around, a little frightened. Evidently, she had thought she was alone. "Thanks. A little low."

Jessara inspected where the arrow hit. "Yep."

"But still impressive for your age," Asha said.

"I'm not trying to be impressive for me age." Vitra drew another arrow and shot the target a little lower than the first. "Damn it!"

Jessara shook her head. "The arrow drops in flight. You need to compensate by aiming a little higher."

Vitra shot another arrow. This time it flew over the target.

Jessara shook her head again. "I said a *little* higher."

Vitra kicked the grass. "How do you do it?"

"It takes practice." Jessara pulled out her bow and drew an arrow. "Practice and muscle memory." She loosed the arrow, hitting the center of the bullseye. "You need to pull the string all the way back to maximize accuracy." Jessara drew another arrow. "Then determine the distance of your target and compensate accordingly." She aimed her bow up just a little. "Hold your breath to steady your aim." The arrow loosed and hit the center of the bullseye again.

Vitra drew an arrow. She pulled the arrow back all the way, aimed, and held her breath. The arrow loosed and this time, it hit the outer edge of the bullseye. She smiled with pride and glanced at Jessara.

"Better." Jessara and Vitra spent the rest of the afternoon practicing. The more Jessara practiced, the more her strength returned to her. She continued giving Vitra pointers along the way.

Asha sat on the side and watched. Seeing Jessara interact with Vitra made her think of their previous conversation about having children. Such a thing would be in the distant future, but she allowed herself to imagine what a life with Jessara and a family might look like. Despite her bluntness, Jessara was tender with children.

The next day, Jessara was back to full strength. Asha was glad she was well but sad because that meant it was time to leave for Enderdale. Asha had enjoyed her time at the monastery, but she knew that they must continue their journey. Tya's offer to stay had been tempting.

Unfortunately, it wasn't an option for the same reason staying in Cosh-gromar wasn't an option. Her presence as a fugitive would put the monastery at risk. If she was discovered, good people would be hurt.

The capital would still take several days to reach. After gathering supplies from the monastery stores and collecting their weapons, they said their goodbyes to the friends they'd made in the monastery. Braun and Tya insisted on walking them out.

On the steps of the monastery, Jessara shook hands with the two monks. "We can never thank you enough for your kindness. I know you don't believe in debts, but if there's ever anything we can do..."

"We appreciate that." Braun bowed his head politely. "Try your best to avoid fires from now on, lass."

"That might be difficult." Jessara grinned at Asha.

Tya laughed under her breath as she walked over to hug Asha. "Thank you for everything, Asha. You've been a good friend. I do hope you find whatever you're looking for."

"Thank you, Tya." Asha gladly accepted the embrace. "I hope you find peace."

Tya turned to Jessara. "Not a lot of people would do what she did for you, Miss Jessara."

"I know." Jessara smiled at her lover.

"Watch out for one another," said Tya.

"We will." Asha took Jessara's hand and enjoyed the familiar firmness of her lover's grip.

Braun put his palms together as if praying. "May this chapter of our soul's journey be bright for both of you."

"Yeah!" Jessara clearly had no idea what to say in response. She overcompensated by putting excess enthusiasm in her voice. "You too!"

Tya and Asha laughed under their breath.

Then the couple turned down the path and began their journey away from the monastery.

Chapter Thirty-Five

On The Road Again

Jessara was surprised by how far off the main path the monastery stood, and it took the rest of the day to get back on the road to Enderdale. She didn't mind the extra walking; it meant more time in the woods with Asha. It was starting to hit Jessara that they were on the last leg of their trip. As much as Jessara wanted to believe that the King would spare Asha and let them work together, Asha's pessimism might be warranted. Jessara had to acknowledge, at least to herself, if not aloud, that the King's mercy wasn't certain.

Braun had drawn them a map through the woods, but it was dark by the time they found the main road. The couple decided to set up camp for the night just off the path. Asha made the fire, and Jessara hunted a rabbit, which they ate along with some rye bread from the monastery. Jessara enjoyed being back on the road with Asha, especially in a warmer region. After eating, they snuggled together and slept.

On foot, Enderdale was about a week away. They walked at a slow pace, neither in a particular hurry.

At the end of each day, the women would make camp, eat their dinner, and rest. They happened upon the occasional traveler, and some would politely greet the lovers, while others would scoff at Jessara or simply ignore them.

The farther south they traveled, the warmer the air grew. They followed the border between the Northeast Woodland and the Steppe, which meant that to the left of the path was forest, and to the right was hilly grassland.

As they were walking on the fourth day, Asha broke the silence. "Hey, Jessara?"

"Yeah?"

"I was wondering if we could stop in Farnsville before we get to Enderdale."

"We can." Jessara stopped. "But why?"

Asha looked at the woods. "I'd like to pay my respects to the family that I...that I failed."

Jessara put her hand on her shoulder. "It wasn't your fault."

"I know. I do. But I would still like to visit their graves."

Jessara thought for a moment. "It's not far out of the way." And to delay their arrival in Enderdale was a welcome bonus.

"About how far are we?"

"From Farnsville? Probably two days."

Asha frowned again. "It'll probably be our last stop before Enderdale."

Jessara gazed at Asha, not sure what to say. Usually, Jessara looked forward to returning to Enderdale because it meant drems and a new assignment. This time, she wished they'd stayed with the Sisterhood or even at the monastery. But she knew no other way to protect Asha. The King would never stop hunting her if she tried to go into hiding, and the next assassin probably wouldn't fall in love with her.

At that moment, Asha and Jessara heard a loud scream from the woods on the left side of the path. They turned to see a woman dart out of the brush, her white linen dress badly torn and bloodstained. Blood ran down her forehead and matted her blonde hair.

The poor woman looked terrified. "Please, help me!"

Asha immediately ran to the woman. "What's going on?"

"Wolves!" the woman cried. "My husband and kids are trapped in our cabin. Please help!"

"Show us!" Asha motioned to the forest.

The woman turned to run back into the woods, and Asha darted after her.

"Wait, Asha!" Jessara tried to stop her.

Asha looked back a second, puzzled. "Come on! We have to help them!"

"Asha!"

But she'd already disappeared into the woods.

"Damnit!" Jessara sprinted after her. *Impulsive little shit!*

"This way." Jessara heard the woman shout from ahead. "Hurry!"

After another minute of running through the woods, Jessara came to a small clearing. She stopped in her tracks when she saw the scene. A log cabin stood before her, but no wolves were in sight. Instead, Jessara saw the woman they'd been chasing standing in front of the house. Asha lay on the ground next to a large man holding a club.

Immediately, Jessara went for her sword. "Fuck m—" But Jessara was cut off as she felt the impact of something on the back of her head.

CHAPTER THIRTY-SIX

BANDITS

Jessara's brain throbbed against her skull like the beat of a drum. When she opened her eyes, she found herself in a dark, musty cellar.

She sat on the dirt floor with her hands tied to a small support beam behind her back, and her legs tied together in front of her. Asha sat behind her in the same position, their hands interlocked with each other's arms.

Another human woman with dark black hair was tied to a parallel support beam on the other side of the room. She looked a little older than Jessara.

"What the fuck?" Jessara struggled in her bounds before glancing back at her still unconscious partner. "Asha!"

Jessara used her shoulder to try to shake her awake. "Asha!"

Asha let out a groan as she woke up and pulled on the bounds. "What in Nara? You're kidding me! Why is it that everywhere we go, I end up tied to a fucking post!"

Jessara scoffed. "Maybe it's because you keep blindly running into kidnappers."

Asha strained. "Bloody Nara! Not so loud; my head hurts!"

"Could be a lot worse!"

"Hey, concussions are no joke. I could have permanent brain damage! Also, how could I have known it was a trap?"

If Jessara hadn't been tied up, she would have thrown her hands up. "'Please come and save my child and husband! They're being attacked by wolves!'" The sarcasm may have been over exaggerated, but it drove the point across. "I've pulled that exact stunt."

"Shut up."

"Umm, ladies?" The other captive woman looked utterly confused.

Jessara ignored her as she continued to mock her lover. "'Come on, Jessara! We've got to help them!'"

"Well, if you knew it was a trap, why did you bloody walk into it?"

Again, Jessara wanted to throw up her hands. "Because I was too busy chasing after your ass. If I didn't know any better, I'd say you like being tied up."

Asha paused for a moment. "Not in this context."

Jessara raised an eyebrow as some pleasant ideas went through her head. "Good to know."

At that moment, a key turned in the door. A moment later, it swung open to reveal the woman who'd lured them along, with a tough-looking bandit. This time, she wore armor made from some type of animal hide. The stitch work was terrible, but she was no longer covered in blood.

As she entered, she looked at the couple with a sinister smile. "Glad to see you're finally awake." When she spoke, she sounded much more articulate than Jessara would have suspected. Perhaps she'd had an educated background.

"Looks like you did a good job fighting off those wolves." Asha's words were full of frost and poison.

The bandit laughed. "Works every time. Nobody can resist helping out a pretty face."

Jessara smirked. "Then why send you?"

The bandit laughed and slowly approached Jessara. Then she cocked back her leg and kicked her in the face.

"Fuck!" Jessara's lip split, and her already throbbing brain jostled around. The shock from the blow was as painful as it was unexpected. Jessara looked up at the bandit with rage in her eyes, as she imagined the many ways she knew how to kill.

The sound of ropes straining echoed in the room as Asha struggled. "Bitch!"

The smile left the bandit's face. "You got a nice garment there. Any father who'd buy something like that for his little girl would pay a lot to have them both back."

Asha gave the bandits a smug look. "Well, joke's on you! I don't have a dad."

"Well then, I guess you're no use to us." The leader turned to the other bandit. "Kill them both."

Jessara had already figured out that a potential ransom was the only reason they were still alive. "But she does have a rich uncle!" It was the first thing that came to mind.

To Jessara's relief, Asha went with the ruse. "Yes! Very rich."

It was a bad lie, but it was too late to change it, so Jessara committed. "And he loves her."

"We really are quite close. He must be worried sick about me." Asha did her best to sound dainty.

"And who's the elf?" The bandit pointed to Jessara.

"She is my...umm." Asha tried to think something up. "Servant."

"Bodyguard," said Jessara, at the same time.

They both looked at each other.

Asha nodded her head decisively. "Servant bodyguard."

The bandit raised a suspicious eyebrow. "She carries a lot of gold for a servant."

"It's my gold. You think I carry my own gold?" Asha lifted her chin to appear more aristocratic. "I get my servant...servant bodyguard to do it. And my uncle loves her too, so you really need to keep us both alive."

"Fine." The bandit looked annoyed but satisfied. "We've already gotten a lot of money and goods from robbing you both. Nice sword by the way."

Jessara's blood boiled at the thought of someone else's hands on her hoplite.

"We're going to give your uncle time to miss you." The bandit slowly paced around the room as she spoke. "Then you're going to write a ransom note and tell us exactly where he lives. Sleep well tonight." She opened the door, and the other bandit exited. Before she left, she turned back to Asha. "Oh, and if I find out you're lying, I kill the elf in front of you and then I slit your throat. Ta-ta." With that, she flashed a smile and left the room.

The footsteps faded.

Asha nodded sarcastically. "Lovely woman. I think we connected."

Jessara shot her a look. "Servant? Seriously?"

"I'm sorry. It was the first thing that came to mind."

"So because I'm an elf, I'm your servant?"

"It worked, didn't it?"

"Excuse me," the other captive said.

Again, Jessara ignored her. "That's racist!"

Asha let out an annoyed sigh. "I'm sorry!"

"Ladies?" the other captive interrupted again.

Jessara angrily struggled in her bonds. "Also, she has my sword!"

"I know, my love."

"She's going to blunt it or something!"

"Can I please have your attention!" the other captive shouted.

"What!?" Jessara and Asha both shouted back.

The captive took a deep breath. "Thank you."

When Jessara looked at the woman, she appeared restless. The woman was shaking as if something were trying to come out of her. Furthermore, the woman was wearing a green wool dress, which was strange. Normally, human nobility wore dresses made of expensive materials such as velvet or silk. Wool was mainly worn by commoners, and even then, never colorful. The only people in the Kingdom who wore colorful wool clothes were elves. Perhaps she'd recently come across an elven merchant.

"Something that may be strange to you is about to happen." The captive's face grew more uncomfortable with each passing second. "Can I have your assurances that you won't freak out?"

"What's going on?" Moments later, Jessara got her answer.

The skin on the woman's face began to reshape. She made a strange bubbling sound as she changed into what looked like an elven man, roughly the same age, with long, dirty blonde hair and a delicate face decorated with eyeliner. His dress changed to a blue velvet doublet with red brocade down the center, and a purple wool chaperon, a kind of hood, which completed his look.

Jessara's eyes widened. "Well, that's a new one."

"What? What happened?" Asha strained to look, but she was tied too tightly.

"Well, she just changed into a man. And he's an elf." Jessara remembered what Aleris had told her about shapeshifters. They could only be in a different form for a limited time, which explained why he was so desperate to get their attention before he changed. She also remembered that it was rare for an elf to be able to transform into a human. This must be a powerful shapeshifter.

"I wouldn't say 'man,' and I wouldn't say 'he,'" said the shapeshifter.

Jessara tilted her head as understanding dawned on her. "Would you say 'they'?"

They nodded. "I would."

"Would you say' elf'?"

The elf looked puzzled. "Well, obviously."

"Right, sorry." Jessara felt stupid. "They just changed into an elf."

"Oh, a shapeshifter!" Asha couldn't contain her excitement. "I've never met a shapeshifter before!"

"Yes." The shapeshifter's face grew concerned. "And these ruffians think that I'm some rich noblewoman from Enderdale."

"Who are you?" said Jessara.

The elf held their head high. "I'm whomever I want to be, depending on the day. Ma and Pa named me Glindarius Montrell. My friends call me Glindar, and so does everyone else."

Jessara could tell that their new acquaintance enjoyed the sound of their own voice. "Well, Glindar, can you tell me how many of them there are?"

"I've seen at least eight. But one of them is out trying to deliver my ransom note."

"How long have you been here?" said Asha.

"Three days." Glindar jumped at the sound of a loud stomp on the ceiling. When they were convinced nobody was coming, they continued. "Any day, they'll figure out that I gave them a fake address."

"Listen, Glindar. It's okay. I'm Asha, and this is Jessara. We're going to get out of here. Believe it or not, we've been in worse situations." As always, Asha was much better at reassuring people than Jessara could hope to be.

Glindar looked skeptical. "I applaud your optimism. But I've been struggling to get these bonds off for three days. They come in every few hours to check and tighten them."

After three days, Jessara was surprised Glindar hadn't used magic to escape. "You couldn't burn through them?"

Glindar's brow furrowed. "What in Nara are you talking about?"

"You clearly study and practice magic," said Jessara.

"I'm a shapeshifter, you simpleton." Glindar huffed. "You can only have one specialization!"

Asha shrugged. "I probably could have told you that."

"Right, I knew that." Evidently, that club had not been kind to Jessara's brain. "The point is that you won't tell on us if we use magic to get out of here."

"You know how to use magic?" said Glindar, shocked.

For a moment, Jessara was offended. "Well, no." She motioned to Asha with her head.

"Wait a minute. Her? But she's human." Glindar leaned in, trying to get a better look at Asha.

"I get that a lot," said Asha.

"I think it's the nose," said Jessara.

"You can't be a shapeshifter." Glindar shook their head. "You were unconscious."

Asha sighed impatiently, probably because she was tired of being tied up, at least in this way. "I'm not a shapeshifter. And you can ask me about my life's story when we get out of here. Jessara, this may take a while. I need you to try to hold your back as far away from my hands as possible."

Jessara leaned forward. "Do what you need to do."

Asha slowly burned the bonds off her hands, accidently burning Jessara a few times, but Jessara was too proud to show it. After Asha's hands were free, she burned the rope off her legs. She then stood up to work on her lover. "How did you end up here, Glindar?"

"I'm a traveling merchant. Being a shapeshifter is quite useful—I can change into whatever face will get the customer to pay the most." Glindar smirked. "Anyway, I happened upon these degenerates on the road. They asked to see my stock. As soon as I showed them, they all drew weapons and forced me to follow them. They were most rude the entire trip."

Asha finished with Jessara's ropes, and then stood behind Glindar. "I'm going to need you to hold still."

"Do be careful," said Glindar, as Asha burned through the ropes. "Ow! Shit!"

Asha recoiled. "Sorry. Hold still."

After a few moments, Glindar was free. They rubbed their wrists and straightened their doublet as they stood. "Now what?"

"We fight our way out." Jessara grabbed her lockpick out of her boot and worked on the door.

Glindar's eyes widened as they glanced between Jessara and Asha. "I told you there were at least seven of them."

"I know." Jessara's tone didn't change.

Glindar acted perplexed. "We have no weapons."

"She shoots fire out of her hands." Jessara pointed to Asha.

Asha patted her lover's back. "And she knows eight different ways to kill people with her hands."

"Seven." Jessara finished with the door and put her lockpick away. "The throat kick requires feet."

Glindar threw their hands in the air. "You're both mad."

Jessara opened the door to find a dusty, cobweb-infested stairway leading up to another door. She signaled for Glindar and Asha to follow her. As they crept up the stairs, the wooden steps squeaked more than Jessara would have wanted.

When she reached the top, Jessara checked the doorknob. Unlocked. She cracked the door and peered through to see a small bedroom with a large feather bed, a crude oak dresser, and a bear skin rug. A bandit sat on a chair leaning against the back wall. Jessara couldn't risk him alerting the other kidnappers; she couldn't take them all on at once without weapons.

Jessara glanced at Asha and Glindar. "Go to the bottom of the stairs."

Her companions complied. Glindar's footsteps were heavy on the creaky steps, but Asha's weren't much better.

Jessara grabbed the door and started counting backwards from five with her fingers. As she counted, she wished she had her headband. It was in the satchel the bandits took, and she felt naked without it. When she reached zero, she pulled the door closed, creating a latching sound.

"What in Nara?" Jessara heard the bandit stand, and footsteps approached the door. Jessara positioned herself to be hidden when he came through. Sure enough, the bandit did not notice her when he stormed out.

From the bottom of the stairs, Asha waved at the bandit with a massive smile on her face. "Oh hey! Can we get some water down here? A little thirsty." As she talked, Jessara came up behind the bandit, grabbed his head, and snapped his neck. She helped his body to the ground to avoid noise. On his corpse was a small dagger and a club. Jessara motioned for Asha and Glindar to rejoin her, and she handed the dagger to Asha and the club to Glindar.

Glindar stared at the club for a moment. "I don't know how to use one of these."

Asha pointed to the head of the club. "Bashy part hits bad guys."

"Thank you," said Glindar sarcastically.

Jessara motioned for her companions to follow her into the bedroom. She listened for a moment and heard the distinct voices of three bandits outside the room. With three opponents in mind, Jessara quickly ran scenarios in her head to strategize. Asha knew spells, but they were in a log cabin, and Jessara had no desire to repeat her incident at the Red Dagger camp. Glindar was a wildcard, but at least Jessara knew they could shapeshift—that might be enough to buy a few moments of confusion.

Having established their assets, Jessara's scenarios all came to the same conclusion; a head on fight with all three opponents would be a bad idea. They needed to be drawn out. She motioned for Asha and Glindar to get against the wall perpendicular to the exit. Then, she walked over to the chair and kicked the leg, causing a loud *crack* as the chair toppled over.

"Damn!" Jessara heard from the other room. "You okay in there, Tred?"

Jessara motioned for Asha and Glindar to stay put.

"Tred?" said another bandit.

"Go check it out," said a third.

Footsteps approached the room, and Jessara tensed her muscles as she prepared herself. She hid behind the doorway, and as soon as he stepped in, she tapped on his shoulder. He whirled around in time to see Jessara slam her palm into his nose, snapping it into his skull. When his body hit the ground, Jessara heard more commotion in the other room. "Shit!"

Jessara turned to Glindar. "Shapeshift." She pointed to the dead bandit.

Glindar threw their hands out. "Are you serious?"

Footsteps approached the door.

"Now!" Jessara hated working with amateurs.

Glindar's skin melded into the shape of the bandit, and as soon as they were done shifting, Jessara pushed them out of the room.

Glindar was face to face with the approaching bandits in the nick of time. "Umm...hello, gentlemen! Not to worry! I merely....umm...tripp ed. But as you can see, I am back on my feet and in tip top shape!"

While the bandits were distracted, Jessara noticed that the one she'd just killed had a dagger. She snatched it and brought her attention back to the bandits outside the doorway.

"The fuck you on about?" said one of the bandits.

"And since when do you carry a club?" said the other.

"Well, I find that clubs can be quite effective. Particularly...umm," Glindar ran their hand on the blunt end of the club. "The bashy part."

Jessara put her face in her palm. There was no way Glindar could keep this up for much longer.

"The fuck's come over—" The bandit didn't finish as Jessara leaned out of the doorway and threw her knife into his throat.

The other bandit spotted Jessara and drew his weapon. Panicking, Glindar swung their club at his head. *Bash!*

The bandit collapsed to the floor, motionless.

"Oh, Creos!" Glindar practically jumped with joy. "Did you see that!"

"Yes, good job." Jessara quickly searched the downed bandits for weapons and found a sword, so she gave her dagger to Asha.

Glindar was gleeful, and swung their club through the air again. "I hit him in the face!"

Asha gave them a congratulatory pat on the back. "Yes, we all saw it."

Glindar was certainly not the type of person Jessara would normally spend time with, but there was something endearing about them.

But it was time to plan their next move. Two windows looked out the front of the cabin. Jessara crept over to one and scanned the front yard. The leader was pacing around the area, along with two other brigands.

"She has my sword!" Jessara raised the blade she'd taken from the bandit and gripped it tightly.

Asha grinned. "I like our odds now."

Jessara nodded. "You take those two. The leader's mine. Nobody touches my sword."

Asha gave an obviously fake cough.

Jessara glanced over at her and grinned. "Well, unless they're good kissers."

Asha gave a satisfied nod.

With that, the trio stormed out the front door. Asha took a dagger in each hand and shot one into each of the bandits.

The leader turned around just in time to see Jessara charging. She tried to ready her blade, but she was already thrown off guard. Jessara kicked her chest, and she collapsed, dropping Jessara's sword. Jessara cocked back the sword she wielded and jabbed it at the bandit, but her opponent rolled out of the way.

The blade dug into the grass as the bandit pulled herself up and kicked Jessara in the back. The blow sent waves of pain through Jessara, throwing her off her feet.

The bandit produced a knife from her boot and leapt on Jessara. At the last minute, Jessara threw up her elbow to halt the descent of the blade. With all her strength, Jessara tried to keep the blade at bay, but the bandit had the upper hand. The tip of the knife was nearly upon Jessara's throat when a ball of flame engulfed the bandit's face.

She screamed, but only for a few seconds as Jessara seized the knife out of her hand, jammed it in her chest, and pushed the body off her.

Jessara sat up, catching her breath, as she glanced over at Asha.

An ear-to-ear grin spread across Asha's lips. "What would you do without me?"

Jessara raised a brow. "Not get captured by bandits."

The grin eased. "Touché."

Jessara pulled herself up to retrieve her sword. She carefully inspected it to make sure it hadn't been blunted or scratched in any way. When she was convinced it was the same, she gave it a few swings. It was good to have it back in her hands.

Glindar threw a fist in the air. "We did it!"

Asha smiled. "Let's find the rest of our stuff."

The trio found an old barn where the bandits had stored their loot. They retrieved Jessara's weapons, her drems, and Glindar's cart and horse. The cart was made of fine walnut wood with ornate, carved flowers. White fringe lined the top, and a large selection of fine quality clothing made up the stock. It was about what Jessara had expected based on Glindar's personality.

Once everything was gathered, they started through the woods back to the path.

"I don't know who you ladies are, but you have my thanks." Glindar led the horse and cart, walking beside the women.

"Any time," said Asha.

"Take a look at my selection." Glindar motioned to the cart. "Any one item is yours, free of charge."

One item? Can't afford to be too generous to the women that saved your ass. Jessara laughed under her breath. "What do you have?"

"The finest garments you've ever laid eyes upon! Name your fabric! Silk, cotten, wool, linen, satin, velvet, I have them all! Looking to impress the relatives or express yourself? You're sure to find something." Glindar's sales pitch sounded like a theatrical monologue, and evidently well rehearsed.

"Thanks." Jessara laughed. "But it's not really my thing."

Glindar laughed too, but tried to stop as if realizing laughing might sound insulting.

Asha looked down at her dress. "And I have a very specific wardrobe."

Glindar stretched their arms as if asking for a hug. "There must be some way I can repay you."

"Let's just say you owe us a favor." Jessara put her hand on Glindar's shoulder. "You know—if we ever need a shapeshifter."

Glindar gave a formal bow. "I would be happy to oblige!"

"Which way are you going?" said Asha.

Glindar pointed to the southeast. "Enderdale. To drop off my earnings at the bank, and sell some wares I've picked up along the road."

"We're heading that way as well." Asha paused for a moment. "We're taking a quick stop in Farnsville though."

Glindar tsked. "A little out of the way for me, I'm afraid. We must part ways when we reach the crossroads. But when you're in Enderdale, please look me up. You can find my house in the main plaza of the elven district. Look for the one with my cart out front."

"We might just take you up on that," said Asha.

"By the way, Asha, was it?"

"Yeah?"

"Before we part, you must tell me." Glindar leaned in. "A human doing magic? How is such a thing possible?"

Asha smirked. "I don't know what you're talking about. Humans can't do magic."

Jessara rolled her eyes.

Glindar grunted. "Come now. You said you'd tell me after we escaped."

Asha held a finger in front of her and wiggled it back and forth. "No, I said you could ask. And you just did."

Glindar tsked again. "Disappointing."

Asha laughed. The trio walked along the path for a few miles until they came to a split in the road. The left sign read "Enderdale" and the right read "Farnsville." Jessara and Asha said their goodbyes to Glindar.

Jessara stored the directions to Glindar's house in the back of her mind. Having a shapeshifter on a future job could be useful. As they parted ways, the couple took the path on the right toward Farnsville.

CHAPTER THIRTY-SEVEN

THE LAST NIGHT

Asha was tired. After the adventure with the bandits, it had already been a long day. The couple decided to set up camp just off the road as the sun set. Jessara went hunting while Asha tended to the fire. The terrain was growing grassier and hillier, and trees became more sparse. They were getting closer to Enderdale.

As she sat by the fire waiting for Jessara to return, Asha thought once again about coming before the King. She still thought the most likely outcome would be her execution. Then she thought about Jessara's promise. Asha had no idea how she'd be able to protect her if the King decided to send her to the gallows.

A few minutes later, Jessara returned with a dead groundhog. It wasn't exactly gourmet, but at least it wasn't rabbit. As they sat eating their dinner, an awkward silence festered between them. As usual, Asha was the one to break it.

"We should reach Farnsville by early afternoon."

"I know." Jessara sounded pained.

Asha paused. She knew what Jessara was thinking, because she was thinking the same thing. "That puts us in Enderdale by evening."

She nodded. "I know."

"This could be…"

"I know."

Silence fell again.

Asha glanced back at the fire. "You looking forward to getting home?"

"Enderdale never felt like home. It's why I'm always quick to take another job."

"You looking forward to your next job?" Part of Asha wanted her to say "no".

Jessara shrugged. "I don't know." She shook her head. "Let's not talk about that right now."

Asha was more than happy to change the subject. "What do you want to talk about?"

Jessara's face softened. "I'm surprised you didn't take Glindar up on their offer."

Asha put her hand on her clothes. "What, and change my dress?"

"Lots of women have multiple dresses."

"Do you have multiple dresses?"

"We aren't talking about me."

Asha raised an eyebrow. "Do you have even one?"

Jessara looked at the fire. "Well, no. But that's not the point. I've always wondered something though."

"Yeah?"

Jessara gently stroked the sleeve of Asha's dress. "Why blue? Wouldn't red make more sense? Flames and all that."

Asha looked down at her dress. "Blue burns hotter than red. Plus, I like blue. Don't you like it on me?"

"I love it. Although, I've always liked green." Jessara paused for a moment. "Strange."

"What's that?"

Jessara seemed to be trying to remember something. "I think you're the first person who's ever learned my favorite color."

Asha grinned. "Well, now the secret's out, I'll use it to ruin you."

They both laughed.

"It's just, I've never learned to talk about mundane things like that." Jessara thought for a second as the smile left her face.

Asha could tell that Jessara was thinking about tomorrow, but Asha wasn't going to allow it. Tonight would be to enjoy each other's company—to Nara with tomorrow. "My favorite bird is the blue jay."

Jessara looked up at her and smiled. "Red-tailed hawk."

"If you could have one magical specialization, what would it be?"

"Telekinesis." Jessara did not hesitate. "If you could change yours, what would you change it to?"

"Telepathy." Asha didn't hesitate either. After growing up with a telepath as a sister, the answer was clear.

"Yeah. And why's that?"

Asha grinned. "So I could know when you're picturing me naked."

Jessara stared at Asha's breasts for a moment with a blank expression on her face. "I'm sorry; what was that?"

They both laughed.

"How old are you?" Asha realized that had never come up.

"Twenty-nine. You?"

"Twenty-five. What about your favorite food?"

Jessara was about to speak, but she stopped herself. "I'll tell you that after we sort everything out in Enderdale."

Asha frowned. "You really think you'll get the chance?"

"I promise." Jessara leaned toward Asha and pressed their lips together. She gently placed her hand on Asha's cheek as they kissed.

As soon as she felt Jessara's lips against her own, Asha knew she was safe. Jessara had proven time and time again to be the most driven woman she'd ever known. She'd put herself in harm's way without hesitation to protect Asha. Jessara put her arms around Asha's body and held her firmly. As long as she drew breath, Asha would always have someone to protect her. No matter what happened tomorrow, she would be safe. Asha smiled as their lips parted. "I love you, Jessara."

"I love you too, Asha."

Asha made a suggestive grin. "How secluded do you think we are?"

"I haven't heard anything in hours." Jessara smiled back. She slowly ran her hand down Asha's face, to her chest, her stomach, and finally between her legs.

Asha breathed out as she spread her knees. Jessara moved her hand up Asha's dress and began to rub her. As soon as she made contact, Asha let out a satisfied moan. The soothing motions of Jessara's finger were giving Asha the perfect sensation. She pulled Jessara's lips back to her own as she enjoyed being fingered by her lover, partner, and protector. As they kissed, their tongues played together in perfect harmony. All Asha wanted was for this moment to last forever.

CHAPTER THIRTY-EIGHT

FARNSVILLE

Asha awoke to the sound of birds chirping and water running in a nearby stream. She was surprisingly refreshed. Despite the stress of impending events, Jessara's fingers worked wonders in terms of distracting her.

After Jessara hunted down some breakfast, they continued down the road to Farnsville.

Thus far, Jessara had been understanding about their detour. "How long are you hoping to stay?"

Asha shrugged sadly. "Not long. I reckon their funeral and burials have already happened. I just want to visit their gravesite."

Jessara paused for a moment, gazing at her partner. "It wasn't your fault. You do know that?"

"I don't know. Maybe not. But it was my responsibility." Asha had gone over the events from Farnsville again and again in her head, and she knew there wasn't much that she could have done differently. Perhaps someday she'd forgive herself. Someday.

They walked for several hours, talking to pass the time. Asha refused to let her anxiety ruin the last few hours they had together, and she enjoyed herself as Jessara told her more stories about former jobs. Her mind even wandered into imagining a life where she and Jessara worked together. It wouldn't be a perfect life. Although she enjoyed adventure, she took no pleasure in killing most of the time. The idea of working for the King wasn't particularly appealing either. But after all she and Jessara had been through, she knew they could work together, and therefore have a life together. Perhaps that could make her overlook the King's past actions.

By early afternoon, Asha spotted some structures in the distance. As they got closer, Asha's heart sank as she noticed a familiar scent in the air. "Do you smell that?"

Jessara nodded with a stern look. "Smoke."

They picked up the pace. Columns of smoke rose from the buildings, but as they reached the edge of town, they slowed down and looked upon the scene in horror. The entire town had been burned to the ground. A few of the buildings had small pieces of wall intact, but otherwise, only black, charcoaled wood remained.

Another scent filled the air, but it was not the smell of wooden embers. Jessara glanced at Asha grimly. "Burnt flesh."

Asha's eyes widened with shock and disgust. "By the Tree! What the fuck happened here?"

Jessara scanned the area. "The whole town."

A pain rose in Asha's chest. She struggled to breathe as she tried to process the atrocity before her. "I don't understand. We're too far into Kingdom territory for this to be a Compact raid."

Jessara shook her head. "It wasn't a raid. It was a slaughter."

"What do you mean?"

"No bodies in the street." Jessara led Asha to the ruins of one of the burnt buildings. Within, they saw the charred remains of nearly a dozen people.

"By the Tree!" Asha grew sick to her stomach.

Jessara pointed to the remains of the structure. "They were forced into the buildings and then burned alive. Whoever did this destroyed the town without a fight."

"Why kill the townsfolk? And why target here?" Asha's voice choked. Questions rushed through her head with no answers. Nothing about this scene made sense.

"I don't know. But they were thorough. They wanted nobody left alive."

Asha's eyes shot to Jessara as a terrible thought entered her mind. "What if this was the Red Daggers?"

"Why?"

"The house fire made a spectacle. They could be trying to cover their tracks or..." Asha gasped.

Jessara took a step toward her. "What?"

"Or they were trying to frame a certain fire sorceress that the Kingdom already feared. This could be my fault."

The idea hit Asha like a runaway wagon, and was as painful.

"No. Don't do that to yourself."

"But what if they did it because of me?" The thought was too terrible to bear. Asha already feared she'd never move past the weight of the girl's life on her conscience. Now she might have the blood of an entire town on her hands.

Jessara stayed silent. She'd witnessed countless deaths before, but even she was at a loss.

Asha gazed upon the charred remains of the people. Some of the remains were...small. She imagined them burning alive while trapped in the building, and she nearly broke down.

Jessara let out a nervous sigh. "I know you probably don't want to hear this right now, but the Kingdom has to be investigating this."

That did not comfort Asha. "And they probably think I bloody did it."

"But you couldn't have. The ruins are still smoking. This happened within the last two or three weeks. You were with me."

Asha shook her head. "It won't matter."

Jessara looked around the town again, as if the ruins of the buildings could provide her with answers. "I don't know what's going on, but you're *not* going to take the fall for this."

Asha sighed. The fragile hope she'd been building came crumbling down. "I guess nothing will be certain until we get to Enderdale."

"We'll be there by nightfall. Are you ready?"

"No."

"Me neither."

Chapter Thirty-Nine

The Truth

Fear hollowed out Jessara's chest. Silence echoed between them as the couple walked the rest of the way to Enderdale. Jessara was still processing what they'd seen, and she feared Asha was correct about being blamed for the atrocity. Many scenarios played in her head of her convincing the King. She thought about it much like planning a battle, except this wasn't a battle, but persuasion—something she'd never been good at.

The one constant was that the King couldn't know that she loved Asha—at least not yet. He'd immediately believe her judgment had been compromised. Perhaps it had. But that changed nothing. Asha could not have burned down Farnsville.

The King had always respected Jessara's judgment. He trusted her. If she confirmed that Asha had been with her at the time of the fire, he'd believe it. After everything that he'd trusted Jessara with in the past, he'd surely listen.

Hours passed, and the walls of Enderdale came into view. Jessara's heart raced as they drew closer.

As the gate to the city loomed over them, Asha stopped and turned to Jessara. "You need to restrain me. My face is going to be recognized within the city. I need to go in as your prisoner."

"I don't think that's necessary." Jessara was unsure of her own words. She expected a witty or sardonic remark from her partner. Instead, Asha maintained an uncharacteristically stern expression.

"Don't argue with me, Jessara."

Reluctantly, Jessara took the shackles out of her satchel and re-strained Asha's hands behind her back. The charade made her sick, but she knew Asha was right. When they reached the front gate, several guards' eyes widened as they recognized Asha. They said nothing, but Jessara saw both fear and hatred in their expressions.

The rest of their walk through the streets of Enderdale was similar. Many guards and citizens recognized Asha. The couple passed by three wanted posters with her likeness, which wasn't a good sign. Jessara could feel her heart pounding as she escorted Asha up the steps to the palace. No turning back now. Two guards were stationed at the double doors at the top of the stairs, both of whom Jessara had seen many times.

One of the guards gave her a satisfied smile. "Jessara, you're back. See you brought a friend."

Jessara put on her normal, impassive demeanor. Usually, she did it out of genuine indifference, but this time, it was to hide the pure terror in her heart. "I need to see him."

"I think he's in his office. Wait here." He entered the palace, leaving Jessara and Asha alone with the second guard. He glared at the prisoner.

Asha glared back. "Got something to say?"

The guard's face twitched in anger. "Nothing to the likes of you."

Moments later, the first guard returned. "Go ahead."

Jessara led Asha through the palace. Portraits of past kings lined the walls. Jessara had been through this same hall hundreds of times, but she'd never given the decor a second glance. Finally, they reached the King's office.

Jessara took a deep breath and opened the door. In the room stood the King, General Harriot, and six guards. Four of the guards held crossbows pointed directly at Asha. Another bad sign.

As soon as the King saw Jessara, he smiled his usual welcoming smile in his blue silk doublet. "My dear Jessara! You have returned. I was beginning to grow worried."

"We got sidetracked." Jessara maintained her impassive demeanor as she glanced at the general. "Harriot."

Harriot nodded. "Jessara." He sounded nearly as impassive.

Jessara wondered if Harriot had mentioned seeing her in the mountains to the King. She still hoped to use his experience with Asha's assistance to try to sway things in her favor. Hopefully, that would still be possible.

"I must apologize for the welcoming committee, Jessara." The King motioned to the crossbowmen. "But she has already escaped once. Capital work bringing her in alive! Guards, seize her."

The guards started moving toward Asha.

"Wait. She isn't with the Compact. She can help us." More desperation came out in Jessara's voice than she intended.

The King was visibly surprised. "My dear Jessara, what are you talking about? Did you know that this woman single-handedly razed the town of Farnsville."

Asha had been correct. This would complicate matters for Jessara. "It wasn't her. It couldn't have been."

The King's brow furrowed. "Excuse me?"

Without realizing it, Jessara positioned herself between the crossbowmen and Asha. "She's been traveling with me for over a month. I think I know who did it though." She might have an angle to prove Asha's value. The Red Daggers were almost certainly behind the destruction of Farnsville, and nobody knew the Red Daggers like Asha. If the King wouldn't let Asha be an asset in the field, perhaps she could trade information on the group for her freedom. It wouldn't violate her oath.

"I see." The King's eyebrows raised thoughtfully. "Guards, take Asha to a cell. It seems we have much to discuss."

The guards moved and Jessara tried to stand in their way. "You don't need to do that. She can provide information on—"

"I will decide what needs to be done." The smile left the King's face, and coldness edged his voice in a way that Jessara wasn't used to.

"It's okay." Asha's voice shook when she spoke. She was trying to be brave, but Jessara could tell she was terrified.

"Do not forget the gloves." The King motioned for the guards to continue.

One of the guards took out chainmail gloves. Jessara glanced at the King suspiciously as the guard locked the gloves on Asha's hands. How did he know that gloves would contain the power of a fire sorceress? He hadn't before. Asha looked at Jessara with fear in her eyes. Two of the guards took hold of Asha's arms and marched her out of the room, while the crossbowmen kept their weapons trained on her. Asha kept her eyes on Jessara until the door closed behind her. *I'll see you again.*

Jessara turned to the King and tried to collect herself before making her case. "I think the act was carried out by a group that Asha and I had a run-in with, a group called the Red Daggers. Asha has been fighting them for some time and can provide invaluable information. She may be the key to capturing them and getting justice for Farnsville."

"General." With his usual firm but formal elegance, the King motioned to the door. "Please excuse us."

Harriot hesitated for a second, and then left the room.

Jessara stared at the King, puzzled. For once, she wanted Harriot in the room.

The King gave Jessara a professional smile. "The general has a different stomach than the two of us."

Jessara's stomach churned. Something wasn't right. "What in Nara's going on?"

The skin of the King's forehead creased. "Watch your tone with me, Jessara."

He'd never been this stern with her before. Usually, he was understanding when Jessara voiced dissent. "Please explain what's going on."

"I am already aware of the Red Daggers." The King's tone and expression didn't change. He made the confession as if it wasn't a confession at all, but merely a meaningless anecdote.

Jessara's eyes widened. "Since when?"

The King rested his hands on the table and leaned over it as he looked at Jessara. "Recently we made contact and came to an...understanding. Listen Jessara, you are my best assassin. You know that sometimes we must do...questionable acts for the right reasons."

"Questionable? They steal children!" Jessara did her best to maintain eye contact, but she grew flustered.

The King nodded with a frown. "I know. Their methods are shameful, but their results are necessary."

"Taking children is necessary?" Jessara found it hard to breathe. This couldn't be happening; her strategy was falling apart.

"Children become adults. As distasteful as it may be, it is better to eliminate them before they become a threat."

"So, you're willing to punish them before they've done anything?"

The King took his hands off the table and paced around the office as he talked. "Imagine how many lives can be saved that way. Have you seen what magic has done to the Compact? Their supreme leader changes every five years or so because people are constantly vying for power. The leader is never the person that is most fit; they are whoever happened to have the power to kill the previous leader. The only reason the Compact has been kept at bay for so long is because of instability within their highest echelons. Governing in the Kingdom is secure because it is stable. Magic users threaten that stability. It does not matter if they are human or elven. It cannot be tolerated."

Jessara shook her head. "But you said that human magic users could be an asset. You told me to bring Asha back alive for that reason."

"I did." The King pursed his lips. "But a wise king must adjust course when new information presents itself."

"What new information?" Jessara broke eye contact as she struggled to hide her emotions. Desperation festered, but she knew she couldn't show it. If the King discovered her relationship with Asha, it would put them both in danger.

The King snapped his fingers. "Eyes, Jessara!"

Jessara forced herself to comply.

The King nodded with gritted teeth. "That is better. As I said, I was approached by the leader of the Red Daggers recently. He offered a wealth of information about magic use. The most interesting thing he told me was that although elves can *learn* to use magic, humans, such as Asha, are *born* with it. In fact, there is an entire hidden cult of them somewhere."

He knew about the Sisterhood. This entire conversation was getting worse by the minute. Every muscle in Jessara's face strained not to give away that she had additional information. "Why does that matter?"

The King took a step toward her. "It means that they cannot be controlled. It means that who receives magic is left up to chance and not merit. When I thought she could help me control magic, I wanted her alive. But she cannot. No one can."

"What about all of the innocent people—innocent children—who have to die?"

"It is a small price to pay for the many thousands of lives that stability saves. I would think that you, of all people, would understand that."

Jessara paused for a long time. He truly thought she'd be okay with this? What kind of monster did he think she was? It took every piece of restraint she had not to glare at the King. "What happened to Farnsville?" Jessara feared the answer.

The King was silent for almost as long as Jessara was. He was sizing her up. "There are some things you need to understand before I answer that question, Jessara. Asha had an altercation with the Red Daggers in Farnsville, and a house was burned down. The Red Daggers are a secret organization. As I said, I only recently became aware of their existence. But the work they do is important—essential even—and that work must remain in the dark, especially now that they operate with my blessing."

Jessara raised a brow. "I can see why that might shake people's faith in you." Poison dripped from her words before she could stop herself. Her attempts to hide her emotion crumbled as the man she'd trusted her whole life revealed who he was.

The King glared at Jessara, but composed himself. "I will let that go, because I know you must be feeling strong emotions right now. We did everything we could to tie the original fire to Asha and *only* Asha. But there were too many witnesses in the town. After you left to go after her, a rumor took root that she was acting defensively against an unknown group of attackers. The rumor led to questions, which led to doubt and even defense of Asha. Groups of humans within the city began to organize in defense of human magic users. They believed that Asha was the future, and that she will be our salvation against the Compact. They did not see the danger posed by magic users, even human magic users. They did not see that if magic is given to people at random, it cannot be controlled. Some of the finer citizens began to petition me to pardon the sorceress. This sentiment had to be contained. They had to fear Asha as I do."

Rage boiled deep within the fiber of Jessara's being. "So you massacred an entire village?"

The King continued his explanation as if he didn't hear the anger in her voice. "When I met with the leader of the Red Daggers, he told me altercations have happened before, but never this close to the Capital. I had heard rumors of such over the years, but usually it occurred in remote villages. The rumors beginning to take hold in the capital threatened the secrecy of the organization, while also making Asha a hero or victim. We both had a problem. We discussed many possible solutions. Cracking down on the rumor? That would only make people think there was something to hide. Making the individual witnesses disappear? Again, it would only arouse suspicion. The people needed to be shown who the enemy was and who their protectors are."

"It was a massacre!" Jessara resisted the urge to slam her fist down on the table.

"It was a sacrifice." The King's voice was as calm as it was unsettling. "And one that I did not make lightly. Doubts about our official line began to make the people fear their King. A healthy amount of fear is good, but too much directed at the wrong place can be dangerous. That fear had to be redirected, and it worked. The rumors are no longer being spread, because people are too busy hating Asha for burning down a village full of innocent people. She is the final key to the puzzle, and her death will allow us to put this matter behind us. The people will forget the rumors of the Red Daggers; they will continue to have a healthy fear of magic; they will honor the dead; and they will be able to get on with their stable existence inside the Kingdom."

Jessara's heart sank. "So, she's to be hanged?"

"Yes."

Jessara tried to remember the arguments she'd prepared to try to convince the King to spare Asha, but everything was falling apart. "That's a mistake. She can still be an asset."

"Have you not been listening to me? The people believe her to have destroyed an entire village. They are demanding her neck."

"You said that you needed information from her. You doubled my reward if I brought her in alive.""

"Yes, I did. Your reward is on the table, by the way." The King pointed to a large sack of drems that, until now, Jessara hadn't noticed. "The information I was seeking has already been given to me by the leader of the Red Daggers. Her execution is the only use I have for her now."

Jessara was disgusted by how willing the King was to throw lives away. She may have killed for him, but her targets had always had a justifiable reason, or so she'd thought. They weren't just wanton slaughter. "As a scapegoat?"

The King's brows furrowed. "What has gotten into you, Jessara? I understand that you do not always agree with my actions, but you have never attacked me like this before."

For a second, she considered killing the King right there. She had her weapons; they were alone. He stood much taller than she, but he was no fighter. It would be a simple matter. She tried to calm herself down as her thoughts turned to Asha, how she'd promised for so long to keep her safe.

Suddenly, the King's expression turned to shock. "Jessara! Are you crying?"

A small tear was running down her cheek, and she quickly turned and wiped her face.

"Eyes, Jessara!"

Jessara turned back to face the King while attempting to suppress more tears.

After a few moments of studying Jessara's face, the King's eyes narrowed with suspicion. "Have you come to care for this woman?"

Jessara breathed heavily. Pain echoed in her chest as her attempts to control her face failed. "She's my mark."

"That is not a 'no.'" The King pondered for a few moments. Finally, he smiled, but it wasn't a soft smile—it was a smile with anger behind it. "It is okay. You have had a long journey, and you have spent a long time with her. It is only natural that you might develop a certain level of *respect* for her. This has happened at least once to every assassin I have ever worked with." The King stared at Jessara's face for a moment as if lost in memory. "It was only a matter of time. Most of your contracts call for elimination. You and I both know if the contract had been only to kill her, you would have done it without a second thought. You likely would have returned sooner, and you would be off doing your next contract."

His words gave her pause. When Jessara had been a child, the King had been the only person with whom she'd ever allowed herself to be emotionally vulnerable. Her trainers punished it as weakness, and the other children took advantage of it. The King had taught her that he was the only one she could rely on.

"But I did get to know her." She spoke as if she were a child again, seeking comfort from the man she viewed as a father.

The King nodded with paternal warmth as his face softened. "I know you did, my dear Jessara, and I know it hurts. I am sorry that I must put you through this. Our business often requires us to fight against our basic instincts. Do you know why I was not allowed to keep my name when I became king?"

Jessara shook her head.

"Because the individual does not matter." The King took a step toward her and placed his hand gently on her shoulder. "My own identity does not matter. My feelings do not matter. All that matters is the Kingdom. I have done terrible things, many of which have been through you. I will continue to do terrible things. Some, I suppose, will also be through you. At the end of the day, somebody needs to do what must be done. It is a burden that both you and I carry together. But at the end of the day, it does not matter whom they are done by. If we did not do it, then someone else would have to. In some ways, we are saving them the pain."

Once again, Jessara was silent, and an impassive look returned to her face.

Finally, the King walked over to his desk, pulled out another sack of drems, and placed it on the table next to the other. "You did your job well, and you deserve some rest. Your journey has been long and difficult. For the emotional toll you have endured, I am throwing in an extra thousand. Get some rest, and come back in a few days. I have another contract for you."

"Who's the mark?" Jessara was confused, but she knew that she wanted to kill someone.

The King walked over to the door and opened it. "General. Please come back in."

Harriot entered and glanced at Jessara, who still had a cold look on her face.

"The name of your next mark is Progmash. He is the chieftain of the orcs of the Northern Mountains."

Jessara's eyes widened as her stomach grew ill. *No. Not him.*

"I recently went to the mountains to try and establish an alliance with the orcs." Harriot didn't sound any more pleased than Jessara had. "They weren't receptive."

Jessara raised an eyebrow and wondered if Harriot had mentioned their run-in to the King. At this point, it probably would've been better if he hadn't. "How was your journey?"

Harriot gave her a knowing look. "Otherwise, not eventful."

Jessara nodded in understanding. He hadn't told the King, which made her wonder what his angle was.

"The Compact is establishing bases in the mountains." The King missed the nonverbal exchange. "If they were able to establish a stronghold, they would be able to mount a large-scale offensive on the northern flank of the Kingdom. If they are successful, the war is over."

"The orcs are neutral." Jessara was surprised to hear herself echoing Asha's sentiments.

"In this war, you are either with us or with the Compact." The King's forehead creased. "It does not only apply to the orcs. You are to eliminate the chieftain, and make it look like the Compact carried it out. It shouldn't be too difficult considering you are an elf. We need the orcs on our side."

Jessara held out her hand, but a scowl remained on her face. "Give me the contract."

The King looked from Jessara's hand to her eyes. "You can come back for it later. I want you to rest. Now are you going to let this business with our young sorceress go?"

Jessara stood silent for a few moments. "You know the answer to that." She turned and started toward the door, but she stopped herself before opening it. Another thought dawned on her. "I have one more question."

"Anything to ease your mind, my dear Jessara." The King gave her a warm smile.

Normally, when he called her that, she took it as endearment. Now, she just felt patronized.

"My parents." Jessara made sure to look him in the eyes. "How did they die?"

The smile disappeared from the King's face, and fear nestled behind his brown eyes. "They were killed by the Compact in a town purge." He looked away.

"Eyes!" Jessara took an almost aggressive step in his direction.

The King glared at Jessara. "They were killed by the Compact."

They both glared at each other for a few moments.

Finally, Jessara's eyes relaxed. "Okay." That one word had more defiance in it than anything she'd ever said to the King. She turned and started back to the door.

"Wait. Your reward." The King motioned to the coin sacks on the table.

Jessara glanced between the King and the drems several times. Then, without a word, she turned to exit, leaving her reward on the table.

Chapter Forty

The Cell

Nearly three hours had passed since Asha had been locked in her cell. Hunger and thirst gripped her, but based on her previous visit to the jail, she didn't expect that would change any time soon. Her hands and legs were chained to a ring on the ground, and she wore chainmail gloves that were locked in place. The gloves surprised her. She hadn't expected the King to figure out how to contain her powers, but he'd been bound to grow a brain sooner or later.

Asha trembled, but kept a strong face. As she waited, she wondered how Jessara was faring with the King. After the day's events, as well as the welcoming committee, she didn't have high hopes for her survival. She was willing to die, but the thought still filled her with sorrow, especially when she thought about Jessara. She would have to watch Asha die—a terrible thing. Asha was reminded of when her spirit mother watched her birth mother die, and the agony of the scream that haunted her dreams. She hoped Jessara wouldn't feel the same pain. They hadn't been together for as long as her parents had been, so she hoped that, after a mourning period, Jessara would be okay.

Despite the dark places her mind went, she refused to show any weakness to her jailors. Occasionally, when a guard walked by her cell, she'd needle them with a chastising remark. If she was to be hanged, she wouldn't give them the satisfaction of her fear.

Suddenly, Asha heard footsteps approaching her cell. They were heavy and rhythmic, the type that belong to someone who thinks they own the world. It could only be one person.

"So, you are the firebrand." The King's fine and colorful clothes contrasted with the dark, dirty, dank cell.

Asha laughed sarcastically. "Oh, that's very clever. Did you think of that one all by yourself, or did you torture it out of some defenseless dissident?"

The King paced outside Asha's cell with an inquisitive look. "You know, Jessara tried to convince me to spare your life. She said you could be an asset to the Kingdom. Is she correct?"

Asha tilted her head and nodded. "That sounds like her."

The King raised a brow. "You would never work for me, would you?"

Asha might have considered it for Jessara's sake, but from the King's tone, she realized that wasn't an option. "You wouldn't spare me even if I did."

The King sighed, almost apologetic. "Under different circumstances, that might have been possible."

Asha's heart sank as the King all but confirmed what she had feared, but she kept her smirk. "Let me guess. You need to blame somebody for the massacre of Farnsville."

The King stopped pacing and stared at Asha with a blank expression. "What makes you think I had anything to do with that?"

Asha leaned in, pulling against her chains. "I could see it in your eyes when Jessara brought it up."

"You must think yourself quite clever."

"I know I am."

"Indeed." The King took a step toward Asha's cell. "I want you to know that I will take no pleasure in your death. Despite my actions against you, I hold no personal feelings of ill will."

"Yeah." Asha dragged the word. "Sorry I can't say the same about you."

The King nodded. "I imagine not. Still, I admire you. Magic is fascinating, and I do wish we lived in a different world—but what you represent is dangerous in our current one."

Asha chuckled; she had to hear this one. "And what is it I represent?"

"Chaos and disorder."

"How do you figure?"

"As I told our dear Jessara, you cannot be controlled." The King resumed his pacing. "I recently learned that you received your ability to do magic from birth."

Asha did everything she could to hide her shock. How could the King have learned that? For a moment, she wondered if Jessara had told him, but she put that thought out of her mind. She trusted Jessara. It was the one thing she could still hold on to. Asha's expression managed to remain blank, and she said nothing.

"You do not need to confirm anything to me." The King sounded pleased with himself. "I know the truth—at least, I know what I need to know."

Asha's lips curled into a nasty grin as she started to put things together. "Oh, I see what it is."

The King stopped pacing again and crossed his arms. "Enlighten me."

Asha leaned as close to the bars of her cell as her chains would permit. "You can't bloody stand that you'll never have access to magic, that it will never be yours to control. You wanted Jessara to bring me in alive because you thought I could give you power. But now you know that's not possible. And even if it was, I wouldn't help you. So you're willing to throw away my life and an entire village just to maintain your power."

The King glared at her. "You do not know what you speak of."

She'd struck a nerve, and her grin deepened. "Don't I? Are you going to feed me some pathetic line about the burden of ruling? The tough but necessary decisions that you make? The need to fight against chaos and maintain order?"

The King cocked his chin in an annoyingly self-righteous manner. "Are you saying that chaos is not worth fighting? That order is not worth maintaining?"

Asha tilted her head as she prepared her diatribe. "You say order, but what you mean is the current order. Your order. Outside of the city, elves are hunted down and killed by human supremacists, but you do nothing because your order depends on elves being seen as lesser. The Compact raids small villages on the border of the Kingdom, but you won't expand your army's resources to protect smaller villages, because they must be focused on preserving your order. Elven mages are hanged—their bodies displayed in the streets—all in the name of preserving your order. You say you want to fight against chaos. What about the chaos of a king who throws lives away like pawns on a chess board? The chaos of a power-hungry tyrant who would wipe out an entire village? You want to fight chaos? Take that dagger of yours and shove it in your fucking throat."

The King was silent for several moments. "A convenient position to hold from that side of a cell."

Asha maintained eye contact. "So is yours."

"Such a mind. Such a tongue. Neither will threaten the Kingdom for much longer."

Asha's face softened almost imperceptibly. "When?"

"Tomorrow evening."

Asha's heart raced. "Aren't you going to try to torture information out of me first?"

The King shook his head as if asked a stupid question. "Torture does not yield accurate information."

Asha was taken aback. "Yet you have Jessara do it."

"She is an assassin, not a spy. I do not rely on her for intelligence. But sometimes, I need her marks to say what I want to hear so we can bring that to the people. The people do not need accurate information. They need information that keeps them hating the Compact."

Asha raised her head. "Wow. You're an even more evil bastard than I thought you were."

The King's forehead creased under his crown. "I suppose I have you to thank for Jessara's new attitude toward me. She has never questioned a contract before, but she spends a month with you, and suddenly, she is begging for your life."

Asha grinned. "I guess I have a certain charm. It worked on your mother too."

At that moment, another set of footsteps approached Asha's cell. A nervous soldier appeared and bowed to the King.

"Pardon me, your highness." The soldier glanced at Asha with what appeared to be guilt in his eyes.

"Speak, soldier," said the King.

"It's done." Something about the way the soldier said those two words made Asha's heart quake. Terrible news was coming.

"The rest of you?" The King's voice dropped.

The soldier shook his head. "Didn't make it."

The King nodded thoughtfully. "Well, at least she went down fighting. There is honor in that."

Please, no. Tears pushed against the back of Asha's eyes like a hammer. "What the fuck happened?"

"Do you have it?" The King held out his hand to the soldier.

"Yes sir." The soldier handed him a long object wrapped in cloth. The King unraveled it.

Asha was horrified when she realized what it was. "Jessara's sword!"

"And you disposed of the body?" The King inspected the hoplite.

Asha couldn't breathe; panic gripped her.

"Yes, sir."

"Capital work, soldier." The King somberly gave the blade back. "Keep it. It is far better than your own weapon."

"No!" Asha yanked on her chains. "NO!" Tears burst through. "You killed her! You fucking killed her!"

The King shook his head as he glared at Asha. "No, you did. You killed her the moment you turned her against the Kingdom."

"She turned against you!" Asha could barely speak through her tears.

"One and the same."

"Fuck! FUCK!" Asha screamed. Her chest hurt and her head ached. Her heart beat so fast, she thought it would burst from her chest. She looked up at the King with more hatred than she'd ever felt.

He looked at her stoically. "You loved her." It wasn't a question.

Asha tried to run against the bars of the cell. "I'll kill you! I'll fucking kill you!" Her restraints held firm as she tried to pull against them. The metal dug into her skin, causing immense pain, but she didn't care. She struggled, shouted, and cursed at the King until finally she fell to her knees sobbing.

The King walked right up to the bars of the cell and leaned in. "You may not believe me, but I truly am sorry for the pain I have caused you."

"Bullshit!" Asha swung her head around as she tried to struggle out of her chains one last time.

"I take no pleasure in what I must do." The King stood with watery eyes. "And believe it or not, I cared for her too, more than you could ever know. But the Kingdom must always come first. I hope that your death is quick and painless." With that, the King walked away, leaving Asha weeping on the floor, and the soldier standing in front of the cell.

Asha realized the soldier was still there. Sorrow was in his eyes, but his pity only made Asha more enraged.

"What more do you want from me?"

"I'm sorry." He sounded sincere.

"Fuck you! Go away!" She sobbed. "Go away! Go the fuck away! Please. Just go away." The soldier left her sight. Asha was alone in her cell, broken and riddled with grief.

Chapter Forty-One

Back To The Gallows

Asha sat silently in her cell. Her wrists and ankles were raw from the chains, her eyes dry and ringed with dark circles. She hadn't slept, and she'd refused food and water when they finally brought it to her. It was evening of the next day. A crowd, more rowdy than the last, could be heard from the jail. Footsteps approached the cell.

Asha looked up to see a guard staring at her. "I heard you're a talker."

Asha remained silent. Her eyes fell back to the ground with no fear or anger left. The King had won. He'd beaten her, broken her, and killed the woman she loved. The last thing she could do was die with the secrets of the Sisterhood. Maybe she'd even see Jessara again, in another life.

"I was there the day you escaped." The guard approached the cell and put his hands on the bars. "Put on quite a show."

Asha ignored him.

The guard took a step away. "What? Nothing to say? Last chance."

Asha said nothing.

The smile disappeared from the guard's face. "Suit yourself." He stood silently for a few moments until Asha heard another set of footsteps approaching. A second guard came into view.

"You're late," said the first guard.

"I'm sorry," said the second. "I was tied up on my last shift."

"Well, it's time. You got the irons?"

"Right here." The second produced a pair of wrist shackles. After unlocking and entering the cell, they released Asha from her chains and replaced them with the irons behind her back.

Asha put up no resistance as they worked. When they released her legs, they led her out to the hallway. As she walked past the cells, Asha recognized some of the prisoners from her first visit, who were even dirtier and skinnier. When she got to the door at the end of the hall, the second guard unlocked it, and Asha was back on the streets of Enderdale.

The sun was inappropriately bright in comparison to how Asha felt. They walked by the hanging bodies of elves on the streets with the same sign that read "magic users." All were different bodies from Asha's last walk. Fresh. Asha imagined her own body up there. It didn't scare her. She just wanted her pain to end.

As they approached the square, Asha spotted the gallows. An executioner with a hood over his head stood next to a marshal in a padded jacket, a golden gambeson, on the scaffold. The marshal was different, but she couldn't tell if the executioner was the same as before. She didn't care.

As she walked, she avoided looking at the noose. The guards led her through the crowd. She could feel the people's eyes on her as they parted to let her through, but her own gaze remained on the ground.

Asha was led up the stairs and placed on the trap door. The executioner came up behind her and placed the noose around her neck—tightening it even more than the first time.

"Hang the bitch!" yelled someone in the crowd.

"Murderer!" yelled another.

Asha didn't look at the crowd. She didn't react to the hecklers. One final tear streamed down her cheek.

The marshal pulled out a scroll. "Asha Weaver. You have committed the following crimes. Treason, magic use, resisting arrest, the murders of several officers of the law, assaults on several officers of the law, the destruction of property, insulting the King, escaping justice, and the brutal and heinous massacre of the town of Farnsville. Therefore, you have been sentenced on this day to hang by the neck until dead. Do you have any final words?"

Asha said nothing, hoping it would be quick.

"Very well." The marshal put the scroll away. "May the Creos have mercy on your soul. Proceed!"

Asha saw the executioner's hand move toward the lever. She took a deep breath and closed her eyes.

CHAPTER FORTY-TWO

BETRAYAL

Jessara stormed out of the King's office, lost for words. Her entire world had turned upside down. She thought back to every assassination she'd ever committed. The only thing that had driven her was hatred of the Compact, for what they'd done to her parents, but now, she was certain that the King had lied to her all these years.

She exited the palace. The guard that had let her in tilted his helmet to her.

Jessara spared him a quick glance and nodded as she descended the stone steps of the palace. Her stomach churned as she thought about all the times she'd defended the King to Asha, how she'd promised Asha she wouldn't be executed.

Jessara had been thinking about how to convince the King for over a month, but when he spoke to her, he'd been so sure he was right, Jessara had almost doubted herself. Even as she heard him defend atrocities, she still wanted his comfort. Visions of the charred bodies in Farnsville returned to her. Who could commit such an atrocity? Who could defend it?

She reached the streets of Enderdale and started toward the elven district. The bar she frequented while in town would still be open. She needed a drink, a strong one.

The walk took her through the noble's district of Enderdale with their lavish clothes and wooden buildings, then through the commoner's district with decent stone construction and modestly dressed people. Most humans she came across ignored her, which was fine with her. She had a lot to think about, and she didn't want to be disturbed.

As she walked, Jessara thought about the Red Daggers stealing children in the night from their parents. Who could give their blessing to such a crime? Most of all, she agonized over what the King had said about her. *You and I both know if the contract had been only to kill her, you would have done it without a second thought.*

Prior to meeting Asha, she wondered if she would have cared about the revelations of the King's atrocities. She always knew that he'd go to any lengths to preserve the Kingdom, but had he always been this brutal? Maybe a part of her had always known the type of man he was; she just hadn't cared.

Jessara knew she was in the elven district when the buildings became shabby and the clothing colorful. Before long, she reached the bar. A smoky fire pit sat in the middle, and tables lined the walls with elven patrons enjoying food or booze after a long day of work. A few colorful oil paintings of forests or lakes hung on the walls, mocking Jessara with images of brighter places. When she entered, she headed straight to the counter.

"Hey, Jessara." The bartender was middle-aged elven woman with graying brown hair, whose name Jessara had never bothered to learn despite being a regular. "What can I get you?"

"Strongest shit you got." Jessara slapped down a few drems.

"You all right there?" The bartender poured her a cup and set it on the counter.

"Tough day at work." Jessara took a gulp and sat down at an empty table in the corner. As she drank, she thought about the next contract the King wanted her to fulfill. She started to think about the layout of the city of Coshgromar—how she could make her entrance and exit. But then, she stopped herself, feeling sick to her stomach. Jessara didn't want to kill Progmash. She'd left the reward because she didn't want to kill for the King anymore.

Jessara had sat in the bar for almost half an hour, when a hooded man entered. Most patrons didn't notice him, but Jessara looked for potentially dangerous people everywhere she went. This one in particular caught her eye, as his walk seemed to demonstrate more status than the people who normally frequented the bar. The stranger scanned the establishment and noticed Jessara sitting in the corner. He approached the table and sat down across from her.

Jessara took a swig and motioned to the chair. "That seat's taken."

"You should think about pacing yourself on the drinks," said a familiar voice. The man brought his head up, but kept his hood on.

"Harriot?" Jessara took another gulp. "I think you're in the wrong part of town."

Harriot scanned the bar, then leaned in. "I'm repaying a debt." His tone was sincere in a way she wasn't used to. After their meeting in the mountains, she didn't harbor as much animosity toward him, but she still didn't trust him.

Jessara met his eyes, hating every minute of it but paying close attention to his reactions. "Did you know about the massacre at Farnsville when you ran into us on the mountains?"

Harriot nodded with a grim expression. "It had just happened when I left. The King told me he figured it was Asha's doing. When I saw you both on the mountains, I knew it wasn't true, so I didn't think it was worth telling you."

Jessara raised a brow. "Why didn't you tell him you saw us?"

"When I got back to Enderdale, it had become the official line to blame Asha. Just suggesting that it could be anyone else would set him off."

Jessara sighed. "He was behind the massacre."

Harriot looked at the ground with a frown. "I suspected that. So, I kept my mouth shut."

"Coward." Jessara leaned in, trying to put as much poison into that one word as she could.

Harriot glared at her. "Think what you want of me. My loyalty has always been to the Kingdom. The King needs a reasonable voice in his ear. I can't be that from a prison cell. I did what I had to."

Jessara let out a humorless laugh. "I'm really tired of hearing people say that."

Harriot looked like he was about to argue, but then he stopped himself and shook his head. "I didn't come here to justify myself, Jessara."

Jessara took another drink. "Then why are you here?"

"To warn you."

"Warn me?"

"The King believes that you've turned against him after that stunt you pulled when you left your gold. There's an ambush waiting in your house as we speak. When you go home, they'll kill you. They've been told to bring your sword to the King as proof of the deed."

Jessara made a fist. "That bastard!"

"I'm sorry, Jessara." He sounded genuine.

Jessara eyed him with suspicion. Why would this man, whom she was pretty sure hated her, stick his neck out like this? Was he setting her up? As much of an asshole as he'd been to Jessara, he'd never struck her as deceptive. "Why are you warning me?"

Harriot shrugged. "I told you; I owe you a debt, and now we're square. Do what you want with the information. But you're now an enemy of the Kingdom, and the next time I see you, I'll treat you as one."

Jessara took a deep breath. She believed him, and began processing the implications of what he'd told her.

"Thank you, Harriot." Not something she had ever expected to say to him.

"Good luck." With that, Harriot stood up and left the bar.

"That son of a bitch." Jessara was left not knowing what to think. Her life, as she knew it, was over. She pondered her next move. The ambush in her house would need to be dealt with, and she had to find a way to disappear. Strangely enough, an unexpected sense of freedom came from Harriot's revelation. She'd been trying to figure out what to do with what she'd learned. She would probably have betrayed the King, but now he'd made the decision for her.

Jessara's mind returned to her lover. She would not let the King hang her. Jessara needed to formulate a plan, but first, she needed to deal with the ambush.

Jessara exited the bar and walked toward her home. The streets were dark and quiet, for there were few street lamps in the elven district and not many patrols. The Enderdale guards didn't much care what the elves did to each other within their own district, as long as they didn't hurt humans.

Because of this, few people walked the streets at night. The occasional thief or pickpocket crept around, but they usually steered clear of Jessara—the ones that were still living anyway.

As she walked, she pictured the layout of her house. A small set of stairs led up to a loft where she slept—only one door in and out. If *she* were planning an ambush, she would have positioned the attackers just inside the doorway, ready to kill as soon as someone entered. However, the door was not the only entrance to her house. A window on her loft could be accessed from the roof. Some nights she squeezed out and sat up there.

Jessara reached her street. Two rows of houses connected with adjoining walls and clerestory roofs. Jessara ran to the end of the row and climbed up the brick wall. The bricks had been thrown together crudely when the houses had been built—fairly typical for a building in the elven district. Jessara found plenty of places to grip as she climbed.

In less than a minute, Jessara made it to the top. She crept over the roof tiles of several houses until she came to her window. Her vantage point gave her a decent view of the entire house. As she'd predicted, several guards—five—lined the walls next to the front door.

Jessara's window was locked, and the key was inside. She quietly picked it as she put on her headband. When the window opened, she took out her bow and drew an arrow. In a moment of hesitation, Jessara realized that she was about to kill Kingdom soldiers—the very people she'd worked with her entire life. But it was them or her...and it wouldn't be her. She took a deep breath and aimed at one of the guards. *So it begins.* She loosed. It struck the guard as the others jumped with surprise.

"Shit!" They tried to figure out where the arrow had come from.

Jessara jumped through the window and ran to the edge of her loft, drawing a second arrow. She leaned over the railing and shot another guard.

Those remaining scurried to the stairs, drawing their swords. Jessara threw down her bow and pulled out one of her daggers. She threw it into another guard before he made it to the steps.

While the remaining guards struggled up the stairs, Jessara drew her sword. She ran down the steps and kicked the nearest one in the chest. He barreled into the other guard, causing them both to tumble. They lay on their backs at the bottom of the stairs as Jessara slashed across both of their throats.

Jessara breathed a sigh of relief as she inspected each body to make sure they were dead. The fight might have been quick, but the implications of it began to hit Jessara. She'd killed Kingdom soldiers, and she was now an enemy to the Kingdom. Enderdale was no longer home and never would be again. The master of her destiny was herself.

It was time to figure out how to save Asha. Trying to do so would be difficult if the King found out the ambush had failed. He'd send guards to comb the city looking for her unless he believed she was dead. She needed help, and she knew just who to go to.

Jessara retrieved her weapons, put on her hood, and exited the house. Her next destination was the main plaza of the elven district, where the wealthiest elves lived. Some of the buildings could almost compare to those of the humans. Almost.

Jessara walked along the streets, scanning the houses, until she saw what she was looking for—Glindar's merchant cart. She approached the front door and banged on it. A few moments passed, and she banged again.

"I'm coming, I'm coming!" Jessara heard Glindar's tired voice inside. The door swung open, revealing Glindar in a nightgown that was so on point for what Jessara knew of Glindar, she almost laughed.

"Jessara?" Recognition dawned in Glindar's sleepy eyes. "Do you have any idea of the hour, you reprobate?"

Jessara put on her professional, impassive demeanor. "I need to call in that favor."

Glindar yawned. "Can't you call it in tomorrow?"

Jessara ignored them. "Get dressed and follow me."

"Damnit. Give me a second." They disappeared into their house.

As Jessara waited, she ran rescue scenarios in her head. None that involved rescuing Asha from the jail itself were workable—too many guards, too many obstacles, and no viable escape. She'd have to wait until the execution itself, and for that she'd need more help.

A few moments later, Glindar returned wearing their regular clothes—well—regular for them anyway. "Where are we off to?"

"Follow me." Jessara led them out the door.

As they made their way through the streets, Glindar was visibly agitated. "Can you explain what's going on?"

There wasn't enough time to ease Glindar into the reality of what Jessara was asking them to do, so she went for the direct approach. "Asha's in prison and will be executed soon. Probably sometime to-morrow."

Glindar looked horrified. "What? What in Nara happened?"

"You haven't heard?"

"Heard what?" It may have been a good thing Glindar didn't know. At least they wouldn't have any presumptions about Asha's guilt.

"Farnsville was burned to the ground, and everyone thinks Asha did it. Seriously, you haven't heard?"

"Look, I'm a traveling merchant, and I've been away from Enderdale for two months. I don't pay attention to local news."

"I need your help saving her." Jessara almost laughed—her plan depended on an eccentric and uninformed merchant she barely knew.

Glindar stopped walking. "Hold on! You want me to help someone escape from prison?"

Jessara stopped and turned to them. "We saved you, and you agreed that you owed us a favor."

Glindar pouted and continued following. "Why couldn't you have just taken a free dress or something?"

Jessara shrugged and answered as if it were a serious question. "I don't wear dresses."

"Well, did she do it?"

"Of course not. She was framed."

"How do you know all this?"

"Because I know the King."

"Well, can't you just take it up with him?"

"No. Because now he's trying to kill me."

"Why in Nara is he trying to kill you?" Glindar was freaking out.

"Because he thinks I've turned on him."

"Why in the Creos' names does he think that?"

"Probably because I have."

"And now you're roping me into this?"

Jessara gave them a pat on the back. "You're catching on."

They arrived at Jessara's house. It was much smaller and shabbier than Glindar's. "What exactly do you need me to do?"

Jessara waited to open the door. "First things first. Would you say that after our little adventure, you've seen enough dead bodies to not freak out about them?"

Glindar's eyes widened. "Why do you ask?"

Jessara opened the door.

As soon as Glindar saw the corpses, they gasped audibly. "Oh Creos, that is a lot of blood."

Jessara pulled Glindar into the house. "Get in."

"What happened h—"

"Shh!" Jessara had neighbors—none that she knew particularly well—but they had ears.

Glindar looked around the house, as if searching for additional attackers. "What happened here?"

"I told you. The King tried to have me killed." Jessara pointed to the bodies. "It didn't take."

"These are guards." Glindar emphasized every syllable. "Actual officers."

"They started it."

"You're mad. What does any of this have to do with me?"

"I need the King to think that the hit succeeded. The problem is, the only people that could tell him that are all dead. Fortunately, I know a certain shapeshifter who owes me a favor."

Glindar's eyes widened. "No."

Jessara tsked. "Yeah."

"No!" Glindar frantically paced around the room. "You want me to impersonate a guard and lie to the King?"

Jessara sighed. She enjoyed the challenge of planning a seemingly impossible task, but she knew the stakes.

"No. Asha needs you to."

That made Glindar stop pacing. "Look, I sympathize with your situation, but I cannot involve myself."

"If Asha hadn't burned through those ropes, then both of us would be dead right now."

"I know that." Glindar grew increasingly agitated. "But you're asking me to commit at least five capital offenses."

"Every time you change your face, you're committing a capital offense." Jessara pointed out the window. "You see those bodies hanging in the streets? Asha will be one of them if you don't help me. And her crime is the same one you commit daily. Does she deserve that?"

Glindar closed their eyes. "Shit."

"So, you'll help?" Jessara was surprised her outburst had worked. She hadn't planned it; she'd merely spoken from the heart.

Glindar grumbled. "Fine, yes."

"I'll owe you one after this."

"More than one."

"You can imitate clothes, right?"

"Yes, but what do I say happened to the other guards?"

"Tell the King that I killed the rest."

"Will he believe that?"

"You've seen me in action—so has he." Jessara grabbed some cloth from one of her cabinets and drew her sword. She wrapped the cloth around the blade. "He'll want this as proof. Tell him you disposed of my body." Jessara hesitated for a moment. She had no desire to part with her hoplite, but more pressing matters were at stake.

Glindar forced an innocent smile. "Then I'm done?"

Jessara shook her head. "No, not remotely."

"What next?"

"After your meeting, I need you to meet me at a friend's house. Do you know an elven scholar named Aleris Rondelio?" Jessara paused for a moment. She'd never referred to Aleris as a friend before; perhaps Asha was rubbing off on her.

"We've met."

"Do you know where he lives?"

"Yes." Glindar let out a long sigh, coming to terms with what Jessara was asking. "What's the plan then?"

"It depends on whether or not Aleris can help us." Jessara knew that Aleris was well respected among other elves in the city. She hoped he'd be willing to use those connections to get her some reinforcements, specifically ones that could do magic. "You ready?"

"No." Glindar's face started to morph into the likeness of one of the guards—a black-haired, blue-eyed, middle-aged man.

"How about now?"

Glindar shook their head. "Still no."

Jessara handed them her sword, and Glindar started toward the door.

As they were leaving, Jessara figured she should at least say something that showed appreciation. "Good luck."

For once, Glindar had nothing to say. They simply turned to her, gave a her thoughtful nod, and exited the house.

Jessara was alone inside the house she'd lived in her whole adult life. She hadn't spent a lot of time there, but she realized that this would likely be the last time she ever saw it. If it had ever felt like home, it might have been harder to leave.

Jessara filled her quiver with arrows, and she grabbed a guard's sword. After taking one last look at her house, she pulled her hood over her head and walked out to the street.

Jessara had been to Aleris' house several times. He'd always been a good source of information on the Compact. Whenever she needed to learn more about its political structure, its secure buildings, or its laws, Aleris would always be her first stop.

He also knew much about the nature of magic. Asha had not been the first magic user Jessara had hunted. When it came to knowing the strengths and weaknesses of magic users, Aleris could always be depended upon. On several occasions, he'd strongly implied that he still practiced magic. At the time, Jessara had paid it no mind. Now she wondered if that could be the key to saving Asha.

It was long past midnight when Jessara arrived at Aleris' home. For a house in the elven district, it was decent. Almost no stones were out of place, and it stood three stories tall with a tiled gable roof. Jessara had always thought it strange that one person should need that much space.

Initially, no one answered when Jessara knocked—not surprising, given the time. After several moments, she pounded the door with more force. Footsteps approached on the other side, and a heavy-eyed Aleris, wearing a linen nightshirt, opened the door.

He immediately recognized her. "Jessara? Can't you come back at a reasonable time?"

"Nope." Jessara barged past him. Normally, she would have exchanged a few formalities, but she didn't have the time.

Aleris shut the door behind her, exasperated. "Please come in. I wasn't sleeping or anything."

"I'm sorry it's late, but I need your help."

Aleris shrugged. "I'm already up, so what can I do for you?"

Again, Jessara skipped pleasantries and explained the situation to Aleris—that the massacre at Farnsville was committed by the King, that Asha would soon be put to death for the crime, that the King had betrayed Jessara and sent guards after her.

Aleris listened intently. Nothing seemed to phase him, which struck Jessara as odd. It was almost as if he'd been waiting for this day. "I feel for you, but I don't understand what you expect me to do about it."

It was time to see if Jessara's suspicions were accurate. "You know other magic users in the city, don't you?"

Aleris was silent.

She shouldn't have been surprised by his reluctance to trust her. After all the times Jessara had defended the King's actions to Aleris, he would be well within his right to suspect a trap. But Jessara needed his help. "The King has already made me an enemy of the Kingdom. It's not like I'm going to turn you in."

"I'm familiar with a few, yes." Aleris was being careful how much he revealed.

But Jessara didn't have time to be careful. "How many?"

"Why?"

Jessara leaned in. "Because I'm going to save Asha, and I need all the help I can get."

Aleris' eyes narrowed. "I don't understand, Jessara. You've always been loyal to the King, besides the occasional snide remark. Why turn against him now?"

Jessara took a deep breath. "Because he killed my parents. He's been lying to me my whole life. It was his forces that purged my village in Anwood—not the Compact."

Aleris gave her a look that she had trouble reading. For a moment, she thought it was guilt, but that didn't make any sense.

Then, Aleris' expression turned to concern. "How do you know?"

Jessara may not have been the best at reading people, but nobody could have mistaken the King's response to her question earlier that night. "I know."

"Very well. Then why not just leave the city? Why save the sorceress?"

Jessara looked away. "Because...she's important."

Aleris looked at Jessara for a moment, then his eyes widened with recognition. "You mean she's important to *you*. Creos. Have you fallen in love? I didn't think that was possible."

"Believe me, I'm as surprised as you are." Jessara felt like she should be offended, but she couldn't bring herself to be.

"Again, I do feel for you. But I'm not going to risk the lives of every magic user I know in a foolish attempt to save your girlfriend."

Jessara raised her head. "She's being put to death for being a magic user."

Aleris pursed his lips. "We're put to death every damn day. Such is the way of the world we live in; she is not the exception."

"We?"

Fear gripped Aleris' eyes as he realized his slip up.

"You're a magic user, aren't you." Jessara had already suspected it.

Reluctantly, Aleris nodded.

This could be the angle Jessara needed. She had something to offer him—to all elven magic users in Enderdale.

"What if it didn't need to be like this? What if you could use magic openly?"

Aleris shook his head. "The only place we could do that is with the Compact. We're not going back."

"I'm not talking about the Compact." Jessara thought about the Sisterhood. "I'm talking about the orcs." She wouldn't break her oath, but she could tell him enough to try to convince him.

"In the Northern Mountains?" This was clearly the last thing Aleris expected to hear. "Why in the Creos' names would they help us?"

"Because I know the chief, and he owes me a favor." Excitement rose within Jessara. "You'll be safe there."

"We'd be bringing trouble to his doorstep."

"It's already there. The King ordered the assassination of Chief Progmash—effectively a declaration of war. We bring that information to Progmash, and he'll give us all sanctuary."

Aleris sat back in his chair. "This is a lot to take in."

At that moment, a knock pounded on Aleris' door. For a second, he looked terrified.

"Relax. I invited someone." Jessara walked over to the door and opened it.

Sure enough, it was Glindar, still looking like the guard. "Let me in, quickly!"

Aleris stood alarmed. "What in Nara?"

"Relax, Aleris." Glindar's face shifted back into its original form. "It's me."

"Glindar? How did you get involved with Jessara?"

"Long story." Jessara turned to Glindar. "What happened?"

"I think he bought it. He even let me keep your sword." Glindar lifted Jessara's hoplite, which she quickly snatched back.

"Good job." Jessara wasn't sure she'd get her sword back, but it was a relief to return it to its sheath.

Glindar turned serious. "There's another thing you should know. When I found the King, he was talking to Asha. She was there when I told him. She thinks you're dead."

Jessara lowered her head sadly. "How'd she take it?"

"How would you?"

"For now, she needs to believe that." Jessara was talking to herself. After her journey with Asha, she'd learned what heartbreak felt like. She thought back to seeing Asha on the bed in the temple. The moment she'd been told that Asha was brain dead. The pain. It was terrible to think of what Asha was going through right now, but it was the only way to save her.

"I know." Glindar rubbed their eyes. "But you should have seen her."

Jessara tried to put that out of her mind and returned to making a plan. "When is she scheduled to be executed?"

"Tomorrow afternoon. You were right."

Jessara turned to Aleris. "Do you have a way you can gather up all the magic users you know? Let me talk to them?"

Aleris stroked his chin. "We have a way of communicating."

"Do you have a place where you all gather?"

"Yes."

"The sanctuary?" said Glindar.

Aleris nodded.

"Gather them." The plan was starting to take shape in Jessara's mind.

Aleris left the room and came back with a strange red orb. He put his hand on it, which turned it green.

"Sanctuary," Aleris said to it.

"Where are they gathering?" Jessara watched Aleris put the orb away.

"Follow me."

CHAPTER FORTY-THREE

THE SANCTUARY

Aleris led Jessara and Glindar down to his cellar. It was dusty, full of old barrels and cheap wine. Cobwebs, whose inhabitants had long since fled, draped the walls. Aleris immediately approached the back of the cellar and waved his hand in front of the wall, which faded away to reveal a hidden door. Jessara and Glindar followed him through it, and they found themselves in the sewers below the city.

Although Jessara was no stranger to moving around sewers in other cities, she'd never been down here before because very few of her jobs took place in Enderdale. Enderdale had a massive system underneath the city to avoid flooding, and most of the junk and refuse in the streets ended up down here after rainstorms. The smell was invasive.

After a half hour of walking, Aleris led the group to another brick wall. Once again, he waved a hand over it, revealing a hidden passageway. After closing the barrier behind them, he led them down the passage. He explained to Jessara that there was a network of almost forty magic users who all had access points to the sewers in their houses. These access points were all sealed with magic barriers in case they were caught.

The home barriers were set up in a way that they could only be broken by the person who had created them. If that person were executed by the guards, the barrier would remain forever sealed. The cave they were currently walking through had been dug thirty years ago—after Enderdale allowed elven defectors to settle in the city. Those who practiced magic never gave it up, but their numbers had dwindled over the years.

After a few minutes of walking, they came to a large, cavernous opening with several torches lighting the walls. Another archway on the far side of the cavern led outside. Several other elves had already gathered.

Jessara studied the opening. "We're at the bottom of the cliff, below the city."

"Yes." Aleris proudly motioned to the cavern before them. "We call it 'the Sanctuary'. We dug out this place so we could have a space to practice freely. Also, so that if anyone ever needed to escape the city, they could. Remember when I told you that when a mage developed a specialization, it alters their body and mind? Because of this, practicing magic is nearly impossible to suppress. For us, it's as natural as walking."

"So Asha wasn't the first to escape?" Jessara had never heard of such an attempt before.

"Not at all. Only the first to do so in such a public manner."

Jessara chuckled. "That's Asha for you." She pointed to the opening. "Can't people see you from out there?"

Aleris shook his head. "It's a fairly secluded part of the city outskirts. But even if someone did happen by, a camouflage spell hides the entrance."

All of these revelations were generating new assets for Jessara. Her plan was falling into place. "I thought we'd have to fight our way to the front gates, but we could escape through here!"

Aleris held up a cautionary hand. "Hold on, Jessara. Nobody has agreed to anything yet."

Jessara knew her plan to offer them sanctuary in exchange for help freeing Asha was solid, but she was no speaker, and these people had no reason to trust her. The life of the woman she loved relied on her ability to persuade these elves; her combat skills meant nothing here.

Aleris began to greet and mingle with the other elves. He told Jessara to wait a few minutes so the rest of the mages could arrive. As they came in, Jessara awkwardly stood in a corner of the cavern. A few elves gave her suspicious looks, but said nothing. *Don't mind me. Just a ruthless assassin that used to kill for the man you all hate.*

One last elf entered the sanctuary, and Aleris clapped his hands to get the group's attention. "That's everyone."

One of the elves crossed his arms. "You'd better have a good reason for dragging us out here in the dead of night, Aleris."

"My friend here has a proposition for us." Aleris walked up to Jessara and put his hand on her shoulder. "I believe we should hear her out."

Jessara's heart pounded as all eyes fell on her. She tried to prepare herself to speak, but she felt as if her vocal cords were tightening.

"Wait." Another elf eyed her suspiciously. "I know her! She's a lackey for the King! What in Nara were you thinking, bringing her here?"

"I no longer work for him." Jessara's voice was a higher pitch than she had intended, but at least she had managed to say something.

The elf put her hands on her hips and glared at her. "You expect us to believe that?"

Jessara looked at the faces of the elves before her. She was sure she'd seen several of them around the city. *You can do this.* She imagined Asha standing beside her, and she was able to get her bearings. This was for her—for Asha. Jessara took a deep breath. "He's responsible for the massacre at Farnsville. The woman that he's blaming for it is innocent. She'll be put to death tomorrow for a crime she didn't commit."

"Why should we care about a human?" said another elf. "It's about time they started hanging each other."

"But what if that could end?" Jessara was desperate to find the correct words.

An elf, who looked significantly less hostile then the rest, stepped forward, appearing genuinely curious. "What could end?"

Jessara imagined Asha had just put her hand on her shoulder. "I can offer you a place where you can openly use magic."

Another elf scoffed and shook his head. "She's wasting our time, Aleris."

Another pointed an accusatory finger at Jessara. "Why should we believe a word you say?"

Jessara knew she was losing the crowd, if she had ever had them to begin with. Asha would have been able to find the right words. She always knew what to say.

"Because I trust her!" All eyes went to the speaker, which to Jessara's surprise, was Glindar. "This woman saved my life—she and the woman who will be executed tomorrow for something that we do every day—executed by a tyrant that we all live in fear of! I vouch for this woman, the accuracy of any information she gives, and the sincerity of any offers she presents."

Jessara looked at Glindar with a nervous smile. After all she'd put them through, she was surprised they stood up for her. Although, they'd been with her every step of the way so far. Maybe it did pay to have friends.

"All right," said an elf. "Speak."

Jessara gazed at the crowd of elves. The imaginary Asha began rubbing her shoulders as she took a deep breath and started to speak. "You left the Compact because you couldn't stomach their butchery. You took a stand. You couldn't be complicit in genocide. But now we face a different sort of genocide."

Jessara paused for a moment. This wasn't as hard as she thought, but it was still a surreal experience. "Elves are all treated as second class citizens. We're forced to live in slums. We're punished harshly for the slightest crimes."

The imaginary Asha put her arms around Jessara and held her tightly from behind. "We're given the difficult jobs that the humans don't want to do. If we wander outside the city, we're faced with supremacists, who at best refuse to talk to us, and at worst, murder us on sight. And the one bit of resistance that gives elves hope—magic use—is criminalized, punishable by death!"

Her voice grew louder. "The bodies of our people line the streets to remind us of what happens when we step out of line. The King outlaws magic because it's a power that he can't control. We've always accepted the way things are, because the alternative was worse. But it doesn't need to be this way. I've made friends with the chieftain of the orcs of the Northern Mountains."

One of the elves scoffed. "The brutes?"

Jessara glared at the elf. "How many times have we been attacked for being 'husks'? Is that really a comment you want to make?"

No reply.

Jessara tried to catch her breath as she pushed through her nerves. "It might not be a land we're used to, but all of you left your home once. Among the orcs, you won't need to hide. You can use magic openly. You'll be safe. And you'll be treated well."

Silence fell among the crowd for a few moments. Jessara held her breath. *I'm proud of you,* said the imaginary Asha.

The elf who'd seemed the least hostile from the beginning took a step toward Jessara. "You can guarantee this?"

Jessara took a deep breath as she pitched the final offer. "The woman that is scheduled to be executed tomorrow is very close to the orcs. She's friends with the chieftain. If she vouches for you, they'll accept you. So the deal is this. You help me save her, we all escape the city, and I take you to the orcs. Then you can live openly as magic users. You'll never have to hide who you are again."

"Some of us have families and friends," said an elf.

"Bring them." Jessara smiled. "It will be a better life for all elves, magic users or otherwise. Any that can fight can help with the rescue. Any that can't will wait for us here in the sanctuary."

One of the elves turned to Glindar. "You trust this woman, Glindar?"

"Yes." Glindar had no hesitation.

"Aleris?" said another.

Aleris looked at Jessara for a few moments and then smiled. "I do."

The crowd spoke quietly among themselves. Jessara's heart was still racing. She'd never spoken like that before, and it was terrifying.

Finally, one of the elves nodded and stepped forward. "What's the plan?"

CHAPTER FORTY-FOUR

THE ESCAPE

"Very well." The marshal put the scroll away. "May the Creos have mercy on your soul. Proceed!"

Asha saw the executioner's hand move toward the lever. She took a deep breath and closed her eyes.

Suddenly, she heard something fly through the air next to her. For a moment, she thought it was her own body falling through the trapdoor, but then she heard a loud scream. Asha opened her eyes to see an arrow sticking out of the executioner.

Asha searched for the source of the attack, but quickly realized that dozens of elves among the people had drawn swords and were attacking guards. Metal clanked against metal. Some of the elves shot off elemental magic, either at guards or into the air. Cracking noises echoed through the streets.

The crowd screamed among the chaos, and they tripped over themselves trying to escape the pandemonium.

Asha watched in disbelief as she tried to figure out was going on.

Another arrow hit one of Asha's guards. An ice shard shot into the marshal.

"Hold still!" A hand reached out from behind Asha and pulled the noose off her neck. She turned her head to see the guard, who'd escorted her before, was holding a key. "No, turn around! Give me your hands!"

Asha was still baffled, but she complied.

Bells rang in the distance. Nearby, guards rushed into the battle, and the smell of blood filled the air.

Asha saw an elf in black fighting her way through the guards toward the gallows. The elf was cutting through opponents with the agility and precision that Asha had only ever seen from one person. It couldn't be.

"Jessara!"

Jessara heard Asha call as she pulled her sword out of another guard. She smiled back and darted to the top of the gallows. A guard attempted to block her path, but Jessara kicked out his knee, and in one swift motion, slashed into his side.

Asha was exhausted, hungry, and parched, but the moment she realized that the woman she loved was still alive, the desire to fight filled her veins. She wanted to live.

By the time Jessara made it up the stairs, Asha's escort had finished unlocking her shackles. She began shooting fireballs at guards in the crowd, careful not to aim at any who were near civilians.

Jessara took her place by Asha's side, sheathing her sword and drawing her bow. "This is becoming a habit."

"You're alive?" Asha fired another spell at a soldier. "But a guard said he'd killed you."

"That wasn't a guard." Jessara motioned to the "man" who'd just unlocked Asha's restraints. They smiled at her.

Asha brightened with recognition. "Glindar?"

"In the flesh." Glindar shifted into their original form. "So to speak." They wore steel-plated armor of elven design.

The number of guards in the area dwindled. The rebel elves were winning.

"All right! Time to move out!" Jessara held out her hand to Asha. "Stay with me."

Asha smiled as she took the hand of the woman she loved. "Always." Even in the midst of battle, Asha knew Jessara's familiar, firm grip. It was clear her partner had come up with a plan, and Asha knew she could trust it.

Jessara, Asha, and Glindar jumped off the gallows and ran through the square to join the rest of the rebel elves. Over a dozen bodies lined the ground. A few were elves, but most were guards. The remaining rebels numbered a few dozen.

Nearby guards attempted to attack the group, but they were disorganized. Each attempt ended quickly, with either an arrow or a spell. Fortunately, civilians had evacuated the area, so Asha didn't need to be quite as precise. That was a lucky break, as she had limited energy from a lack of food and water.

After rounding a few corners, they came to a manhole.

"Get in one at a time!" Jessara pointed to the top, and one of the rebels removed it, allowing the elves to begin descending.

Asha was not looking forward to a trek through the rat-infested sewers, but she wasn't going to complain.

"They're coming!" One of the rebels pointed to an approaching platoon of guards.

"We need to hold them off!" Asha began lobbing spells.

"Get in!" Jessara shot arrows at will. "I'll follow!"

"No! I'm not leaving!" One of Asha's spells managed to set two soldiers on fire.

"There isn't time! None of this means anything if you don't make it!"

Asha formed a large fireball in her palms until it grew to twice the size of her head. She threw it at the platoon, and the explosion shook the street. Those in the center of the blast were disintegrated; those at the edge were either set ablaze or pushed back.

Asha breathed heavily and fell to her knees. The spell had taken much out of her.

"Asha!" Jessara rushed to pull her up.

"I can't lose you again." Asha looked up at her. "We escape together, or die together."

Jessara hesitated and then smiled at her. She held out her hand and helped her lover to her feet.

Asha looked back at the manhole. Only a few of the elves remained to descend, but they were running out of time. The platoon faced massive losses after Asha's attack, but those remaining were closing in.

"You need to save your energy for running." Jessara scanned the incoming enemies. "No more large spells."

"Fine."

* * *

Jessara put her bow on her back and drew her sword as the remaining soldiers clashed with the remaining elves.

One swung his sword at Jessara. She blocked it and stabbed him in the gut.

Another charged. She clicked his blade to the ground and drew a dagger with her other hand. Without skipping a beat, she shoved it in the attacker's throat.

She looked to her side. One of the guards was pulling his sword out of one of the rebels. Jessara threw her dagger at the guard, catching him on the side of the head.

Jessara rushed over to the downed guard, dispatching another along the way. She retrieved her dagger and glanced over to see how her partner was doing.

Asha continued to shoot fire at incoming guards, but she appeared to be slowing down. Doubtless, she was running out of energy.

"That's it! Come on!"

Jessara glanced over to see Glindar jump into the sewer. They were the last of the group.

Jessara and Asha darted over to the hole. Asha jumped in first. Jessara drew her bow, and as she jumped, she downed an incoming guard.

Jessara landed on the floor of the sewer, bracing her knees. A quick scan found Glindar lying on the ground with Asha standing over them. The rest of the rebel elves had already run ahead.

Jessara put away her bow. "What happened?"

Glindar groaned loudly. "I hurt my ankle when I landed. I can't walk."

Jessara threw her hands up. "You've got to be kidding me!"

Glindar grumbled. "I'm not used to armor! I'm not used to any of this!"

"Shit!" At that moment, Jessara heard boots from a soldier hitting the ground behind her. Instinctively, she drew her sword and cut him down before he could recover from the drop.

Then, she turned back to her companions. "Asha! Help them get their armor off, or they'll be too heavy to carry."

Asha began to strip Glindar of their armor.

Meanwhile, another soldier landed in the sewer. Jessara attempted to knock her off her feet, but the guard kicked at her, making her stagger. The swing of the guard's sword forced Jessara to jump backward. Then she mounted a deadly counterattack before the assailant could recover.

As the soldier collapsed, another jumped down. She took out a dagger, and the moment the soldier's feet touched the ground, she buried the weapon into his knee. His scream was short-lived as Jessara took her sword and stabbed it through the man's neck.

"Jessara!"

Jessara turned to see that Glindar's cuirass was off. She darted to Glindar and picked them up, swinging them over her shoulders. "Run!"

Another guard jumped down behind them. Asha shot off a fireball at the soldier and turned to follow.

They rushed through the sewers as soldiers continued to pursue. Occasionally, Asha would shoot a spell to delay their advance.

They couldn't run fast because of Glindar, but fortunately, the soldiers faced a bottleneck to get troops into the sewer. Jessara felt herself growing exhausted, and she was relieved when they finally saw the passageway to the sanctuary. "That's it!"

Three soldiers closed in from behind.

Suddenly, Jessara heard additional footsteps coming from in front of them, and she saw four soldiers rounding the corner. "Fuck me!"

Asha panted as she ran. "They must have come through another entrance!"

Jessara tried to pick up the pace, but she was exhausted. Her body begged for rest, and her lungs burned from the heavy breathing. But she refused to quit.

***

Asha shot fire at one of the advancing guards, who was pushed into another. In the nick of time, Jessara and Asha managed to make it to the passageway before they were cut off. Jessara and Glindar went in first, closely followed by Asha.

Asha was running out of breath, and she grew lightheaded as the strain from spells and hunger caught up with her. She pushed as much as her body would allow, occasionally glancing behind. Soldiers continued entering the passageway in pursuit.

Asha looked ahead and noticed some kind of light at the end of the tunnel. She wasn't sure where the tunnel was leading, but considering how desperate Jessara was to get there, it must be safety.

Behind them, a soldier reached within sword range of Asha. She'd been delaying shooting fire for fear of a cave-in, but she had no choice. Before the soldier could slash at her, she fired a spell into his face. A loud *crack* shook the tunnel as the man screamed in agony.

Asha's fear was warranted, as the ground began to shake. "Cave-in! Go! Go! Go!"

Dirt dropped rapidly behind them. The screams of soldiers being buried alive echoed. Every shred of remaining energy Asha had was poured into pushing herself to get to the end of the tunnel.

She screamed in pain as she pushed her body to its limit. The opening was approaching, but so was the cave-in.

Both women yelled. They reached the opening as dirt came down inches from them. Asha threw herself at Jessara and Glindar, pushing all three of them the rest of the way as the passage sealed behind them.

Asha lay on the ground, exhausted but relieved. She strained to catch her breath as she heard an unexpected sound—applause. She looked up to see that she was in a large cavern, and almost a hundred elves stood before her—clapping and yelling in celebration.

Asha looked at Jessara and smiled. They both laughed.

As the adrenaline wore off, Asha processed what had happened in the last hour. She started with the most important fact. "You're alive. Bloody Nara! You're alive!"

"Yeah." Jessara's voice was soft and gentle.

Asha practically jumped on Jessara and started kissing her. As the reality that the woman she loved was still with her set in, she grew more desperate to kiss the lips she'd thought she'd never kiss again. Every time she pulled her mouth away from Jessara and opened her eyes, the sight of her lover made her yearn to return to those lips.

An older elven man, whom Asha had never seen before, approached the women. "I'm sorry to interrupt this, but you can kiss after we get away from the city."

"Right, sorry." Asha did not want to stop, but she knew he was right. She got off her partner and helped her to her feet. "Who are you? Who are all these people?"

"I'll explain later." Jessara brushed dirt off herself. "But Aleris is right. We need to move."

CHAPTER FORTY-FIVE

SUNSET

The humid air outside the city of Enderdale had never felt so relaxing to Jessara, and leaving the city had never been so liberating. She knew that she was leaving her former life behind, and she couldn't have been more content. As she, Asha, and the rest of the elven refugees fled, Jessara kept her hands locked with Asha's the whole time. Now that she had her lover back, she'd never let her go.

The group tried to put as much distance as they could between themselves and Enderdale. It was slow due to the size of the group, but as Enderdale shrank behind them, Jessara knew that she and Asha were safe.

Along the way, Jessara filled Asha in on what had happened in the last day. She told her about the deal she'd made with the elves to receive sanctuary in the Northern Mountains. Asha expressed worry that this idea could provoke the Kingdom to attack the orcs. But as soon as Jessara told her about the contract on Progmash's life, Asha agreed that a confrontation between the orcs and the Kingdom was inevitable.

Jessara also told her about the conversation she had had with the King—about his confession regarding Farnsville and her revelation regarding the death of her parents.

Sunset was drawing closer. Enderdale stopped being visible several hours prior, and the group decided it was safe to make camp. They set up tents and unpacked provisions. A forest off the path provided an adequate amount of cover for the site.

As the others unpacked, Asha dragged Jessara to a small hill next to the campsite. Jessara was all too happy to join her. She'd been waiting for some time to be alone with her.

"Perfect view of the sunset from here." Asha's face glowed as they both observed the bright orange and yellow colors against the clouds.

"Absolutely gorgeous." Jessara gazed at the sunset, and then at Asha's beautiful blue eyes. She let out a sigh.

"So, you were right all along."

Asha grinned. "You'll need to be more specific."

"I deserved that." Jessara chuckled. "You were right about the King. The kind of man he is. You were right."

"I'm sorry. Any regrets now that that part of your life is over?"

Jessara thought back to when she'd been alone with the King in his office. "Yeah. I didn't kill him when I had the chance."

Asha looked pleased. "Get in line."

Jessara could barely make out the Northern Mountains in the distance. "After the King realizes Progmash knows about the assassination contract, a storm will come to the Northern Mountains. It may take time, but it'll come."

Asha took a step toward her partner. "And we'll be there to meet it. The orcs, these elves, the Sisterhood, you, and me. And I wouldn't bet against us."

"But in the meantime." Jessara took Asha's hand and pulled her close. "I just want to enjoy the view." She gazed into Asha's sparkling blue eyes as she brought their bodies together. Once again, she was whole in the arms of her lover's embrace.

"No beauty in the world could match it." Asha slowly moved her lips closer to Jessara's.

Jessara felt them press soft and gracefully against her own. The warmth of Asha's body was home. The familiar scent of lavender on her lover filled Jessara's nostrils. As they kissed, Jessara felt a cooling breeze against her skin. When they parted their lips and opened their eyes, the light of the sunset illuminated Asha's gorgeous face. That was the face Jessara wanted to see every day for the rest of her life.

Asha smiled. "You kept your promise."

Jessara nodded thoughtfully. "I always will. Also, one other thing."

"Yes?"

Jessara grinned. "Venison stew."

Asha let out a confused laugh. "What?"

"My favorite food. Venison stew."

Asha smiled back. "Roast mutton."

They paused as they took each other in.

"I love you, Asha."

"I love you too, Jessara."

The future would come, and their trials would be many. But at present, they were safe. With the sunset in front of them and Enderdale behind them, the assassin and her sorceress kissed once again.

THANKS FOR READING!

Thank you so much for joining Jessara and Asha on their adventures together. Working on this book has been an important part of my life the last several years, and I could not be more excited to share it with you.

If you enjoyed my book, I would love to hear your input. Leaving reviews really helps authors like me with exposure, and it helps readers decide if a novel matches with their interests. If you are willing and able, please consider leaving an honest review on whichever platform you bought this book from.

Jessara and Asha's story will continue in *Heist of the Assassin and the Sorceress.*

ACKNOWLEDGEMENTS

A huge thank you to all those who helped make this novel possible.

To my wife Jess. Our relationship was my major inspiration for the relationship of the main characters. Also thank you for all the wonderful advice and ideas you gave me during this process. You helped me overcome writer's block on several occasions, and you helped give me the confidence I needed to finish this book.

To my father. As a retired professor of anatomy and physiology, you were a valuable consultant with regard to injuries and medical treatment.

To my mother. You were the first person I discussed the world of Dremeria with and the first person who made me feel like I could turn this book into something.

To Cassandra Medcalf. As an author, you helped guide me through a process that I was brand new to. Thank you for all the great conversations about publishing! Thank you for being an amazing beta reader with invaluable input. To anybody reading this, I strongly recommend checking out Cassandra's *Fixer Upper Romance* series and her new book *Foul Play*!

To Kyle. As one of my first beta readers and my book bestie, you gave me so much encouragement. Thank you for letting me bounce ideas off you for hours!

To Joshua. Thank you for letting me pick your brain for hours on linguistics.

To all my other beta readers who provided amazing advice and suggestions all around.

To Mary. My amazing editor. You taught me so much as my high school English teacher, and it was wonderful to reconnect so I could learn even more from you.

ABOUT THE AUTHOR

N. R. G. Selove is a queer autistic writer, podcaster, disability advocate, political activist, and professor of communication studies. He lives in Virginia with his wife, daughter, and two dogs. His hobbies include video games, long walks, arguing, and long discussions about T.V. shows and movies with his wife. He's a hopeless romantic who loves love in all of its beautiful forms.

www.ingramcontent.com/pod-product-compliance
Lightning Source LLC
Chambersburg PA
CBHW071744110726
47908CB00006B/1698